The
Songbird
of Venice

Also By Victoria

Henry's Spare Queen Trilogy

Lady Margaret's Disgrace, the Prequel
Lady Margaret's Escape Book One
Lady Margaret's Challenge Book Two
Lady Margaret's Future Book Three

Find Victoria online and on social media:
Author Website: *victoriasportelli.com*
Facebook: victoriasportelli

Dear Reader

If you enjoy this book,
please, leave an honest review
on your favorite review site.
I deeply appreciate your feedback and support

Thank you so much!

www.VictoriaSportelli.com

The Songbird of Venice

VICTORIA SPORTELLI

Creazzo Publishing
Sioux Falls, South Dakota

Creazzo Publishing
401 E. 8th Street Suite 214-1194
Sioux Falls, South Dakota 57104
USA

ISBN 978-1-952849-12-1 (paperback)
978-1-952849-13-8 (ebook)
978-1-952849-14-5 (audio)

Credits:
Cover Design: Jennifer Quinlan
Interior Design: Wordzworth.com
Editor: Margaret Diehl
Image: Elle Belle Design

Names: Sportelli, Victoria, author.
Title: The songbird of Venice / Victoria Sportelli.
Description: Sioux Falls, South Dakota : Creazzo Publishing, 2024.
Identifiers: ISBN: 978-1-952849-12-1 (paperback) | 978-1-952849-13-8 (ebook) | 978-1-952849-14-5 (audiobook)
Subjects: LCSH: Orphans–Italy–Venice–History–18th century–Fiction. | Vivaldi, Antonio, 1678-1741–Fiction. | Arranged marriage–Fiction. | Music–Fiction. | Aristocracy (Social class)–Italy–Venice–History–18th century–Fiction. | Social conflict–Italy–Venice–History–18th century–Fiction. | Statesmen–Italy–Venice–History–18th century–Fiction. | LCGFT: Historical fiction. | Romance fiction.
Classification: LCC: PS3619.P674 S65 2024 | DDC: 813/.6–dc23

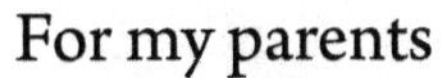

For my parents

Contents

Italian Words

I sprinkled Italian words throughout the story to give you a flavor of Italy. Information about early 18th-century Venetians is in the Author's Notes after the story.

bambino, baby, male / bambina, female / bambini, babies
borsellino, purse
buona, buone, buon, good
" fortuna, fortune
" giorno, day
" pomeriggio, afternoon
" sera, evening
" notte, night
camicia da notte, nightdress
campo, field before a church with buildings around it
Capo degli Anno, head of the year (January 1)
cara, dear one
cena, dinner
Cina, China
colazione, breakfast
da, de, di, (all the same), of
degli, della, of the
denari, money
Dio, God / Dio Mio, My God
donna degli notte, woman of the night
doxe, duke (modern is doge) / doxeressa, duchess
grazie, grace to you (thank you), / tante, many / mille, million
il conto, the count / il contessa, the countess
il granda, the great one (woman) / grande, women

il grando, the great one (man) / grandi,, men
mia / mi / mio, my
mi dispiace, I am sorry
maiordomo, head of servants
marito, husband
moglie, wife
nonno, grandfather
orinare, urinate
ospedale, hospital (old term for an orphanage)
palaso, palace or great house
perdonami, pardon/forgive me
per favore, for a favor
pieta', piety
pio, charity
pranzo, noon to 2 pm meal
rio/s, waterway /s
Serenissimo Principe, Most Serene Prince
Sette e' Mezza = seven and a half
si, yes
sono, I am
umanita = humanity
vestito, dress, gown
zecchini, gold coins
zuppa, soup

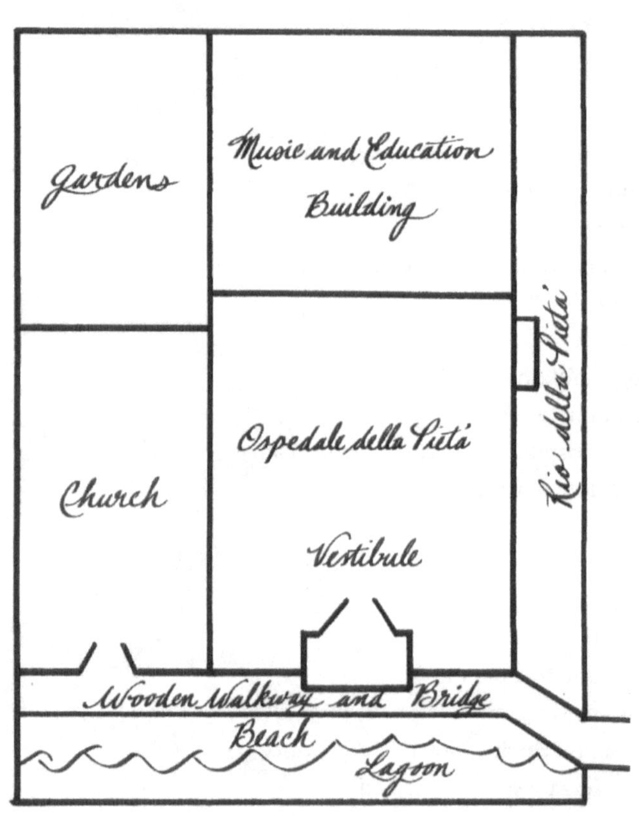

Gardens
Music and Education Building
Ospedale della Pietà
Church
Vestibule
Rio della Pietà
Wooden Walkway and Bridge
Beach
Lagoon

1723

Spring

"And hope. Always hope."

–Mark Buchanan

1

Pio Ospedale della Pieta'

Laguna della Venezia

April 5

As I rocked the newborn on my chest, she lifted her head. With unseeing eyes she faced the opposite direction and dropped her head against my heart. Her baby smell wafted to me; I sniffed in and sighed. When I was sure she was asleep, I kissed her head.

I pray one day I will have one like you. Little One, you are well formed. Your foot is not twisted like Carmela's, who needs crutches. Your mouth is not deformed like Stella's. You smell sweet. Who pushed you through our infant window and abandoned you? I yawned. From where did you come? Too poor to keep you? Set aside because you are not a son? Did your mother die birthing you? Is that why you wailed so? Mother Superior tells us nothing, just hands you over. Would I knew my story.

Oh, this rocker! I shifted on the cushion to no avail. Doomed never to birth one of my own, I can only hope for employment to raise another family's *bambini*. I sighed aloud; the babe stirred not. *Think not of what never can be. Yet my heart aches for the husband and family I will never have. Ah-h-h. Wishing gets me nothing. Enjoy this pleasure while I am still assigned it. Oh Lord, if I may never wed, I beg You, send me to a family. Girls younger than I are hired; why not me? What are Your plans for me, Oh God?*

Gazing at the portrait above me, I whispered, *I look to you, our regal Il Granda Patronessa smiling down at us abandoned ones. I pray for the repose of your soul and thank you for your generosity in giving us this home. May you already be in heaven. Per favore, ask God to send me my future. Who comes?*

"Your whisperings are so calming, Zia. You must prepare for they will soon arrive. I can take her."

Arching my back to ease my ache, I replied, "Warm her bed, Sister."

"I walked her. I sang; I rocked. I even used that 'Nee-e-e nah naw. Ne-e-e nah naw' phrase you taught us. I could not quiet her."

"You were unsure so she felt your nervousness. Stay calm. Think loving thoughts. Move slowly."

While Emelia rubbed her hands together and apart on the sheeting, I uncovered our newest sister, shifted the babe's head into my hand, and balanced her body over my right arm. Keeping the swaddled bambina flat, I laid her in the small bed and covered her to her neck. When she did not stir, I gestured Emelia to back away, led her across the room, and closed the door behind us. Hand over my mouth, I covered another yawn. "The day nurse will see to her now."

"Why do you kiss their heads before you lay them down?"

"A prayer for a good life."

"Will you be able to sing and play?"

"Certamente. This is my favorite performance, all light, joyful songs."

"Why is it always eight days after Easter?"

Since you could speak, you have peppered me with questions. You ought to remember my answers for you are old enough to be assigned a little sister of your own to raise. "Ask Mother Superior. Must hurry. If she cries, pick her up and do as I did." I left the nursery and descended the stairs to the second floor.

Anna Maria is twenty-seven and still here so I am not the oldest. Can I accept I may never leave? That worry saddens me. Stop fretting. Dress and warm my voice for the concert. Be a good example. Act happy. Smile at those returning from Mass. At the dormitory door I released an audible sigh, forced myself to smile, grasped the handle, and entered the room for us Big Sisters.

2

From my seat at the harpsichord, I watched the il grande women and their daughters enter through our vestibule on the zero floor, the only public space in our home. The women and girls doffed their capes and masks and handed them over my sisters who took them away. Always aware of rank and curtseying as needed, our guests chatted as they roamed from small group to small group through sunlight shooting golden beams from the windows. Tall candelabra around the room and beside the singers' platforms shrank the shadowy places. The scent of beeswax wafted toward me. Women fanned themselves and looked about. When the procession appeared in the doorway, I played a loud flourish. Our guests sat. Pairs of Littles, aged four through nine, entered the hall holding boughs of fresh flowers and leaves curled around heavy wires. *The cheerful uniforms of yellow blouses and skirts are the same every year.* The girls stopped in the aisle and held high flower-bedecked arches, and the room smelled like spring.

Violin and bow in hand, Anna Maria led the procession. Halfway into the room she smiled as our guests applauded her. Singing the first song, other Bigs entered under the flowery arches as I accompanied them. They stood on the two platforms or the floor before our all-female audience and finished the sprightly tune about spring and nature blooming. Like me, each wore a pale blue, collarless blouse with sleeves to the wrist over a dark blue, floor-length skirt and black slippers.

Anna Maria played her first solo as I accompanied her. She received loud generous applause, curtsied her thanks, and waited for quiet. She said, "The Sisters of Saint Maria of Humility greet you this fine spring day. We residents of this hospital are honored by your presence. We hope you enjoy our concert." She curtsied again before leaving the hall. I slipped from the bench as she exited and took her place center front of the singers.

With our hair brushed back and fastened at the nape, we, who range from ten to twenty, appeared alike enough to be sisters. The Littles departed with their blooms before we began the next song. Knowing what the audience expected of me, my heart beat fast. I held my breath and exhaled slowly through my nose. My chest rose as I filled my lungs. *The first high note must be pure and at a perfect pitch.* I opened my lips and, with my sisters, gave all that was in me: my love for music, my life's blood, every phrase an offering from my heart. The ladies' applause lifted my spirits high as the chorus curtsied. I stepped forward and offered my interpretation of the new song Padre Vivaldi had composed. At their applause I lowered my head, curtsied and stepped back into the chorus. When voices called "More" and "Again," I repeated my solo.

The choral part of our annual spring concert ended a half hour later. Anna Maria re-entered so she could lead the violinists' portion of the program. Then other musicians on the lute, mandolin, or cello filled the rest of the program. For our final song we singers stood on both sides of the musicians and performed together. As the applause faded, we separated, me to the harpsichord and they to their hostess roles. As usual, Anna Maria left because she hates talking to our patronesses. *The best day is living in music, singing and playing for myself. Singing and playing for others to enjoy makes this a good day.* I played the introduction for the next part.

From the doorway Padre Vivaldi signaled; three eight-year-olds and five-year-old Chiara entered with their violins. Two girls, aged twelve and nineteen, accompanied them. After their playing I saw Padre smile at them and wave the group to leave. Violins and bows in hand, three Bigs re-entered the hall to replace the Littles. From the doorway Antonio Vivaldi, priest, violin teacher, and composer, conducted the group. Playing his newest concerto, one girl played the fast, slow, and then fast variations on the theme while the others accompanied her. During the solo part I wondered. *How will he do it? Two concertos a month for the next six years? How can he have that many tunes in his head?* At Padre's wave in my direction, I took up my last part as an accompanist. The group departed after generous applause from our guests.

Stop playing the song in my head. Abandon it. Rejoin the world. While I dislike my next duty, for my sisters, I will be courteous. I left the harpsichord to stand in the hostess's place. The smell of sweets and tea assailed me, and I felt my mouth watering. I swallowed hard and turned away from the food side of the room.

Curtseying to the women who approached, I greeted each saying "Signora" and her family name and added, "We are so happy you came." I then greeted the signora's unmarried daughters with "Donna." If I knew not the name or the guest was new, I started with, "Signora, you are so kind to speak to me." I smiled and accepted each compliment before turning to my set speeches. "I am grateful to be one of the chorus." or "I was only one of the soloists," or "Each is as accomplished as you think me," or "Your attendance means so much to all my sisters." I ended each encounter with, "We appreciate your attendance and patronage."

Stop the song in my head. Focus. Three sentences and welcome the next patroness. If one asks a question, I must answer as if I have never heard it before. Glad the line is short this year. I hope they also greet and compliment my sisters.

The il grande women of Venezia stood in small groups to converse as they waited. Other choristers had already reached the serving tables on the other side of the room. Looking beyond the three remaining women in line, I announced, "The ices and refreshments are ready."

The women waited for the highest ranked il granda to approach the serving tables. The rest followed by rank. At the left table one girl scooped mountain ice into a crystal bowl; the second poured a chosen syrup to flavor it. At the second table a row of girls stood ready to offer small tarts, terrone towers, and squares of lemon, vanilla, and chocolate cakes after a guest pointed at her choices from large trays.

For each il granda or daughter, a girl followed to carry her bowl and plate. The rest of the chorus had placed small tables about the room and moved the chairs to create islands for conversations.

After the ladies had seated themselves, a girl carried a tray of cups and saucers to place before them. A second girl followed with a silver teapot holding a pad on the bottom to protect her hand. She poured tea, and a third girl followed to offer a small tray holding the honey pot for sweetening the beverage. Mother Superior crossed the room, stopping at each table to visit. Other sisters supervised the table workers. The whole orphanage was hard at work.

Would that I could send an ice down my parched throat. Finishing my hostess duties, I returned to the harpsichord. I saw a small girl pull her hand from the lady holding her in line. She dashed to intercept me.

"I liked your solos. Are you the one they call the Songbird of Venezia?"

I smiled at the child dressed in a pale green velvet gown with cream-colored silk poking above the neckline and through the sleeve slits. The child's golden ringlets bounced as she shifted from foot to foot. Her blue eyes sparkled.

"My name is Grazia. Donna, yours is…?"

"Lucietta." She rushed out, "I want to sing like you, but Nurse says I breathe wrong. How may that be? I have been breathing all my life!"

I stifled my chuckle by pursing my lips. "If you like, I can show you. Will you stand beside the harpsichord bench?" I waved the girl forward and followed. *Whose child is she? Spirited little thing. No one may touch a ranked even if she is only a child. Be cautious.*

I sat on the bench to face my student, who looked at me with wide eyes and a broad smile. "Breathing to sing is not the same as breathing to live. Follow along, Donna Lucietta. Keep your shoulders down." I touched my fingertips to my shoulders and tapped them. Lucietta copied me. "Place your hand over your stomach as I do." I exaggerated the motion and sucked in air through my nostrils. "I breathe in and my stomach goes out. I pull in my stomach, and my breath comes out through my mouth as I sing." I inhaled and exhaled a soft "A." "If you try, out may come a note."

"I did it! I did it!" squealed Lucietta.

"Very good. Practice breathing to sing every day until you need not think about the steps; you just do it."

"I want to sing now!"

"Very well." I faced the harpsichord and played a light, two-handed glissando. "Do you know the song, 'Little Lamb'?" At Lucietta's nod, I requested she keep her hand on her stomach to guide her breathing. I tinkled the introduction, nodded, and we sang.

The sun is high and time to wake

To the meadow we shall climb.

Adventures await us, dear,

Wait not for another time.

"Remember your breathing, Donna Lucietta. "

"It is hard!"

"Yes, it is." I began the second verse.

Running across the meadow,

Taking cool sips from a stream,

Time to go home, little one

To dine, my lamb, then dream.

I softly sang the harmony so Lucietta could hear her own voice.

Running across the meadow,

Taking cool sips from a stream,

Day is over, little lamb.

To bed, to sleep, to dream.

Time now, my sweet, for dreams.

I turned and saw a few il grande had been our audience. "Your madre is calling."

Lucietta made a face. "Donna Zorzi is not my madre. She just wants to be my madre because Papa has ships and farms and is handsome." Lucietta leaned forward and whispered, "I also heard her say he is rich." She turned and dawdled her way to the il granda who had brought her.

I returned to playing while our patronesses finished their refreshments and conversations. After the last women had exited through the vestibule, I jumped up to join Caterina in rearranging the chairs into rows for the performance next week.

She sneered, "How kind of you to join us."

"Did you notice the directress of the Choral Conservatory in the last row? I think she came to hear you. Is that why you sang two solos?" I picked up two chairs and followed her. "Were you auditioning to become one of them? I hope so."

"How easy it is to be the most important singer, complimented every time you open your mouth."

"Caterina, you are the true soprano, not I. You go from middle C to high C with no notes between, but I cannot. I can sing only the bottom half of the soprano range. Your high C can be as loud or soft as you want. I can only reach it if I sing to it and at full volume—and that only sometimes."

"But you sing lower notes than I."

"That only makes me an oddity."

"The donnas admire you."

I extended my arm as if to hand something to Caterina. "Dear Sister, I pass hostessing to you. Also, next year you may stand in front and have all the solos. I will sing from the back row." *Now, smile as if you mean it.*

Caterina harrumphed, "Not likely."

Together, we picked up tables and stored them in the closet at the back of the hall. *Being famous has done me no good. I am still not employed. Anna Maria may choose to spend her life here, but I like going outside. I want to live in the world but only if I can keep singing. Music is vital. I cannot live without it. I will not. I returned for another table. What if I must leave the Venezia and live elsewhere in the Veneto region? Think not on it. Pray.*

I followed Caterina to the closet and closed the door. As I waited to be alone, my stomach rumbled. *Food first. To the dining hall. Then the Chapel. How shall I start? Per favore, Dearest God, I beg you. Send me a future.*

3

Palaso Delatesta

Rio del Pestino

April 13

"Papa, my daughter is at me from rising to bedtime. Lucietta starts politely, then she wheedles, cries, and stamps her foot. After I said "No," she has kicked her nurse and refused to eat. She is impossible."

Giovanni shifted in his soft, well-worn leather chair. Antonio poured a Soave from the Murano crystal decanter into its matching goblets and handed one to his father. He took the second leather chair and sipped. On the desk beside Giovanni, one candle in the candelabra sputtered. As they drank, flickering light danced against the wall of books in the cozy room.

"Son, you have spoiled her. She is almost ungovernable. Now you bear the fruit of your weakness. Lucietta is as strong-willed and stubborn as her namesake. May she rest in peace."

"Last week she wanted this Grazia from Ospedale to be her

nurse. This week she asked me to marry her! She has threatened to throw herself into Canale Grande if I wed Donna Zorzi. Says she hates her and will not accept her. She wants this Grazia to be her mother. What am I to do?"Antonio swirled the wine, drank, and stared at the golden liquid. When he heard no response, he added, "Perhaps you could speak with the Mother Superior about a position for this girl. We could replace Lucietta's nurse. Papa, what do you think?"

"Once that poor girl is in the house, Lucietta would campaign even harder for you to marry her. Imagine the scandal. The Grand Council is voting next month to delay the next counting five years to give us time to recover from losing the war. The Ninety-nine refuse to re-rank themselves and an overwhelming majority appear to approve the measure. Even so, at the next counting, we could lose our place. Be sent down fifty, maybe a hundred ranks. Made an example. Two hundred fifty years of hard work undone over a single decision."

"Signor Zorzi will no longer permit me to see Maria. 'Family honor' her father said before he sent me away."

"Pontenuevo again. He loved Lucia so much, he gave in and permitted her to marry below her rank. Her death devastated both of you. His sorrow is now revenge, and he is so powerful he thwarts your efforts to find a wife and have an heir. He wants you as alone and bereft as he is."

In a dejected tone, Antonio listed, "Threats, promises, support, contracts. Whatever." He drank. "Last eligible donna of the second hundred gone. Those lower are even more afraid. Our family joining our exclusive class is costing me dearly. The law declares nobility may only wed nobility. But who? How?" Giovanni watched his son empty his glass. "Another glass before bed?" At his father's nod, Antonio stood and reached for the decanter.

Three days later, Signor Giovanni Delatesta met the directress of the orphanage. Straight backed, Mother Superior sat behind her desk with her fingers interlaced and her clasped hands resting on the desktop. A woman of rank, she wore a deep yellow silk garment and a dark beige veil covering her forehead, hair and shoulders. Signor rested on a cushioned chair before her. As Signor Delatesta explained his dilemmas, he glanced at Mother Superior's hands and realized she was older than her youthful face showed. After he stopped, the directress's silence was long.

"I understand your problem, Signor. I may have a solution."

"I am eager to hear it, Mother Superior. If you are successful, I will be both grateful to you and generous in my support of your fine institution."

4

Pio Ospedale della Pieta'

April 16

My three knocks were light, tentative. After hearing "Enter," I walked into Mother Superior's office, stood before her desk, and clasped my hands at my waist.

"Close the door. Sit."

She would not permit me to sit if I were in trouble. What is this about?

"You will prepare yourself for an interview one hour after we dine. Wash your face and hands; shine your shoes. Wear your choral garment. Wait in the chapel."

"Mother?"

"A father and perhaps his son." Mother Superior raised her brows. "Which is more important?'

"Always the father."

"Speak only to answer questions. Ignore the son unless he

addresses you. Sister Santina will fetch you and chaperone."

"Yes, Mother. Thank you, Mother."

I climbed the stairs to the second floor, entered the Big Girls' wing, and prayed. *Grazie mille, God. May it be employment. A chance to leave. Start a life. Priests say a woman's hair is her glory, and we must cover it before all men but our husband. Brush my hair, tie, and hide it as I do for the* patrons' *concerts. My glory is my singing voice. Today speak low. Be modest and honest. Eat? How can I eat when my future may be arriving?*

Standing beside my bed, I brushed my hair as I hummed a tune. I stopped when I realized I was singing to myself. *Deep breaths to calm me. Only five. Do not become lightheaded. Pray in the chapel. Housekeeper or nurse? I care not as long as I am in the world.* I took more long strokes as I mentally listed my accomplishments. Gazing at a high window of wavy blown glass pieces held together with iron strips, I wondered how I looked in a mirror. *Forbidden, to prevent the sin of pride.*

As I twisted and pinned my locks, I considered. They say *I cannot join the Conservatory and sing as Caterina might. Not qualified? Hah! I sing better than she. I am the famous one, not her.* Standing tiptoe at the window, I turned this way and that, but I saw only faint waves. *Stay here; teach others, and gain responsibilities until I answer only to Mother Superior. Join a convent and spend my life in prayer and good works. Not much different from each other.* I added more pins to be certain my hair would not fall. *Leave and labor for a family. Could be good or bad.* I donned my choral robe and buttoned it from neck to ankles. *First time anyone has asked for me. My only chance to leave? Am I an unfortunate doomed to live confined? No matter what The Recitation says, I know the world does not want us.* Through the arm slits, I picked up my scarf. At my nape, I tied the ends and pulled the sides over my ears. I tucked the front, so it covered my forehead to my brows. *Attired to be seen by men, I am a marble, armless statue. Act calm.* I sighed again before I left the Big Girls' room.

On the first floor I met several girls who noted my outfit and murmured, "Buona fortuna." I nodded my thanks and strode into the chapel. After crossing myself and genuflecting, I sat in the second-to-the-last pew. *The fat, three-wicked candle on the tall wooden pillar right of the altar reminds me God is present. The lights from altar candles on each side of the golden crucifix are steadier than my nerves. Deep breaths. Per favore, God.* I started my first prayer with *Let my future be arriving.*

I looked up. *Blessed Mary, watch over me. The high stained-glass windows tell Bible stories but give little light. The candles add to the stifling atmosphere.* Beneath my robe, I clasped my hands, bowed my head, and spoke The Recitation. "I am a child of God. I am here because He has willed me to live. Our Lord has…"

Later, Mother Superior escorted a pair of men into the concert hall and bade them sit on upholstered chairs that had been set in a corner. On the small table between them, a Murano decanter held the finest Valpolicella of the Veneto and matching wine goblets. She poured the liquid into the crystal glasses before excusing herself. The men sipped but spoke not. Sister Santina, well-dressed and wearing a headdress to cover her forehead and hair, opened one of the double doors and stepped into the hall. Hidden, I watched as she strode twelve feet into the room.

"I am her chaperone. Say or do anything untoward or upsetting, and we shall leave. You will never see her again." Sister Santina announced, "We present Grazia."

In ghostly white, I floated into the empty room and stopped

halfway between Sister Santina and the visitors. I watched as the men looked at each other with wide eyes.

The elder spoke. "Thank you, Grazia, for seeing us. This hall is large and echoes. If it pleases you, Chaperone, may she stand closer so we may speak in normal voices."

I looked at Sister, received a curt nod, and halved the distance between myself and the men. *Wearing velvet and silk. Sit at ease as if they are il grandi. The same high foreheads and wavy brown hair. Thick brows over gold-flecked brown eyes. High cheekbones, full lips. Related for certain. Puffed clothing announces they are ranked. Deep green full-length coats, knee breeches and vests. Gold trim, large golden buttons. Lace-fronted shirts and lace at their wrists. More wealth. White silk stockings, shining golden buckles on black shoes with heels Il grandi height. Holding matching black velvet hats with gold and green feathers. Likely, their colors. What can they want from me? Sing just for them like a paid parrot? Not unless ordered. In their home? Never!*

I felt a wave of power from the elder. The younger stared. A chill struck my nape and coursed down my back.

"Grazia, what is this room?"

"Signor, this is our choral hall. In addition to our frequent concerts, twice each year, we perform for the signori who are our benefactors. Other times we sing for the public."

"What is the balcony over there?"

Not needing to follow his raised hand, I kept my eyes on him. "We sing from the balcony. The men sit on this level."

"Do you speak with them?"

"Oh, no. We sing from above; then we leave."

"Why are you wearing a garment that covers all but your face?"

"We wear this in the presence of men. We are modest and

careful because we want to be judged by our moral character and accomplishments."

"Did you not give a concert three weeks ago for their wives and daughters? You wore regular clothes, walked among the women, and talked with them."

"True, Signor. Each spring we give them a concert and a tea. Because they are women and girls, we may be among them."

"How many years are you?"

"I am eighteen years, three months."

"What are your accomplishments?"

"I keep accounts, am practiced at running a household, and bargain well with merchants. I cook and know how to supervise others cooking. I keep a book of recipes for foods, medicines, and cleanings. At fourteen, I was trained by the sisters to run Ospedale. My whole fifteenth year I did so with no help. We lived well, yet I kept down expenses. I am cautious with coins, Signor. Now, I am training a girl so she may run Ospedale for a year and be ready to serve a family as I can do already."

"Impressive. In what else you are accomplished?"

Does he want a nurse to raise his grandchildren? I stole a glance at the younger man, who held his impassive expression. Arms still at my sides, I clenched my fists. *Change not my stance. Stand firm in the protection of the Lord.*

"Signor, I speak, read, and write Venetian, French, Latin, German, and a little Greek. I play the harpsichord and the lute. I sing and read music. We learn the latest dances. I can also teach manners, etiquette, and the proper behavior toward the il grandi. I am trained in mathematics, literature, and philosophy and can teach those as well as reading. I also sew, mend, and embroider." *Have I had said enough without appearing to brag?*

"Are you the Grazia who is famous for her voice?"

I narrowed my eyes. "Signor, I sing only for the glory of God and only at home. Never for coin or fame. My sisters and I hold concerts to thank our benefactors for supporting Ospedale. Without them, we orphans would have no place to live, no place to learn to serve." I stiffened my spine, glared, and spoke with force. "If your intent is to hire me for one task and then to charge fees for others to hear me sing, know I vowed to God never to sing for money. You cannot make me do it. Ever."

"I am glad to hear that, Grazia, for we would never do that nor permit it done to you. Keep your vow."

I curtsied. "Grazie, Signor. I believe you are a man of honor."

"We see you are well qualified to be a housekeeper or a nurse. Grazie for seeing us."

I curtsied more deeply. "I am grateful to be considered to serve your honorable house."

I turned and followed Sister Santina toward the open door. *I pray to you, Oh Lord, that theirs is an honorable house. Per favore, God, let me have a life, even if it is to work for others. If it be Your will, set me free.*

After the pair had departed, Giovanni looked at his son. "At the end, she showed some spirit. I like that. Fair skin, pert nose, pleasant voice. Blue eyes that went icy when she spoke of her vow." He paused. "If the Council will permit it, she will do. I will see Mother Superior about the matter."

"I want to see the girl again without that masking. I may need a wife, but I do not want a fat or misshapen one."

5

Pio Ospedale della Pieta'

April 19

Against the deep green linen of my only formal dress, my hand looked alabaster. *Whom do I meet that I must attire and groom myself so? How important is she?* I finger-wound tendrils at my cheeks and fluffed my curls. To calm myself, I hummed one of Padre Vivaldi's tunes.

With a straight back, I held the railing as I descended to the zero floor, our only public space. Girls who saw me smiled or nodded as they backed away. I nodded to Sister Santina and followed her into the choral hall. Stopping just inside the doorway, I gasped. To steady myself, I grasped the door frame with my right hand. *My hair is not for a man to see. I should not be dressed like this! What is happening?*

As if in a trance, the young man stood. Mouth agape, he stared.

I felt his gaze unclothe me. *Where is his father? What does he want?* I looked to Sister.

"You are safe. I am here," averred Sister Santina. She gestured, "Signor, per favore, sit" Composing himself, his face turned impassive as he did so. "Today, you two meet to learn more of each other."

I stood behind chair she indicated and clutched the top of its wooden back. Sister gestured me to sit. As I did, she moved her chair closer to us, so he could see her but I could not.

Our knees are only five feet apart. Too close. Too close. Do not flee. Sister is here; she will protect me.

"Buone giorno. I did not mean to surprise you."

"Buone giorno, Signor."

"I am Antonio, eldest son of the house Delatesta. My father is Giovanni. Ask of me what you will."

"Are you hiring me?"

"No. I seek a wife."

I looked over my shoulder for confirmation; Sister nodded.

So serious. So stiff-backed. Is he nervous or does it represent his character? Become a wife? Unheard of! Lord God, have you answered my prayers? Dare I accept this stranger? "Are you il grandi?" At his nod, I added, "Why are you not looking among them?"

"You are beautiful and have a pleasant speaking voice, but I want more. I want an accomplished wife, who can run a household and raise children. I can give you a family."

"You think I have no family."

"Do you?"

"Not in the way il grandi think. Here, we are sisters; we raise and teach each other. We are happy here." I looked away. *Marriage and children. At my age, this may be my only chance. Is it a good one?* I looked back but only at his chin. "How ranked is your family?"

"We have held ranks in the low one hundreds for over a century.

One hundred third among over eight hundred."

High, indeed. Close to the first Ninety-nine, yet not one of them. "Per favore, tell me of your family."

"You met my father. My mother died eight years ago."

"I will pray for the repose of her soul."

"Grazie. You are kind." Antonio continued, "Stefano is my younger brother. He and his wife, Polonia, have a four-year-old daughter and two sons, three and one. My sister Violante, Father's youngest, married Il Conto Benedetto degli Bollini of Ferrara. They reside in a palaso in the city and a villa in the countryside. Their sons are four and two.

"I am thirty. My wife died giving birth to our daughter, who is now five years." He relaxed his shoulders and added, "You met her at the concert earlier this month. Lucietta."

I smiled. "She is a charming child. We sang together. "

"She is quite taken with you. Now I see why."

"If she likes me, hire me to be her nurse, and she will become accomplished." I watched Antonio shake his head.

"I wish to marry again."

Why me? Orphans have no rank. Marrying me will do nothing to raise his. Would he respect me and treat me well? Hide me away? How desperate is he for a wife that he would consider an orphan? He needs heirs and expects me to provide them. Does that make me a wife or a brood animal?

"I want the firstborn of a farmer, a store owner or a merchant, so I can be both his wife and his helpmate." I watched his eyes soften; he made a small smile and then hid it.

"I am a merchant. We sell grains and animals from our farms in the Po Valley where our family originated four hundred years ago.

Stefano runs those. We sell our goods throughout the Veneto. We Delatestas are trusted wherever we trade. We owned three ships but now have only two." Antonio shrugged, "Trading by sea has been has been harder of late."

"Since we lost control of the Mediterranean in the Seventh Ottoman-Venetian War. The Ottomans reduced us to sailing only the Adriatic Sea. Not much trade there." I smiled at Antonio's surprise. "We are confined, Signor Delatesta, but we are aware of our world." *Once fabulously wealthy, many il grandi have suffered since the war. What is his position now?*

"May I ask what they call you?"

"The outside world may call me a songbird, but I am Grazia."

"Which do you prefer?"

"You may call me 'Grazia,' Signor Delatesta."

"Per favore, say 'Antonio.'" He gazed at me in silence for what seemed a long time. "Grazia, we live in Palaso Delatesta, a fontego-shaped building on rio del Pestino near the corner of the rios San Marina and del Mendicanti. Our warehouse is the water floor with three floors beside it. On the primo floor, we entertain in two large, public rooms, have an office and a music room. The family lives in six private rooms on the secundo. The servants live on the top floor. Behind the house are a large vegetable garden, an herb garden, and a lovely flower garden. All walled, of course."

Telling me they are prosperous. Eager to convince me living with him will be pleasant. "Have you music in your household?"

"We have a harp." He shifted in his seat. *Whose, I wonder.* "You said you play the harpsichord. I would make one your wedding gift."

"A kind offer, sir, and something I would need should I teach your daughter to sing and play." *Ask it.* "Do married il grandi women sing and play music in their own homes. I must have time each week-day to sing and play. I cannot do without it."

"You would have time."

We stared at each other. *Ask another question.* "Who is your housekeeper?"

"Sabina. Her husband is Tomaso, our maiordomo. Their daughter and son also work for us. We have long hired whole families and kept them for as long as they will stay. Tomaso was born in our house, and his parents served mine."

"I am an orphan. I have no dowry. No rank."

"You would be a Delatesta, a one hundred third like me. If you are willing, my father and Mother Superior will settle matters."

"You still want me to be your wife?"

"Si."

"Why?"

"Because I like you. Because you are accomplished. Father, who is never wrong about people, says you are a woman of worth. Because I would be proud to have you on my arm."

"Grazie mille for your offer of marriage...Antonio. I will pray on the matter. Mother Superior will write your father soon." I stood; Antonio rose and bowed. I curtsied and departed with Sister Santina following me.

Marriage! To such a man. Stiff-backed, but he has a deep, pleasant voice. No warmth. Yet an il grandi! A family! Chiseled chin. Handsome. Smells good, a manly scent. Well spoken but cautious. What does he fear? Frowned when I said Mother would write. Not accustomed to asking? Expected an immediate yes? I will ask her about them. I schooled my expression to neutral as I approached the stairs and hid in the dormitory.

I sat on my bed as I considered. *Married. Can sing and play daily. Supervise the housekeeper, not be one. Raise his daughter and any children we have. Hire a nurse, not be one. His father seems nice. He is offering me a family. Oh Lord, is it a good one? Remember Padre Nicolo's Sunday sermons. No one is perfect; nothing is. Especially not me. Do not expect him to be so.* I heard noises on the stairs and stood.

I remained silent throughout supper and answered no questions while returning to the dormitory after Vespers in the chapel. I readied for bed and said The Recitation with the others. With coverings to my chin, I stared at the ceiling. *No more practicing for hours. I will miss rehearsals with my sisters and our performances. I will miss seeing Padre Vivaldi or his teasing me. Here more than half my life is music. Married, much less.*

Yet, I will be in my own household, setting menus, making decisions. I can set my own times for playing and singing. Songs I like, not what performances require. May I also leave and return when I choose? Climb the bell tower to view the city and the lagoon? What of the rumors about the city's failing economy? With their high rank, I wager they are not suffering. Not if they can afford a harpsichord.

Refusing to respond when my sisters asked why I was smiling, I rolled to my side as Caterina extinguished all the candles but one. *Life outside this place! A husband. My own household. A chance for children! Thank you, God.*

6

❧

April 23

I followed Sister Santina to the choral hall. *Why am I present-ing myself dressed as I did four days ago? Do I meet the father or Antonio? I have not asked Mother Superior to write. What do they want now?*

Sister stopped me and stepped through the doorway. "We present Grazia."

I walked into the hall. Sitting alone was a gray-haired elder. Dressed in black brocade and silk, white hose, and black shoes, his face showed no expression. *Taller heels than the Delatestas. Who is he?* With one leg extended and a glass of wine in his left hand, he looked relaxed and confident. Around his neck he wore a gold and sapphire emblem on a ring of large, flat, gold links. His lined face bespoke sadness. I froze at the way his eyes examined me from my face to my feet; the tight line of his mouth and the hardness of his stare frightened me.

The chain and emblem. One of the Council of Forty? What could he want with me? When he gestured I was to approach, I unwillingly

31

stepped where he pointed.

"Grazia, you are a beautiful woman. I know of your many accomplishments and high moral character. I find you a suitable wife for my only son and heir. You and he are close in age and will live long, happy lives together. I expect you to bear male children, give my son heirs."

I remained silent as he continued. "The Golden Book at the Palaso Doxe lists families of ancient Venetian origin; Pontenuevo is in it. Admission to the book was closed in the year of Our Lord, 1297. Any family arriving after that is of no consequence. Married to my only son, you two will live in a wing of your own in Palaso Pontenuevo on Canale Grande. You will have new clothing each season and wear beautiful jewels. You will dine sumptuously each day and live a life of ease. Skilled nurses will raise your children. All who know me will receive you, befriend you, and tout you. You will do no work but for charity or to support Our Mother, the Church. We also have other homes. A villa south of the city is on the coast and another palaso is in the hills of Montagna Lozzo where we look down at the valley. In my world, you need only order what you desire. For every healthy grandson you birth, I will reward you more and more. Richer clothing, more jewels, your own gondola.

"Know whom you are joining. My family has been among the First Ninety-nine since they started the system—almost five hundred years. I rank thirty-seven. The next doxe comes from within The Forty. Do you accept this offer of marriage into my family?"

"May I ask questions?" He sipped his wine and give a curt nod. "Have you other children?" At Ponteneuvo's glare and head shake, I looked down. *A father with one son is not a family.* I looked up and saw the man's face had remained a mask. "Signor Pontenuevo, you are important, very important. You have the single girls among the First Ninety-nine from which to choose. Why do you seek me to be your son's wife? I am an orphan and no one of importance."

Pontenuevo set his glass on the table beside him. "That is why I choose you. Marriage within my circle would create connections I do not want. You come to me—to us—unencumbered by family or alliances. That is to my advantage."

Two offers of marriage in the same week. Thank you, God, for your generosity. Which to choose? "Signor Pontenueva, you are more generous and beneficent than I deserve, but I cannot agree to such a match without first meeting my intended. I look forward to your next visit when you introduce me to your fine son. I will give you my decision after we have met and talked."

Glaring, Pontenuevo stood and stepped to me.

Do not cringe. He cannot force me. Frozen, I stared at his empty chair.

In a voice dripping with danger, he hissed into my ear. "If I accept you, my son accepts you. My offer is the best you will ever receive. Mother Superior will convince you of the wisdom of agreeing to this match. I expect a written answer by Tuesday morning."

I waited for his hard steps on our wooden floor to fade. *His tone, his glare. He expected immediate acceptance. No, obedience. Something is not right. I feel it. I must ask Mother.* "Sister, I…"

"No! Speak only to Mother Superior."

I fled the room and Sister Santina followed. "Where are you going?"

"To the chapel!"

The next morning, I dismissed Anzola from making purchases and stood on the dock outside the kitchen. When the fish seller's boat approached, I waved the others back to give us privacy. I crouched and set yesterday's empty basket on the boards. Taking his offering, I whispered as I slowly inspected each item. "No smell. Caught this morning?" At his assent, I changed the subject. "I have questions."

"This is your regular Saturday order."

I barely moved my lips. "Whisper. What know you of Signor Pontenueva?"

"Very dangerous. If he learned I spoke of him, he would destroy my family." He paused. "But I like you. One of the First Forty. Wears his emblem everywhere. Has enemies."

"His family?"

"A daughter died. A son never seen outside their palaso. Born nineteen, twenty years ago. They say he has strange eyes, talks funny, is simple. Plays with miniature soldiers. "

"What else?" I picked up another fish and held it up as if to scrutinize it.

"After the first two, his next son was born early, dead. Deformed, they say. Shortly afterward, his wife died. He remarried, tried again, and failed with her too. He let her join a convent. No wife since."

I spoke loudly. "You are right; these are the best we have seen in a month. I give you the regular cost, plus two soldi for the freshness of your catch."

"Grazie," said the fisher as he smiled recognition for what I was paying. He pocketed the coins and took the empty basket. After he turned his gondola and oared up the rio, I waved the next boat forward. I finished making purchases for the kitchen from the other sellers and handed the items to the kitchen helpers. After I locked the door, I returned the coin purse to Anzola and strode to the chapel.

I knelt in the front pew before the lit candle, mentally talking to it as if it were God, not His representation. With hands clasped against the wooden railing, I prayed for guidance. I leaned back and mulled over what I had learned. *The Golden Book. Is he telling me only the First Ninety-nine are important? Are true Venetians? Healthy daughter, but not sons. How did his first wife die? Let the second one go to a convent? Two are not a family. When the father dies…*

What is wrong with his son that he is not seen? Might he be a simpleton? What if he is and it is hereditary? How do I get healthy, smart children from a father who may be neither? How do I birth smart children from a man with a boy's mind? What will happen to me if I… fail? Suddenly, I straightened and fear assailed me. "What if… what if he wants to try again with me and claim his son is the father? He said 'we.' Is he so powerful he thinks he can do anything? Once I am in his household, will he… Dear God, Blessed Mary, protect me! Once caught, he will never let me outside. How do I escape this?" *Great and Good God, I beg you, give me guidance, a plan. Something.* I leaned forward against the pew back before me and pressed my hands together so hard my fingertips paled.

7

April 25

After supper Mother Superior walked me through the garden of trees, flowers, and sprouting vegetables. She settled on the bench farthest from the house and patted the seat beside her. Mother waited until she heard me sigh.

I pointed. "Last week that was a bud. Now look. I can even smell its scent."

"You have decided."

I glanced at her and nodded.

"You choose Antonio because he is young and handsome, not because of his position. That is not wise. Pontenuevo is more powerful and much richer."

"Antonio has a brother and sister; they have spouses and children. That is a family. A father and son is not a family. When Signor Pontenuevo dies, his son and I will be alone with our children. No family. No support. No protection."

"What else are you thinking?"

"Antonio talked of his farms and ships with pride. I see a vigorous man who will work hard to keep what he has and gain more. He hinted times are hard. You know I can be frugal. Both families want heirs, but I believe I can be more help to Antonio. Teach him to need me for more than sons. Pontenuevo needs me for only one thing. What will he do to me if I do not produce sons?" Mother Superior glanced away. *What does she know? What is she hiding?*

"Signor Pontenuevo is very strong, a powerful man, but is his son? Is he powerful enough to keep me and our children safe, to hold and even increase his wealth in these troubled times? I have not met him, and Signor said I would not. What does it say of the son that I cannot see him? I will not walk into church and marry a man I have not met, not talked with. A complete stranger? No."

"You forget what Pontenuevo can do for you by being among the First Forty."

"Mother, I have prayed over this. I would be a curiosity. Women would fawn over me and be polite when men were present, but you know how they are. I am so much less than they, and they would be sure I knew it every moment of my life. Gestures, looks, words, snubs. They will insult me a thousand ways without men noticing. Among the Second Hundred, I may find a friend. At least I would be in a family."

I held out my raised left arm and extended my pointing finger. "This is the doxe, highest position in the Veneto. The eight hundred go to the ground." I dropped my thumb three inches below my finger. "Pontenuevo and son are only that much lower." I leaned to point my right hand finger a meter below my thumb. "This is the Delatestas. I know even this is too high for me. Mother, the truth is that I am lower than the lowest of the eight hundreds. Not even on the list.

"The Second Hundred women will insult me the same, but I will be busy running a household and raising a family. I will be useful, needed. I will be more than a body birthing sons. Even a distant brother and a sister can visit and I could lean on them."

"Pontenuevo will not be happy with your decision. He will make you pay; he will make us pay."

I guessed aright. "He has threatened you, my sisters, our home."

"He is not subtle."

I looked away. *Buzzing has ceased. Silent birds rest in the trees. The sun will soon set.* "That he would threaten you and my sisters reveals his true character. No. I will not submit, no matter how many dresses and jewels mask his threats. You must protect yourself and the others. I must protect myself."

"You are tired. We will talk again in the morning."

I looked into her eyes and held them. "Mother, we can talk here until dark. We can move to the chapel and talk until dawn. You may sit behind your desk, and I will stand before you for as many days as you wish. I will not change my mind. I will not marry Pontenuevo's son."

"Buone notte, Grazia."

I stood and curtsied. "Buone notte, Mother." I left her.

8

April 26

After Mass I approached Mother Superior. She raised her brows. "Your eyes are red and you look tired. You tied back your hair with a cloth and not with a ribbon. You are in work clothes."

"Mother, I have been thinking. May I speak with one or both Delatestas in your office before the end of this day? I want not to write what they must know." At her nod I curtsied. "I will be in the chapel."

Within an hour a girl told me to report to Mother. "Per favore, will you meet me outside her office with a glass of water?" The girl nodded.

Outside the waiting room I dipped two fingers into the glass to dab my eyelids and did the same to cool my cheeks. The water eased my tight throat. I returned the empty glass and tried to inhale courage as I stiffened my back. *I can do this; I must.* Only then did I reach for the door handle. Grateful the waiting room was empty, I gave Sister Iseppa a wan smile. Without smiling back she gestured me forward. I saw Mother Superior first. Senior Delatesta rose from his chair and caught my eye; I nodded and curtsied.

"Buone giorno, Signor." I curtsied again. "Buone giorno, Mother." They repeated my greeting.

"Per favore, do sit," requested Mother Superior.

Signor waited for me to sit first. *A gesture of respect. So different from the other.* "Antonio is away?"

"No. He expects you summoned us to refuse him. He said he could not bear to see your face when you say no."

I grasped my left fingers with my right hand, placed them in my lap, and gazed at them. "Does he still want to marry me?"

"Si."

"Signor, you may advise him otherwise after you hear what I say. Afterward, I leave to your good judgment to do what is best for your family." When no one spoke, I looked at him and continued. "On Friday Signor Pontenuevo asked me to marry his son." I corrected myself. "No ordered me. First, he promised me clothes, jewels, houses, a luxurious life. He reminded me how important I would become by marrying into his family. When I asked to meet his son, he turned on me." I saw Signor nod. "Later, he threatened Mother Superior to harm Oespedale if I do not consent."

"That sounds like Pontenuevo," smirked Signor. "You are right to be afraid of him."

"I do not want him to harm you, Antonio, your family, your businesses." I paused. "Your lives."

"You think marrying Pontenuevo's son will save us? It will not. He has been our enemy for years. Nothing you can do will change that."

I gazed into Signor's eyes. "Why?"

"It is a long dispute of no consequence here." Signor leaned against the back of his chair.

A trade war?

"Pontenuevo did not think to ask you until he learned Antonio did."

"How did he know?"

"He has spies. Many in Venezia do; secrets are almost impossible to keep."

"I must save my sisters and Ospedale."

"I assure you, Ospedale has many powerful friends who will keep it safe. Pontenuevo has enemies. Last year, they passed over him, and he did not become our new doxe. Yet he expects to be the next one." *Signor chuckles as if he knows something Pontenuevo does not. His face turns serious; he has decided.* "Child, what are you going to do?"

I looked away. "Refuse Antonio."

"And marry a Pontenuevo?"

"No. To protect Antonio and Ospedale, I will go far away into a cloistered convent, never to be seen again." *Never to see the world again. What a price to pay to keep my sisters safe! My heart grieves.* "He could not harm Ospedale or your family for that."

Signor pushed himself to the edge of his chair. He reached and lay a hand over mine, and whispered, "What do you want, Grazia?" He waited.

A family. Children. A life beyond here. If his family is my only chance, then I must take it. A cold husband is still a husband. "I want to wed Antonio." I felt tears coming. *Do not cry Do not cry.*

Signor smiled at me. He looked at Mother Superior, cocked his head, and raised his brows. At her nod, he instructed, "Wait here, Grazia. Do not leave." He strode out of the room and closed the door behind himself.

Did I say something wrong?

Mother rounded her desk. "Do not cry, my child," she said as she drew me into her arms. I pulled away to look into her face and sniffled. She stroked my back. "I know how badly you want to live in the world. If you did not like a post, with our help, you could leave and find another. Marry and we can no longer help you. Marriage is permanent; you cannot leave it. Are you certain you want to marry? Do you favor him enough for a lifetime together?"

I shrugged, but I also smiled.

Just then, the door opened and Antonio stepped through. I pulled away from Mother. He bowed. "Mother Superior." Then he turned and stared into my eyes. "Will you marry me?"

"Si."

Antonio opened his arms, and I walked into them. He hugged me hard. *Such strength! He will protect me. Warm. Feels good to lean against him.* Against my ear, I heard his strong heart beating fast. *Maybe not so cold after all.* "He will never have you," he promised. I looked up, and Antonio kissed me. Not knowing how to respond, I froze. When we finally parted, I tucked my head under his chin and inhaled his man-scent.

Still in his arms, I heard, "I should not have done that."

"No you should not," Mother admonished. "Release her. No more kissing or touching until AFTER the marriage ceremony."

"Yes, Mother," we said in unison. I giggled.

"Grazia, eat something. Then wait in the chapel. These signori and I must write a marriage contract."

Grinning, I nodded to Mother, Signor and Antonio. I walked around my espoused and closed the door behind myself. I beamed at

Sister Iseppa and kissed her cheek. Then I bounced out of the room and hummed my way to the kitchen.

Late that afternoon, Mother Superior summoned me to her office.

"You must pen the letter to Pontenuevo in your own hand. Would you like help to word it?"

She is asking, not telling. Is she treating me like an adult because I am now espoused? "Si, per favore."

Mother handed pen, ink and paper across her desktop as I pulled a chair to the edge of the desk and picked up the quill.

Ask now or I may never know. "Why is his family named 'new bridge'?'

"His family arrived before the Golden Book closed. Before they built their palaso, the family ordered a bridge built across a side rio, so they could walk to church instead of ordering a gondola. Only the second in all the city besides Ponte Rialto. They renamed themselves 'Pontenuevo' and informed the il grandi they considered themselves to be one of them. Since then, their increasing wealth made them one of the Ninety-nine, then among the First Forty." She pointed to the writing implements before me.

"How do I start?"

"Everything starts on the left. Two centimeters from the top write 'To Signor Nicolo Pontenuevo.'" We continued, she advising and me writing. I finished, signed and dated the letter; then I handed it over for inspection.

To Signor Nicolo Pontenuevo

I am most grateful you asked me to marry your son. To join your family is an honor too far above my station. I know I am most unworthy, and I fear stepping into such a prominent place from my low one. I am certain I would not fit into your world and be the credit to your family and to your position as you would need me to be. Per favore, accept my sincere, heart-felt apologies for not accepting the honor of becoming a member of your most noble family. Per favore, extend my deep regrets to your son.

Yours in Christ,
Grazia of Pio Ospedale della Pieta'
26 April 1723

"Well done." Mother Superior folded the letter and held a wax stick over the candle beside her. "After I seal it, I will send it to Pontenuevo's home. The gondolier will wait and hand it only to him, so he cannot claim he never received it." She sealed the letter by stamping the dripped wax with the metal Ospedale symbol, which then she set aside.

I watched her blow on the wax to set it. "Why send it tonight when tomorrow morning is soon enough?"

"I want him to learn it from you first, so he is prepared for questions or gossip. Tomorrow may be too late." She set the letter before her and admitted, "Rumors may make it already too late, but at least we will have tried. Grazia, until the Delatestas escort you into the church, we must guard you every moment."

"Would Pontenuevo charge our home to take me by force?"

"He hates the Delatesta family that much. You will stay in the third floor attic. No leaning out windows. No going outside. No meeting vendors at our kitchen door. No dining in the hall. Take every meal from the kitchen before or after we eat. No practicing in the music building. No rehearsals. No performances. To keep you

46

safe, you must not be seen again until you are guarded the whole way to the church ceremony.

"You will attend Mass once a week, but never on the same day. Your sisters will never call your name nor speak of you. Find a hidden spot and tell no one where it is. You must have a secure place should attackers storm us to remove you."

I felt my eyes widen. Mother reached across the desk and grasped my hand. "I am sorry my child, but this is not punishment or a prison. I am trying to protect you so you have the future you desire. To bed. I will hand this letter to a gondolier to deliver before I re-lock and bar the main door."

We stood. Mother gazed at me for a moment before she turned and I followed. I watched her descend the stairs. Candle in hand, I slowly climbed the stairs to my dormitory room. Each step included a prayer I would remain safe until I became Antonio's wife.

9

April 29

After Mass in the church attached to our building, Mother sent for me. I met her in the dining hall. She stood beside the head table as she faced the room and I had my back to it."My child, you have done well to hide and remain silent. Your sisters know nothing, but they are guessing wild things. Look disappointed despite what I tell you.

"Signor Delatesta sent word. The Council received the petition and documents requesting they consent to the marriage of Antonio of the house Delatesta to Grazia, orphan, of the Pio Ospedale della Pieta'. Drop your head and sag your shoulders." Mother looked over my head and frowned. I knew many would look away and heard girls scratch benches against the floor as they sat. "Now comes the waiting. The Council meets not in June, July, or August except for a critical matter. They will either accept the petition step in May, or you must wait for the summer or longer. Look disappointed; refuse to speak, fill a plate, and leave. That should quell the girls' gossip."

Saturday, I sneaked into the office. "Mother, I have searched every place I can think of from the vestibule door to the storage area under the roof. Nowhere have I found a spot where searchers could not find me. I sleep not for worry. What can I do?"

She leaned back into her chair and sighed. "I know every part of this place, and I too lack…" Sister looked away; I waited. Suddenly she commanded, "Grazia, swear to our Holy Lord what I am about to tell you, what I am about to show you, will remain a secret. No matter the cost, no matter the pain, swear you will die with this secret unspoken." I knelt, placed my hands together in prayer and so swore. "Gather cleaning supplies. Go to the chapel. Dust and polish. Should anyone enter, ask them to return after you have finished. Stay until I come to you."

"Yes, Mother." I stood and departed. Later I was re-dusting the already clean pews when Mother arrived.

"Did anyone enter?" I shook my head. "Sit." She joined me. "When our order converted this home to meet our needs, we attached our small church to our west wall. You walk through an old outside doorway right into it. We also added the educational wing behind our building. As long as you do not leave or look out windows, no one knows where you are in our compound. I have already locked the church's entry door so Father may enter only by our main door. A sister sees no one else is about before we open the church to our neighbors. You are safe unless we are invaded.

"Before I was born, thieves pillaged the church for coin. The bishop commanded the thieves to return the coins on pain of excommunication both for those who had robbed us and for any who accepted the stolen coins. They returned the bags, some at the bishop's office, some at our front door. Since then our supporters send their donations directly to the bishop's office."

"When I was learning to run Ospedale, each week you gave me

a bag of coins to purchase food. I was proud of my frugality." *Do not brag.* "I returned the bag and tried to have a few coins remaining."

"We charge almost everything, including the cloth for your red uniforms; we send the receipts to the bishop's finance office. After I send in my monthly list of charges and their accounts match ours, they pay our debts. However, each Monday after Mass, the priest hands me our allotment to purchase food. I save the unspent coins; and, once or twice a year, we eat very well on a holy day. No one dare rob a priest so he is safe. Everyone knows we have no wealth here so we are safe as well."

I nodded. "An excellent system." I frowned. "Why do we then hold two concerts and a tea each year for our benefactors?"

"From whom do you think the Church receives coins to record in our account?"

"Oh-h-h!"

"Bring your cleaning rags."

Sister led me to the priests' robing room. "This corner room used to keep a priest's vestments. It hides a secret." She watched me look at the plain wooden walls. She opened the vestment closet. "Watch." Sister drew aside the sister's winter capes and pushed on the back wall on the top left and at the bottom left corners. The back wall sprang forward and stopped when it touched the garments. Mother Superior gestured.

I stooped and looked left. "I see nothing but blackness. I smell an old dusty place."

"Exactly. On your knees clean the place all the way to the other side of the altar, especially any spider webs. Then return."

As I worked I dusted and passed a wooden box of papers and a small bag of coins. *Clean well; I may need to hide here.* I backed my way to the opening and turned myself around as Mother had instructed.

"Pull the leather strap to close the door from the inside.' After I did so, I heard a muffled, "Now push the door open."

I placed the dusty rags on the closet floor, crawled out of the hole, dropped the rags into the room and stood. I closed the back wall, replaced the capes and shut the closet door.

"Grazia, remove the dust from the floor." Mother brushed my back with the last clean rag. "Remove the dirt from your knees and clean where you stand. Tonight, when all are asleep, I will place a dark blanket inside the hole. If you must use it, crawl all the way to the end of the altar and cover yourself. Even if someone finds this place, he will look inside and see blackness. Beware, Grazia, you must breathe slowly. With no other air, you cannot stay long. If you get lightheaded, you must leave. Try to stay inside the closet."

Mother watched me clean myself and the surrounding floor. "How did you get so dirty, Grazia?"

"I found a spot everyone has been missing for months, Mother. It is clean now."

Mother Superior nodded at my answer, turned and left.

I hide so I may have a family and children. Even if he is cold, I can bear that. I will miss practicing daily and performing with my sisters. Will I still have my music every day? I must have times when I may be alone to sing and play. Teach his daughter and any children we have to love and play music as much as I do. I will not abandon music. I can insist on that.

Not be a servant or raise someone else's children. This marriage is like a business contract. I leave here to live in the world and have a family. I will bear my own children, run the household and raise the children. He gets a well-run household and, God willing, heirs.

Wait until I am certain Mother is in her office to return my supplies to the cleaning closet and then eat. Tonight, I will sleep in my hiding place with the secret door ajar. Before dawn, I will leave. Hide in the attic unless we are invaded.

In the attic I turned onto my side on the pile of blankets on the floor, I fell asleep thinking about Antonio. I dreamt he gazed at me with loving eyes as we walked a sunny garden of blooms, and we smiled at the bambino in my arms.

10

Palaso Delatesta

May 4

At a tap on my shoulder, I opened my eyes and blinked at the darkness. "Silence. Shoes. Follow," came in whispers.

How did she know tonight I was hiding among my sisters?

The figure rounded the end of my cot and slipped past Caterina, who was snoring softly. Because the windows were still black, I moved from memory. I exited the dormitory and silently closed the door. Descending the stairs behind Sister Iseppa, I guessed her destination before we reached the first floor. "Enter. You are going outside." Swathed in a dark robe over her nightclothes, Sister gestured toward the office door and turned down the hall to her own wing.

Mother Superior smiled at my wide eyes. "The Council agreed to hear Signor Delatesta's petition for your marriage to his son on the twenty-fourth, three days before they adjourn. They want to meet you. If their refusal is not immediate, you will wait past summer for them to reconvene and issue their judgment. However, you may wait even longer. They work at their own pace."

"How do they decide?"

"The Council of Forty follows the rulings the censors state regarding our laws. Factions for and against your union will parlay for supporters. Politics, power or money are always the reasons for their decisions.

"If they refuse the petition, may we still marry?"

Mother shook her head. "None of the first three hundred marries without Council approval."

"The danger."

"You cannot avoid it. You may not prepare to meet the Council here. Your sisters must never know what you do outside. Let them think you were hiding. You will return after dark. If anyone asks where you have been, smile and say nothing. Speak not of what you saw or did." At my nod Mother pointed to the chair holding a dark blue gown. "You will wear one of my vestitos. You will be covered with the half-mask and the black hooded cape and gloves everyone wears outside this time of year. Away from our door no one will know you. The gondoliers will protect you. Dress quickly. You must arrive before dawn."

Holding a lit candle, Sister Santina led me through the kitchen to the pier. From a gondola beside the boards, a gloved hand reached into the small circle of light as a voice spoke. "Secura." *A password?* Sister handed the candle to a sister behind her and accepted the man's hand. After she settled in the bow, the hand reached again.

"Secura mia donna."

"Silenzio," hissed Sister.

I took the large gloved hand. Also caped and masked, the man squeezed my hand, then helped me into the boat. I sat and reached for both rims to steady my emotions. *Warm voice. Called me his! Not so cold after all. Just careful. Our first gondola ride together!* From the kitchen dock, the boat slipped up the narrow rio. My eyes adjusted, and the world stayed dark gray as the boats swirled away the mists in their path. Over Antonio's head, a dark figure rowed as the boat ahead preceded us. Behind our gondolier, I spotted the bow of a third boat. *Guards front and back. So careful.* I smiled and nodded to the figure before me; he smiled back.

The boats zigzagged northward as I gazed left and right at the dark buildings. *Will I see the Canale Grande? Travel on it?* At the juncture of a wide rio we turned left onto a smaller one. The buildings were large and grand.

A pre-dawn glimmer touched the water. At the end of the second house, the boats turned left toward a pier with the front boat circling to stop beside ours. Masked but wearing no capes, three men searched the area behind us with their hands on sword hilts. Antonio left my boat. Standing on his pier, he scanned the area. As he reached for Sister's extended hand, I noted the back boat mirrored the first one.

Long legs. Under his cape the tip of a sword peeking out. Do all men go about armed? I raised my arm and felt my hand squeezed again. I tripped on my cape as I tried to stand on my seat. Antonio grabbed my flailing hand and lifted me. He stepped back and lowered me until my feet touched the boards. The warmth of his hands raced to my heart. A harsh cough stopped me from speaking.

I turned to follow Sister. Two guards opened a massive, nail-studded door, and we passed through. To the right of the narrow stairs before us stood a pair of tall doors from below the water line to high above us. The boards had jagged bottoms rotted from being in the water. The upper and lower locks were bigger and thicker than a large man's hands. Sister grasped the railing and started up the steps. I gazed upward at a window centered between the top of the stairs and the door tops. A guard looked at me. *Cement railing and stairs cannot burn. Stairs only wide enough for one person at a time and a landing halfway to the top. A guard to call the alarm or throw hot water on attackers. Attack from whom?*

At the top of the stairs, Sister and I stepped into a small room. *Only big enough for two swordsmen to block the way.* I scraped my shoes against a thick, rough rug. Pegs on the left wall held capes above an empty long box below them. *For masks, gloves, scarves? A landing place to separate the outside world from the inside one.*

A second pair of doors opened to a grand hall well lit by candles. I saw marble floors, and cushioned benches on either side. In the center, stood a table with a gold-streaked glass vase filled with flowers. Both behind us and at the other end of the long hall ahead, pre-dawn glimmers lit the windows and parts of the floor.

An older woman in a crisp white apron gestured us to follow. Sister and I passed an archway to our right. I peeked left through a wide arch into a salon before we turned right. We took stairs to the second floor, turned right again, and entered a room with a wide bed jammed into a corner. On the table before us stood a lit three-tiered candelabra.

"Per favore. Ladies, do not leave this room. After you break your fasts, knock on the door. Someone will take the tray and lead the seamstresses to you." She pointed to the table with pottery mugs and a carafe beside a tray laden with fruit, bread and cheeses. "I am

Sabina, the housekeeper." She left.

Sister removed her gloves and stuffed them into the cape's side pockets. She pushed back her hood, untied her mask and dropped it at the end of the bed. We both undid our ties and draped our capes at the end of the bed. I removed my mask and set it upon my cape. Sister Santina led the prayer and we sat. I asked, "Sister, why do we wear white masks to the tips of our noses and down our cheeks? Why do we go out caped and hooded in black?"

"From mid-September through May, Venetians travel covered to protect their identities and to move in privacy. Men meet, do business and write contracts without the whole town knowing. Once a boat is in a rio or the Canale Grande, everyone looks alike. Covered, women are safer because no one knows who is rich, who is not. The heat of the other months is too great to be swathed. Business falls back, and women travel not at all or with more armed escorts than in the cooler months."

I pulled another chunk of bread from the loaf and topped it with a slice of rosemary-flavored goat cheese. "The gondoliers know who goes where."

"If any of them speak or spies, he and all his family are banished. They may never return to Serenissima. A harsh punishment indeed."

"Do people spy on one another?" I chewed my last bite as I listened.

"I expect so. Most often, household servants pass information and gossip for denari. As we have only sisters of the cloth and you girls, no spies." Sister drank the well-watered wine and set down her empty glass. "Nothing we do is important enough to pass. Until this matter."

I took the empty tray to the door, knocked twice and set it on the floor. Before I could back away, a girl opened the door, bent, pulled the tray to her and closed the door.

A troop of women entered carrying bolts of cloth and wooden boxes with leather handles. They laid the bolts on the bed. One woman emptied a box of slippers, shoes, and short boots of various sizes and colors. She lined them with the toes pointed to the wall. Two others opened boxes of small balls of thread, scissors of various sizes, needles in cloth swatches and other sewing equipment. The final case held brushes, assorted combs, ribbons and strings of pearls. A young woman sat at the table with a parchment, quill and ink pot before her.

"Sono Signora Fiamette Barbo, head seamstress. Donna, may we help you disrobe? We must measure you for a vestitio for your presentation to the Council."

Tall and stately. Her simple dress matches her gray hair as if she wants to disappear. Not shine so her work does. Her dove-gray vestito has a modest, plain neckline with long sleeves loose for easy movement. No lace. No hoop or multiple slips for fullness. Her helpers are also dressed in the same clothes; their hair is also bound in buns at their napes.

I looked to Sister Santina. At her nod, I lifted my arms and accepted the women's ministrations. I stood bare-footed in the middle of the room in my sleeveless undergarment. Barbo stepped around me. Using her right hand with fingers and knuckles tucked under, the seamstress touched me across my throat. She called, "Throat thumb to four." The girl with sun- colored hair sitting at the table wrote something. Barely touching me, Barbo called other strange measurements. She used her first finger for neck to shoulder and said, "Shoulder one." Neck to waist was "thumb to four plus thumb to one." The woman continued until she had all the measurements she wanted.

Next, another helper, who looked to be the older sister of the first girl, stood beside the footwear and called me to her. With my hand on the wall to steady myself I tried one right shoe after the other. When the woman was satisfied, she called, "Slippers green. For shoes yellow. For short boots blue for height."

Released, I stepped to the bed and wrapped myself with my cape. Sister was speaking with Signora Barbo. I sat on the bed and eyed the bolts to my left. *All light or medium colors. Are deep colors reserved for married or older women or for winter? I fingered an end. Not linen. Soft, light. Not cotton. Smooth. Silk? I imagined names. Cloud, cream, apricot, peach, shallow sea, sunshine sea, seaweed, leaves, sky blue, sea blue, sun yellow, gold. The cream and pale yellow stripe is nice. I like the flower bouquets on the other cream best. Not that they will ask me; I know nothing of fashion. This is a bigger life than I imagined. Huge house, servants, beautiful clothes.*

I walked to the pair in conversation and heard Sister grumble, "No, no. Not those ugly panniers from the French and English courts. They are an abomination that deforms God's creation and wastes fabric. We will accept a circle of fullness but not deformity."

"You want her to be the young innocent she is," agreed Signora Barbo.

Sister nodded. "No pushing up breasts or even showing the tops. No display of ankles or bare shoulders. We will have modesty or she will not appear!"

"Si, Sister. Would you like to help select the fabric?"

I followed and watched as she loosed bolt after bolt and draped the fabric over my caped shoulder. I heard, "Too pale. Dulls her skin. Does not complement her eyes. Dulls her hair." Three bolts remained, the medium blue with waves in the weave, the yellow, and the floral embroidery on cream. The women dismissed the yellow because it was too close the my hair color.

"If you will accept either the blue or the cream, I will present them to Signor Antonio and he will choose which he prefers."

"I like the cream," I volunteered.

"He will select the blue; men usually do," muttered Sister.

Why am I not allowed to choose? Do men rule everything, even their wives' clothing? Will I want to get around that? How? Something to learn later… not until I know more of the outside world. For now, accept.

While the two seamstresses used the table to cut and to rough sew together pieces of linen, a hairdresser arrived. She was dressed so differently from the others that I stared; I remembered my manners and looked away. Her hairstyle was fashionably formed and decorated with enameled colorful pins. She wore an ornate dress of dark blue with lace at the squared neckline and at her elbows. Her tiny waist was accented by hoops under her skirt. The front insert of her skirt was cream silk with birds and flowers embroidered on it. She looked rich.

I sat sideways and held the back of the chair while the hair dresser, addressed only as "Mademoiselle," walked around me with her hand to her chin. She lifted segments of my locks, twisted them this way and that and pinned them on my head in assorted places with U-shaped thin metal pins. Sister Santina rejected each effort as "Too adult. Too complex. Not appropriate for an innocent." That the woman declared "I am a French maid!" did not change Sister's sour expressions.

What is a French maid?

After several more refusals of styles, the woman stood back.

"You do it!"

Sister parted my hair from the middle of my forehead to my crown. She started a braid at the part and curved it against my head as she braided it almost to the end. Sister handed the unfinished braid to the French maid. She started a second braid at my temple and handed that to me. Then she took a square of hair before my ear, braided that strand and tied all three together with a thread. Sister created the same three braids on my right side. "Can you make a complex knot of braids at the back of her head with her free hair flowing down her back?"

Mademoiselle smiled. "Watch." She draped the braids over my locks. As she formed and pinned, Sister held the box of pins for her. The women looked at each other and said "Lovely" in unison.

"Sister, how do you know this style?"

"It is a classic. Modest and subdued. The older men will remember it is a symbol of innocence."

I burned to see myself, but spotted neither a polished metal nor a silver-painted Murano glass mirror. I turned to the women stitching and smiled at their approving looks. One held up the top of the model of a dress with the sleeves attached. Another held what was to be the skirt. The women looked to the head seamstress.

I wore the sample garment seams out. The women adjusted and ran lines of stitches where to take in, blue thread, or let out, red thread.

"Too low," decreed Sister as she eyed the straight line of cloth across my chest that barely covered my nipples.

"First finger to the first knuckle higher?" asked Barbo.

"Second knuckle."

"Too high. They will refuse her because they think her a child, not a young woman. Compromesso. Two fingers higher?"

"Agreed."

The women gathered up their goods and refilled the boxes. Signora Barbo exited the room, and her staff followed.

"I am hungry."

"We will sup at home. Dress."

I donned my uniform, a red, short-sleeved dress to my ankles. I fastened my embroidered linen belt at my waist and slipped into my shoes. We donned our masks, capes, and gloves. Sister knocked on the door. Sabina escorted us to the inner door and left.

Under the watchful eyes of the guard at the window, I followed sister down the cement stairs. We exited the outer doors and walked the pier. Our party returned us the way we had come. The whole way home, Antonio and I stared at each other, but I neither smiled nor spoke.

Sounds of the city accompanied us. Church bells announced sunset. From open windows I heard bits of conversations and parents calling children to bed. At our dock Sister ordered the men to remain in the gondola. First Sister and then I clutched a pier pole as we exited the gondola. I felt a burning at my back, but I dare not turn to see if he still watched me.

Sister Iseppa let us into Ospedale, locked and bolted the door. "Everyone is at chapel. Change in Mother Superior's office. In the kitchen, food awaits you. Sleep in your hiding place after everyone is in their dormitories. Do not appear until the morrow. Remember what Mother told you if you are asked about your absence. Buone notte."

Thursday, I stayed indoors while everyone else stood on the rooftop to watch the annual La Festa di Sensa. From my perch in the kitchen, I ate as I imagined the lagoon filled with colorful boats. The bishop marrying the doxe to the sea, and the doxe throwing a wedding ring into the lagoon as the symbol of our fair land marrying the sea from which comes Venice's wealth. I heard a resounding shout from the viewers and horns.

The ceremony is over. The city will party all day and into the night. In the dining hall my sisters will enjoy the delicious food I have just eaten. The rest of the day they will do no work, play games, sing and dance with each other. Time to hide in the attic.

11

Palaso Delatesta

May 24

I stared at my first vestito da donna as it hung from the wardrobe door. *So much skirt. So beautiful.* I touched the delicate flowers in one of the small bouquets that dotted the cream-colored silk. *Such fine stitching. Must be hard not to pucker such delicate cloth.* I crossed my arms over my waist and hugged myself. *For me! A ranked woman's garment. So pretty. Fashionable. To be admired, not usable like my uniform.* I stood tall. *I will look grown up and important.* I lightly touched the fabric gathered at the waist and drew my hand down. *Such Wealth. Just the fabric and its embroidery would feed Ospedale for a year.*

"Come child. You must prepare. The seamstress and the hair dresser wait," said the housekeeper.

I pulled off my shoes, undid my waistband and pulled my uniform over my head. "I bathed and washed my hair last night. Why this now?"

"Fashion. I must wipe your body with rose-scented water before you dress. These days, being clean is not good enough."

Sister snorted her disapproval. "Leave. I will not have strangers see her naked; I will do it." After the woman closed the door behind herself, Sister ordered me to remove my chemise. Sister held a small bowl of rose-scented water and a piece of wet linen. "Pick up your hair."

As she wiped my back, face, arms, and legs, I shivered. "Cold. Can you not pat me dry?"

Sister's answer was to pick up a second piece of linen and walk around me fanning the fabric. I kept shivering. "Your new chemise is on the bed."

Cream silk, like the dress. I picked up the slippery cloth and lifted it over my head, Ducking to get under it, I was astonished as it slid down my body. My skin tingled as the scooped-neck sleeveless tube caressed me. *So this is how il grande women start their days!* Because touching my body without cause is forbidden, I felt the fabric at my thighs. *Light as air. Only to the knees to aid walking.*

Four women bustled in. As instructed, I sat on the bed. An assistant handed me footed silk stockings, which she showed me how to don and pull to my knees. I fastened them in place with cream ribbons tied in a bow; the ends tickled my calves. I pushed my feet into the cream-dyed leather flat-heeled shoes. The dresser started matching ribbons under my arches, crossed them over my insteps, encircled my ankles, tied the ends in back and tucked the ends under the ribbon.

The woman instructed me to stand, approached and started placing an item around my rib cage and to my hips.

"No! You said nothing about her wearing a corset."

Fiamette Barbo retorted, "No need, Sister. Venetian women

have been wearing these for over a hundred fifty years. The dress will not fit without it. This is Venezia, not a provincial city. Every respectable woman wears one. Proceed."

As Sister crossed her arms over her chest and glared, the assistant laced, tightened the lacing and tied the bow at the back of my waist. The corset forced me to stand straighter. I looked down at my breasts, which the *corestto* had pushed upward. *This is why Sister wanted a high front.* I turned to admire my *vestito* again.

Signora Barbo stepped beside me. In a quiet voice, she reported, "He chose the blue. Then he asked, 'Which does she prefer?' You may be marrying an attentive man." *Attentive and kind.* "Use the chamber pot now; it is almost impossible afterward. We will turn our backs. Then dress and hair."

I inspected the linen underskirt. "Why is this layered?"

"One layer around your middle gives you a thin waist. Adding layers below hides your hips and gives you greater fullness to your ankles."

I raised my arms and bent toward the women. The seamstresses placed the underskirt hole over my arms and drew the skirt over my body as I straightened. One tied the waistband behind my left hip and dropped the ends down the remaining hole. Putting me into my dress was more complicated. As Barbo held the bodice upright, the three assistants held out the skirt in a high circle to prevent creases. I slipped under the skirt, inserted my arms into the sleeves and waited as the head seamstress lowered the bodice over my torso. When the skirt dropped over the underskirt, two assistants pulled the sleeves into position while the third faced me to secure the waist seam across my natural waist. I wriggled into the fitted bodice that must be laced to below my waist.

"Stop!" commanded Sister. "I ordered the cloth to be two fingers higher, not lace."

"The bodice is three centimeters higher as you had ordered. You did not specify it to be fabric. I used lace that matches the lace at the ends of her sleeves," huffed Barbo.

While the women argued, I looked down at the alabaster lace. I drew my fingertips across its delicate softness and sighed. I chose. "Sister Santina, the lace lays flat across my chest. The holes are so small, the lace is like fabric. When I look down, I see nothing of my breasts. Neither will any man, no matter how tall he is. Thank you, Signora Barbo. This lace makes me feel like a woman, not a girl." I watched Sister's jaw drop as the seamstress harrumphed her triumph. "Seamstress, the lace at the ends of my sleeves are so long they cover my hands when I lower my arms."

"It announces you are a donna. Lace-covered hands symbolize you do no work. "

"I am not a donna."

"When you dress as a donna, they will think you one. I predict you soon will be." We smiled at each other. "I will lay the flap across your back and do the laces myself." I gave Signora Barbo my back.

Mademoiselle appeared and styled my hair as before. She stood on a chair, so I did not have to sit and crease my gown. She made the three braids, which she laced between my fingers. *Fun this may be, but do not giggle. Be a lady.* At her instruction, I turned so she could do my right side. Standing with my back to her and facing Sister Santina, I waited as she created the knot.

When she reached for a pair of hair clips of tiny muli-colored flowers that matched the flowers on my gown, Sister stopped her. "No hair decorations. She is a maiden." Mademoiselle sighed her resignation and replaced the items in her apron pocket.

As I moved away, one of Signora Barbo's assistants helped her off the chair. Mademoiselle brushed and finger-curled my hair. Before she left she whispered into my ear, "C'est magnifique." *I wish I could see myself. Sister frowns, but Barbo is smiling.*

Sister and Signora Barbo prepared me to depart. *Aha! A cape is so big, the sleeves wide, and the hood deep to cover so much vestito and the high hair styles like the French maid wanted. I am trussed like a stuffed chicken. I cannot take deep breaths in this corset. Add a mask, and I will only see ahead. Donnas are as confined by their clothes as they are by custom. Should I stumble, I could not rise without assistance. Il grandi are escorted to protect them from falling as much as being protected from thieves.*

Sister led me from the room. At the stairs, I clutched the railing with my black-gloved hand and was careful to set my second foot on each step before I took the next one.

12

Palaso Doxal

Piazza San Marco

Masked and caped, I walked beside Signor Delatesta to Mass at Santa Maria di Formosa with two armed guards ahead of us. Sister Santina on Antonio's arm and two more guards followed.

After Mass, we crossed the campo to gondolas. I grasped the cape and my voluminous skirts, took Signor's hand and stepped into the vessel. Signor Delatesta gestured. I took the seat inside the black-fabric-covered wooden shell in the center of the gondola. Facing backward, I sat and clasped my hands together. Sister climbed in and sat beside me. We pulled in our feet as Signor dropped the cloth and sat facing us on the outside seat. *A tiny window on each side. For air?*

I tried to take a deep breath. *So difficult. My steps were small, my breathing is shallow, and now my skirts fill our seat. My clothing is a prison. Should the boat capsize, I will drown. Please God, let me arrive safely.*

Soon, out the door window, I saw wide water beside us. *Il Canale Grande! Gondolas everywhere. Some with rooms like ours. Very fancy. Boats move as if on important business. Sister is right. We all appear to be the same. Nothing to see on the water.*

In the boat behind us, Antonio and the guards scanned the canale for approaching gondolas. They waved away any who turned their vessels toward our party. The one party insisting on getting close. Through the hole, I saw the tip of a sword waving; the gondola disappear.

Now abreast, the boats commanded the middle water as I looked through the side peephole. Servant women with baskets on their arms stepped in and out of shops along the side of the canale. Colorful signs over doors pictured the products within: bread, cheese, wine, fruit and more. Street sellers standing at small tables or walking while carrying their items called to passersby. The smells of warm bread and cooked meats assailed me, and my empty stomach rumbled. I heard strange languages spoken. Too enthralled with the colors, smells, and sounds of Venice to notice, I did not realize our boats were heading toward the wide water of the lagoon.

After the gondole entered the lagoon, they turned to face Piazza San Marco. I saw only water. At our turn to dock, guards exited the first vessel, cleared the area, and held our boat against the cement platform. Signor Delatesta helped Sister and me from the felze and the boat; we stepped onto the platform and took the steps to the piazza floor. Antonio, and the other guards followed.

I gasped at the huge sunlit piazza with its two pillars. Beyond the impressive building to my left stood the bell tower. Right of us was the Palaso Doxale. Above the portico was the loggia; above that the palaso wore white and pink marble tiles in a diamond pattern that covered the walls to the roof. Beyond the pałaso, I admired the domes of the Church of San Marco. In the sunlight they glistened like golden onions. Right of the pałaso front I spotted a rio and another massive building to its right. We faced a distant tower with a bell and a giant clock face showing the hour. I admired the figures on the top, plus the lion of St Mark holding a book.

Signor Delatesta raised his left arm and led me into the piazza. He had positioned me so I was walking on a shining, white marble path while he walked on gray stones. Looking about, I saw white lines in some kind of pattern on the piazza floor.

Behind me Sister ordered, "Look down!"

I looked up and saw painted statues on the corner of the palazzo. A bare-breasted woman wearing a green leaf between her legs. A brown tree trunk, then a man wearing a similar leaf. *The Creation of Adam and Eve or after The Fall?*

"I said down!"

I obeyed.

Our party proceeded down the side of the pałaso. In the piazza, groups of men strolled and talked, but I spotted no women. Under the walkway and between the portico's arches, scribes sat at tables as they wrote for the men standing before them. I saw the end pillar was shorter and fatter than the rest. *Something large and important above it. Do not look up so Sister speaks not and draws attention to us.*

We turned right and faced tall carved doors guarded by four armed men. Behind my left shoulder, I felt Antonio standing close. Signor Delatesta left me, strode to the lead guard and handed him a parchment. The man read it, re-rolled it and handed it to second guard with words I could not hear.

To my left, I noted four dark wooden men hugging the corner of the church. Before I could wonder who they might be, Signor raised his left arm. I stepped forward and set my hand on his forearm. Only Signor, Antonio, Sister and I passed through the wide doorway.

We strode a little way into the long hall before we turned right toward steps, a landing, more steps, and a window at the top. After we had reached the window, we turned right to a new set of stairs. This set had a carved ceiling painted white. The landing half way up the stairs had a niche on each side with a statue in each. Looking up, I saw another window. We climbed and turned right again. I felt warm under my clothes and cape. *Another set! How high must we climb?*

Tired, I paused, and everyone except the guard waited for me to catch my breath. Looking up, I noticed the ceiling on this third set of stairs was both carved and covered in gold leaf. Each flat place was painted. *Each set of stairs is more decorated and contains bigger statues. Want us to climb and climb so we know we are being taken to an important place filled with important men. Impressive, but not subtle.*

Again I lifted my cape and skirts with my left hand. Again seventeen steps to each landing. *Take a deep breath. Stop counting.* Because I heard Sister's heavy breathing behind me, I leaned a little more heavily on Signor's arm and he slowed our pace.

Signor Delatesta whispered, "The Golden Staircase."

The next set of stairs was also carved, featured gold leaf, and included paintings in the ceiling's circles and the wall's ovals. I spotted what might be a room at the top. *I care nothing for the decorations or statues. I want this climbing done.*

We entered a small room. The guard opened half a double door and disappeared. Wooden benches lined the walls. Ceiling-high double doors at one side looked to be the entrance to an even bigger space. A sentinel at those doors leaned back to listen at the door crack; he called two names. The men stood to enter the next room and we were alone.

Signor chose a bench and sat. Antonio stood in front of me and faced the room.

"Grazie mille, no. Signor Delatesta, I am too nervous to sit, and I do not want to wrinkle my dress."

"Call me 'Papa' so it appears we are already family." *Papa. What a lovely word!* His smile broadened. He explained, "We are called by rank so many men may be called before us. It could be hours." He patted the place between Sister and himself so I sat. "We want to appear relaxed, confident. You need to be rested and calm when we enter the Council chamber."

"Has this room a name?"

"The Square room."

"What is beyond those tall double doors?"

"The Anticollegio Chamber. Members discuss matters of finance, trade, and diplomacy there."

"Where will we go?"

"To the Il Camera Grande degli Consiglio Grande e Doxe. The grand room of the Great Council of the Doxe. Most just say 'the salon.' The new leader of the Veneto is Signor Alvise III Sebastiano Mocenigo."

I will never know who is my papa. Accept this one and love him. "Papa." I spoke with all the warmth I could muster. "Why is your son not seated?"

"You are the only women in the room. His eyes warn any man who enters not to stare."

I arranged my cape and skirts. *Tall collar. Broad shoulders, thinner waist. Wide stance, as if he were on a ship. Left hand on his hilt. Might that signal a warning? He trimmed his hair since last we met. They wear the same green and gold velvets with white trims. Delatesta colors? The gold filigree on his blade shield bespeaks wealth. Papa wears a gold signet ring. On Antonio I see only a thin gold earring in his left ear. Perhaps when one is rich, one needs no jewels to prove it. Everything they wear is fine indeed. Even the boots to their knees are heavy leather that shines as if they are new for this day. So much wealth.*

I looked to either side of Antonio's back as I watched two men enter from the same stairs we had climbed. They looked winded and in a hurry. They sat in a corner; I ignored them to gaze at the ceiling. *Tintoretto's work. Also, a painting on each wall, Mercury with the Graces, Bacchus, Minerva, Mars, also his. From my lessons, I recognize the master's hand.*

I grew warm inside the gloves, mask, and cape. I felt a trickle of sweat at my nape. Shifting did not catch it; I pressed my hand against my neck so my hair would dry the wetness. I heard the Campanile bells call noon. *How much longer must we wait?* "Papa I am too warm in all this. If I sweat, I may stain my dress. Wet under my arms would embarrass us."

"Sister, per favore, remove your outerwear and assist Grazia to do the same."

Sister Santina pocketed her gloves, dropped her hood, and removed her mask. She stood, removed her cape and set aside her things. I watched men glance at her, dismiss her and look away. I pocketed my gloves, stood and faced Sister. I pushed back my hood and heard a man's gasp. Sister unfastened and removed my cape. For the first time, strange men saw my hair. The curls cascading down my back would have touched my backside if it had not been so masked in fabrics. I untied my mask and passed it to Sister.

Papa Delatesta stood and took my hands in his. To the sounds of hissing from a corner, he uttered, "Not a donna, a regina."

"They hate me."

Papa squeezed my hands. "No. child, no. They compliment you. Those S-S-S noises are men's ways of expressing their admiration of your beauty. To speak of you or to you would cause a challenge and a sword fight so they make S sounds instead." He added, "It is good Venezia is a republic. If we had a queen, she would be so jealous she would banish you. Sit. We will visit."

I noted Antonio's arched back and his head moving from side to side. The men became silent. *He glares at them and they look away. Yet he has not seen me.* I sat. "Papa, what will happen inside?"

"The Senate Room is much larger than this one and can hold the Ninety-nine, but do not be afraid. Rarely are they all present, perhaps only three to four dozen men. We will walk toward the doxe who has three to five men sitting on either side of him. Some of the First Ten. They accompany the doxe whenever he is in public, and a few stay with him in private too."

"They guard the republic so the doxe cannot make secret alliances, plan wars, or do anything important without republic approval. We learned that at Ospedale."

"Good. About thirty more may be present. Sometimes you can tell how the men will vote by with whom they sit, but usually they are mixed. Of those numbered Eleven to Forty, some may be in attendance. The other fifty-nine may listen, but they may neither speak nor vote unless our laws state the matter is of a certain importance. Often a few of those are present."

A pair of men walked to the sentinel, who let them enter the way the guard had gone.

I leaned toward Papa and whispered, "If he is there, I think I will faint."

"Note him not. He may be of the Council of the First Forty, but he is only one man. As I am your escort, you will place your hand on my left forearm. Antonio will stand on your other side and a little behind. I will nod; you will curtsey. The petition is mine so I am the only one to speak unless they ask you a direct question."

"I will look to you for permission to answer."

"You are clever and a good girl."

"Will they vote before us?"

"No. The Censors Office will have three to five men present. They report the laws that affect my request and their ruling on my petition. Only the those of the Council of Forty may ask questions, disagree, converse. The First Ten decide when to vote. I expect we will wait the summer for the decision. Politics, my dear, includes bargaining among the patricians before they vote." I nodded as if I understood. While we had conversed, more men had entered and had passed through our room. The bells in the Campanile rang the thirteenth hour and still we sat.

"Delatesta!" called the door guard.

In unison we three stood. Antonio turned and gasped, "Dio mio!" I grinned at him, and a bolt of heat coursed through me. When I realized I had raised my heels to stand taller, I set them down. I felt my heart throbbing and a warm glow coursing through me. *Surprised. No. Shocked. Proud and possessive too.* I saw Antonio clamp his mouth shut as he continued to stare. I tried to keep looking at him, but the rush of blood to my face and the hammering of my heart overtook me. Failing to quiet myself, I dropped my gaze. I saw his extended hand and was about to take it. Sister hissed, "Not yet. Not here," and I dropped my hand to my side.

"Follow me!" from Papa startled me. He softened his tone and spoke my name. Papa accepted my hand on his left arm and led me toward the double doors now opened. Antonio and Sister followed. My stomach grumbled.

Papa must have heard, for he leaned his head close to mine. "Mine too. I promise you a good meal afterward."

13

We passed through without my having to press my skirts to my sides. Without looking at me, Papa whispered, "Smile." We began our slow walk down a long hall. From the high grills on the left wall, I heard men's voices. The guard opened the door; we turned left and stood at the corner of an enormous room.

A Tintoretto mural covers the entire opposite wall. Seventy feet long? Is this another waiting room? Per favore, God, let no one notice us.

The sudden silence in the room told me God's answer was, "No." I felt Antonio at my left shoulder. *Hiding me from their view. Grazie mille* I thought as I made a small smile I hoped only he saw.

Forty feet ahead of us the guard held open the next door. I followed Papa into a small L-shaped room with benches on three sides and an exit door. In an enclosed inner room, the man behind an opening covered in bars instructed, "Nobles, no one goes before the doxe armed. I will hold your weapons until you return."

Papa and Antonio turned the corner of the booth and handed up their swords and fighting knives. Then each removed a knife from his right boot. Antonio removed one from his left boot as well.

"Come sit" instructed Sister as she sat far from where she had dropped our capes and masks. Her soft smile gave me confidence. *Despite your sometimes harsh ways, you do have a kind heart.* The men sat together and whispered. While we waited bells rang the fourteenth hour.

Admiring the carved panels on the door we were next to go through, I thought *I hope it is the audience chamber. I am hot, tired and hungry too.*

A new man opened the other door, looked at Papa and said, "Signor Delatesta, the doxe welcomes you to his Council Room."

We entered the large room that could hold two hundred men standing. I placed my hand on Papa's arm, and we walked toward the opposite wall. Above the half panelling, the ceiling and walls were so filled with gold leaf and paintings that I did not know where to look first. High on the left wall was a zodiac clock pointing to Gemini, a door, and a clock pointing halfway between the fourteenth and fifteen hours.

On both sides and behind us, two rows of wooden seats lined the walls. *Less than a third filled. I am glad.* I counted eleven steps to the wide and deep platform. The dais on top was three steps higher and against the back wall. On it sat men in the eleven armed chairs, all carved in a dark wood. A triangle above the middle chair marked the doxe's place. In unison Papa and I stopped halfway to the steps. The doxe, dressed in rich, almost regal garments, wore no crown. In armed chairs on either side of him sat five il grandi as richly attired as he and also all in black, the color of restraint and good behavior.

"The sister is not one of us. She may not stay," ordered a man seated against the wall to our right.

Papa looked at the speaker. In a ringing voice, he announced, "My daughter-to-be goes nowhere unchaperoned. Sister Maria

Santina stays."

"I agree," said one of the Ten, whose voice also echoed. No one challenged him.

I had heard Sister stop halfway to the dais. I guessed she would glare at the first speaker and start praying. *For success, I hope.*

Ignoring the attack, I stared at the wall behind the dais. From corner to corner, from the tops of the chairs to the ceiling. One painting. Jesus carried up by angels, a kneeling doxe on the ground, and a holy man in black in the right corner. *Magnificent. Another Tintoretto.*

At the head censor's announcement of the Delatesta petition, I returned to the real world. Papa nodded and I curtseyed to Doxe Alvise III, Sebastiano Mocenigo. From left to right I met the eyes of each of the Ten. I smiled at Papa as he lowered his arm. Lowering my stiffened shoulders, I held my left fingers with my right. My arms formed a graceful arc with the lace covering my hands *Be at ease. Breathe. Only a half smile.*

Three men in black sat before a table in the right corner with closed double doors behind them. Before them lay books and parchments. They appeared ready to speak, but a Ten surprised everyone when he did not call for their reports.

"Buone giorno, Grazia."

I looked at Papa. After his nod, I replied to the Ten, "Buone giorno, Signor."

"Did you enjoy your ride here?" I nodded. "Why?"

"Standing on our roof gives me only a glimpse of Canale Grande and the top of the bell tower in the Piazza. Being in the city is very exciting."

"Is this the first time you have left Pio Ospedale this year?"

"No, Signor. This is my second."

"Tell us about your first."

"Three weeks ago. Monday, the fourth day of this month. Accompanied by Sister Maria Santina, we rode in a gondola to the Delatesta palaso. Their housekeeper escorted us to the guest wing. I spent the day in a room with seamstresses, a shoe maker, and a hair dresser. At dusk, the housekeeper escorted Sister Santina and me to the pier, and we rode a gondola home to Ospedale."

"Did you see Signor Delatesta?" I shook my head. "Did you see Signor Antonio?" I nodded. "What said you to each other?"

"We spoke not. He only escorted me."

"Did you travel masked and caped?

"Both Sister and I did." I added, "As did Signor Antonio."

The man nodded and a second Ten began. "How long have you lived in Pio Ospedale?"

"All my life, Signor."

"How old were you when you arrived?"

"I do not know."

"We know you sing well. You are famous for it. Singing is your favorite thing to do, is it not?"

"Si, Signor. Music is my life. I love playing the harpsichord. I love other things too."

"Such as…?"

On familiar ground, I relaxed my shoulders again. In a soft voice, I said, "I love to greet my new baby sisters and rock them. They arrive afraid, hungry and crying. In the nursery I sit under the portrait of Madre Nostra to comfort and feed them. Sometimes I rock them all day or all night until they feel safe and are calm. I also pray for Madre Nostra." I shrugged. "I am always a little sad when I hand them over to the big sister who will raise them. My big sister left for a convent several years ago."

"Who is Madre Nostra?"

"Our Mother. Not really our mother. We call her that because she gave us our home and spent many ducats to fund Ospedale. We know not her name, but from her portrait we can see she was an il granda. In gratitude I pray for her every day—even though the painting is ancient, and likely she is already in heaven for a long time."

"Grazie, Grazia. Censors, what is your report?"

As a Censor stood, I resisted the temptation to take Signor's hand. *No. I am grown. Fear not this formality.*

A censor picked up a thick book and announced, "In 1297 Anno Domini, Venetian law closed the Golden Book listing our nobility to include only those born in nobility. A later law forbade the marriage between a patrician and a common person. The law is still in effect."

The same censor picked up a second thick book. "Law 321 of 1430 states all marriages involving anyone in the first Ninety-nine families of Venezia must be approved by the Great Council of all numbered families. The House Delatesta was not one of those families. The amendment of Law 321, Amendment 14 of 1490, applied because the House Delatesta was then in the high two hundreds, and the amendment had added the second hundreds. This amendment also changed the approval needed from all numbered families to only those from the Council of the First Forty. Amendment 81 of 1545 added the three hundreds, but, by then the House Delatesta was in the one hundreds. Since the House Delatesta joined our ranks by membership in 1580, it has always obeyed our laws and amendments." He set the book on the table and sat.

A second censor stood with a different book in hand. "Law 322 of 1506 states, 'Documents of parentage must accompany any request for marriage to one of the Ninety-nine. Amendment 15 of 1580 added those ranked in the second hundreds to Amendment 14. I testify we recorded Antonio Delatesta's birth. We approved his first marriage and recorded the death of his first wife. Signor Antonio Delatesta is thirty years, widowed, and eligible to marry again." The man sat.

A third censor, the head of the group, stood. "The parentage of Grazia of Pio Ospedale della Pieta' is not part of our records. Nor is the status of her parents."

A frisson of fear coursed down my back. My stomach fell; my face froze. *Does he know my parents' names?*

"Mother Superior showed us Ospedale's records book, which I copied." He lifted a parchment and read, "Bambina delivered into our care on twenty-three April in the year of our Lord 1705. Born sixteen January, three months old, weight 5.3 kilograms, healthy, holds up head when on stomach, sweet disposition. Mother and father known, father ranked within the noble family Habsburg of monarchia austiaca. Mother is nobility as well. Assigned to big sister Orelia, age twelve years."

He looked up, "They have categories of orphans: Orphan One, handed over by her Venetian mother, who named the Venetian father." I saw some men shift in their seats. "Orphan Two, handed over by her Venetian mother, who refused to name the Venetian father. Orphan Three, handed over by her Venetian mother, who declared the father was not Venetian. Grazia is none of those." He picked up a second parchment. "In my presence, Mother Superior wrote this statement: 'I am Sister Maria Corolla of the Holy Order of Saint Maria of Humility. On an errand on twenty-three April in the year of our Lord 1705, I left Ospedale and saw a young woman lay an infant on our platform. Before she could close the window and deliver her bambina into our care I stopped her. She spoke Latin, not Venetian. The poverty of her garments hid her true station just as her accent and Latin revealed it. I asked questions, which she answered. I returned inside. At the platform, I spoke my signal; she laid her bambina on the platform and closed the window. After accepting the babe from her mother, I announced I had found her and turned her over to the nearest sister. As God is my witness, I swear she gave me the information I required as to her name and her origin and that of Grazia's father. Neither was Venetian, but from the region northeast of our republic, the monarchia austiaca. Their births were of noble rank to be equal to or higher than the House Delatesta. I refuse to reveal that information or how I verified it, a policy of our organization.' She signed and dated it the twenty-seventh day of April this year."

A First Forty stood. "As we know not her parentage, we cannot permit this marriage into the Il Grande House Delatesta." He sat.

Two seats down, another First Forty stood. "I concur."

On the opposite side of the hall, a man stood. "Pio Ospedale categorizes the orphans in a way we … recognize. We all know there is no problem with this lovely girl marrying into our ranks. While she is foreign born, she is as noble as we are. Venetian nobility may only marry nobility; that law is inviolate. True, there is a Venetian law barring the marriage between foreign nobility and ours, but consider this: Grazia may have been born of foreign parents, but she has been raised Venetian and has no ties to any foreign country. In my mind, that makes her Venetian. I advocate we send the matter to the Council of the Avogadori."

The third censor stood and announced. "The law also states

nobility from a foreign country may not marry Venetian nobility to avoid foreign entanglements. Grazia arrived as an infant and has no foreign entanglements. As she is Venetian raised and trained, she could be an exception. Our laws allow the Council of the Avogadori to make that exception."

A man to our left rose. "I advocate the Avogadori consider what an asset Grazia has been to the cultural life of our city. I believe she is as Venetian as any other daughter raised among us.

Glancing left and almost behind Antonio, I spotted a man giving a tiny nod and standing to speak against our marriage. Without turning my head, I pushed my eyes right and spotted a wrinkled hand on a black leg pointing. When it moved the tiniest bit, another man stood to advocate rejection. *Him! Not brave enough to stand, he directs others to do his bidding. Coward!* I lowered my lids to calm myself.

The head censor stood. "I have additional information. I was the censor to whom Mother Superior spoke. I looked into her eyes; I heard her voice. I am convinced she spoke the truth. She was Sister Maria Corolla when the foreigner handed her the infant now named Grazia. When asked in Latin, the woman admitted she was the mother. She neither understood nor spoke Venetian. Asked her country, the woman answered, 'monarchia austiaca.' Asked the father's name, origin, and rank and hers, Grazia's mother vowed she told the truth. 'Seek me not; tell her nothing. Give her a good name, a good life' were the bambina's mother's last words. She turned and disappeared. Sister Maria Corolla, now the Mother Superior of Ospedale, named her Grazia, a ranked lady's name."

The man next to Pontenuevo stood. "Mother Superior arranged this match for her pet orphan. She lied about the girl's origins to achieve it."

"Mother Superior NEVER lies!" resounded in the hall from behind me. Sister Santina continued, "I arrived at Ospedale a year after Grazia. Sister Maria Corolla told me the story when Grazia was three years old. She had no reason to lie, then or now. After fifteen years working with her, I should know. Mother Superior never lies."

"I am the First Censor, trained to recognize lies, forgeries, and falsehoods. I say Mother Superior spoke the truth to me and wrote the truth. Trust my work or dismiss me."

A Ten replied, "First Censor, we respect your skills, but we will deal with your challenge later. Let us concentrate on this petition. Per favore, sit at your will."

Another of the Ten asked, "Grazia, you have a fine voice. Why are you not in the Conservatoria?"

My silent sigh steadied me a little; I looked up. "When I was eight, the directress of the music conservatory asked for me. Mother Superior told her I was too young to be among much older girls. When I was ten, the directress asked again, and Mother Superior said my voice needed more maturing before she would consider it. When I was twelve, I asked Mother Superior to go to Conservatoria Grandi. She told me of former directress's requests; then she refused mine. When I asked why, she replied, 'You have a fine voice, Grazia, but a fine voice is not the only requirement. You do not meet the other requirements, so this new directress will not accept you. Let it go, child, it cannot be.'" Because I shrugged and dropped my gaze, I missed seeing men in the room give each other knowing looks. Much later, I learned only their daughters, whether born inside or outside a legal marriage could be a member of the famed Conservatory. The Delatesta men knew what Mother Superior had meant, as did the doxe and every other of the First Ninety-nine in the room. At that moment I did not.

Another man seated on the dais complimented me on my fine voice and asked me to sing for them.

"I regret, Signor, I must decline."

"I have heard you have perfect pitch and a pure voice. I am a Ten; I am asking you to sing."

"Signor, when I was twelve, I was refused entry into the Conservatory. At that time, I responded by vowing to God I would sing only in my home, never anywhere else. I also vowed never to sing for fame or fortune. Signor, I will not break my vow to God."

"Not even to sing for Doxe Mocenigo?"

I curtseyed to the doxe. "Singing for you, Serenissimo Principe, would be a greater honor than I deserve, but I will not break my vow. If I marry Antonio, I am certain Papa Delatesta will be honored to invite you to his home. There, I will sing your favorite songs. If it is not to be, I am certain Mother Superior will extend the same invitation. I can sing for you there because that is my first home." *Curtsey first to the doxe and then to the questioner. Stare at the questioner until he looks away.*

Papa's quiet, "Well done. I agree," warmed my heart. Still facing forward, I smiled and made a tiny nod, which the Ten thought was for their leader, not Papa.

A Forty shifted the mood when he asked, "Grazia, what are your accomplishments?"

I turned my face to him and used my sweetest tone. "Signor, I play the harpsichord and the lute. I am a trained housekeeper." After I listed the specifics, I added, "I am also a trained nurse." I finished with all I could teach.

"A long list indeed. In our world, we call that person…a wife." Laughter ensued from a few, but from not from a Ten or the doxe, who held their impassive expressions. *What are they thinking?*

From the other side of the room, I heard, 'This girl is fair and talented, but granting this petition sets a dangerous precedent we dare not…"

Spent, I dropped my chin and mouthed silent words.

A man demanded, "What is she saying? Is she cursing us? What threats does she mouth? Is she …" he ranted.

"Grazia? Grazia!" called Signor Delatesta as he grasped my hand. Startled, I looked his way. "What are you saying?"

"The Recitation," I whispered. "A kind of prayer."

Papa announced my answer.

Doxe Mocenigo instructed, "Grazia, speak aloud this Recitation."

I knew everyone watched me as I turned to seek Sister's permission. After Sister Santina nodded, I stiffened my spine and turned. I looked from right to left catching the eye of every man before I looked into Doxe Mocenigo's eyes. I spoke every word in a loud, firm voice.

"Every morning we rise, stand beside our beds, and speak The Recitation in unison. Every evening, we stand beside our beds and say The Recitation. If anyone upsets us or accuses us, we think The Recitation. It is Io e' Bambina della Dio." I stopped to be sure no one interrupted me. I spoke each word as if I was addressing His Holiness, the Pope.

"I am a child of God. I am on earth because Our Lord has ordered my birth, my life. I will follow God's plans for me. I will live the teachings of His son Jesus. Like the Blessed Mother Mary, I will be pure, holy, and obedient to God's will. He who speaks ill of me speaks ill of God. He who calls me names says nothing about my honor or my character and reveals all about his lack of both. God placed me on earth to do His will, and I will obey. I am a child of God."

The silence was long. I did not move, but continued to look into the doxe's eyes and wait.

A weak voice stammered, "Censors, is she or is she not one of. ..

"Enough!" roared a Ten.

"…ours," mumbled the man as he dropped to his seat.

A different Ten said, "Signor Delatesta, we have what we need regarding your petition. You will receive the Council's decision in due time."

Signor Delatesta nodded deeply and offered me his arm. I nodded to the doxe. I placed my hand on Papa's arm and we turned to leave. I saw Antonio's arm and lay my left hand on it and gave him a tiny sideways smile.

Sister Santina stepped aside as we three passed and followed. Escorted by my supporters, I left the hall wondering if every man's eyes followed me.

14

Palaso Delatesta

"Did we feed you enough, dear Grazia?"

"Si, Signor…I mean Papa. I especially liked the cold soup of sautéed leek in cream. The herbed peas were excellent. The early asparagus fried in olive oil was delicious. Thank you for the strawberries, my first of the year. I regret the manzo was too heavy for my stomach. I do like beef other times."

Papa walked me through their flower garden. Its scents of roses, jasmine and gardenia soothed me. At a bench, he stopped. "My dear, I leave you here with Antonio and Sister. I have not allowed my son to speak all day; also, I commanded your attention as we dined. I am certain he wants to talk with you."

"Signor Delatesta, no matter how the Council decides, I shall ever be grateful for the best days in my life. For teaching me what a papa is like." I kissed his cheek and blushed. I sat at Signor's direction and watched him depart.

Antonio joined me on the cement bench.

Sister gestured as she ordered, "More space between you."

Antonio complied before he told Sister, "I will hold her hand!" Palm up, he set his hand on the bench halfway between us.

"Sister, I am going to take his hand. If you sit between us, we will stand and hug so you cannot separate us." I smiled at my intended and lay my hand on his. We curled our fingers together. *Warm hand and voice. I do like him.*

Sister glowered but said nothing.

"Grazia, you were magnificent."

"Sister said to be honest and to speak from the heart."

"They expected an ignorant mouse who dares not address the il grandi as if she were one of them."

"I am not one of them, but they have held power so long, they have forgotten we are a republic. Each citizen is free to speak. Did you note Pontenuevo ordered when your opposition was to stand?"

"I did. So did the Ten and the rest."

I felt dejected as I uttered, "They will make us wait only to say no."

"Pontenuevo may convince them to wait the summer or longer, but that is to our advantage."

"How so?"

"The more often he tries to rule over the Forty and order his desires, the more determined some will be to stop him. Among themselves, they will talk against him." Antonio explained, "They did not elect Pontenuevo to be the next doxe last year when Doxe Il Camero died. They eliminated him after the second round of voting. Thwarted, he will overstep himself. One of two things will happen. He will stop our petition—a future I do not want. If he gains that power, next he will try to take more power from the Forty." He winked at me. "Or the Ten and the rest of the Forty will vote in our favor to tell him he not only failed to be doxe, but he will also fail in this. A warning to stop trying to manipulate the republic…them. Papa and I believe we will win because too many want Pontenuevo to lose." He squeezed my hand. "Then we are married!"

Such a voice, such an expression, such determination. He is warmer than when we first met. His firm hand gives me strength. How his gaze warms my skin, all of me! I want him! Per favore, God, may I have this dream? He is in a good mood. Ask now.

"May I ask a question?" He nodded. "Who are the Avogadori?"

"Nine men of the ranks numbered from eleven through forty plus one of the Ten. They are charged with deciding exceptions to our laws."

"Is he…"

"No." They serve for five years and must wait another five years to be appointed again. Pontenuevo may not serve for another year, but I doubt he will be invited. The position is a powerful one, and the Ninety-nine who vote who will serve as an Avogadori like to pass around that power."

"May I ask about another matter?" At his nod, I said, "Antonio, you said your family is noble and ranked one hundred third among them. I was taught nobility was from birth and only inherited. At the meeting the first censor said nobility was closed in the year of Our Lord 1297. He said your family joined in 1580 by membership. *Do not ask directly. Not understanding is less threatening.* I do not understand what 'by membership' means." *His looking away bodes ill. Will he yell at me? His face shows embarrassment and something else. His deep breath warns me. Smile and cock my head to look friendly.*

"The Black Death."

"I read we suffered it several times, especially in 1575. Many Venetians died."

"That plague killed almost one-third in the city. Decimated the nobles, too. Venezia suffered and needed their wealth replaced. In 1580, the Great Council opened nobility to responsible families—for a cost." I said nothing, He ended his silence with, "Fifty thousand ducats."

I gasped and grabbed my lips between my teeth.

Antonio shrugged. "Families who have been noble for centuries are listed in The Golden Book. They think we are upstarts and call us the 'very new nobility.' We have been noble one hundred forty-four years, five generations. We think that is long enough to be one of them, but they do not. We are listed in the Silver Book. After the last plague in 1630, they again sold entrances into the Great Council, so now they are the upstarts, not us. We Delatestas may need two hundred more years to cross the barrier to become one of the Ninety-nine." He smiled. "Unless there is another plague, and we survive."

Ask something else. "Is Lucietta well?"

"She is. We keep her in the nursery when you are here. If she sees you…we do not wish to disappoint her if the Council refuses our petition."

"A wise move given her age and lack of understanding."

"Do you realize you have Doxe Mocenigo in your pocket?"

"How? He spoke not. His face was a mask."

"His eyes lit when you spoke of Madre Nostra and said you prayed for her. Your tone showed you love her." Antonio leaned toward me. "Your Madre Nostra was his grandmother's mother."

Sister interrupted us. "Grazia, never reveal what you know to anyone—not even to Mother Superior."

"No, Sister."

"Your invitation to sing his favorite songs, whether here or at Ospedale, was a brilliant move."

I demurred, "My invitation was sincere."

"Exactly. Sincere and honest and kind. You showed your true character in everything you said and did. Mocenigo cannot vote and does not speak in public but his influence is private, subtle. Those who will decide our fate will likely follow his will. He appears to be only a figurehead but he is more. He leads Venice and the Veneto and is important to our allies. Since he has been in office only a year, factions in the Forty are vying for his support. How goes our petition will reveal something of his leanings. It is all very political." Antonio looked at my drooped shoulders and lids. "And very tiring."

"It is late."

"Yes, Sister. Will she be well guarded while we wait?"

"Every moment."

"Per favore, wait here while I summon your escort home."

"I must change into my Ospedale garments." *I hate to leave him! I want to be his wife. Per favore, God, give me to him. Soon.*

Still holding hands, we rose. Eyes burning as he looked at me, Antonio bowed and offered me his arm. I lay my hand on it and gave him a small squeeze. The narrow path forced us to walk with our shoulders almost touching. Antonio whispered; I listened.

May Sister permit us to keep our heads together.

Summer

"Summer will end soon enough,
and childhood as well."
—George R. R. Martin

15

Pio Ospedale della Pieta'

June 15

I plopped into the chair before Mother Superior's desk and began my daily report. "This is a busy month." Mother Superior did not smile. "Two new bambini, and next week is Midsummer. My sisters are already agog about the coming fireworks and feast. They flit, gossip and forget their duties. I am trying to herd a flock of squawking chickens." Mother laughed. "Next they will be aflutter about the month in the mountains. Will we be ready?"

"If it is too hot in the city, we may leave sooner or stay longer. Freedom from indoor lessons, running about, climbing hills and experiencing the natural world is always welcome this time of year." Mother continued, "This will be Caterina's last summer. She expects leave for Conservatoria Grande after we return."

"I am happy for her." *Brava, Caterina! May you become famous and touted. You have earned it.*

"You will then be the oldest Big. Except for Anna Maria, of course. What will you do should the Council refuse the Delatesta petition?"

I shrugged and looked away. *Pray they say yes. Pray the Delatestas still want me.* "I think not on it. I want to enjoy my summer in the mountains and face the future when I must." I turned to Mother and discussed the travel plans to the convent of her fellow sisters in the mountains.

Four weeks later, the orphanage came alive before dawn. Eleven sisters assigned girls their seating, and joined their charges in the barges that were sturdy enough to transport both people and goods. The girls waved addio to the three sisters who stayed behind. On the way we passed boats transporting goods and workers into the city.

After we reached Mestre, the sisters disembarked and assigned their charges to a wagon. By full sun the party was beyond the town and climbing the road north. Supply wagons followed us. The first wagons brought up road dust, and those in the latter wagons covered their mouths with scarves and coughed often.

Five more miles north our train turned left at a Y-shaped inter-section. A half mile later our party stopped at a large farm. A tall wooden fence surrounded the compound of a house, a barn and other buildings. The Bigs taught the Littles how to lay blankets on the grass and stand small tents over them. The farm family served a delicious meal at long tables under an arbor of large leaves and green grapes. We feasted on roasted eggplant, beans drizzled with olive oil, salt and pepper, a salad of greens, bread and a bite of roasted chicken. Each girl received a wooden mug of well-watered white wine. Each Big took charge of several Littles as they sat on the ground. Only the sisters sat at the table with our hosts. Emilia and I took the infants into one tent and slept with them so the girls who had held and tended them all day could sleep uninterrupted. The men driving the wagons camped outside the compound.

After three more days of arduous travel and fifteen more miles, we arrived at the gates of the Convent of Santa Maria Umanita on the Mountain. Tired, thirsty, and hungry, our heads drooped in the midday sun. The Madre Suprema of the convent and Madre Suprema of Ospedale greeted each other with hugs. Sisters in brown veils and novices in white ones streamed out the wall gate, passed the leaders in conference and attended us. They took the babes into the convent, helped the girls leave the wagons, and took them and the remaining foodstuffs, gifts and travel boxes inside the convent walls.

The drivers of the supply wagons left the tents and other supplies against the outer wall and accepted pail after pail of water for their oxen. The men drove the animals down the hill before pulling out feed from a wagon. By evening, they would arrive at the town in the valley below us.

Settled into their rooms, the Littles napped. Chiara objected to napping, so Sister Iseppa told her she could stay awake and watch over the babies and toddlers as they slept. Anna Maria, Caterina and I supervised the big girls, who brought the goods from the outer wall into the storage rooms for the journey home. Three Bigs left to attend the babes. At dinner a hearty bean soup, salad and bread filled everyone's bellies. As we ate, a sister read from the Bible. Dinner finished, the Mothers Superior stood in unison and led the hall in The Recitation. The Bigs readied the Littles for sleep and fell into their own beds, two in each room with a Little. The convent was asleep before the sun had disappeared behind a mountain. As the next day was Sunday, after Mass all of us spent the day in prayer, singing or at rest.

16

Convent of Santa Maria di Umanita in the Foothills

July 17

After each morning's Mass and a meal, we left the convent. In the shadows of tall trees we heard lessons while exploring a meadow, or on a trail toward a beautiful view. We learned of nature and animals, followed tracks and trails, and memorized the names of the mountains, trees, herbs and flowers, which scented the air.

Each day, we girls spoke a different language: Latin, Venetian, French, German. With schoolroom tablets left behind, practice was oral memorization and conversation. After the midday meal we stayed within the cool convent walls for vocal and instrument lessons. Anna Maria led violin practice and Caterina led singers. I loved creating harmony with two other girls while the rest sang the melodies. After the heat of the day had waned, we were free to run, climb, jump streams or lie in the grass to imagine figures in the clouds. Supper included a Bible lesson while we ate then bed. July was gone and half of August had passed.

I sat in the shade with my ankles crossed and seven month old Livia sitting between my legs. She clutched my fingers as I hummed a tune and gently swung her arms to the song's rhythm. Bright-eyed, Livia gurgled her happiness. Someone called my name, and I looked up the hill. A memory flashed. A young woman wearing a sister's brown habit and a white novice's veil stood at the corner of the convent wall and stared at me. Her turneddown mouth and her eyes bespoke sadness. She had a small brown mole below her right eye. The sister turned her back and walked down the side wall before disappearing behind the convent.

A second memory flashed. In the shade I was relaxing against a tree. The same sister, now in a brown nun's veil, stood in the same spot and was staring at me. This time tears glistened on her cheeks. A strong feeling pulled at my heart, and I stood. Before I could move, another brown-veiled sister arrived. She took the woman's hand and led her inside the walls as the younger woman's veil masked her lowered head. The memory faded and only the sky remained.

I remember! I was little, four, then five? No five, then six. Two times. A memory! I did not dream her face, that sadness, the tears. She was real. Why do I dream of her in the sky? I looked at the convent and saw walls of gray blocks, a bit of grass and sky. *Because I was little and craned my neck to look up the hill and saw lot of sky.* My heart jolted. *My mother!*

Mother Superior and a girl approached. "Grazia, I called your name. Did you not hear me? Anzola, take Livia and keep her until bedtime. Grazia, you look stricken. What is amiss?" Mother sat beside me and placed a hand on my arm. "Grazia?"

I waited until Anzola was out of hearing. Looking up the hill, I murmured, "I saw my mother. Here. When I was little. Twice. After the second time, I tried to look for her among the sisters, but I could not find her."

"Not so. You were three months old when the woman who birthed you handed you to me. If I had seen your mother here or anywhere I would have remembered her. Grazia, most of our girls think they see their mother. At the market, walking beside a rio, other places. They want it so much they imagine it and then believe it. You are drowsy from the sun and daydreaming a wish. A falsehood."

Still looking up the hill at the sky, I shook my head. "No-o-o. My memory is genuine. She had a brown spot under her right eye. Like me." I nodded several times. "I saw her. I did."

"If you saw a sister from this convent, she was observing all the orphans, not you alone. If she shed tears, they were of pity for all of you. That you could not find her is proof you imagined her." When I shook my head, Mother commanded, "Grazia! Speak The Recitation."

I lowered my eyes to my lap. In a flat monotone, I recited, "I am a child of God. I am on earth because Our Lord ordered my birth, my life. I will follow God's plans for me. I will live the teachings of His son, Jesus. Like the Blessed Mother Mary, I will be pure, holy, and obedient to God's will. He who speaks ill of me speaks ill of God. He who calls me names says nothing about my honor or my character and reveals all about his lack of both. God placed me on earth to do His will, and I will obey. I am a child of God."

"You are a child of God. If Our Lord had wanted you to be with your mother, she would still have you. God has plans for you. Searching for a mother who left you and whom you have wished for and then dreamed is not part of His plans. You are imagining a fanciful wish. Abandon the lie."

"Her blue eyes. The brown mole under her right eye. Both like mine."

"Accidents of birth, nothing more. Many people have blue eyes, even some of your sisters. A mole on her cheek does not make a woman your mother. Grazia, no more talk of this. Ever."

After I gave her my reluctant nod, Mother changed to the matter for which she had sought me. She mentioned the Delatesta petition. I stiffened my back and made my mouth a line and my face a mask. *Her face. She has bad news.*

"Your situation is unique. Never before has one of you been accepted into Venetian society. If other orphans ever learn of this, they will falsely believe they too can climb into the ranks of nobility. You have done as we asked by telling none of your sisters of your possible rise. We must protect our other girls. If you succeed, they must never learn of it. We will tell them you left to work in Verona. That is far enough away from Venice. If you leave us, you may never return, never write to us, never attend a spring concert, never attend a Conservatory performance, recognize no one from Ospedale. We must abandon you as you abandon our world. Are you prepared for that?" At my clipped nod, she continued.

"Do you recall when you were a Little? Some of the Bigs ordered you, made you feel small, and challenged you when you started singing in the chorus at six years? They put you in your place, even when you could do more than they."

"Age, music abilities, sewing, scholarly pursuits, more. At Ospedale, we rank each other several times over. A few demand we keep it, and they enforce every rank, often with insults and blows."

"Marrying into the il grandi will not benefit you. Those above you will ignore, insult and spurn you. Those below one hundred three will resent you for climbing above them. You will have no women friends. No support. You will live apart from the rest of society."

I did not change my expression. *Let her take my silence as agreement.*

"Should the Council deny the Delatesta petition, what will you do?"

In a flat voice, I replied, "Become a housekeeper or nursemaid to a family somewhere in the Veneto. Never to return; I know the law."

"In a life at Ospedale or here, you would find caring and support. We would respect and appreciate you. You could live your life through music. We know how much music means to you. All the days of your life you would walk in music and be among friends."

I turned and look into her eyes. "Mother, why have you changed your mind? You released me. Are you telling me you have changed your mind?" *No answer? Only silence?* "I am leaving Ospedale and I am not coming here. If the Council denies the Delatesta petition, I will find employment away from Venice. I want to live in the world."

In all my years I had used that tone with Mother Superior only once before. Afterward I had become immovable. After a pause, she spoke a harsh, "I understand." For now, Mother retreated. She stood, brushed down the front of her habit and walked up the hill.

How could she deny what is true? My heart knew it then; I know it now. They sent her away, so I can never find her. Not even if I become one of them. She is wrong. I gasped at my newfound awareness. She is wrong! I shivered. She can be wrong! My spine tingled, and I shook my head in shock. I nodded to myself. They are like me. Sisters can plot to gain what they want. They can hurt and be hurt. They are good women but they are human, flawed. Only older. Sometimes wiser. Not perfect. Not always right!

I looked up the hill at the convent walls. *I will not let her lock me away. Not here nor at home. If I do not marry, I will go into the world and work. If she refuses to release me, I will ask Signor Delatesta to find employment for me. Say it aloud as proof.* "I … will … leave."

On 30 August we departed from our summer retreat. The girls, now brown-skinned, strong, and trim from their hikes and activities, were ready to return home. Not me. We followed the same route and stayed in the same places. At Mestre, barges met us and ferried everyone home. Reluctant to return, I took the last barge.

Girls in the front boats exclaimed about how new Ospedale looked. It shined pale pink with white trimming the main door and the windows. The girls bounced out of the boats, filled the pier and jumped onto the sand beach in front of our home. Standing at the main door, Sisters Iseppa, Orseta, and Marina beamed with pride. They escorted us inside to show us our walls had been repainted white. The sisters had polished the floors and every piece of furniture and had washed all the bedding.

At the main door, I smelled re-stained wood. I noted the polished nail heads and new door handles and locks. "How could we afford this?"

Behind me, Sister Santina said, "I suspect it is a sign of support from our benefactors. A warning to Pontenuevo not to threaten us."

17

Pio Ospedale della Pieta'

September 8

She does not chatter and is a quick learner. She will do well. I left the laundry room with Anzola, the new housekeeper in training. "We schedule every other Tuesday washing day. Never Mondays because the girls bring down the washing and inspect each piece to mend and hem as needed. The alternate Tuesdays are for the sisters. We do not touch their things." When Anzola asked no questions, I continued to the kitchen and watched her supervise the serving of the midday meal.

I took a stool to the hall doorway and relaxed against its frame. *Have heard nothing from the Delatestas. No word, no letter. Perhaps it is politic not to contact me. Perhaps they contact Mother. If they have, why has she not told me? The Council is again in session. Is she keeping ill news from me? Then again, perhaps she knows nothing as well. After all, the petition is not as important as matters of the state. Papa said it could take months. Perhaps four is not so long after all. Perhaps… perhaps. Stop.* I sighed, stood, and joined Anzola, the kitchen helpers and the cooks. I ate in silence as they talked of tomorrow's menu and reported the vendors' gossip.

Before supper I arrived to give my daily report. I looked at Sister Iseppa and received a head shake. *Neither a message nor a letter today. Something must be amiss.* I stepped to Mother's door, knocked and heard, "Enter." Mother leaned back in her chair and listened. "Continue with your duties. Grazia, you have become quite accomplished. Should I fall ill, Sister Iseppa will lead. I shall instruct my staff to call upon you to supervise the girls and our household."

If she is trying to convince me to stay, she fails. Until I know my future, be agreeable. Do not defy her. "Mother, you do me more honor than I deserve. Should you need me I will endeavor to follow your wishes."

"To supper and Vespers." Mother rose. She placed her hand on my shoulder and walked with me to the dining hall. *Smile. Hide what I am thinking of her attempt to win me.*

The next morning I decided to attend Mass in secret. The second floor balcony was linked to Ospedale by a door the musicians used to gain access to the balcony where they played for every service. I opened the door only a few centimeters and listened to Padre Nicolo saying Mass. I looked through the decorated brass grate and spotted two men looking up at my sisters. I watched as they spoke to each other. *I could see them. Could they see me? Had I revealed myself?* Before I could step back I heard a disturbance below. Emelia shifted her cello as she looked as something. She uttered, "Run!" and moved her chair as if to block something.

I turned and raced down the hall. On the floor below I heard doors bang open, someone scream and male voices commanding. Heart pounding, I fled to the chapel. *Might they also come over the back wall and through the music building? Please God, not near the chapel.* The sounds of heavy feet climbing the steps to our first floor came closer. I closed the door as quietly as I could and raced for the second door. In the priest's robing room, I opened the closet door, touched the corners, and closed the outer door. On my knees, I pulled shut the secret door. Grabbing my skirt front in my mouth, I dropped to my knees to crawl to the end of the alter. Hearing male voices in the chapel, I froze. *Trapped.*

"Inspect the next room," ordered a deep voice. Behind me I heard the closet door open and heard the rustling of fabric. I held my breath. "No one here" was so loud it sounded like a shout. "Stand outside the door to keep anyone from entering. We will find her."

I prayed no one was in the chapel, but I could not be certain. I heard boots, running and men ordering. Then the noise faded. Another man's voice startled me because he sounded so close. "No one here." Another voice ordered, "Search behind that door." Again the closet door opened and fabric rustled. "The chapel is secure," the second voice reported. The first voice ordered, "Stand outside the chapel and guard that no fleeing intruders try to hide inside." Careful to be silent, I lay down and closed my eyes. *Breathe slowly. Pause. Short, silent breath. Pause.* Fear made me light headed; I think I fell asleep.

I woke to Mother Superior's loud voice. "Oh Benevolent God, thank you for saving us. Padre Nicolo threatened to have the searchers excommunicated as they stormed our home. Someone ran from the church and local patrollers came to our rescue. The girls are all safe, and the patrollers drove out the intruders who had come searching for one of our own. They arrested them and took them to jail for trial. *Thank you, Our Lord, for saving us. She is in a front pew informing me what happened through prayer.*

"The chapel balcony door is locked as is the door between our concert hall and the church. Our vestibule door is guarded until it can be repaired. I sent word to Signor Delatesta. His men now guard our entrances and both ends of our rio with the city's patrollers guarding the beach, the vestibule and our back wall. I go now to the hall where everyone waits for me. Everyone should remain where they are until after Vespers. I will come again before I go to bed. Until then, let us remain calm and quiet. Lord, continue to protect us."

After I heard the chapel door close, I crawled to the secret door and opened it enough for me to get air. I gulped great breaths until I felt awake again. I sat with my back against the wall and my feet down the way I had hidden. With the secret door open just a crack, I knew I could hide again if I heard a noise. *How many times did one or more of them attend Mass looking for me? Stupid me! I thought I was safe. I thought they had forgotten me. No more attending Mass behind that door. No more sneaking peeks out windows. No more humming tunes to keep myself company. The attic at night; here during Mass.* Hours later, I heard noises and returned to my hiding place. From inside the altar, I heard Mother lead Vespers, and the girls leave for bed. I stayed inside and took in air from the crack.

Some time later, Mother Superior returned. "Everyone but you and I are abed. Come out now."

I crawled out, closing the secret door and the closet door. After I stood, I grabbed Mother Superior about her waist and clung to her. She hugged me back and stroked my hair. "There, there, child. You are safe now. You are safe." I could not stop myself as I sobbed my relief. Mother drew back and held my face in her hands. She kissed my forehead, and I lay my head on her chest and hugged her again.

"I have never needed a mother more than I did today. Grazie mille, for being my mother and protecting me." Tears coursed down my cheeks.

"No matter how much you and I disagree about your future, I will not let you come to harm. No one invades our home. No one takes away one of our girls. In the morning I will speak to the bishop about this incident." She brushed away my tears. "Come with me. I have prepared a hiding place for you under the roof. You will sleep there. Sister Iseppa will leave food for you there. During every Mass, you will hide in this closet. I doubt we will be attacked again, but we will be careful anyway. Now to bed."

For a week, I followed Mother's instructions. She reported Delatesta's men still guarded us. They also inspected everyone who entered our chapel for Mass and allowed only locals to attend. Mother suspended all concerts until further notice. Sister Iseppa reported to me the town was in an uproar over the incident. *Is it because of the loss of concerts or because of the invasion? At least I am a bit safer with no concerts.*

Feeling more confident, I slept in my own bed. I dreamed of the morning I had dressed for the presentation of the Delatesta petition. A need woke me. The room was lit by a single candle on the corner table next to the chamber pot. Seated, I shook my head. *This dream means something, but what?* I padded to bed and snuggled under my coverings. I recalled the Council room, the Doxe, the Ten. Images and words drifted past my mind. "Pio Ospedale categorizes the orphans we recognize. We all know there is no problem with this lovely girl marrying into our ranks. I advocate acceptance of this petition. Orphan One…Venetian mother. Venetian father." More images. My apprehension rose. "The woman admitted she was the mother. She neither understood nor spoke Venetian. Mother Superior arranged this match for her pet orphan. No doubt she lied about the girl's origins to achieve it. I have heard you have perfect pitch and a pure voice. I am one of the Ten. Sing. In our world, we call that person a wife. Is she or is she not one of…ours."

Startled, I sat up in the darkness. *One of ours? How can I be one of theirs?* My eyes stared at nothing as I relived the Council chamber. Every word and gesture held new meaning. Shock stopped my breath. I took a shallow breath to *One of theirs! We are not all orphans. I gasped. I am a bastarda! We are all bastarde! They support us, but they dare not admit who we are. To protect their families, we must leave the Veneto if we leave Ospedale. Damn them all for their evil deeds! They play with women and then they and we offspring suffer for it all our days. God, you may condemn me to Hell for that wish, but I care not. They deserve it.*

I flung myself to the other side of the bed and covered my head. *O Dio Mio, io e' bastarda. She keeps their secrets. All the Sisters know. I dare not face them. They will see in my face that I know. I cannot face them. I will not.* I turned on my back, uncovered my head, and stared into the darkness.

I searched my memory for past words or signs that proved me right; I found them. *Caterina joined the Conservatoria Grande because she is one of theirs. I was refused because I am not.* As dawn broke, my thoughts and fears continued unabated. When I did not rise, Pelegrina came to my bed. At her question I remained silent. She touched my forehead and announce me fevered.

Sister Santina arrived, felt my forehead and declared me ill. After the other girls had left, Sister tried to give me a sip of water, but I clamped shut my lips. Sister departed. I pulled my bedding over my head. By the time Sister Iseppa arrived, the rising warmth in the second floor dormitory had added such heat my skin was hot to the touch.

"She must drink to cool the fever. Pelegrina, stay with her. Force her if you must."

But I would not be forced. Not to drink. Not to rise. Not to eat.

While the rest of the house attended Vespers, Mother Superior arrived at my bedside and dismissed a sister she had sent.

"What is this nonsense about not drinking or eating? Rise, Grazia, and take your place."

"Which place, Mother? The one you prepared for me. Or the one I want in the world?" Sheet to my nose, I stared hard and watched Mother's eyes. *I know you now. You will not release me.*

"Your place in this household, of course. You must set a good example. You have lazed away for too long; you are safe now and must resume your duties."

"When I was sixteen and seventeen, you prevented me from being hired because you need my voice. Now you want me to join your order and take your place. Still sing for the benefactors who donate to keep Ospedale open and prevent us from marrying."

"I permitted your to petition to marry."

"You do not expect them to approve, do you?"

"I have no control over that."

"You do if Pontenuevo is helping you. I know who we are. Bast..."

"STOP!" roared Mother. "You will never say or think that word again. You are orphans. Say it." When I clamped my lips together,

Mother tried to soften her tone. "We care for you. We train you to serve God. He placed you into His world to do His will. One of those things is never to say what you are now thinking. Swear you never speak that word." I gave her silence. "Grazia, I know this is hard for you to hear, but we do our best for you, for all of you. Your ingratitude hurts me, hurts our order, hurts your sisters."

"I may never marry because of what I am, but I refuse to do what you want of me. I will not take up the order; I will not serve Ospedale all my life. Do the Delatestas know what I really am? Why have the Delatestas not contacted me, visited? What have you told them? Why have you changed your mind about releasing me? Why will you not let me leave to work?"

"You are a willful and disobedient girl. It will go as God wills it. How Our Lord wants you to serve Him will be so."

"No, you want me to serve you." I turned my head away from her stare. "You are using God's name to serve your own ends."

"If you do not drink or eat and die, God will condemn you to Hell for ending your life."

I shook my head. "Our Lord knows why I do this. I need to explain nothing when I face Him. He will judge my actions in response to yours."

Mother Superior rose. "So be it. I wash my hands of you." Mother Superior left and not even the closing door sounded.

Lord of Hosts, per favore, give me a sign of Your will. Your will not hers. I pray for Your understanding, Your forgiveness. Oh God, per favore, give me a sign of what I should do.

Hearing the girls chatter as they tromped the stairs, I rearranged myself and pulled the covers over my head. Upon seeing my lump, the girls' voices dropped to whispers. I fell asleep to the soft sounds of the others readying for bed. I heard them say The Recitation, but I did not join them, not even in my mind.

On the morrow, my tongue stuck against my upper mouth. My legs cramped. When I tried to shift my position, my stiff back refused to loosen. Before dark, a headache racked my brain and my thoughts grew muddled.

18

September 17

Late in the afternoon, Signor Delatesta and Antonio arrived unannounced.

"Mother Superior, we have heard nothing from the Council. More important, we have heard nothing from you or Grazia. My son sent three letters. If she did not receive them at your retreat, she should have received them upon your return. Why has my son received no reply?"

Mother Superior stiffened. "She has been ill. You are too late. Grazia is dying."

Delatesta demanded, "What did the physicians say? What have they done for her?"

Mother Superior's expression flattened. "No need for physicians. I know her disease."

"NO physicians!" roared Antonio.

"Find her!" ordered Delatesta.

As Antonio stormed out of the office, he heard his father's accusations. "Why have you failed to care for her? Has Pontenuevo…"

In the hall Antonio spotted two girls about thirteen sitting on a bench. They glanced up at him. Startled, they turned away their faces. He grabbed the nearest one by her skinny arm."Where is Grazia?"

"You cannot go there! It is forbidden." She twisted her arm back and forth as her face flamed. Shrinking toward the wall, the other one began to pray.

Antonio kept hold of the first girl's arm and dragged her. When the girl tried pulled back by setting her heels, he snatched her up by her waist and carried her with head forward like the prow of a gondola. "Tell me!" He found the correct door and cared not that he bounced the girl against the wall as he climbed. At a landing, he inspected more doors. Antonio released the girl, who scampered down the stairs as he called Grazia's name.

On the landing, Antonio faced a window with a door on each side of him. He opened the left door, and a half dozen little girls yelped. He turned, opened the other door and entered.

"Grazia? Grazia, where are you?" The line of neat beds on either side of the room was empty. He looked left at the second bed from the doorway. In a jumble of coverings he spotted a lump with strands of golden hair sticking out. Antonio knelt bedside. "Grazia." She did not respond, so he lifted the covers.

"Dio Mio! What have they done to you! Grazia, speak to me." He received no response. He caressed her face. "Grazia, wake. It is Antonio. I have come for you." He saw her eyes flutter open, then close. He heard a soft, "An…tonio?"

"I am taking you home." He pulled back the coverlet and wrapped Grazia in the sheet. He picked her up and sat on the bed to arrange her on his lap. His arms enfolded Grazia. He felt her move. She whispered, "Imprisoned…no drink…prayed." Still holding her,

Antonio stood. "You are mine now. You are safe."

A covey of Littles chattered in the doorway. "Who are you? Why are you taking her? Where are you going?" They backed away and fled into their room as Antonio approached.

At the bottom of the stairs Antonio heard his father's commanding voice. "I repeat. If you want her returned, send a sister to chaperone. We both want her reputation intact."

Sister Sabina answered, saying, "I will attend her. I am fetching two capes and a mask."

Antonio blew into Grazia's face but received no response. "You are safe. I have you. Physicians will heal you." He grimaced at her lack of movement or response.

Sister draped the cape over Grazia and tucked the ends under her bare feet. With mask and cape, Sister concealed herself and led Antonio through the kitchen and outside to the dock and the gondola. Already seated in the back, Delatesta reached up and accepted his son's bundle. Antonio helped Sister into the gondola's front seat and took the middle seat. He leaned back to balance the boat.

"Home!" ordered Delatesta.

No one spoke. Sister stared at Antonio's back. Antonio stared at his father and the bundle he cradled. If anyone on the rios looked their way or stared, no one in the boat noticed or cared. At their dock Antonio disembarked first and reached for Sister Santina. Then he took Grazia into his arms and sped to their opened door. Antonio was already at the stairs when his father disembarked and ordered the gondolier to fetch their physician.

19

Palaso degli Delatesta

Antonio sat on the bed in the first bedroom in the guest wing. "I will not surrender her."

Sister pleaded, "Per favore, it is untoward. To be in your embrace with only her sleeping gown, a sheet and a cape between you." When Senior Delatesta and a physician entered, she backed into a corner to watch the men.

As he approached, Signor Nengro instructed, "Lay her in the bed."

"She thinks herself alone and unprotected. If I lay her down, she will die. Papa or I will hold her until she knows where she is," responded Antonio.

"Is anything broken?"

"Her heart. They did not deliver my letters. She believes we abandoned her. She stopped drinking. Likely stopped eating too."

Senior Delatesta glared at Sister Sabina, who looked away.

No physician ever touched a woman and neither did Signor Nengro. Giovanni and Antonio watched the physician lean and closely examine her face and hands, smell her breath, and place his ear over Grazia's heart without touching her.

"She needs warm water. A dribble at a time until she will accept it. Every few minutes. When she rouses, water with highly diluted honey. After she is aware, warm vegetable broth or well-diluted fruit juice. No food or meat until I permit it. Her stomach has closed. We must open it slowly. If she orinare, she will live, but it may take three, five, even seven days. Despite her youth, her recovery may be slow and long. Pray she is still strong enough to live.

"Why is her breath so bad?" asked Antonio.

"Liquid deprivation. She may complain of headaches and have muscle cramps as she heals. Expect her mind to be confused, unable to concentrate. Full recovery may take two weeks or longer. I will look in on her tomorrow evening. Pray for her."

20

September 19

Dawn peeked around the edges of the closed blind slits as I roused. *Bells again? So far away. Why have I not noticed before how often church bells ring?* I tried hard to think. *Where am I?* Afraid I was still home, I opened my eyes only to slits. Not home. *The room I dressed in? Good.* I opened my eyes. *What day? Sister asleep on a cot?* Nearby church bells pealed a special call. Distant ones echoed them. *Sunday. God, per favore, forgive me for missing Mass.*

Sister wakes. "May God give you a good day, Sister." My dry throat made me cough.

"And to you, child."

I closed my eyes as Sister resettled her habit. *Her head covering is askew; I may not see her hair. Hide under my bedding.* A door opened, and I heard Sister requested broth and a tray. I heard Sister close the door and mutter, "No Mass again. I have much praying to do."

When I sneaked a peek, Sister had finished breaking her fast and was handing over the tray. The girl reported the family was at Mass and added, "They will visit you after their meal." I moved my legs to ease their stiffness. When I shifted to my side, my right leg cramped so hard, I yelped.

"What is it?"

"My right leg hurts. Also my left."

"Your muscles stiffened with your lack of liquids. Drink more. Have you made liquid?" At my head shake, Sister said, "You must orinare to be out of danger. I will order a cup."

After slowly finishing warm water, I dozed to the faint sounds of voices. Later, the door opened, and I opened my eyes. Padre Vivaldi's red hair glistened in the sunlight as he called my name. *Will he force me to leave? Does my fear show?*

"Child, I learned how ill you are. I am grateful to see you." He knelt beside my bed, took my hand and rubbed it warmer. "You may have refused the violin for the harpsichord, but I still care what happens to you. Mother Superior informed me you refused food and drink in protest. What protest?" Padre stared down at me, but I remained silent. "You are safe here, child. Sister Sabina guards you, and there is a boy at the door to call alarm. Have you stood?"

Before I could respond, Sister answered, "She has not even sat upright. She wears only a sleeping gown. Padre, per favore, if you will step aside, I will cover her shoulders with my shawl, so she may sit with modesty."

I leaned on my elbow, pushed myself upright with effort and grabbed the covers to keep myself sitting. Sister draped a shawl over my shoulders, but the effort to sit became too much. I fell against my pillows.

After sister stepped back, Padre rejoined me. "Grazia, are you refusing to sit like you refused to learn the violin when you were five? Is this a trick to stay here?"

"No more," instructed Signor, who had entered the room. "As you can see, she is too weak to move." He turned to Sister. "Has she made…?" At her head shake, Signor turned to Padre and announced, "She must before we can even think of moving her. She is still in great danger."

Danger? From what? Oh-h.

"I would speak with her alone—with Sister supervising, of course. I will get the truth from her." Padre Vivaldi waited for the door to close behind Signor. "Confess. You are stronger than you pretend."

Using his teasing voice. Eyes twinkle as if he knows I am defying authority again. He knows me well. Oh, how I love his music, his ways, him. "No, Padre. I ache. Am so tired. I drink because Sister or they insist. I want to sleep and sleep."

"You are disappointed and fear you will not gain your desires." You sleep to avoid what you must do." He winked. "You could return home and heal there."

He says that for Sister to hear, but he already knows my desire. Better to die here than return. With effort I shook my head. I whispered,"Why did Mother Superior change her mind about helping me marry?"

Padre leaned in and whispered back, "Perhaps she realized what she was losing." He cocked his head knowingly. He announced aloud. "You are fortunate; no one outside knows the Delatestas spirited you away. Become stronger. Prepare yourself, child. Father Rudolpho is coming for you. In masks and capes no one will recognize you or Sister Sabina. No one will know you left so your reputation will remain unsullied." Padre stood and spoke a blessing as he made the Sign of the Cross of Jesus. Then he leaned, kissed my forehead, and whispered, "Buone Fortuna. I hope you win." At the door he nodded to Sister. "Keep her pure." He knocked twice; the door opened and closed behind him.

I pushed myself to my elbow and sipped from the cup that had arrived and which Sister held for me. I lay back. *What she was losing? Not who? I closed my eyes. What am I? A "voice" who brings in money. Benefactors donate. Despite my vow, I sing for money. In the mountains I supervised the girls; she called me "their leader." With Caterina gone, I am second eldest; she wants me to lead Ospedale. To follow her. No. Replace her after she is gone. To her I am a "what" not a "who."* Sister insisted I drink again. I leaned forward and finished the water. I closed my eyes. *I know what I am, but who am I? I decided. A singer. A player of the harpsichord and lute. A housekeeper. A nursemaid. Possibly a wife. What if they demand I never sing again as a condition to marry? Am I willing to give up what has been my life? If we are allowed to marry, can I ask I have an hour each day for my music, for myself? If I must work to live, will singing privately after work be enough? What if I am hired in a house with no lute or harpsichord or worse, no love of music? Will I survive it? Would I want to?*

I thought of each possible future condition about music in my life from wonderful to awful. I prayed for strength to do what I must. A condition to marry must include at least an hour a day for myself and my music. If no marriage, will Signor Delatesta help me find work? If he does, I will insist I get to sing. Of course the best employment would be in a house that includes music. As a nurse I could offer my skills. I prayed as I considered each possibility. At last I was calm enough to decide what to do next.

Stay here if they will have me. Then leave whether by marriage or employment. Remain in the world. What I have seen is so wonderful.

More must be even better. Wait here. Refuse to leave. Do what I must to stay until my future arrives. She is so powerful. If I return, she will never release me. No longer home. It would be my prison. Fatigue overcame me. With effort, I pushed away pillows and rolled to my side, drew the covers to my nose, closed my eyes and prayed. *Blessed Mary, save me. By the time I wake give me a plan.*

The late afternoon sun cast shadows and lit only a spit of the floor beside my bed. I woke but kept my eyes slits against the light. *Men rule the world; I require a man's protection. Ask Papa Delatesta's help. Without it, I am lost.* I flicked open my eyes. *A lap? A servant girl sits beside me.*

Eyes just slits, I whispered, "Can you reach Signor Delatesta at once?" The girl nodded. "Per favore, tell him I am in danger. Only he can save me." In full voice, I asked, "Per favore, I thirst." After the girl left, I called, "Anyone here?" Sister responded and arrived at my bedside. "Thank you for coming with me, Sister. You save my reputation. I owe you so much."

The woman harrumphed, "Did what I must. We will not have a scandal ruin our reputation. Father is coming for you. Dark will cover us." She told me the Delatestas had come for me and how they took me away.

I have but an hour or two. Will Signor save me?

Bowl and spoon in hand, Papa bustled into the room, greeted Sister and strode bedside. "Buone pomeriggio, beautiful one. I have a warm broth to strengthen you. Keep this inside, and we will consider something more substantial." He took the stool and sat with his back to Sister; he waited for me to shift my pillows and lean against them. "When my daughter Violante was ill, she insisted I feed her so I am quite accomplished at this. Open."

The half-filled spoon approached, and I swallowed. "M-m-m."

"I will not rush you. Let your stomach decide whether to keep each swallow before you take another." He whispered, "Problem?"

"My stomach says wait," I announced. I saw Papa had blocked Sister's view. In the pauses between servings we whispered. I started with, "She changed her mind. If she gets me back, she will stop the marriage."

"Why?"

"Wants me to replace her. Will imprison me to force me."

"When?"

"Sending Father Rudolpho tonight."

Papa spoke aloud with force. "Slower. You want not to toss your success." He whispered, "You want me to stop him?"

I accepted the spoon and nodded. "Keep me here. Chaperoned."

"If Council refuses?"

"Find me honest employment outside Veneto?"

"Scandal."

"Care not. Want my freedom. Marriage or work." I accepted another spoon.

"Will marry if permitted?"

Again, I swallowed before I nodded.

"Done."

My eyes filled. He gave me another spoon. "Will start inquiries in case of need."

I swallowed and announced, "Enough. Grazie mille."

"Close your eyes child; lie against your pillows. If you lie flat, your stomach may return its contents."

Rising, Papa jostled the table where a bowl was ready to accept the contents of my stomach should it revolt. After I heard the door close, I closed my eyes and prayed as I fell asleep.

The sky had darkened and bells announced sunset, I woke. Handed a cup by Sister from a tray a servant held, I sipped warm, honey-laced water. Signor and Father Rudolpho entered. *Do not smile at Signor or Padre will think me well enough to move.*

"Girl, it is sinful you make me labor on the Lord's Day. Your fault. Your sin, No one will travel this night so they will not see us. You return home now."

My stomach roiled at Padre's words. I sat up, leaned over and tossed what little occupied my stomach into the earthenware bowl at my bedside. Father jumped back to avoid being splashed by the acrid liquid. I coughed and coughed as I lay back and held my throat.

Signor Delatesta defended me. "I told you she is still too ill to travel. You have caused her to lose what little she swallowed. Move her and she will die. I am responsible for her safety and her wellbeing. She will be here when next you visit."

"I will return tomorrow night. If she does not accompany me to Ospedale, I will remove Sister Sabina. Her reputation will be ruined. No one will have her, including Ospedale. She will spend her life wandering the lanes as a donna della notte."

I watched Signor stiffen at Father's words. "Father, I will escort you to your gondola" he offered in a cold, flat tone. He gestured toward the door. As Signor passed Sister, he murmured, "Buone notte, Sister Sabina."

The servant girl, who had backed into the corner at the men's arrival, left the wall and poured the remains of my cup into the vomit bowl. She lifted the bowl and carried it well away from her as she departed.

Sister Sabina stepped to the bed and tucked the linen sheet and silk-topped covering around me. "Sleep child. You will be better in the morning."

"Sister, what does a lady of the night do?"

"Nothing about which you need to know. Say your prayers. By morning, God will have made you better."

Autumn

"No one has ever measured,
not even poets,
how much the heart can hold."

—Zelda Fitzgerald

21

September 20

Refusing the cup Sister offered, I sucked in my lips and shook my head. "Enough of this nonsense! You will drink. You will orinare. We leave tonight."

Signor Delatesta entered. "Not drinking?" Signor made mild, disapproving noises. "We cannot have that. Sister, if you will permit me, I will sit and persuade her." Signor watched Sister sit on her cot and remove her rosary from a pocket. As soon as she lowered her head in prayer, he turned to me and sat. "A vegetable broth. Per favore, sip." He watched me obey; I whispered, "Delicious." He whispered. "By the time Father Rudolpho arrives, you will have a new, well-respected chaperone." Aloud he said, "Sip again. Good." He returned to whispering. "We will keep you as long as need be. No one will remove you without your permission." Again aloud, he asked, "Per favore, sip."

"I have not seen Antonio. Is he angry with me?"

"Sip." Signor glanced at Sister to see she was not listening before shaking his head. "Do you remember him carrying you out of Ospedale?" At my head shake Signor reported all Antonio had done. He finished with, "He kept you in his lap, in his arms. He urged you to drink and kissed your forehead each time you did. All night and into the next day."

I felt my cheeks warm. He smiled. "I forced him to release you and to leave. Sister put you into a sleeping gown and to bed. He is desperate to see you, but I refuse him entry."

"I do not understand."

"I can stop any talk of improper behavior if he has not been in your presence. If the marriage ceremony is not to be, you will leave for an employment with an unblemished reputation. You can swear you did not see him after he secured your freedom."

I looked past Signor to be sure Sister was not listening before I asked, "Signor, does he still want to marry me?"

"Papa," he corrected. "Most certainly."

"Papa, I know what I am and…"

"You are an orphan."

"We both know better." I sipped as requested. Despite how the broth warmed my stomach and soothed me, I knew what I had to say. "My marrying into your family will bring you scandal. On the next counting you will lose your rank. Fifty, maybe even one hundred places. I will have caused it and you will hate me. Better I release you from your petition, leave Venezia, and take up work."

"No, child. We rose to this position once; if need be, we can do it again. We need you; Antonio needs heirs. You need us; you will have the life you desire and children, God willing. We will be your family."

"No women will invite me into their homes; they will not enter this one. You will lose business because of me. "

"So be it. To us, family is more important than one contract or several. Women may shun you, but men will continue to work with us, of that I am certain. Worry not about rejection. You will be so busy raising a family that you will not have time to care." He watched my finger trace the embroidery on my silk coverlet. "Antonio and I and all in the household will protect you. Do as we do; pray God shows us His way."

"Si, Papa, as you wish." I finished the cup, and Papa placed it on the table.

"Sister Sabina, I have succeeded. I leave her to you." Papa stood, nodded to Sister, and departed.

After the evening bells rang, Father Rudolpho strode into the room. "Is she ready?"

I spotted Papa behind him and noted how straight-backed he stood. Before Sister could respond, I replied, "Father, you are kind to visit me, but I am not leaving. I will wait here until the Council of the Ninety-nine decides."

"If it should refuse the Delatesta petition?" he snorted.

"Under the watchful eyes of Signor Delatesta, I will remain here until I leave for an employment."

"Remember, once employed, you can never return to Venezia."

Dare I ask him to find work in monarchia austiaca? Live there. Perhaps find her?

Father ordered, "Sister, prepare to leave."

"Sister Sabina, per favore, express my gratitude to Mother Superior and to all the sisters. They made my life most pleasant and trained me well. Each of them will be in my daily prayers. Mother Superior may be disappointed with me, but I will always love her."

"Wait Father. I want you to meet someone." Delatesta signaled and a portly woman with her gray hair fastened in a knot at her nape entered the room. Unsmiling, she nodded to Father, to Sister Sabina, then to me. "This is Signora Pallavisi, the widow of the most famous leather worker in Venice. Her son runs their shop on Canale Grande. She is Grazia's new chaperone and will remain with Grazia until she is married or until she reaches her place of employment. Now you can testify Grazia has been under proper supervision even before Sister Sabina departed for her home."

"Delatesta, God will punish you and your whole family. Your actions are an affront to me, to our Holy Mother Church, and to the proper order of our society. Come Sister; we leave this household with its unholy deeds. Sister frowned at me, shook her head and followed the priest.

I waited to smile my gratitude to Papa until after the door had closed behind them. I felt my shoulders drop and the pain in my neck ease. My whole body relaxed and I sunk into my pillow and bedding. With my chest loosened, I breathed deeply. Eyes closed, I imagined light and freedom. Papa's lips brushed my forehead. "Sleep," he whispered. I barely heard the door close. I was half asleep when an urge woke me. "Signora Pallavisi, per favore, call for a girl to assist me." Afterward, I asked the girl to report to Papa I had orinare.

22

October 5

I sat in sunlight stitching the front of a pillow. Beside me Signora Pallavisi sewed a garment for one of her granddaughters. We worked in silence because Signora had already told me her life story. To avoid spreading gossip, I had shared very little about Ospedale. I looked at the pear tree and admired how the gentle breeze created a rhythm of sound.

Even the wind can sing. But not I. So many days have passed. No music, no singing. I feel as if time has stopped, as if I am being punished for not returning. Never to solo, never to sing with my sisters. No more concerts—ever. Caterina will live such a wonderful life. Dress like a two or three hundred. Traveling to great cities to perform for royalty and the famous. Touted, praised, and honored. She will have many solos and be given flowers, clothing, even jewels by her admirers. I am happy for her and sorry for myself. What if I am never permitted to sing again? Could I bear it? How would I survive that?

No music here. I am only half alive. Antonio does not want Lucietta to know I am in the house. I can't even sing to myself for fear she will hear me and cause a scene. Marriage or employment. Will I ever have an answer? I picked up my needle and bent over my work to hide my face.

Late in the afternoon I heard the house door slam open and looked up. Ahead of his father, Antonio dashed into the garden and toward me with an unrolled parchment in hand. "Beloved! The Council has approved our match." He raised the document. "Our permission to marry."

I beamed. *Beloved! He called me beloved!* I had missed the rest, but I understood his happiness and the parchment he waved. Fabric in hand, I stood and waited for him.

"Son! Do not touch her. Not until she is your wife!"

Antonio stopped, took hold of himself and bowed. "Grazia, have I your permission to ask the priest to announce our banns of marriage for the next three Sundays?"

His eyes sparkle! He wants me! I bobbed a curtsey. "Antonio, you have my permission. I will count the days."

"As will I, moglie futura mio."

My future wife! I love those words.

"Leave!" commanded Signor. Antonio saluted me, spun on his heels and strutted toward the house.

Papa approached. "Antonio forgot to tell you there are conditions. You may never again enter Ospedale or ever attend a Conservatory concert. Nor any event where the girls of Ospedale may be performing or present. You may never seek your mother, your father, or their families. Finally, you may never travel to or in monarchia austiaca. Do you agree?"

I clutched my hands together and lowered my eyes. *The first two prevent any girl from ever hoping for my freedom and position. Cut me forever from my moorings. Harsh but understandable. How did they know my mind that they demand I do not seek my mother, my origin? I sighed. If she had wanted me, she would not have taken me out of the country. If my parents had changed their minds, they would have returned for me. More than eighteen years. Never returned. Likely will deny me if I succeed in finding them. Hopeless. Wait! They did not forbid me to sing or to play the harpsichord or the lute. I still have my music! Music, song, marriage, and God willing, children. Everything I prayed for.*

The Delatestas fought for me, saved me. They want me because they need me. That is something. More than I would have wandering a foreign land searching in vain. More than being just an employee. Accept. Keep my music. Have a family, not work for one. Be glad … and grateful. I met Papa's eyes. "I agree."

"Here you are guarded, and I will not permit you to leave this house until your wedding day. I will inform the censors they must come to you to sign the documents. I will arrange it."

Papa stepped forward, enfolded me in his arms and hugged me hard. "Daughter. How long I have waited to say that! Our Holy Mother the Church has decreed couples may marry only on a Tuesday, Wednesday, or Thursday. I will ask for Tuesday, the twenty-sixth day.

"We have much to do, so we begin now. Per favore, accompany me to your sleeping room. You have paint colors to order and furniture to choose from our attic. If you do not see what you want, we will order it. Tomorrow the seamstresses will arrive to make your wardrobe. Shoemakers too. This evening you will dine with us, and we will introduce you to Lucietta." Papa placed my arm through his and escorted me toward the house as he told me of his other plans. Signora Pallavisi followed.

Her room. Pink walls, pink curtains, pink bedding. White-washed furniture. I hate it. I turned right. "Papa, what is that door?"

"Beyond is Antonio's bedroom. I moved from these rooms after my beloved Francesca died and gave them to Antonio and Lucia. I suggest you change this room. Make it yours."

"Grazie tante, Papa." I offered, "Perhaps we can save her mother's vestito for Lucietta."

"From what I learned from my Francesca, by then, the fashions will have changed several times."

"Papa, if I am getting new dresses, having Barbo make a new dress for Lucietta for the marriage ceremony will help her feel special and included. Anything that is not pink. That was Lucia's signature color, was it not?" Papa nodded once. "I dislike waste. We can have Barbo cut the old vesititos apart and make Lucietta clothing for wearing at home.

"Also, I want nothing of Lucia's." I lifted my chin as I looked into Papa's eyes. "Not a hairbrush, not a comb, not a single piece of jewelry. Per favore, save it for Lucietta for when she grows and wants such things." At his nod, I asked, "Have you a portrait of Lucietta's mother?"

"Si. We removed it from this room and placed it in the attic."

"I prefer you keep it there. After Lucietta leaves the nursery for the girls' bedroom, I would like to place it over her bed." Papa nodded. "I will not let Lucietta forget her mother, but I will not replace her. I am not Lucia, I am me, myself."

Papa patted my shoulder. "You will be a wonderful mother to Lucietta. Do as you wish; you understand girls better than I. Let us proceed to the attic to choose furniture."

After Papa, Antonio and I had finished dining, Lucietta stood in the room's archway only a moment. She squealed and dashed. With arms opened wide I turned in my chair to hug Lucietta as she threw herself into my arms. "Nurse said I am to have a new mama. She did not tell me it was you. All the way here I prayed it was you and it is!" The child flung herself from me, around the table and into Antonio's arms. "Grazie mille, Papa, grazie mille! For getting me the mama I wanted." She crawled into his lap and kissed his cheek. "May I call her Mama now, Papa? Per favore, may I?"

Antonio laughed and petted her. "You may. You will also obey her. Starting now." Lucietta leaned against Antonio's chest.

"Papa is she the one the servants have been whispering about? Is she why I was not allowed into the guest wing?"

"Si. We will not be married until the end of the month, so she will stay there with Signora Pallavisi until then. I repeat, you will do as your mama asks starting now."

Lucietta snuggled against him. "Si, Papa." She noticed her grandfather. "Buone sera, Nonno."

As Papa returned Lucietta's greeting, I watched father and daughter. *Spoiled or very much loved? I will soon learn.*

The next day I was busy until cena. Signora Barbo and her helpers had arrived early and a shoemaker as well. The women stood aside as he pulled pieces of leather from a pail of steaming water. As he dried them with his rags, he instructed me to sit and remove my slippers. The leather was warm as he formed one piece around my left foot and instructed his helper to hold it against me. He formed a leather against my right foot and held it.

"What are you doing?"

"Signora, I am making a mold. Later, I will pour plaster inside. When it is dry, I cut away the leather and have the molds I need to make your footwear. You need not do this again. Your Signor sends his order, and I make your footwear around these molds."

Hand made shoes instead whatever fits from the market. In the same city but in a different world. "Very clever, Signor. Grazie for being my shoemaker." When he looked at me strangely and shrugged with his head to his right shoulder, I knew I had done something wrong. *Should I not thank workers? Are il grandi expected to be rude? I have much to learn about dealing with their tradespeople.*

As I sat with my feet encased in cooling leather, Signora Barbo distracted me with three beautiful garments. "Signor Delatesta ordered these vestito for you." She pointed to the dark blue, the forest green, and the deep russet gowns she had lain on the bed. *Before the Council agreed to my marriage? What would he have done with them had they refused? I knew. Sent me to my employment well dressed.* I smiled to myself. *Both kind and generous. Antonio, you are blessed to have such a papa.* I looked more closely. *Modestly scooped necklines, sleeves slightly puffed at the shoulders then more fitted to my wrist. Neckline and wrists are plain. Full skirt, but not as full as the formal cream gown. Fewer underskirts for home.*

"Signora Barbo, why are you my dress designer?"

"Because you will be an il granda, and I must dress you to fit your rank. I know what an il granda needs from the skin out whether you are at home or out socially. If you will let me choose the colors that suit you, I will send the garments you will wear at home during winter. For now, per favore, order the gowns you need for social events and for winter as soon as you know them. After Epiphany, send me a letter and I will return it with a date for you to see me for your spring and summer wardrobe. Always be one season ahead, for I am very busy."

"Do you serve the first Ninety-nine?"

"No, each household has its own seamstress staff. I serve the first half of the one hundreds. That you rank so high among them means you will be fourth to choose fabrics, trims and laces, and fashion patterns."

I eyed the woolen garments. *Even without lace, they are very fine. Suitable for this weather, but they may be too light for winter.* "Will they fit?"

"I used my previous measurements to sew them. Permit me to help you. If they need alterations, I will take the other two and return them in the morning."

After the shoemaker and his helper left, I donned the underskirt, but I needed to gather fabric around the drawstrings for it to fit. Needing help with the top half of the vestito, I said, "I can reach into the sleeves, but I cannot fit them tight nor can I lace the back. How will I dress myself?"

Signora Barbo talked as she helped me. "Every il granda has a French maid, a well-trained single girl. She manages your wardrobe, dresses you, fixes your hair each morning, and knows fashions, powders, creams, and such. These dresses are for wearing at home, never outside or when entertaining visitors. Only a French maid can prepare an il granda to be seen." Even with her pulling the laces together, my bodice was loose. "Donna, you are thinner than you were. Now that you are eating again, the dresses may soon fit. I suggest we leave them for now."

"At every meal, I am hungry. I agree." *I forgot to eat pranzo. That is why I feel weak.*

She showed me fabrics for autumn and winter dresses for wearing to entertain guests or to simple events. She even showed me a soft pelt. As I caressed the fur, Barbo suggested she make me a winter cape with the hood and cape lined with the mink for warmth.

I gazed into her eyes and whispered, "Can they afford my having such luxury?"

Her eyes sparkled. "Donna Grazia, they are rich, very rich. They can afford anything you want. They do not rank one hundred three with seven hundred other il grandi families behind them for naught. You may even live long enough to see them become a Ninety-ninth." I felt my eyes widen as she gave me a broad smile. "I suggest we add a muff." She gestured. "You place your hands inside to keep them warm. Very elegant." She added, "And appropriate. If you turn a cuff on your hood, everyone seeing the mink edge will know your cape is lined."

I only dreamed of being a shop keeper's wife. Simple clothes, shoes from the market, a cotton cape for summer and a woolen one for winter. Two cool dresses and two warm ones was all I could imagine. I smiled back and nodded agreement.

What I have received this day is already so much more than that. This is how rich people live. In time I may become accustomed, but I think I will always be a bit surprised. She says they are very rich. I will stay grateful and appreciate what Papa and Antonio give me. I want to be a good il granda, not a greedy one. Better to be generous with my time and talents and charitable to others.

I watched the women pack up all the goods scattered around the room and depart. Signora Barbo was the last to leave.

"Permit me to brush your hair and to tie it back with the green ribbon. You will be ready to dine." After she did so, Signora Barbo curtseyed and departed.

I picked up a polished, silver hand mirror, which someone had added to my room, to look at myself this way and that. *With my hair pulled back, I look serious—no, severe.* I loosed a tendril above each ear and examined myself again. *Better, softer.* I smiled. *I look more myself when I smile.*

As I walked to the main stairs, I noted paintings lined the hall. I also admired the small tapestries, the carved wall tables with vases of flowers, painted pitchers, and foreign items in tall glass front cabinets. *I need to know the importance of each item. Best I ask Papa about these decorations before we are married. Afterward I will be too busy supervising Lucietta and ordering the household.* I descended the stairs and stopped at the dining room arch.

Antonio jumped from his seat and bowed. "Buone sera, Grazia. You are as beautiful as ever, but I expect you are in every color."

I smiled at his remark but thought *Not pink.*

"Buone sera, Papa. Grazie tante, Antonio." I watched Antonio round the table and hold the chair to Papa's left; I stepped to take my place.

After I sat, Antonio leaned forward and whispered so close to my ear I felt his breath. "Twenty days." I blushed and sucked my lips between my teeth to hide my smile. He removed his hands from the chair top and stepped back. "Papa, I did not touch her."

My back is to the window; I cast a shadow on the table. Is that bad luck? Dinner of broth, pasta, and fish with boiled vegetables was filling. *No dolce? Perhaps only on Sundays or holidays.* I listened to their discussion of the day's news. *Ask no questions; learn by listening.* After Papa asked me what I wanted explained, I made two requests for clarification, which Antonio answered.

How much they are father and son. They speak in clipped phrases and need not explain; they finish each other's sentences. Same prominent

forehead and hairline, same timber in their voices, even similar gestures.
I heard noises on the stairs. *She chatters as she walks. Must curb that.*

I met Lucietta at the arch and blocked her way. "Lucietta, you are a big girl now. You must behave like an il grande even at home. Your nonno is the head of this family and rules us all. Always you curtsey to him first; you greet him first. 'Buone sera, Nonno.' Then to Papa. Then to me. You do not run into anyone's arms or crawl into anyone's lap. You wait to be summoned, and you walk. Do you understand?"

"Si, Mama." She fidgeted and tried to look around me to Antonio.

"I will sit, and you will practice." After Lucietta did as I had instructed, I called her to my side and placed an arm around her shoulders. "Well done, Lucietta. You may lean against the chair arm. Tell us what you learned today."

"I speak better French than German, but I practiced both. I practiced my letters. On a piece of paper, I trace my name with my finger. I must do it perfectly before I may use a pen on paper." She heaved a sigh. "I hate stitchery; Nurse says my work is terrible."

"Tomorrow, after your midday meal, I will fetch you. Ladies often sew in a group, and you need to be skilled enough to join them. We will sew together, and you will improve."

"Yes, Mama," replied Lucietta in a flat voice.

I gave Antonio a sideways glance and a tiny nod.

"Lucietta, I would like to see you next."

She approached Antonio, intending to crawl into his lap. She pouted and frowned when he grasped her shoulders and stopped her.

"Papa! I am your little girl."

"Not so little anymore. You must learn to behave like a big girl. So you will become a donna. I am pleased you obeyed Mama." He had spoken in flawless German.

"Jawohl, Papa." She approached her grandfather, kissed him on the cheek, and uttered, "Gute nacht, Nonno." She repeated her kiss and farewell with Antonio, then me. Lucietta walked to Nurse, took her hand, and left the room. We heard no chattering on the stairs.

"I am going to miss her in my lap."

"It will be more special when you limit her doing so," I advised. "I suggest you use it when she is sad or before bed when you go into the nursery to say buone notte. But not tonight. She needs to feel its loss before she can appreciate your gesture of love."

"I concur. Her behavior needs improving. Grazia, you have made a good start." Papa lifted his brows. "Expect her to defy you, for she is willful."

"I do not want to break her spirit. Just mold it to better use." I changed the subject. "Papa, tomorrow, may I visit with the housekeeper and the cook? I want to learn how Sabina runs your household."

"Our household. Ask what you wish. Go where you will. Supervise the emptying of your new room. The plasterers arrive early Monday to redo the room."

Since I had arrived, I had not been able to play or sing. First, I was ill. Then so Lucietta would not know I was here. Since the announcement I had found the harpsichord out of tune and unpleasant to play. I strummed the harp, but it is also out of tune. *I miss playing. I feel empty without it.* Instead I go to my room and quietly sing my favorite tunes. Before I sing each of Padre Vivaldi's songs, I say a prayer for his good health.

That afternoon I fetched Lucietta from the nursery and brought her to my guest room. I sat and drew her to my knees. "Show me your work." Lucietta brought forth what she had hidden behind her back. I examined the cloth and pointed, "This is a good stitch. As is this one and this one. This is not so bad a beginning." I turned over the fabric. "Do you knot your threads?"

"Nurse does it for me."

"I will teach you how to tie knots. After you learn that, you will thread your own needle and use a scissors. When you are skilled in the basics, you will practice one stitch at a time. Stand close and watch." We worked atop my knee before I sent Lucietta to a stool to practice knotting the ends of threads. "Make three perfect knots, and we will walk in the garden."

23

October 18

"Well done, Lucietta, a long line of perfect, straight stitches. You may now sew a seam."

"Mama, per favore, no more stitching today."

I cut the last thread from my completed cushion cover and set it in my lap. "Bambina, are you ready to tell me what is upsetting you?" I watched her drop her head and rub her skirt fabric between two fingers. Her gesture of distress. "Lucietta, I cannot help you if you do not tell me what it is."

Lucietta gaze at the ground. "She is coming. I hate her!"

"Who is coming? Why do you hate her?"

"Claudia! On her last visit, she pulled the head from my best doll. My gift from Papa for my birthing date. Every time she comes, she breaks something and she laughs at me. I hate when she laughs because it means she has done something bad."

"What else has she done?"

"She orinare on my bed and said I did it. She is mean to Giacomo and pinches him when his nurse or mine are not looking. He is so frightened of her. When she does this." Lucietta curled her fingers around her raised thumb and gestured up and down. "He orinare in his pants and weeps. She laughs at him and calls him a baby." Lucietta looked into my eyes with such hope. "You are my mama now. Will you stop her?"

"I will do what I can. For now, you to Nurse and I to my room. I must sew the silk back to this cover and order the pillow stuffed."

By the end of cena, I had gained both men's approval of my plan. Lucietta entered, greeted the family, and came to me as I had requested. "Lucietta, we are going to a special place where we speak only the truth. Come with me." I took her hand, stood, and escorted her out of the dining room. We turned right toward the back of the house.

At Nonno's office door Lucietta balked. "I am not allowed there."

"True, but this time is special. We invite you because Nonno and Papa want to meet with you." We stepped back to follow Papa and Antonio into the room. Papa took his leather chair; Antonio stood next to him as I sat in the other leather chair and drew my daughter into my lap. I whispered into her ear until Lucietta nodded. "Lucietta has things to report about her cousins' visits."

In a halting voice, Lucietta began. Her father and grandfather nodded or said something encouraging like, "What other things has Claudia done," and her voice became stronger. She included several incidents she had not told me. Lucietta ended with, "Papa, I know you told me to be nice to Claudia, but it is hard. Very hard. She does not like me, and I do not like her back." Lucietta hid her face inside my embrace.

"Papa, Antonio, I have a plan. Will you hear it?" They voiced their agreement, and I outlined my ideas.

"Your plan is good, daughter; but I must be the one to put it forth and enforce it. That will I do. Per favore, make arrangements tomorrow. Lucietta, come here." Papa placed her on his lap. "You are most fortunate of girls to have a mama who loves and protects you. What do you say to your mama?"

"Mama, grazie mille for helping me." She thought a moment and added, "Mama, if she finds my dolls, she will break them to pieces."

Smiling, I leaned forward as if to conspire with her. "Not if we place them in a box under my bed in my room. No child may enter. If Claudia enters my room, I will spank her. If she harms your dolls, I will spank her twice." *Her smile is a beam of sunshine on a dark day. No wonder Antonio's resolve melts when she smiles like that.* Lucietta kissed Nonno and Antonio before she dashed into my arms, hugged me hard and kissed my cheek.

"Off to bed. Nurse is waiting outside the door." I smiled at Lucietta's perfect curtsies and buone nottes. *How she tugs at my heart. She reminds me of when the Bigs mistreated me because I joined the chorus at six. Coddled and spoiled she may be, but she has a good heart. She loves completely. One of her strengths.*

"Grazie, Papa. Grazie, Antonio, for your support. A mother's first obligation is to keep her child alive. The second is to keep her safe, and protect her when need be. For the first time, I feel like a mother. No one will hurt our little girl, not even another family member. I will see to it."

Such a smile. She learned it from him. His eyes, so warm! Even from here, I feel his heat. I repeated his nod. *We are one in this. Is this how marriage feels? Warmth. Complete agreement. Heat. Leave now. Before I say something to spoil this moment.*

"Who is Zia?"

"What?" I clenched my fingers as I felt my cheeks warm.

"Walking by the salon earlier today, I heard you mumbling. You said 'Zia,' then mumbled something more."

I looked at Papa, who shrugged at me. *Caught!* I looked back at Antonio, who hid his feelings with that blank stare of his. I loosened my fists and spread my fingers against my thighs. "Sometimes, I talk to myself. When I do, apparently, I use the name my sisters often called me."

"Oh."

Do not do that again. What if they think me odd and change their minds? Stand. Nod. "Buone notte." I headed to the stairs to bid Lucietta buone notte with a kiss.

For several moments, neither man spoke. Unbeknownst to me, I became their topic.

"Grazia told you how much music means to her. That she wants time each day to play and sing. Music is as much a part of her as is her breath. Have you noticed Grazia hums when she is happy? I have heard her in the garden, at her needle, and when she walks about. Did you hear her beyond the arch just now?" At Antonio's head shake, Giovanni chided, "Antonio, pay closer attention your wife to be. Grazia hums when she is happy. Notice when she does and when she does not. Use it to know her mood and to respond, but never tell her or she will stop." Antonio stood to leave. "Grazia loves you already. You need to love her in return—and be honest."

"I am going out."

"Son, remind her you were alone for five years. Explain what you did. Perhaps, she will understand; she may even accept your reasons. She will not understand your continuing that relationship.

Someday, somehow, she will learn of her, of them. You will break her heart and kill your marriage. Why are you willing to risk that?"

"She need never know." Antonio left.

Giovanni shook his head in disbelief.

24

October 20

Beneath masks and capes, they wear a finery I have never seen. Jewels even when traveling? A nurse for each child? A French maid and an English valet? So many cases. Il Conto is imposing and even taller than Antonio. He only glances and their servants know what he wants. She is so beautiful. Do I curtsey because they are nobility or remain standing because they will be my family? No one told me how to act. Best I curtsey. "La Contessa."

"Do rise, Sister. We are a family. I need no such recognition within this house. I am Violante." After I repeated her name, Violante murmured, "He is always Il Conto degli Trevino. Everywhere. If he likes you, he will invite you to address him as Il Conto."

Given my lack of rank, his refusing to even recognize me would be no surprise. Nod. The less I speak, the better.

Violante twined my arm in hers as we strode to the salon. *She is kind to take my arm. I will remain standing when she sits.* Violante stopped at the entrance. "I hope you change this room. I have always hated the curtains she ordered. Using a bit of Venezia's official colors is acceptable, but this…" Violante gestured, "is too much red and gold, too bold. Her taste lacked subtlety." *The first criticism I have heard of Lucia.*

Her vestito is a muted dark green. The richness of her gown lies in the weave's *texture, the quality of her lace, how perfectly it fits her. What she will think of my room?*

"These walls need re-painting."

"What colors did your mother choose?"

"Cream walls with soft green and blue fabrics with a dash of a pale yellow here and there."

"I, too, like those colors. Grazie, for your good advice."

"A more important matter is Lucietta. My brother indulges her every whim. Spoiled and perhaps untrainable. Like her mother, she whines when she is denied. We must train children even before their first steps. I fear you may be too late to save her. I know she will give you trouble."

Is she testing me? Just nod. "When we are alone like this, may I call you 'Sister'?"

"You may."

Do not look surprised. "Sister, I suspect the men wait for us to join them. Shall we dine?" *Step back; wait. She has precedence.*

Conversation during the meal started in pleasantries. I heard news and the men's concerns related to their businesses. Like Violante, I remained silent. Near the end of the long meal, Violante stood.

"Per favore, Papa, excuse us. Grazia will show me her room."

Papa dismissed us.

At the top of the stairs, I asked, "Do you wish to see my room in the guest wing?"

"I know Papa; your marriage room is already complete. How

you decorated it will tell me of your tastes."

I held my breath as Violante opened the door and stepped inside. I entered as she walked the room and looked around.

"Your perfume faintly scents it. Good." She stopped at my dressing table. "This was my mother's."

"If you want it, per favore, take it home with you."

"No, I have my own. It looks nice with the other furniture. I dislike painted furniture."

Another criticism.

Violante caressed the table, which was half-filled with jars of creams, bottles of fragrances, and other womanly items. "When I was a little girl, I loved standing beside this table and watching Mama being prepared to attend social events. Her French maid gave me my first lessons how to look like a young woman ready to marry." Violante looked up. "You do have a French maid."

"Mademoiselle Charlotte Garon arrived last week. She informed me she had placed my clothes in the wardrobe, and the table is ready for me. I know nothing of French maids. Is everything correct?"

"It is. Where is she?"

"Eating with the servants in the kitchen."

"That will not do! She will leave you. A French maid is not a servant. She eats every meal alone in her room. A servant brings her a tray and removes it. Throughout the town, the maids talk to each other. Be careful; she knows all your secrets. Do not gossip with her or reveal family matters."

"I will be careful." *Oh no, she looks around the room again because she dislikes the colors.*

"You chose pale colors, but why did you have them painted in this fashion?"

"The faint blue on the ceiling represents the sky. I carried it down the wall of the entry door because, from the bed, he will see it when he wakes." I felt my cheeks warm as I admitted, "Antonio likes blue." I rushed through "I thought three pale yellow walls were too much color. I asked them to start with cream on the top of each wall and graduate to a pale yellow for the bottom fourth. Sunrise?"

For the first time, Violante smiled. "Unusual, but well done. And subtle." She stepped to me and pointed. "That door leads to Antonio's room. Remember this most important advice: always keep that door open. He may choose not to visit you, but you must always be available to him. Being denied his husband's right is the worst thing you can do to a man. If you destroy his confidence in his manliness or damage his pride, he will go elsewhere. Do you understand?"

I nodded. "Always the door is open and always be glad to see him."

Violante guessed, "The sisters told you nothing of what happens between a husband and wife, did they?" My eyes widened as I shook my head. Violante placed her hand on my arm. "I will speak with Antonio and explain. Worry not. All will be well between you." She took another long look around the room.

"I want to kiss Alvise and Zago buone notte. Come and meet them."

25

October 21

Standing back from the tumult, I recalled the quiet, graceful, and dignified entrance of the degli Travinos into the household. The noise, confusion, and loud talk that marked Stefano and Polonia Delatesta's arrival was overwhelming. Claudia kicked at three-year-old Giacomo and pushed him against the wall in her effort to make a grand entrance. To no avail, her mother pleaded with her daughter to behave. The family nurse stood against a wall and clutched the baby close to keep him safe.

"Enough!" shouted Papa. Everyone froze. "Why must your every entrance into my house be like this? I will have order! Polonia. Hold your daughter's hand and keep her with you. Go to your room and do not rejoin us until both of you are quiet and better mannered. Leave!"

Papa glared at Stefano, who looked away. The head of the family went to one knee. In a gentle voice he said, "Buone giorno, Giacomo. I am glad to see you." He offered his hand. "Would you like to come with me into the salon?" Papa waited for the boy to decide. He smiled and accepted his grandson's hand. "You are too big a boy for me to carry. Let us walk together."

Lucietta and I remained outside the salon archway. Papa and Giacomo entered, followed by Il Conto with his wife on his arm, Antonio and Stefano. Miro's nurse ended the procession and stood against the wall on the left side of the arch. In the same order, each chose a chair or a place on a sofa.

I leaned right and whispered, "Remember the order. Giacomo is your cousin and our guest. Be kind."

"Yes, Mama."

Lucietta curtseyed and then greeted each adult in the correct order of precedence.

"Nonno, if you wish it, I will walk with Giacomo to the nursery." With her grandfather's permission, Lucietta approached and offered her hand. "Buone giorno, Giacomo. I am happy to see you. Our cousins Alvise and Zago are already in the nursery." At the door Lucietta whispered to Giacomo. Together they turned; Giacomo bowed and Lucietta curtsied. They disappeared and Miro's nurse followed them .

"Il Conte, may I present Grazia, Antonio's fidanzata. He watched me curtsey low and nod deeply. After I rose, Il Conto's response was a brief, curt nod.

"The boys will live in the nursery. I have other announcements," declared Papa. "Il Conto, with your permission, I would like both your nurses to supervise all four boys. The girls may not enter the nursery or disturb the boys wherever they may be." Giovanni accepted Il Conto's consent with a smile. "As to the girls, Lucietta will sleep in the future girls' bedroom with her nurse attending. Claudia will sleep in your room, Stefano. Polonia is to supervise her every move. At no time may Claudia be alone."

"Papa, why may not Claudia sleep with Lucietta?"

"Because Claudia hurts her cousins, her brothers, even Lucietta."

"How so? She is good to them."

"No, son, she is not. On her last two visits, Claudia orinare on Lucietta's bed and claimed Lucietta had done it. She pinches Lucietta and pulls her hair when no one is looking. Claudia breaks her dolls and toys. What she does to her brother is worse." Giovanni glared at Stefano. "Giacomo still orinare his bed and his clothes because Claudia pulls on his…" Papa glanced my way and chose the words. "his boy parts until he wets himself."

Papa gave Stefano no time to think. "All she needs to do is make a rude gesture, and he wets himself in fear of what she will do to him if he does not. Son, Miro is not yet one, but he already may fear his sister. Learn what she is doing to him when no one is looking."

I noted Il Conto bristled and glared at his wife. She gave him the tiniest head shake.

Antonio spoke next. "Brother, we all know sons are more important than daughters. For a time, Claudia had your attention. Now you give it to Giacomo and Miro. She creates scenes to draw your attention. She cannot punish you for ignoring her, so she hurts them."

"Remember when we were young?" joined in Violante. "I pitted you, Michielo, and Antonio against each other, lied about one or the other of you teasing or pinching me or pulling my hair. When Mama caught me and punished me, I stopped. As for the girls, well, girls snipe at each other. I am certain that Lucietta having more clothes and dolls is part of Claudia's jealousy. Claudia sees Antonio pay more attention to Lucietta than you do to her. Claudia may be only four years, but she is sneaky and dangerous. Take her in hand, brother, before Polonia ruins her."

"Lucietta is no saint," countered Stefano. She gloats about her wealth and position. She criticizes Claudia's clothes and hair. Lucietta acts the queen and talks to Claudia as if she is her servant. I find her behavior intolerable."

I enjoyed their shocked expressions when I said, "I agree." Antonio's expression went flat and cold, but I spoke my mind anyway. "Lucietta is indulged and spoiled. No one has curbed her high spirits nor insisted on better behavior. To turn a horse too hard will surprise the horse; it will balk and defy its owner. Lucietta is like a high-spirited filly. I do not want Lucietta broken like a horse. I want her to learn to contain her high spirits. Learn when and how to use them. I plan to turn her gently, step by step, until she finds herself on a better path, one she thinks she has chosen. That takes time and a steady hand; I will give both to my new daughter.

"With my guidance, Lucietta will keep her good spirits like her Zia Violante and still know when to speak and when to be silent. Lucietta will become a well-behaved, proper Venetian donna, of which this family will be proud." I looked at Papa. "With that in mind, I have already taken her in hand." I turned a steady gaze on Antonio and held his eyes. "If Antonio will let me have her."

No one spoke. More silence and still no one spoke. The maior-domo filled the entryway; Tomaso announced, "Signor, cena is ready."

They will stand, leave, and sit in order, but where do I fit? Is he so angry he will not offer me his arm or seat me as before? Will I be last to leave? Must I seat myself? The shame! He stands and gestures! I smiled, stood and squeezed his arm in gratitude at his saving me, even as his eyes warned me of his anger.

The lack of conversation created a stiff atmosphere at the table. We started the zuppa course, and everyone partook of a spoon or two. Il Conto glanced my way before he broke the silence with, "Stefano, I am curious. When do you begin the olive harvest?"

Stefano answered. Il Conto's genuine interest drew him out, and Stefano talked about some of his farming methods and plans.

After I picked up my spoon and traced a path away from me through the broth, I cleaned the spoon bottom on the opposite side of the bowl. I brought the spoon to my lips and sipped. *There is a kindness within his stiff posture and formal ways. I think I am going to like him. I want our family to be like his, well ordered and calm. Not chaos and inappropriate behavior.*

Friday everyone was careful with their words and cautious in their actions. Claudia ignored Lucietta and glared at everyone else. When I tried to engage her in conversation, she gave shrugs or one-word answers and looked away. I left her alone.

I remained silent as the surrounding talk was of persons and histories I did not know. I learned Polonia had a brother, and Stefano had sent a message they were in town. From Polonia's expression, I guessed she did not want to see him. Bored, I stared at the painting of Piazza San Marco on the wall.

"Grazia."

I looked up and smiled at Antonio, who was standing before me.

"If you will come with me, I have something to show you."

The salon went silent as I followed him, and he turned left at the archway. He stopped before the closed door of the music room. I had not returned to it since I had found the harp under its dusty cloth cover. Antonio bowed, gave a flourish with his arm, and opened the door.

I stared at the transformation. *Redone? Ceiling to floor drapes cover the room. Even the fireplace and its wall.* I saw the lower half of *the window covered by the same gold brocade. A harpsichord stands so morning sunlight will light the instrument. The five-candled chandelier on the pillar left of the bench will light the music sheets. He has given me back my music, my voice. Indeed, a good man.*

From behind me I heard, "Try it, Cara."

I entered and sat. Antonio moved to the curve, raised the top and set the lid stick. I played a glissando low to high. "Tuned perfectly. You changed the room."

"The tuner refused to tune it. He informed me setting a fire or letting cold air seep down the chimney it or around the window frame puts instruments out of tune."

I nodded and began a soft song that covered most of the keys.

After I finished, he said, "I had the fireplace sealed with boards, ordered the draperies, and bought the pillar and chandelier." I glanced at Lucia's harp in the corner. Antonio said, "I moved the harp to give you more room."

"I did not hear him tuning it."

"I had the work done while we were at Mass. Are you pleased?"

"Pleased and grateful. Grazie mille, Antonio. My first song is only for you." I played the introduction and sang about a beautiful garden as I gazed into his eyes. While smiling back at him I almost lost the words.

"Another, per favore."

"Padre Vivaldi composed this for me. It is my favorite." I played the whole concerto. Because I was out of practice, I only looked at the keys. Finished, I looked up into Antonio's shining eyes.

"Thank you for my gift," I murmured, "I regret I have none for you."

At his throaty, "You are my gift, Cara," my heart leapt to my throat as my cheeks warmed. As I slid off the bench, he stepped toward me. *If I let him kiss me, I fear we will not stop.* I raised my hands. "Not until Tuesday."

At his deep-throated "Tuesday," I spun on my heel and left.

26

October 26

At a knock and "Time to rise," I stretched my legs and arched my back as I lifted my arms above my head. *A husband and a family. All I have prayed for. More than a simple shopkeeper's wife, I will carry a rank I never dreamed. Grazie mille, Dio Mio. Blessed Mary, watch over me and keep me worthy of God's grace.*

At the second knock, I threw off my covers, stood, and wrapped my robe about me. "Enter."

Zanetta, Sabina's eldest, led the party, who brought in hot water, filled the tub behind the screen, and departed. "Soon to be my signora. After your bath and scenting yourself with rose-scented water, per favore, go to your new bedroom. Signora Barbo will dress you."

Surprised, I watched Signora Barbo curtsey to me. *To me! I have my rank even before the service.* I nodded my approval and disrobed. Dressed, coiffed, and ready, I sat and gazed into the mirror of my dressing table. *I love my gown, my hair, the jewels Papa sent up.* Barbo approached from behind me to lay the veil decorated with Burano lace over the diadem in my hair. When she draped it over my shoulders, I grasped her hand. "Signora Barbo, I am well pleased with my gown. Your sense of fashion is superb, as are your skills in fitting. I like that the lace across my chest and at my cuffs match this veil, as if it is a family heirloom."

Barbo smiled into the mirror. "Long ago, my great-grandmother stitched the lace to the veiling for the Delatesta family. My grandmother and mother served your family; now I serve you."

"Thank you for your excellent service, Signora; I look forward to our continuing to work together."

Barbo gave me a half smile. "If you will stand, I will fluff your skirts. All are in the salon and await you."

I am more elegantly attired than I could have dreamed. I donned the matching silk gloves, and Barbo opened the door.

Stopping in the archway, I sought the only eyes that mattered. As I watched his eyes widen and his chest lift, I gave him a half smile. We stared at each other until Papa coughed; I looked his way.

"Grazia. After the ceremony, I sign for my son. With your permission, Il Conto has agreed to sign for you."

I turned to Il Canto and curtsied low as my skirts bellowed, "I am honored, Signor Il Conto Degli Travino."

His curt "My honor," warmed my heart as I felt my face flush.

Barbo stood behind me and helped me don my cape and mask. I looked at Antonio but thought of Il Conto. *You could have suggested Stefano do it. Your signing means more to me than I will ever be able to express. How to thank you? You deserve her love. I will give you mine. Do not cry. Not even one tear.*

I stepped into the hall as the others left the salon to don their capes, masks, and hats. I lifted my hood and hid behind it and my mask. With Violante on his arm, Papa led the party. Antonio followed alone. Il Conto escorted me with my hand on his arm. Stefano and Polonia followed.

Two guards led, and two followed. *Am I still in danger, or are they an honor guard? Each man wears a sword. Custom or need? Worry not; I am with my family—my family. Precious words.* As we walked beside the rio to church, I looked across the empty canal and saw others also for church. I ignored their stares. "Il Conto degli Trevino, you have my love and devotion. I am at your service."

Looking straight ahead and without smiling, he replied, "You have mine. He is more fortunate than he knows. Be not afraid. Show him the jewel you are."

At the bridge over the rio, I stopped. *No sides. Just a brick arch. If I trip, I could fall off the edge and drown. Not safe! not safe!* Il Conto looked at me. "They are only dangerous when it is icy. Worry not. I have you." I clutched his arm tightly and leaned toward him as he took me across the arch and onto the campo. We walked across the field to the church.

In church I spotted the children and their nurses already stationed on the women's side. We women took our places before them and the men moved to their side of the church.

Violante squeezed my hand and whispered, "Longest Mass in your life. Concentrate."

I nodded. On my other side, Polonia harrumphed and whispered, "Forever is a long time. Last chance to run."

Run indeed! Run into his arms. The priest entered; I crossed myself, and Mass began. After the benediction most left, but some stayed to watch us marry. The household stood behind us as Violante and Polonia took my cape and mask. I heard whisperings of approval behind me. Stefano took the other men's outerwear. At the altar and before the priest, we stood in a line: Il Conto, me, Antonio, Papa. *Antonio's garments of vibrant green and deep gold complement my gown. Family colors. Does he see I wear the blue he first chose when I was preparing to meet the doxe? Do men notice such things?*

Father began, and I turned my attention to him. I had learned what I was to say, but the words had escaped my mind. I was glad the priest said the words first and I only had to repeat them. After I removed my right glove, Antonio place the gold band on my wedding finger. I smiled at Antonio; he squeezed and kept my hand. After the benediction and Father's permission to give his bride the kiss of peace, Antonio kissed my lips. *Short, chaste. Is that his best?* Papa and Il Conto followed Father to a table beside the altar to sign documents.

Antonio took my other hand in his and turned me to face him. "Buona fortuna, mia moglie."

"Buona fortuna e futura, mio marito." *Good fortune, good future, my husband. May these words always be true.* Antonio held my right hand as we turned to the household. The men spoke blessings, and the women wished us well, happy, and many healthy children.

The feast Violante had arranged for us was an array of my favorite dishes. We started with bowl of squash soup. The next course was scallops in a butter and white wine sauce.

We cleansed our palates with a small plate of pickled carrot slices, leek leaves, and mushroom caps. The main course was roasted beef, baked assorted fall vegetables shiny with olive oil, and warm bread. A new wine accompanied each course. With the roast, Tomaso served the Valpolicella Antonio and I like. Surfeited, I asked if we might wait an hour for dolce and the adults agreed.

At the children's table, Claudia announced, "I want my dolce now. The food was terrible, and I … want … my … dolce!"

"Polonia, take Claudia to your room. If she leaves quietly," said Papa, "I will have your dolce sent up. Wait for my call to return to the family."

Polonia glared at Stefano, scraped her chair legs against the floor and stood. She stomped to the children's table, thrust her arm toward Claudia, pulled her daughter to standing and left the room. We heard the start of a whine stopped with "Silenzio!" The nurses informed the boys their dolce were in the nursery, so they followed the women out of the room.

"Lucietta, per favore, come here." *Draw her in. Let her lean against me.*

"I need to speak with …" *Say it so she will become accustomed to the words my husband. And to my new position.* "Lucietta, per favore, go to your room with Nurse. Do not take the stairs until Claudia is in her parents' room and the boys are in theirs. Supper will be informal, so you may wish to wear the same vestito or a more comfortable one if you like. If you wish, you may visit the boys in the nursery. Remember, you are their hostess and be kind. You may go now."

I like his hand on the small of my back as we leave. Tomaso nodded to us as he opened the door. *My hand warmed as he took it and twined his fingers in mine. Warm eyes. Shoulder to shoulder. May we always be like this together. A cool wind, but a warm sun. Cannot stay outside too long. I remember this bench. I can be in his arms now. We are married.*

I turned and lifted my heels and chin to meet his lips. *Warm. Pleasant. He is teasing my lips open with his tongue. O-o-oh.* I tilted my head and leaned into his chest. His embrace tightened. With my lips burning, and my heart racing, I forgot all but sensation. *Cannot breathe. Air!* I pulled away and thrust my head into his chest.

I gasped, "No more. Need air. Too soon." I felt his silent chuckle and considered pushing him farther away, but he stopped and kissed my head.

"Enough for now. Let us sit," he said as he led me to the bench. Antonio sat with his hip to mine. I took a deep breath and leaned my head against his shoulder. "Such a day. I am overwhelmed."

"Grazie for choosing my favorite color."

"I especially like the way the blue changes as the pattern moves like waves. Like the sea I think."

"I remember the fabric, and that you preferred the embroidered cream. Both suit you well. You are beautiful and I am a most fortunate husband." Antonio brought his arm around my shoulders and his other hand holding mine. Warmed, I sat in silence. "I do not want a Claudia. You are gentle but firm with Lucietta. I approve." *Permission.* He paused. "Welcome to our family with its good parts... and not so good ones."

"As formal as is Il Conto degli Travino, I have seen his eyes when he looks Violante's way."

"His family disapproved of their ancient line being joined to a merchant's, no matter how wealthy. Not even her dowry moved them. Il Conto vowed he would marry her or no one else. As he is their heir, they had to agree." Antonio extended his left leg and relaxed his back. "Violante is smart; she learned how to be a contessa and to fit into his world. I know you will do the same here."

Is he warning me or only telling me what he expects? Smile back. "Will you tell me when I behave as a donna should and instruct me when I go amiss?"

"Of course." Antonio paused and added, "Producing two sons

won Violante a bit of their favor."

As I must as well. How do I do that?

"They are well matched and appear content. Not so Stefano. Papa warned him, but he refused to listen. After I met Polonia, I also knew she was presenting an image different from her true self. After I married, he insisted on doing the same. Now he is paying the cost of his rashness."

I looked at the pebbled path and my feet. *Say it and be done.* "Antonio, I am afraid."

"Our marriage will be like Violante's, not Stefano's."

I released a deep sigh and looked away. "I know nothing about being a wife…in our rooms."

Fingers still entwined, Antonio turned me until I faced him. "On your body there is a door to a secret place. Tonight I will open that door for the first time, a husband's right." His eyes and mouth smiled. "I will teach you the world of pleasures within that place and all over your body as well." He kissed my fingers. "That, I will enjoy very much."

I blushed and shivered.

"You are cold." At my nod, Antonio rose and took me into his arms. I relaxed within their warmth. "Fear not. We will have sons… and daughters too." I returned his kiss. *Soft lips. Longer than our first kiss at church. Very nice.* I felt myself melt into him. His tongue flicked into my mouth and startled me, but I moved not. Released, I lay my head against his chest. and murmured, "Time for dolce." Antonio held me close as we returned to the house.

Feel well warmed…What door?

In the salon, after we had enjoyed dolce and beverages with the adults, I excused myself to bid Lucietta good night. When I opened the door to my new bedroom, I found Garon waiting.

Open the door to his room before I start. Pray she knows what I need. No talk. Nod.

Garon returned my nod and began the nightly ritual of preparing me for sleep. Garon turned away to lay my underskirt upon a chair. In only my mid-thigh silk camicia I wiggled my toes against the plush rug that lay between my table and the bed. Garon pantomimed; I pulled the garment over my head and exchanged it for a small bowl of l'acqua degli rosa and a small, soft square of hemmed cotton. Garon turned to the guardaroba to store garments while I grazed my flesh with the moistened cloth. I sighed in pleasure that the braziers had warmed the room and that Garon had thought to warm the rose-scented water. I dropped the cloth into the empty bowl and placed it on the dressing table.

Draped across Garon's arms lay a white silk something. I whispered, "What is it?"

"A night garment. Traditional for a bride."

Thin with tiny straps. Cups my breasts and falls away. Slit to my hips on both sides. She held up the garment; I raised my arms. It slid down my body. *I am wearing nothing.*

Garon pulled back the bed coverings, fluffed the pillows, and gestured. I stepped to the bed, sat, lifted my legs and pushed myself closer to the middle. *Three pillows wide. Plenty of room for both of us. He is broad shouldered but not thick.* I shifted and lay back against a pillow. Garon lifted the coverings and placed them over me; I grabbed the edges and held the top, blanket and linen sheet to my chin. Garon smiled, grasped my clenched hands and lay them atop the silk, embroidered, down-filled coverlet. She unfolded my fingers and patted them. "Buone notte, Signora." Garon left.

Still taking deep breaths to relax, I heard soft noises from beyond the open door. Spotting a streak of candle light against the wood, I flung the covers aside and jumped out of the bed. Looking around the room, I realized my dressing table bench was farthest from his doorway and took to it. I grabbed the bench's edges to steady myself as I tried to slow my breathing. I looked up. Antonio stood in the doorway wearing only a bit of fabric about his waist. I gasped. *So that is a man! Well-muscled. Trim, yet strong looking. Hiding what beneath that cloth?*

I snapped shut my jaws, dropped my gaze and pulled my knees together. I clutched my hands in my lap. I could not think, not even to pray.

The rug suits the colors of this room.

"Open your eyes. Look at me."

His footsteps had made no sound. Why on one knee?

Antonio wrapped my hands in his and warmed them. He opened my fingers and raised my right hand to his lips. He kissed my wedding ring, lifted his head and smiled. *My heart races; I feel my cheeks color. I know not what is coming, yet I fear it.* He rose with my hands in his; I had to stand. Antonio kissed my forehead, then each cheek. His kiss upon my mouth was sweet and unhurried.

Not angry I do nothing in return.

Antonio stepped backed and took me with him. He stood us beside the bed. When he released my hands, they fell to my sides. Smiling, he tapped my chin with his pointing finger. I watched him walk around the room, blowing out candles. Only embers from the two braziers lit the room. I stared at Antonio's shadow on the floor as he locked the door, turned and stepped toward me.

27

October 27

I woke. *He is touching me from his breath against my hair to the leg he has thrown over mine.* He draped his arm across my waist. Lifting my lids, I noted the line between his light shoulder and his sun-darkened forearm. *Not trapped. Held, cradled. Such a night! A little pain. Then pleasure! Such pleasures. Warmed. Then hot. Every part of me. I will always remember his words, "Now you are mine. Forever." He whispered, "Cara." I am his dear one. He is mine.*

A knock startled us. "Signora, time to dress for Mass."

Antonio lifted his head to kiss my temple, rolled away, stood and disappeared into his room.

I sat up and looked for my camicia between the sheets. Before I located the gown, I pulled out Antonio's loincloth. *A red-brown stain? Why?* I scooted out of bed, dropped my gown over my head and shimmied as it fell. I stuffed Antonio's stained covering into a dressing table drawer. After unlocking the door, I turned and walked away. I spoke to behind me, "I must wash."

"Oui, Madam," replied Garon as she carried in a pail of hot water with a linen sheet draped over her shoulder. Behind the screen, I soaped, rinsed and dried my face and body. *The private parts of me are sore. Breasts too. Such a night!*

From the slit between the screen panels, I watched Garon pull back the covers to look for something. She frowned, looked around, spotted the partially opened drawer and pulled out the fabric I had stuffed there. She folded the fabric and put it in her apron pocket. I heard her mutter, "Leave it in the old man's office for him to find." *Whatever that is, it is a private thing between Antonio and me! What right does Papa have to it! Why would Papa need that old thing? It is ours! Say nothing. Ask Antonio about it or let it be?*

I love his hand on the small of my back as we enter. I hope my small push back and smile tells him I like it. Wonderful smells in the hall from below. A hearty colazione to come. To Papa's left already sat il Conto. Opposite him sat his wife. After I sat beside Violante, I watched Antonio step behind his seated father to his place opposite me. Stefano seated Polonia beside me and strode around the table to sit beside his brother. As we faced our husbands, and I sat between the women, I thought *Rank. Always rank.*

"Buone Giorno, Violante. Buone Giorno, Polonia." After each responded, I wondered why everyone else was looking so expectantly at Antonio. Tomaso strode into the room with a large wine goblet on a silver tray. He placed the goblet in front of Antonio. *Wine? Why are the men grinning? Even Tomaso as he stands behind my husband. Why is Antonio smirking at me?* Antonio picked up the goblet, waved it in a circle to each person at the table, lifted it toward me, and then down it in one gulp. Everyone applauded. Not knowing what else to do, I reluctantly joined them, much to their amusement.

Zanetta entered with and held the tray as her father served a cup of cafe or te' to first Papa and then to the men by rank. I leaned to Violante and whispered, "What was that drink?"

Violante smiled at me before she leaned and whispered back, "The traditional drink a husband must swallow in one gulp." At seeing my wrinkled forehead, Violante added, "Red wine gone sour to vinegar for strength, honey, spices. To fortify his spent manhood."

As my cheeks burned, I stared at the cup before me. *Wish I could disappear.* After I felt my face cool, I sipped my te' slowly to keep hidden. When I looked up, they were chatting among themselves. From the next tray, I took a plate with bread on it. *If I do as they do, only a moment behind, I will not embarrass myself. Or my family. My family. I have a family! Be nice to Polonia; she frowns. Ahh, the soup course.*

"Polonia, I hope you will tell me of your life on the farm."

After Zanetta had removed the bowls, Polonia responded, "Not much to say. I manage the children and the household while Stefano is gone all day. Sometimes, he stays overnight on a distant property."

"That must be hard for you."

"Certamente, I am alone most of the time. Claudia is my comfort."

As Polonia complained further about her circumstances, I imagined walking fields in sunshine, climbing the hills, and dangling my feet in a cool stream. At last, Polonia wound down and returned to eating the main course of lamb and vegetables. I commented, "To one born and raised in the city time in the country sounds lovely."

"Hah! You would not think so if you were stuck there for months on end."

Do not invite her to visit. I lack the authority. I forked a piece of lamb into my mouth and chewed. *I do not want to hear her complaints for days or deal with Claudia.* I saw Antonio speaking to il Conto, and Stefano looking my way. I smiled and nodded. In return, he gave me a raised brow and a small shrug. *He knows; he understands. Turn.*

Violante was much more cheerful describing living in Ferrara and the Este Castle; she talked of the cathedral, parks, concerts, and social events. She described their summer estate in the country. We ignored Polonia's snort of derision when Violante invited Antonio and me to visit as soon as possible but omitted Stefano and her.

Papa excused us. Discussing Il Conto's travel plans, the men stayed at the table. Before I departed, I signaled Tomaso to pour more wine. *Obvious, but I need to give instructions to the household so they become accustomed to me.* Polonia had left to supervise Claudia, and Violante for the nursery and her sons. I sought Lucietta.

That night, I wore the matching robe over my camicia. I suspected Antonio was naked beneath his blue robe patterned with pale ships. Standing beside the bed, I murmured, "I locked the door."

Antonio drew me into his arms and started a kiss that I felt it all the way to my toes. Such *a way to begin!* As I responded, his fingers danced down my back, creating tingles where they tapped. He sat us on the edge of the bed. I giggled as I started sliding off the silk coverlet. Antonio held me as we slid to the floor; we both laughed as we went. His lips touched mine, and he plunged his tongue between them. I froze. He helped me to stand. Antonio threw the coverlet, blanket, and sheeting across the bed. Smiling, my husband gestured and bowed; I sat. On one knee, Antonia began caressing my ankles as the candle by the door sputtered dead.

28

October 28

After Mass and a hurried meal, Stefano and his family departed more quietly than they had arrived. First, Papa sent Polonia and Claudia to the gondola with their maid. Stefano sent his sons and their nurse into his gondola. He smiled at me. "Sister, you are a lovely addition to our family. Antonio is a fortunate man." He kissed me on each cheek. After shaking hands with his father and brother, he bid us farewell. Before he stepped into the sunlight, he heaved a great sigh and straightened his back. Papa, Antonio and I followed and stood on the dock to wave and watch as the boats traveled up our short rio and turned left onto Rio San Marina.

Antonio placed my arm through the crook of his. "Il Conto stayed until yesterday because he likes you. Said you are more an asset to the family than he thought you would be. Reported to me Violante gave you excellent advice, including how to deal with your new dressmaker." He added, "You need to visit her soon." Together we watched the gondolas from three of the houses on the other side of our rio travel to San Marina and turn left or right. He nodded toward the final gondola. "Our neighbors slowed to see us."

"I suspect they are relieved I have only one head."

Antonio chuckled and Papa laughed outright. "Well said, daughter. I have business to attend." Papa left us.

As we turned toward the house, a chilly wind picked up. Antonio said, "Grazia, I conduct business sometimes in our home but more often outside it. After pranzo on Mondays and Thursdays, I leave. Often I return well after you go to sleep so I do not see you until morning. I will continue that practice." He gestured me to enter and I preceded him up the stairs.

"Does Papa do that too?"

"No. He conducts most of his business weekdays after Mass and colazione. Sometime, he serves pranzo and continues after midday if he must."

"When you are gone, may I have Lucietta join Papa and me for cena? She is old enough to learn table manners." We climbed the stairs and had reached the entry and the oval table and flowers in the large Murano vase swirled with gold streaks.

"As you wish." Antonio glanced toward the office door. "I must consult with Papa."

"When you have time, I have several financial matters to discuss with both of you. Per favore, schedule when we three can meet." At Antonio's assent I waited in the hall; Papa invited me into their sanctuary. I learned about our weekly food budget, including feeding business associates at pranzo, the wages of the staff, the household budget and more. Papa handed me the household record book and suggested I use it until I am ready to start one of my own.

I sent for Lucietta. "Time for music. Finish your lessons later."

I showed her the music room and explained how her father had remodeled it for us. After uncovering her mother's instrument, I suggested. "Let us try the harp." I sat and strummed the strings and was pleased to tell Lucietta it was tuned. She stood beside me and I showed her how to pluck a simple tune. "Would you like to learn to play the harp? If you do, I will ask Nonno to find a teacher for you."

"It is so big," she said as she took my place.

"A teacher will bring one your size for you to start on. By the time you are ready for your mama's instrument, you would be a skilled player.

"I would like to try it," admitted Lucietta.

"I will talk to Nonno for you."

"Grazie tante, Mama."

"Back to your lessons, now." After Lucietta left, I stayed and played and sang for an hour. *Feels so good to be back. Good that I start immediately. I want my daily playing to be so much a part of our routine that no one challenges me when I come to this room.* I looked about. *I need a case with drawers for music. If there is none in the attic, I will ask Papa what I may use.* I left the room with the household book in hand.

Standing at the base of the stairs, I pondered where to work. *Not on the dining room table; I need a place to store the book, receipts, and such. Not in a guest room; Polonia or another guest might learn our finances. A desk in my bedroom is private. Locked. Servants or Garon cannot pry.*

At pranzo I announced I had found a desk in the attic and had ordered it placed in a corner of my bedroom. After our main meal of the day, Papa provided me with the paper, ink well and pens I had requested. I was so busy I had not called for Lucietta and ignored Garon's announcement of cena. I did not lock the accounts book in my desk until Antonio arrived to escort me. He expressed his approval as I pocketed the key. After he escorted me to the dining room he departed. As I had requested, Lucietta joined Papa and me.

"Where is Papa?"

"He is gone on business. You will see him tomorrow." Lucietta behaved well and followed my gestured hints, laid her napkin on her lap, put her hands together, bowed her head and listened to Nonno pray. Afterward, I walked her to the nursery, kissed her buone notte, and headed for my bath.

"What do you know of Fiamette Barbo?"

Garon washed my back as she answered. "She owns the House of Signora Barbo. Barbo is to be married, but all dressmakers are called 'signora'. Her house serves the families numbered one hundred to one fifty. She can serve that many because she has two dozen women working for her either in her shop or in their homes."

"What do you know of dressmaking?" I asked as I shifted in the bath and reached for the soapy rag Garon offered.

"I learned from the doxe's wife to the ninety-ninth, each family has its own dressmakers and seamstresses. The rest of the il grande hire their work. The styles come from Paris, the fabrics from around the world. Woolens from England, rare silks from Cina through India and the other silks from Sicily. Cotton from the Ottoman empire, linens from the low countries."

I stood to be wrapped in a linen sheet. I stepped out of the bath. "How do I hire Barbo?"

"You send a note requesting an appointment. She returns it with a date and time on the bottom. When you arrive, you choose the fashions, fabrics, trims and such. She sets the costs and the date for the fittings. When a vestito or your whole order arrives, you owe the money. If you do not pay her upon delivery, she drops you in her order of service."

"Rank in everything."

"Si, Signora. In the fabrics as well. Each season, you are fourth in line to choose. You may not have the fabrics or trims of those above you."

Naked under my robe, I sat at my table. Servants emptied and cleaned the bath while Garon dried my hair. "Signora, your hair is your glory. So long and just the right amount of curl. I am sorry you must now bind it." She raised a handful and commented, "Your marito is a fortunate man." I saw her concerned face in my mirror. "Signora, I must tell you. You are already late in choosing your winter vestitos. I suggest you sent a note to Signora Barbo in the morning. Tonight, I will make you a list of what you will need to wear in the house, going to Mass, entertaining afternoon guests, and for special dinners and socials."

"Grazie, Garon, for taking such good care of me. I think Barbo may already have begun my winter at home garments. I have much to learn, and I rely on your help. Do you accompany me when I see Barbo?"

"No, Signora, I may not. In the morning may we discuss what colors best suit you?"

"Si. Remember to order a bath every evening Signor is away. Buone notte, Garon."

Garon handed over the brush, said, "Buone notte, Signora" and departed.

In the mirror I looked at the open door behind me. *He has been in my room. Why can I not go into his? I will touch nothing. Just look.* I picked up the candlestick to my right and walked toward the open doorway. *The bed is massive with tall posts in the corners and has so high a sleeping place I would have to jump to reach it. That or need something two or three steps high. Three chests for clothing.* I tried to lift a lid but it was too heavy. I looked up and spotted two metal brackets. *A place to set his sword?* Against the third wall was a screen that hid his metal tub and his chamber pot chair. *Everything dark wood, large and masculine. Very like him.* At a small table I looked at his hair brush and comb. I lifted a bottle of dark liquid and sniffed. *His fragrance. That is why he smells so good. Leave now. If I stay longer, he may smell my fragrance and ask why I entered his room.*

The next day I woke alone and met Antonio downstairs for Mass. After we broke our fasts, Garon appeared in the archway with my cape and mask in hand.

"Because we are husband and wife, you need no chaperone. Though cool, it is sunny today. Would you like to see the city?" At my assent Garon dressed me in the hall. He escorted me to the outer hall and donned his cape and mask. A gondola waited at our dock, and we sat together on the cushioned seat in front of the gondolier. We leaned against velvet pillows and drew a heavy woolen blanket to our waists.

"A gondola with a felze box would block your views; I ordered an open one so you could better see the sites. The day is ours. We will stop whenever you like. "

Antonio put his arm around my shoulders and drew me close. He had taken the windward side so I would feel warmer in the sunshine. We turned left and traveled the rios until we reached Canale Grande. Looking right, I asked, "The Rialto Bridge?"

"On our way home, we will proceed northward and ride under it. That way are the lesser homes on the Canale. The greater ones are close to the Rialto or south toward the piazza."

I admired the cream and pink stone buildings and noted they had no water gates, just wide docks in front of tall, ornate, recessed entrances. At the lagoon we turned westward and headed toward four small islands surrounded by tall, gray stone walls to the water. I spotted church steeples. Antonio expected my question. "Those islands are monasteries for different orders of monks. They never leave them."

"How do they eat?"

"They have gardens, chickens, geese. I know not if they order from our island or the mainland."

"Beyond them I see San Giorgio Maggiore Island. From my old rooftop I had only seen it from a distance. I would like to see that church and its island."

We stood before the gleaming, four-columned front, and I craned my neck to see the top of the pediment. A Benedictine brother stepped out of the left of the three doors and offered to give us a tour. Once inside, we stopped often; Brother Sebastiano pointed and talked of the architect Palladio's designs for the main sanctuary and the side altars. He named the artists of many paintings, but I only recognized two, Tintoretto and Ricci. We exited the church, and he talked of the old bell tower of 1467 that stood beside the old church at the edge of the square. I looked away as Antonio pulled coins from his beneath his cape and handed them to Brother Sebastiano with our thanks. *The walls are taller than the tallest man. The monks can walk about and live away from the eyes of the world.*

They had locked the old church against visitors so we proceeded to the main square. Food and drink stalls provided our midday meal, which we enjoyed as we watched other visitors wander about. *We talk so easily together. I like his company. I would like to hold hands, but none of the other couples do not. I will not reach.* Just then, Antonio's hand brushed mine as he looked at me and smiled. I had expected we would have to signal for a gondolier to leave the island, but the man Antonio had hired was waiting for us at the main dock.

As we left the island, I looked away from where I knew Ospedale stood and toward Piazza San Marco and the doxe's palace. We landed at the stairs.

"No one walks between the pillars. Bad luck," warned Antonio. He pointed to the winged Saint Mark atop one pillar and explained the statue atop the other pillar was of Venezia's former patron saint, Saint Todaro, with his foot on a dragon. I nodded my understanding. *No need to tell him I already know who they are. Let him shine.*

Past the pillars we stepped left, and walked beside the library and turned the corner to see the outside tables of a restaurant Antonio had said has been there for centuries. Two tall men in black uniforms stood beside the entry. I watched them open the massive double doors for two men who entered and turned left. For a moment, I spotted waiters in white coats and gloves carrying golden trays of covered dishes to tables of men dressed in black. I spotted no women. *Perhaps couples eat in a different area.*

As we continued walking, I noted the piazza was even larger than I had thought. Across the piazza and above us, birds wheeled and called. At one arch of the doxe's palace, a man stood throwing bits of bread into the air. Birds swooped close to him to catch food midair while those on the ground pecked at each other to gain what had fallen.

The afternoon light softened the edges of the buildings, monuments, and statues and left a glow in the air. *This is why we are Serenissima, a city both serene and beautiful day and night. Might the many windows hold candles, so we may walk the piazza at night and admire its beauty? Some moonlit night, I will ask Antonio to show me this place again.*

At my request we climbed the three hundred twenty-three steps of the bell tower for a commanding view of our island and two nearby ones. Antonio pointed out features in the square. I was most impressed by the golden domes of the church of San Marco, the four horses over the main entrance, and the golden mosaics within the arches. Because the sun was within an hour of setting, we did not tour the doxe's church but returned to the steps and took our gondola up Canale Grande.

Antonio explained the grandness of each home is determined by how many stories each building had above the water level. "Also the ornateness of decoration and the number of windows facing the canal. If the home also stands on a corner of a rio, that also reports a family's wealth."

A golden light caressed the eastern side of the Canale so those homes simmered and seemed magical. The white marble arches and window trims gleamed as the stone walls' colors softened. The gondola sped up. Nearing the bridge, Antonio leaned toward me, pointed to a four-storied house with three windows on each side of tall, dark wooden double-entry doors. The top three floors had seven front windows. Antonio whispered, "Pontenuevo."

At the Rialto I leaned back and stared at the marble arch above me as we passed under it. On the bridge and on both sides of the canal, people were closing shops or hurrying homeward.

Past the bridge the most magnificent palaso was faced in gold sheets with gleaming marble arches and window trim. At Antonio's instruction the gondola slowed and took a side rio.

"See that small, pink, two-story house on the corner with only one large front window with the flower box? Vivaldi lives there with his father and many siblings. Likely crowded in there. Bought by the coins his patrons gave him."

"Why is Padre not serving a church and living with other priests?"

"Not strong enough. Breathing problems. His father or one of his brothers goes everywhere with him. Carries his medicine should he wheeze and takes him to a physician if it's bad enough."

That is why he took the contract to write concertos for Ospedale. To pay for his home. "Does he leave for a warmer clime in winter?"

"I do not know. One winter I did see him wearing a heavy cape with his head wrapped in a woolen scarf so I saw only his eyes. Cold is his enemy."

The sky darkened as we turned right into a rio and shadows crept toward us. We took a smaller rio that appeared to lead us away from home. Before I could ask why, Antonio pointed to a small house with a tiny window on either side of a recessed door and a wooden dock so short that only one person at a time could stand on it.

"Niccolo Polo's old home."

"So modest."

"They moved to a larger home after Marco returned from Cina." He added, "We all start small and move as we do better." Further north Antonio pointed right and told me that was where the Jews lived. I glimpsed down a lane with small houses crowded together that were two or three stories high. They looked neat and clean, but the narrow lane was crowded with people all dressed in black. The men wore hats; the women covered their faces with veils and walked arm in arm in pairs. They put their backs to the walls when men walked past them. I smelled strange foods cooking and wondered what Jews eat. We passed two streets and the area disappeared.

"Where the Jews must live." *I am aware of the laws forbidding Jews to live among us Christians and of the gates locking them into their neighborhood from sunset to sunrise. We had been taught Jews were needed for trade, but had to be locked away for Christians to be safe at night. I wondered how true that is, but I said nothing to Antonio. I doubt I will ever meet one to inquire about their lives.* The wind picked up. Antonio pulled the blanket to my chin and we stayed close.

"The lagoon is large and water choppy. To the left is Mestre on the mainland."

"I see ships and docks. Are those extensive buildings behind them warehouses?" At Antonio's assent, I thought *So many ships, all without sails in their rigging. Unusable because of the Ottomans.*

At a corner we turned and took rios I did not know. Antonio named them as we took them. South on Mendicanti. Then we jogged left on San Marino and right down our rio. On our dock Rocco stood with a torch in hand to light our way. Leaving Antonio to pay the gondolier, I hurried inside and up the stairs to the warmth within.

Saturday the lines were long after Mass. Because I had little to confess, the padre asked me about my wedding. I kept my answers short and revealed only what the priest demanded. I was happy he could not see my flushed face through the screen as he asked about my nights with Antonio. I was glad to close the confessional door behind me and kneel in a pew. *If I have done nothing sinful, why does the priest ask about our private times? What did the priest ask Antonio?* I completed the few prayers required for my penance, stood and met Antonio and Papa in the back of the church. I could not look at Antonio as we walked home for pranzo. I was glad he asked no questions.

Monday was All Saints Day and a High Mass with a long sermon on which I tried to concentrate and failed. I understood little of the theology the priest said we must believe. Our pranzo was a merry one, with special foods and lively talk. Freed from lessons or sewing, Lucietta joined us as we four sat in the salon and visited. No one came calling so Papa ordered a small table and took a puzzle box from a bookshelf. We put together a puzzle of our peninsula as Papa and Antonio taught Lucietta and me the major rivers and cities. After cena we put together a second puzzle of the Veneto. I had not realized how far northeast our region extended. More than halfway to Vienna Papa revealed.

Tuesday was All Souls Day. After another High Mass we ate before we boarded gondolas for the cemetery on the mainland. I was glad for my new fur-lined hooded cape, which protected me from the worst of the blustering wind blowing through the markers. My puffy muff protected my gloved hands. A ten-foot marble statue of a guardian angel with outstretched arms marked the Delatesta site.

We watched as Papa laid flowers on his wife's grave, prayed and repeated the process at his first-born's marker. Because Michielo had died at sea, no body lay beneath it. Antonio took Lucietta from my side and stood before Lucia's grave. As I watched him bend over to talk with her, the wind blew their words away. Lucietta laid flowers at her mother's marker, kissed its top and sought the comfort of Antonio's arms. I felt sorry for her loss and then sorry for myself. *I have no mother to mourn. Only a vision of what might be true.* We returned home in silence and spent the rest of the day apart and quiet. On our way to our rooms, Antonio reminded me he had resumed meeting prospective clients Monday and Thursday evenings.

29

November 3

After Mass I was leaving colazione and in the hall when Tomaso handed me a note. I broke the wax seal, read and announced, "Oh no, she will not!"

"Who will not do what?"

"Papa, I must go to the dressmaker immediately. She is much mistaken if she thinks I will wait a month to see her. We are one hundred three not one hundred forty. I require a gondola and two guards."

"I will escort you."

"Grazie, Antonio, but no. If you come, she will think I cannot do this alone and count me weak. I am not weak! She will learn that today. Papa, I require a pouch of gazetti and soldi so the pouch is large and heavy. Equal to one hundred zecchini."

"For what?"

"I am going to teach Barbo I am not to be trifled with. She will not insult me! Others pay their dressmakers upon delivery. I will give her an advance and ask for prompt service."

The men watched me settle into the gondola. I heard Papa comment, "No mouse, that one. Pity the dressmaker."

At the dressmaker's door I ordered my guards, "Wait here. Let no one enter." Inside, three women looked up from a bolt of brocade as I removed my mask.

"Buone giorno, Signora Barbo." I nodded to the mother. "Buone giorno, I am Signora Antonio Delatesta. You are…?"

"Signora Gasparo Druscho. Madelena. This is my daughter, Donna Clara."

"Your number?

"One hundred twenty-eight."

I gave her a sweet smile and reported, "As I am one hundred three, I believe I have precedence." The mother nodded to me and gestured to her daughter; the pair stepped back. This time I had a full view of Signora Barbo, again dressed in gray with a knot of her dark hair at her nape.

"Signora, each season I am fourth to select my fabrics and to place my order. As I would never presume to choose before the three ahead of me, I expect others to accord me the same respect." I turned to the Druschos. "I am agreeable to having you stay during my appointment if you will wait your turn."

"We will wait, Signora Delatesta."

I caressed the dark green brocade the woman had been holding. After I picked up the bolt, I smiled and handed it to Signora Druscho, who grabbed it and clutched it against her chest. "I would not think of taking it from you, Signora Druscho." I turned. "Signora Barbo, what have you to offer me?"

I admired the pile of fabric bolts on several tables and chose; then I approved designs from the pile of drawings. I touched the dark green warp with a black weft. "This changes color when it moves, very dramatic. Signora, from where does this marvelous silk come?"

She shrugged, "Calabria or Sicily. They have been making it for centuries. They say the skill came from Cina."

Now, to win you to my service. "Signora, you are busy, but I need this at once. The doxe is coming to dinner soon, but I do not know the date. I will wear this for him." From the corner of my eye, I saw both spectators' jaws drop. "The deep rose I will wear Christmas Day." I listed other garments I needed before Christmas Eve. I finished with, "I will wear the blue with the gold trimmings for Festal, so I want that by the end of January. The rest are for spring, so I want them before Easter."

"This is a large order, Signora Delatesta."

"Certamente. I know payment is due when you deliver my order. As I have asked for so much and at speed, would you consider another arrangement?" At Barbo's uncertain nod, I continued. "I am accustomed to paying something when I order, but I think you deserve more than usual." I extracted the pouch from my borsellino. "I have one hundred zecchini to offer you now. Will that do?"

"Si, si, signora, si," came Barbo's excited response.

I handed over the pouch as if it were nothing. "I expect we will do this each season if it meets with your approval."

"Certamente."

"I will wait for a list and costs for all I have ordered." I caressed my deep green/black bolt. "Oh, I almost forgot. Per favore, may I have a piece of each of the fabrics of my vestitos? My signor wants them in hand when he chooses the jewels I will wear with each."

From the corner of my eye, I spotted the mother's and daughter's eyes widen. I placed the paper and fabrics in my borsellino, pulled the strings taut, and hung the bag's strings over my wrist. "Grazie, Signora Barbo. I look forward to working with you again."

"Signora Delatesta, I am pleased to serve you."

"Signora Druscho, may I watch as you choose your fabrics?" *Be polite and complimentary so they speak well of me. Invite them to visit me at home.* They took longer than I did, and Clara fought her mother over every fabric, color and trim. *A strong-willed girl. Her taste is better than her mother's yet she must fight for her choices. Remember that with Lucietta.*

I bid the dressmaker and the Druschos farewell, donned my mask, stepped outside, and lifted my face to the sky. *Bright day, clear, but I feel more cold coming.*

As I rode home, I reviewed my success. *Just the right amounts of imperiousness and kindness. They were polite about my invitation. I hope they come. At first Barbo appeared surprised then angry to see me. My confidence unsettled her. The more I chose the more she warmed. Especially when I selected the green black. Very expensive. Who are the other three that they passed on such richness?* I smiled to myself. *The Druschos are sure to gossip. I hope I did not speak wrong about jewels. One set should be enough for a while. Papa or Antonio? Papa.*

I regaled Garon with my success, who laughed and congratulated me. "You are smart to ask for the patches. You have proof of what you chose, and she cannot change the fabrics for something less."

I refused bread and cheese, saying, "I have forgotten hunger; I will await cena."

I asked Lucietta to show me her room and Nurse's sleeping corner within the nursery. Nurse explained she could better hear Lucietta in the night with a curtain instead of a door. In front of

Lucietta I asked Nurse of Lucietta's progress. I praised them both for Lucietta's success in learning her letters. I spent the rest of the afternoon listening to Lucietta's lessons. Hand in hand I walked her to cena.

After I dismissed Lucietta, Papa commented, "She is behaving better. No longer runs and says buone notte. Takes Nurse's hand and speaks more kindly to her. What have you planned for her next?"

I explained and he approved. "Papa, I must tell you what I did without your permission. A spur-of-the-moment decision we may regret."

After I informed Papa of my comment regarding jewels, he instructed, "Wait a time and then bring your patches to my office."

I gasped. Papa had emptied the desktop of all but the chandelier. Under it sparkled sets of earrings, necklaces, rings, brooches, and bracelets. I looked up with a question in my eyes.

"Two centuries of collecting. Lucia brought her own jewelry. These are Delatesta, last worn by my wife, God rest her soul."

"Papa if I wear any of this, I will need Antonio and four guards to protect me from theft!" I watched Papa's slow smile.

Papa patted my shoulder. "Never fear. We always protect you, jeweled or not. The patches?"

Together, we decided on the diamonds for the deep green, the rubies and diamonds for the Christmas dress, and the sapphires and diamonds for Festal. "The emeralds and diamonds for the cream vestito you wore your wedding day."

"Do I wear an entire set at the same time? Is it not too much?"

"You vary how much you wear depending upon the occasion. Perhaps just a brooch and the small earrings for a special afternoon guest. Oh, I forgot. We also have pearls for day wear. I will bring them out another time. You will look lovely in any of this. My Francesca would have been proud to see you in them." I colored at Papa's loving looks.

I kissed his cheek. "Grazie tante, Papa."

Papa escorted me to a chair and sat in his stuffed, leather-upholstered chair. "You have been married over two weeks. If women want to meet you, they will arrive one hour after pranzo. You will meet them in the salon with tea and a plate of dolce, fruit and decorated breads. They stay for an hour and then go visit someone else. You must dress to receive guests, engage them in light conversation and escort them to the door. I expect some will be curious about you; no one came today so be ready tomorrow."

"Si, Papa. Buone notte." I kissed him and left. On the stairs I decided *Never ask where he keeps the jewels, coins, any wealth. If I am never told, no one can force me to reveal it. Leave it to Papa and Antonio.*

I slipped deeper into my scented bath water as I released the tensions of the day. I fell asleep thinking about entertaining the Druschos for tea.

30

November 8

Papa, Lucietta, and I went to Mass without Antonio because he had already left for the Great Council meeting of the ranked, which is usually called during the second week of the month. *He said they are only summoned when they are needed, but they must be ready to serve. I wonder how often they meet.*

After pranzo, I paced the salon. *Five weeks since the wedding and still no visitors. Well dressed, hair fixed, wearing pearls. All to no use. They will not come. Call for Lucietta and give her treats.*

"Mama, why are we dressed? Who is coming?" She munched on a biscotto.

"No one is coming today. Perhaps next week. This is a special day just for us." I began. "I have noticed your good behavior. Your Papa and I are pleased. We have decided you are getting ready to leave the nursery and to live in the girls' bedroom. Like a big girl."

Lucietta's eyes widened. "Now?!"

"Not yet. You must prove yourself worthy. We have five tasks for you. Five good qualities we want you to have. When you succeed, we will reward you."

Lucietta's eyes narrowed. "What tasks?"

"The first is to be polite. You will say 'per favore' when you want something and 'grazie' when you receive it. To Nonno, Papa, me, anyone who comes into our home. Even to the servants."

"They are servants; they must do what I tell them. Why must I ask them and be grateful?"

"Nurse asked this of you before, and you refused. Now Papa and I insist. Servants are persons too. They know their responsibilities. Your being polite to them is a formality all proper ladies use. With servants, with each other, with everyone. Learning this now will help you all your life. Others will think well of you; you will be a proper girl, young lady, then woman. Have you noticed how polite I am?"

"I thought that was because you are new."

"No, child. It is because my training began when I was younger than you."

"What is my reward?"

"Something very good. How many fingers have you?"

Lucietta held up hands and splayed her fingers. "Ten."

I held up two fingers. "For now you will practice being polite for ten days plus two. How many is that?" At her "twelve," I continued, "Nurse, Nonno, Papa, I, and everyone else will watch. If you have been polite all day to everyone, before you go to bed, Nurse will give you a soldo. When you have twelve coins, you take them to Papa, who will be very proud of you. The next day, I will give you your first gift."

"Two surprises, one from Papa, one from you?"

"We shall see. Would you like another biscotto?" I raised my brows.

"Si, per favore."

"Well done." I offered her the tray. She waited.

"Grazie, Mama." Lucietta picked up a almond studded one. "Mmm. Good."

"See. Not so hard after all."

At cena I reported starting Lucietta's first lesson and asked for their support. "Per favore, gentle reminders as needed." After the men agreed, I lowered my head and clenched my hands at the table edge. "No women are coming. Because of what I am." Papa placed his left hand over my right. "Worse, your friends no longer come here on business matters. Their wives demand they abandon you." I looked at Antonio. "You leave on Monday and Thursday to contract business with their husbands. They reject you because of me. Because of me even more bad things will happen to us. Our future holds declining income, failure, social isolation. Perhaps something even worse. All my fault."

"Not so, Grazia," said Papa. Business has declined since we lost the war. Fewer contracts with more families vying for them. The winter storms will make sailing even more dangerous. It is only a cycle. We will be fine."

I shook my downturned head. "Kind words, only partly true. What I feared has happened. I am hurting your family."

"Our family," corrected Papa. "We will survive this hard time as we have survived for centuries."

My tears plopped on my uneaten food. Antonio came to me. Bending over, he kissed my temple. "I would not trade you for an eightieth or a sixtieth, or even a thirtieth. Per favore, stop crying. We will be fine." Again I shook my head. Antonio scooped me into his arms. I put my arm over his shoulder and cried against his neck.

Antonio carried me upstairs and into my room. Garon dashed past us and closed the door. Antonio sat on the bed and held me close as I cried out my sorrow. I finished and wiped my face with the pocket cloth he handed me.

"I still see my friends, but you have lost your sisters. I meet business associates to learn of possible contracts, but women do not visit you. Cara, I am sorry for your loss, but I do not know what to do to help you. Perhaps in time they will change their minds."

I shrugged, and he kissed my cheek. He held me close and kissed me again. Afterward he called Garon to help me to bed. After she left I thought *Tomorrow I will play and sing all morning. Remember music is my air. Forget the world.* I prayed for acceptance until I fell asleep.

Antonio returned to his father now reading in the salon. "Papa, they are more unkind than you know. They talk of the next ranking and wonder how far we will fall."

Giovanni set his book on his lap. "I am aware."

"I thought they would accept her into our social rank even if she is foreign-born." Antonio look away and his father waited. "I like her. Very much. She's spirited. Already our lives are better, calmer. But what of our business prospects? What of my future children's acceptance in society?"

"Let us leave that to the future. Much can happen between then and now. I see how much you like Grazia, even admire her, but I also see you have not given her your heart. Is it Maricella?"

"No. As much as I appreciate her, she knows I will never love her. Her hold on me is my sons." Antonio glared at his father. "I will never give them up."

"Lucia might have charmed the doxe, but could she have looked straight into the eyes of a Ten and refuse him?"

Antonio shook his head. "She had charm and grace, but not Grazia's strength. Her determination."

"Son, not every woman dies in childbirth. Your mother bore four children; only the wasting sickness could take her. In both her family and in mine not one woman died bearing children. If you withholding your heart until she survives a birthing, that may be too late. Once you lose her love, you may not get it back. Ever. Antonio, which do you value more? Acceptance and our rank or the needs of your heart?"

Antoni shrugged, stood, and walked off.

Giovanni mumbled to himself, "I pray you choose aright, son."

31

November 16

Midmorning a messenger in the black, red, and gold official livery of the republic arrived. He presented a packet to Papa and left without waiting for an answer. A servant called me from the music room, and I met Antonio at Papa's office door. We entered and saw the large gold envelope with the red seal and three red ribbons hanging from it. I sat with a thump. Antonio closed the office door, and I held my breath as Papa broke the seal and read aloud:

To the Honorable Giovanni Delatesta:

My wife and I will dine with you on Wednesday, the twenty-fourth day of this month at the twentieth hour. We look forward to hearing your daughter's beautiful voice. Enclosed is the music of my favorite songs. Nine other guests will accompany us, plus one, who will accompany Signora Delatesta.

We look forward to a pleasant evening.

Yours in Christ,
Alvise III Sebastiano Mocenigo
Serenissimo Principe degli Venezia

"Dear God, he is coming. He is really coming."

"You invited him, daughter."

"I expected him to wait until at least January. Even spring."

Antonio added, "He could not have timed it better. We need social approval and his visit will give it to us. No one insults the doxe or his choices. Who might be the other four couples and who is the odd one?"

"That we will soon learn," chortled Giovanni. "The doxe's aide will arrive to help us prepare."

I jumped up. "I must inform Signora Barbo I need the deep green black by Tuesday night! O Dio Mio! I must have that vestito! Papa, have you paper and pen? Will you send a messenger to Barbo?"

As I scribbled, Papa and Antonio consulted. "We have not entertained this number since your mother's fiftieth birthing date celebration. We need to add every board to the table to seat fifteen and we need more chairs."

To Signora Barbo:

The Doxe will be here on Wednesday, the twenty-fourth, at the twentieth hour. I need the deep green by Tuesday night. I am at your disposal for fittings, and I am grateful for your speed in finishing my vestito. I shall express my gratitude in person after the event.

Yours in Christ,
Signora Antonio Delatesta

The first time I have written my title. It looks lovely on paper.

"Who sits where?" I asked, but received no answer.

Tomaso knocked. "Signori, the doxe's aide has arrived. He is already walking this floor."

"An urgent message to be delivered at once," said Antonio as he accepted my note and handed the folded paper to Tomaso.

"May I follow you? I need to write what I need for Sabina and Rosa." I grabbed a book from a shelf, plopped a paper on it and grabbed Papa's pen and inkwell. I balanced them atop the book until Sabina appeared. She walked behind us carrying the inkwell, which appeared each time I held out the pen. After the aide had left, I again plopped into a chair and set the book, papers, pen and inkwell upon Papa's desk.

"Considering all we must do, I am anxious. Papa, Antonio, may I read you my notes? I do not want to forget or do anything amiss."

At their nods I began, "Six guards. Two at our entrance, two at our first floor front, two at the back to guard the garden entrance.

- The doxe chose music first, dinner after.
- They gather in the salon for sweetened wine and nibbles. Escorted to the music room.
- After my performance, cena.
- Twelve guests; the aide gave you the seating, Papa. May I leave it in this room and fetch it as needed? Grazie.
- At your signal, Papa, or the doxe's, women back to the music room after dinner for men to talk in the dining room or the salon
- When summoned, we women to salon, enjoy the dolce, converse, and depart when the doxe signals

What shall we do if the odd one is Pontenuevo?"

"Leave him to Antonio and me. You are the gracious hostess, amiable and accommodating to all. Please list the menu."

"Entry: two sugared light wines and nibbles. Cook and I will decide on those. Soup is beef broth spiced with ginger. Prima piatto is fish. Depending upon what is available, sautéed scallops sprinkled with cheese or baked whole stuffed sea bass filleted, served with capers and olive oil. Venus clams in a white wine sauce over pasta if the others are not available. Then salad or an ice to cleanse our palates. Second piatto is roasted beef dotted with whole cloves, with bowls of vegetables, saffroned risotto, bread. You choose the wines for each course, including with the dolce. The aide asked us to surprise the doxe. What dolce do you recommend, Papa?"

"We have enough to do today. We can make that decision tomorrow. Consult Rosa now; I expect she is already making plans. Tell her to order whatever she needs. I will order the beef myself."

Before I passed him, Antonio put his arm around my shoulders and kissed my temple. "Worry not, Cara. All will go well."

I hugged him around his waist and received a second kiss. "Cook" I murmured.

As I turned, Antonio commented, "You could have worn your marriage dress."

Papa laughed. "Son, you still have much to learn about women. Come with me to the butcher's. We need to get out of her way."

I closed the door and hurried down stairs to the kitchen.

32

November 24

After Mass a messenger delivered an enormous bouquet of fresh flowers. With it came a card. "We look forward to our evening together. Yours in Christ. Signor and Signora Alvise III Sebastiano Mocenigo."

We stood around the hall table and admired the white, yellow and pink roses in a deep blue Murano vase rimmed with gold.

Papa said, "A traditional gift. That vase is even finer than ours. An heirloom our family will treasure always."

"The colors contrast well with the mahogany table."

"How do you know it is mahogany?"

"Sabina and Tomaso walked me through the house and taught me about everything I saw. Asian carpets, Ottoman artifacts and portraits, the maps on the walls and all the imported objects you have in your collection cabinets. Thinking I know nothing of worldly goods, the women may test me and I am prepared."

Papa smiled at Antonio, who looked surprised. "Son, do not underestimate your wife. She is much more than beautiful."

Antonio grinned. "Papa, I appreciate her more every day."

I blushed and distracted them with, "From where did the white chairs in the music room come?"

Papa said, "From church. For a donation, they lend them. We will return them tomorrow."

Before midday, a procession of delivery men carried in the five bouquets in the colors I had ordered: white, blue, and yellow. The three for the dining table were long and low, so guests could talk over them. The other two matched but were tall. One I had placed in the music room and the other in the salon.

"Magnificent," I commented to Antonio as I admired the completed dining room. The gold-edged Murano crystal sparkled, the colorful maiolica blue and gold rimmed dishware gleamed, and the silverware glowed. Silver candlesticks with tall white candles decorated the spaces between the floral arrangements. "The flowers cost almost as much as the meal. They are out of season. From where did they come?"

"A family of florists keeps a glass house on one of the outer islands; they force grow flowers all year," he reported.

"Their capes and masks! I forgot where to place those."

"Everything in Papa's office is locked. Tomaso's son will stand at the door for our men to give him the items and will stand guard. You must prepare your room, Cara. The women may want the chamber seat. Garon must stay in your room. The men will use my room."

"I will close the door between our rooms."

"Buone. Cara, time for you to prepare." He walked me to my door, kissed me lightly and waited for me to disappear.

Garon fixed the last diamond clip in my elaborate hair style. I stood and tugged down my bodice to display the roundness of my breasts. Garon puffed up my sleeve tops to show the wealth of cloth I wore and reached under my vestito to fluff the back of the under-skirts and the skirt. I was admiring my image in the mirror when Papa knocked. I faced the door. "Entrare."

Tray in hand, he took three steps into the room and stopped with his mouth agape. Tomaso waited in the hall. "Daughter, I have never seen such a fabric."

I swished the skirt. "The color shifts as I move."

"I like the modest depth of the square cut at your neck. No lace or sheer fabric?"

"You said to wear diamonds, so I had Barbo remove the sheer fabric insert. I have it for a new look later." I stepped forward. "Oh Papa, so many jewels! Per favore, tell me what to wear."

Papa pointed. "The more elaborate necklace, the earrings with the dropped diamonds, and the ring with the large rectangular dia-mond center and round diamonds around it. This necklace will light up your face, where everyone will be looking. The earrings will move as you sing and draw their attention. The ring will remind them who we are." Papa watched Garon fasten the necklace clasp and as I put on the earrings. He handed me the ring.

"Papa, I want only my wedding band on my right hand. May I wear the ring on my left? I put it on. See, it fits my middle finger." Papa tuned to hand the tray to Tomaso.

Turning back, Papa extended his left arm. "Daughter, I am proud to escort you and introduce you to our doxe."

Garon stayed behind to prepare my room to be seen, to guard its contents and to serve any woman who needed it.

I pray all goes well and credits the family. I must sing better this evening than I have ever done. God, Jesus, and Blessed Mary stand beside and behind me every moment. If I embarrass the Delatestas, I will never forgive myself. Inhaling and exhaling a deep breath to calm myself, I turned the corner on the stairs and took the last steps. Calm washed over me the moment I saw Antonio's jaw drop.

"Dio mio, Grazia, you are beyond stunning! You are a queen."

"If that is true, you are my king. This evening I follow your lead and depend upon you to do things aright." When he offered me his arm, I took it and bathed in his stare. At a noise below Papa took his place to greet our guests. Antonio stood to Papa's right, as I did to Antonio's.

The doxe and signora arrived first. The other guests ascended the stairs after having removed their outer clothing. Without moving his head or appearing to speak, Antonio told me their rank and sur-name before each couple stepped to Papa. "2, Cavasa; 8, Monagario; 15, Gradenigi; 24, Vallaresi; 37, Pontenuevo. You know the last one."

I curtsied and greeted each guest then I grinned. "Padre Vivaldi, you honor this house and me." I took both his hands in mine.

"No, Signora Delatesta, you honor me. I am happy to accom-pany you." He leaned toward me. "He sent me your music."

I took Antonio's arm and followed Padre into the salon. I watched as the doxe and his wife greeted each couple and visited for a few moments before the next in rank moved forward.

Do all the first Ninety-nine dress so extravagantly? The women wear black, as I had expected; their fabrics include silks from Damascus and Cina; two wear brocade. No domestic silk. Their vestiti use so much fabric with flounces, pleats of accenting fabrics, and puffs larger than mine. Their skirts are also fuller than mine. The black shows off their large, varied jewels, and they wear far more jewels than any set Papa showed me. Their wealth is far above ours. The men wear similar fabrics in their waistcoats with flared bottoms and britches over white silk shirts and stockings. They are so rich we look poor in comparison. The doxe is not as tall as I thought, nor as imposing. He has warm eyes. Her formality matches his, but her expression is a mask. Antonio and I stayed in the background as several couples approached Papa to speak to him. Neither of us saw what was happening behind us.

Lucietta peeked around the corner of the salon and spotted a signor dressed in black wearing a gold chain with a green and gold emblem. He held no wine glass and stood away from the people who filled the other end of the salon.

"Why are you sad, Signor? It is a party."

Pontenuevo's eyes popped at the barefoot child standing before him in her night camicia. The shock of seeing Lucietta for the first time froze his face and locked his body. In a hushed voice, he marveled, "You look like your mama."

"Papa says that all the time. Mama is in heaven. Have you met my new mama?"

"Si."

"She is teaching me to be polite. Am I being polite?"

"You are being very polite, Little One."

"Grazie. I want to make you smile."

Pontenuevo gave her a small one and a silent sigh as he continued to stare.

"That was not so hard. Signor, Mama is going to sing. She practiced every day, so I have already heard her. Mama is very good."

One man in the salon noticed a little girl in her night clothes talking to one of their own. "I see we have an uninvited guest," commented Signor Cavasa in a light tone.

Every head turned toward the archway. Rather than dash away,

Lucietta pulled out her gown's sides and curtsied. "Buone sera, signori e signore." She entered the room straight backed and as regal as if she were wearing a formal vestito. I spotted Nurse peek around the archway and disappear. Lucietta stepped to her grandfather. "Nonno, may I stay?"

"No, you may not. Speak 'Buone notte' to our guests."

With each farewell, Gracia curtsied. "Buone notte, Nonno. Buone notte, Papa." She froze. "Papa, I forgot the most important man!" In a loud whisper everyone heard she asked, "Which signor is the doxe?" She colored as several women tittered. Antonio leaned to her and pointed to the couple on the gold divan by the window.

Lucietta marched to the pair and curtsied more deeply than she had before. "Buone notte, Signor Doxe. Buone notte, Signora Doxe."

"Buone notte, Lucietta."

"We are pleased to meet you," spoke Signora Mocenigo after her husband.

"Grazie, Signor Doxe. Signora Doxe. I must go now."

She turned and curtsied. "Buone notte, Mama." I tried hard not the smile and failed. I took her hand and escorted Lucietta as she nodded left and right. Lucietta stopped to curtsey and say farewell to the first man she had seen. Beyond the archway, Lucietta asked, "Was I polite, Mama? I tried to be polite. I made the sad man smile."

"You were very polite and kind. I am proud of you. However, you must return to the nursery." At Lucietta's, "But I want…" I stopped her with "No." I noted her coming pout. "If you promise not to come down again, you may sit on the top step and listen to me sing. I will leave the door open for you. Promise to return to your bed afterward."

"I promise."

"You are a good girl. I know you will do as you promised." Lucietta lifted her arms, but I did not respond. Instead, my skirts ballooned around me as I crouched. My heart filled with Lucietta's hard hug and her "I love you, Mama." I watched Lucietta take Nurse's hand and disappear up the stairs.

"She is a bold and spirited child."

I stood and turned my head to see Pontenuevo beside me. "She is her mother's daughter. For which we are grateful."

"Grazie for that."

"Signor Ponteneuvo, won't you escort me into to the party? The others miss you."

"I doubt that." Still, he raised his arm.

I placed my hand on his forearm. "Please escort me to Padre Vivaldi. We must consult before the concert."

The music room filled and became warm. At the first song, a hymn of praise to God, Padre tried to set the pace, but I insisted on my speed and he relented. I noted the doxe's small nod of approval and relaxed. Next I sang a popular song about riding a gondola down the Canale Grande. Thirty minutes later I curtsied to warm applause. Doxe Mocenigo stood and offered his arm. Signora Mocenigo accepted Papa's arm and followed us to the dining room. The doxe seated me to his right and sat at the head of the table. Signora sat opposite him, with Papa to her right. Each took her or his place as the doxe's aide had set. I glanced Antonio's way and saw his eyes sparkling at me. I sucked in my lips to hide my smile and looked at the man across the table.

We dined with time between each course to allow for light conversation and for our stomachs to settle. Between courses, the doxe talked to me about music; I inquired of his family. *His voice is soothing, and his manner warm. I am enjoying the evening. I may never be in his presence again, but I will always remember his kindness to me.* I listened as he turned and visited to his left with Signor Cavaza and Signora Gradenigi.

Between the fish and the beef courses, we cleansed our palates with an ice sweetened with sugary lemon water. Padre Vivaldi regaled the table with his story of my refusal to play the violin and my insistence at learning the harpsichord. After he ended they looked at me. I explained, "I could not sing with a violin under my chin. I chose the harpsichord, so I may accompany myself."

"Fortunate for us you insisted, Signora Delatesta."

That the doxe addressed me means approval. Perhaps now the others will do more than ignore me.

The servers Papa had hired next delivered the slices of roasted beef spiced with cloves. Other waiters followed to offer platters and bowls for each guest to select the rest of their main course.

At the end of the meal, I saw the doxe's glance and tiny nod at his wife. "Ladies, let us leave the signori and visit in the music room," she said.

Signora Mocenigo led us out of the dining room and into the music room. I followed last. Two sets of three chairs sat in the middle of the room. As they had stood in the dining room, the women sat by rank. Nervous, I remained standing. *How do I converse with these women? Better to be silent than speak and be thought a fool. I know not their usual topics, yet I fear this silence.*

"Signora Delatesta, the dinner was magnificent. I enjoyed the sea bass, and your cook prepared the beef to my liking; I love clove."

"You are kind to say so, Signora Mocenigo." At Signora's gesture, I sat in the last open chair in the second set. "Signora Delatesta, your vestito is distinctive. The color changes from black to flashes of green-black as you move. The skirt is the correct shape for this season, and the bodice accents your jewels well."

"Grazie, Signora Cavaza."

"I remember that bolt," added Signora Vallaresi. "We of the first Ninety-nine passed over it. Too bold and not just black."

"I am honored you remember it, Signora, and I am grateful no one else wanted it. The moment I saw it, I had to have it. That it was not popular makes it distinctive and me memorable."

"Well and good for you," said Signora Gradenigi. "In the salon I found the combination of your vestito and red-and-gold striped draperies behind you garish. It forced me to close my eyes to prevent a headache."

I turned Bianca's insult with, "I agree. Such a sight is garish." I paused but a second. "I will change the room."

Signora Mocenigo addressed me. "Signora Delatesta, do you play the harp?"

"I regret I do not, Signora."

Signora Mocenigo said, "Domenica, you play well. Do play something for us."

Signora Vallaresi approached Lucia's harp in the corner and sat. Signora Monagario commented, "It shocked me to see a child invited into the salon after she had disobeyed her nurse and inter-rupted us."

Signora Mocinego gestured to me and patted the chair Vallaresi had vacated. I moved to sit beside our guest of honor. She addressed the others. "Did you never peek into a party your parents hosted, try to grab a treat or interrupt the conversation to be noticed? I did. More than once!" Signora Mocenigo laughed. "Have not one of you also done the same?"

The women began tales on themselves from their childhoods to outdo one another. As they talked and laughed about their small misdeeds, Signora Vallaresi played a soft melody. Gazing at the woman speaking, but not at me, Signora Mocinego said, "You stood your ground and turned the conversation away from yourself. Well done, Grazia."

Without looking her way, I replied, "Grazie mille, Signora."

In the dining room, the doxe said, "Harp playing is my wife's way of informing me she is done with visiting. I suggest we finish our port and send for our wives." Mocinego emptied his goblet and stood as did the others. Giovanni's small nod sent Tomaso to the music room.

The salon was now dotted with small wooden tables so our guests might set down cups and plates. The sweetened coffee was black and strong. A new sweetened wine was also available. Each plate held a miniature biscotto with one end dipped in bitter chocolate. The second dolce was a square of cinnamon cake with a sugary topping. Third was a small, round tower of almond terrone. *Men may pop pastries into their mouths, but we women must cut tiny bites with small forks.* The men finished all three desserts, but most of the women took only a bite from each. When Signora Mocenigo set down her plate so did the other women. I had taken a bite of terrone and lowered my plate to answer a question from Signor Mocenigo so my other dolce were untouched when I set the plate on the table beside me.

The final course over and conversation dying, the doxe held out his hand for his wife. All rose. Each signor shook Papa's hand and extended generous compliments about the evening. Two guards preceded the group to inform those at the door the doxe was leaving.

I said farewell to the couples as they departed and spoke a warm "Buone notte" to Signor Pontenuevo. Padre Vivaldi squeezed my elbow and spoke his approval of me before following the others. *He liked my performance. I still matter to him. He still wants the best for me. I will always try to be his friend. Perhaps in my new rank I can aid him in some way.*

Papa and Antonio accompanied the party to their gondolas and watched as the guards' gondolas sandwiched the doxe's gondola between them. I knew Papa and Antonio would continue to wave from the dock until the last gondola disappeared into the night.

Meanwhile, I supervised the servers emptying the dining room table of everything but the flowers and the tablecloth. I pulled vases from the bottom shelf of the serving cabinet and closed the doors. Tomaso set a knife and wooden board before me, and I worked quickly re-cutting stems and placing flowers in vases.

Papa passed the archway without seeing me but Antonio stopped.

"Why are you taking apart the bouquets?"

Without looking up I replied, "I am making gifts for everyone who helped us." I placed greens among the blooms in a vase, set it aside and looked at Antonio. "Per favore, help me deliver them."

"Time for bed. Do that in the morning."

"Too late." I started with another vase. "Did Papa go to bed?"

"He is in the kitchen paying our friends' servants before sending them home. Come now, Grazia. This is unnecessary. The servants expect nothing from doing their duties."

"Our demonstration of appreciation will mean more because it is unexpected and immediate." The first table arrangement was only a few fronds drooping from the bowl. I began disassembling the second bouquet. Antonio said nothing. "Antonio, I would like to take the bouquet in the music room to Rosa and her family. If you will join me I can carry the salon one to Tomaso and Sabina's door." Antonio sighed and walked down the hall.

I met Antonio at the base of the back stairs. He hugged the first bouquet to his chest and carried a candle holder in his other hand. Leading the way, he asked, "You seldom looked at me all night. Why?"

"If I had looked your way too much, they would have thought me weak and dependent. I glanced your way as often as the other wives looked at their husbands. I matched them so they might consider me like them."

"Good thinking. You were confident and strong. Especially how you treated Pontenuevo. I am proud of you."

In the shadows the candle created, I watched my feet to avoid a misstep. "Grazie, mio marito."

On the third floor Antonio stood in the middle of the servants' hall. I placed the salon bouquet beside Tomaso's door and placed a small card in the blooms. I took Antonio's bouquet and did the same for the cook's family.

"What is on the card?"

"'Grazie mille for your hard work in making this evening a success.' I signed each 'The Delatesta family.' One more trip and we are done."

After we had delivered bouquets to the doors of Biaso's and Roccco's families, I left the last vase at Garon's door. At the bottom of the back stairs, I said, "Two more tasks and I am for bed." Antonio dropped his chin with a questioning look. "Bid Papa buone notte. Fetch a rose."

33

November 25

Just before noon we attended the last morning Mass. On the women's side of the sanctuary, I released Lucietta's hand and looked at the priest's back. As the Mass began, I spoke the first required response before jumbled thoughts and images overtook me.

The best night we have enjoyed together. Who cares for sleep with such a husband! If I glance his way, I will blush. I am alone among strange women. No, never alone again. I am with him; I have a daughter beside me. Papa. A family. Was the evening a success?

I relived each moment with the doxe and his wife from their arrival to their departure. *What could I have done better? Not my music. There I know I am skilled and confident. That is important. My confidence shows in the way I moved and gestured to accent the words. The music the doxe chose was a good mixture of sacred and popular. The singing range suited my skills well. My practicing every day but Sundays has kept me sharp. Padre is an excellent accompanist. My curtsies modest at their applause.*

Food? Delicious. He praised it. Served with correct rests between courses. Placements? His aide set those. Did I smile too much? Not after

I followed the women's examples. I was polite to the doxe and the man to my right. Nodded to the woman opposite me and remained silent as she took over the conversation. Demonstrated good manners.

The music room. There, I was nervous. Stiff. I could have been warmer, my tone sweeter. Was I right to follow the Signora Doxe's formality? Did what they expected of me. Their rank is too high for them to visit me. Might one take me under her wing? I shook my head. Neither expect it nor hope for it. Not to be. Pray for a few curious women ranked below me to arrive. Start with them and pray for one or two to become friends. Would like that. She could tell me how to succeed in this life. I need to learn so much. What only other women know. Must fit in. Want him to be proud I am his wife. Children next. Please God soon. I woke from rote action and response in time to hear the benediction and join the final "Amen" of the service.

After rising and taking Lucietta's hand, I followed Papa and Antonio. Lucietta copied my pensive mood and looked down too. Papa took Lucietta home. We stopped at the bridge. Antonio signaled for a gondola and helped me step into it. He escorted me to Signora Barbo and waited outside.

Inside two women stepped aside as I took both Signora's hands in mine. I praised the excellent fit of my vestito and reported how successful had been our dinner with the doxe and his chosen guests. I repeated Signora Mocenigo's compliments about my gown. I thanked her for her prompt service and released her hands. She looked down at the full pouch I had given her. I added, "I look forward to your delivery of the rest of my order. I know we will continue to work together well. Expect my appointment request for my spring clothing after Epiphany."

She bobbed a curtsey. "Certamente, Signora Delatesta, I look forward to seeing you. I appreciate the arrangement you made regarding how you compensate me."

She fingered the pouch in sight of the others. *They will ask and she will report how grateful I am for special treatment. If I have not started a new way to pay her, at least gossip will report we Delatestas are both generous and well funded.* "Buone giorno, Signora Barbo." I nodded to her clients and strutted out the shop door.

At the entrance hall, I pocketed my gloves and removed my mask before handing over my outwear. Papa and Lucietta were waiting in the dining room. The alabaster linen cloth still covered the table, but the napkins were new.

"Ah, colazione and pranzo together with zuppa first. Just what I wanted," said Antonio. We four sat and received bowls of steaming chicken broth as Tomaso supervised, and his daughter Zanetta and his son Filippo served.

Their mood is light, happy. Because all went well? Because we thanked them with flowers? No matter which or both. The house feels happier, as if it absorbed all the good from yesterday. And last night. I smiled at Antonio, who responded with a smile, a warm gaze and a brief nod.

I smell roasted chicken. Grateful for new food. No remains of last evening? Hope they are enjoying our leavings; they were delicious. I will speak to Rosa. We must consume all meats and dolce before Advent begins. No waste.

After Zanetta had cleared the table, I waved Nurse into the room. She set the cup of soldi beside Lucietta. "Papa, Antonio, Lucietta has practiced being polite for a dozen days." I smiled at my daughter. "She did so without missing a day, and I am pleased with her. Lucietta?"

She stood, walked around the table and placed the cup beside her father. "Mama said I was to bring this to you for proof."

Antonio hugged her. "I am pleased. What happens next?"

"Mama hinted you might do something special. Afterward she will give me my first gift. She will give Nurse the coins, and I must add a new task and start again." At his "Something special?" Lucietta nodded, gazed into her father's eyes, and repeated, "Something special."

"Let me think." He paused. "They are bringing ice from the mountains. Would you like to enjoy a sweetened ice as we did this time last year?"

She flung her arms about his neck and yelped, "Si, Papa! Now, Papa?"

"Now." He rose and scooped her into his arms. "Per favore, excuse us. We are on an errand." *Good Nurse, you already have Lucietta's cape and mask in hand.* Papa and I watched the happy pair depart hand in hand while they guessed what flavors might be available.

"Nurse? I would speak with you." Though she is older than I by at least twelve years, Nurse started at my calling her to return. I smiled to calm her nervously clutching her hands together. "Do you always wear a gray dress under your apron?" At her "Si, Signora Delatesta," I asked another question. "What days are your own? I am unaware of your schedule."

"Signora, I am single and have no family in the city. My family works on a farm north of Mestre. I take no days for my own."

I turned to Papa, who was still seated at the table. "May we give Nurse a two week span or from Christmas Eve day to after Epiphany to spend time with her family? I am willing to attend to Lucietta and to keep her studying while Nurse is gone." As I looked toward Papa,

I furrowed my brow. *She must have a name. Why have I not thought to ask it? How unkind of me.* I gazed at her with what I hoped was a kind face. "I do not know your Christian name."

"It is Angelica, Signora Delatesta," she replied curtseying as if to apologize for being so familiar with me."

"Grazie tante, Angelica, for being such a skilled and accomplished teacher for our Lucietta. I have been remiss in telling you how pleased I am with your good work. I am sorry I have not said it before." Hoping for his confirmation of my compliment, I looked to Papa.

"I agree. Angelica, not only are you a good and faithful nurse, you have missed times away from your duties. You may leave December twenty-third and return after Epiphany. I will make the travel arrangements and pay for your transportation. You will also receive your pay while you are gone. We want you to lose nothing. Only gain time for yourself with your family."

Nurse curtsied to Papa and exclaimed, "Grazie mille, Signor, for your generosity and the time with my family!" She smiled, curtsied to me and said, "Signora, I am most grateful you suggested this. I will write my family today." She curtsied again before she strode to the stairs with a bounce in her steps.

"Well done, daughter. I had become so accustomed to Nurse's constant presence, I had not considered she might have a family. Now to Lucietta. What is her first gift?"

"I will show her the girls' bedroom and tell her she is earning her way out of the nursery. As she is our first and oldest daughter, her next gift will be to choose its new color."

"Her next task?"

"Manners. She has already begun to learn to dine properly. I will teach better curtsying and other behaviors. How to remove gloves, hold a teacup and so much more. Even after a dozen days she will continue to learn how to be a young donna, but this is her formal start."

"After she completes manners?"

"Each task is more challenging. Three is completing lessons without complaint. That will earn her the right to go to the attic and choose her furniture. She dislikes stitchery. Four is improving her stitchery by working one hour each day with Sundays free. For that she will choose the draperies, her bedding and decorations. We will place her mother's portrait in the room. The fifth task is the hardest: be obedient without challenging you, Antonio, me, or Nurse. She will earn her move into the room. That may take a while."

"It will, indeed."

"What will also be difficult is each skill adds to the ones before. I expect we will be at this until spring or even summer. We must be patient with her. Had she started when she was two or three years her training would be easier."

"I see you plan well ahead. What will happen after she is in her new room?"

"If she maintains all five behaviors daily for a month, she will earn an extra special gift from Antonio and me." Papa raised his brows. "I will take her to Barbo for a new wardrobe with hemlines to her ankles."

"She will be thrilled!"

I grinned at his approval. "By twelve years of age, she will be ready for hems to the floor and can be called 'Donna Lucietta.'"

"Daughter, you are an excellent mother."

"Grazie mille, Papa. Your saying so means the world to me."

Winter

"No winter lasts forever;
no spring skips its turn."

—Hal Borland

34

❦

December 20

On the walk home from Santa Maria de Formosa, I watched Papa, Il Conto, and Violetta step around ice patches. Holding Lucietta's hand, I did the same. As we approached our door, I looked back. I saw Polonia, Claudia, and Stefano. But not my husband. I told Lucietta to walk ahead, waited for Stefano and held him outside. "Where is he?"

After the bridge he turned and disappeared."

"Did Antonio say where he was going?" Stefano looked away and shook his head. *He knows something; I see it in his eyes.* He gestured me to precede him. At colazione, I watched each man. They avoided looking my way. I observed them making concerted efforts to hold each other's gazes as they talked about I knew not what. *Something is wrong.*

Hours later we women and girls were still sewing in the salon under the light of four chandeliers on the tables among us. Violetta and Polonia visited, but I only spoke if they asked me questions. My mind reviewed the families' arrivals two days ago. I thought of every interaction, every meal since then and our times abed. I could find nothing amiss, nothing for which he could reproach me. *Why is he gone? Where has he gone?*

I overheard an interchange between the girls.

"Do your parents do something special on your saint's day?" asked Lucietta.

"Of course! On my saint's day, I ask Mama for my favorite foods, lamb stew, warm buttered bread and half a glass of wine."

"My Papa and Mama do the same. I asked for roasted chicken and biscotti dipped in chocolate."

They looked away from each other and returned to their stitchery. I looked toward the archway and sighed.

I missed hearing Lucietta report to Violetta that she had used good manners at table for twelve days. She bragged she had seen her new room, and that we had delayed her next lesson until after Epiphany. Later Violetta reported Lucietta's remarks to me and that both Polonia and Claudia had heard her. I looked toward Lucietta, ready to chide her in front of her cousin.

Violetta distracted me with, "My housekeeper informed me the spices we use now cost quadruple what they did before we lost the last war. The price of sugar from the West and fabrics from the East too."

"Do you know why?" I asked.

"Both the Spice Road and the Silk Road no longer end in Venice by ship. Because the Ottomans rule the Mediterranean, the goods now go overland and end in Munchen and Nernberg. They are exacting revenge for our high prices for transporting the goods into the continent, and we are now paying them much more than what we once charged them."

"What of sugar? Papa said serving sugar is a status symbol for the wealthy. Using it for the doxe's visit cost almost as much as the food."

"At least you two can still afford them. We cannot and must do with pinches instead of pouches," grumbled Polonia.

"After Epiphany, I will use much less and less often. Change my menus; design simpler meals. I will not bankrupt my family to prove we are wealthy. Harder times are already here." I turned. "Polonia, if you have recipes using local herbs and spices, I would appreciate your sharing them with me." Polonia's response was a shrug. *No help there. Consult Rosa.*

Just before cena I heard the door; through the archway, I spotted Antonio. I stood to meet him, but Violetta stopped me with a question about the meal. By the time I had answered her, Papa called us to dine. We stood for prayer, sat and waited for the soup course.

I caught Antonio's eyes and raised my brows. He grinned at me before thanking Osana for the soup and lifting his spoon. After cena we adults sat in the salon, and the evening ended without my being able to speak to my husband privately.

Warmly wrapped in my heavy vesta, I sat at my table and face the door between our rooms. *If he does not come to me, I will go to the door and call him.* I held my breath. *Am I brave enough to walk into his room if he does not respond? Why not? He walks into mine.* I heard his night noises and waited.

"Cara, you are too far away."

"You were missing from Mass to cena."

"This is the only day I dare leave for a week. Remember the season. I left to examine the progress on your Epiphany gift. On my way home I encountered friends who invited me to dine with them.

Refused to accept my excuses. Mi dispiace, Cara. I let the time slip away and did not realize it until almost sunset. Perdonami?"

My first test at forgiveness. What he said sounds reasonable. What choice have I? I stood and smiled. "Certamente, mireto mio." I opened my arms to him. "You raise my curiosity. What needs progress? A hint?" I walked into his arms to accept his embrace and kiss. At his laughing refusal to tell me, I lay my head against his chest. His heart beat steadily. *No hint of distress.* He kissed my hair, nibbled my ear and nuzzled my neck. I felt his hands undo the band at my waist and reach inside my robe. He sat on the edge of the bed and pulled my hips to him to kiss my belly. Instead of telling him what I thought was growing inside me, I gave myself to his loving ministrations.

With so many family members to talk with, the days passed quickly. Lucietta was kinder and Claudia more polite so I worried less, but Claudia still slept on a cot in her parents's room. Each day I paid special attention and made time to be alone with Claudia, who liked it and even hugged me one evening before she left for bed. Evenings the men played card games. They are something I had never seen in Ospedale. I watched from behind Antonio but understood nothing of what I saw.

Violetta drew me away to introduce me to a double deck of cards, four suits of one to seven, a king, a knight, and a soldier. She and Polonia taught me to play Tressette. At first. I was terrible and asked many questions. After three evenings, I won a game. Then they taught me the children's version, much simpler. I started with one 7, gained two more, and won that game too. *Playing cards with my new sisters is so enjoyable. They said tomorrow night, they will teach me Sette e' Mezza.*

Each night with Antonio was better than before, a bliss I had never imagined. Each morning he loved me again. After he left I would fling my arms over my head and stretch like a lazy cat under coverings still warmed by our togetherness. Garon had taken to bringing me a pail of hot water so I could wash before I dressed for Mass. When she knocked on my door, I stopped savoring my union to answer.

Dressed for church, we met in the main hall and acted so respectable. I knew his soft eyes and side glances me held a promise. We would be one again when next the dark hid us from the world.

35

December 24

Christmas Eve morning, I reached for Antonio, but he rolled away and bound from the bed toward the door.

"Not this day, Cara, nor this night. The Church decreed this is a holy day of abstinence."

"Then you know what I want for Christmas Day night." When he turned in profile, I could see what my words had done to him.

"You have become a temptress. I am closing the door. If I even smell you, I may lose my will. Would you have me on my knees before the church doors every night for a month? A long time ago I saw a man making that penance for giving in to his passions. Do not touch me. Do not even look at me!"

I laughed in happiness at my newfound powers as Antonio disappeared and closed the door. I quieted and called for Garon. As he had demanded, I neither looked toward nor spoke to Antonio as we donned our heavy fur-lined winter capes and gloves. Looking about, I noticed two other couples ignoring each other. *Glad I am to be part of such a passionate family.*

During Mass I worked hard to pay attention to the service and the sermon. I feared what I might have to confess. After Mass, every confessional had a long line. The march from Mass was as silent and as solemn as had been our march to it. Colazione was only vegetable broth and bread devoid of herbed dipping oil. Pranzo was the same. I wondered if cena would be as well. All day we sat in the salon and did no sewing, no singing, no card playing. No one spoke; I was tempted to nap. I stayed with the others so as to be less of a temptation to Antonio.

Cena was a fragrant risotto rich with, onion bits, and sautéed mushroom slices, but I wondered why no cheese. Then I remembered meat and dairy are forbidden on fasting days. *Have I become so accustomed to this kind of life that I have forgotten how to fast?* I ate more than usual because I thought we would fast until Christmas morning. We put the children to bed and waited. As the church bells rang the twenty-third hour, we drank cups of steaming broth to warm us before attending Midnight Mass, a High Mass with no sermon. Instead, the bishop read from the Book of Saint Luke of the birth of the Christ, of hosts of angels singing Hosanna and of the shepherds arriving.

On the way home I shivered all the way despite my heavy cloak and hood. Even with thick gloves, my fingers felt frozen inside my muff. Tomaso took our outerwear. With both hands I held the cup of hot broth Rosa handed me and sniffed the heat spiraling to my nose. *Too hot. Blow on the liquid and try again. Heaven down my throat! May it reach my bones.* I stepped into the dining room and halted with my mouth agape. A sumptuous meal filled the table. *Barely room for candles. What is all this?*

Antonio blew into my ear and whispered, "Midnight supper.

No colazione. No Mass in the morning. Cena will be at the fifteenth hour." He seated me and we adults feasted. Surfeited, I crawled into bed alone, patted my belly buone notte and fell asleep.

I knew not the time Antonio entered my bed. He kissed me in several delightful places and I stirred. When I complained he had interrupted my dream he murmured, "Dream on, Cara. Ignore me." He knew I would not.

36

December 25

Past the noon hour Antonio and I wandered downstairs; we were the second to the last to enter the salon. Several minutes later Il Conto and Violetta followed. At the appointed hour, Papa led us to the Christmas feast.

In each of our soup bowls, lay a large orange. *Such luxury!* We set those aside and the broth arrived. Conversation was light and pleasant as my family ate. Each course was served in order of rank. Papa first, Il Conto and around. With the soup we enjoyed a creamy spread of salted cod on bread. We were served the traditional rice and peas followed by scallops in a white wine and butter sauce. This year the third main dish was risotto blackened with squid ink. Fearful of the taste, I nibbled a tiny bite. *Unusual but delicious!* I ate it all. Except for Miro, the children sat at a separate table and ate the same foods we did.

When Claudia started to object to the food, I said, "Polonia, with your permission." With a full mouth, she nodded. I told the nurses, "On Christmas the children may eat whatever they like and pass what they dislike. No fussing now. Each of you chooses what to eat." I turned back to the adults and saw Il Conto smiling at me. The adults ended the meal with cafe or 'te or white wine. The children were offered sweetened pomegranate juice Our desserts were terrone and small spice cakes.

We spent the evening in the salon. On the floor Giacomo showed Miro how to roll wooden toys about and pretend to be a farmer plowing, planting and harvesting imaginary fields. Polonia scowled at them. Trying to engage Claudia, I asked how they spent Christmas on the farm, but her responses were shrugs and short answers. The men drank wine as they talked of economics, crops and the Ottomans. We women spoke little. Violetta became bored with us and left to take her sons to bed. With the men still talking, Polonia and I escorted our girls upstairs and parted in the hall.

The next day, after attending Sunday Mass, the nurses took the children home. We adults celebrated Santo Stefano's Day by wandering. Friends and families met, walked together and chatted as they travelled from church to church. At each we prayed for Stefano, our first Christian martyr, viewed nativity scenes and left a small donation. Silent yesterday, today the walkways and rios bustled with people, happy sounds and singing.

At home we honored Stefano on his saint's day; Rosa had prepared his favorite foods. Papa told stories of Stefano's birth, his childhood and his many accomplishments. Papa thanked Stefano for his hard work and commented how his work on the farms has become even more important to our family. We congratulated him on his fine family and toasted him. Because I had drunk a little too much wine, I excused myself, climbed the stairs and plopped into bed for a nap.

37

December 27

Il Conto, Violetta and their sons left for home. Stefano's family said farewell to them and left for Polonia's brother's house for the day.

After pranzo, Antonio excused himself and said he would be gone the rest of the day. Other families dined and partied with their friends and neighbors the week between Christmas and the new year; we had stayed home. *Because of me, they do not invite us. Do nothing. Say nothing. Like the family, pretend this is what we choose.* I knew he went to visit friends' families and to socialize with business associates.

He does not take me with him for fear they will snub me or refuse him entry. Better I stay home than humiliate him. I cannot forget what my past has done to my family. I have gotten the family I want, but has he? Will he stay happy with me when this continues. Perhaps for years. I spent the rest of the day entertaining Lucietta until we joined Papa for cena. I read to Lucietta until I sent her to bed. Picking up my current book, in the salon I snuggled under a lap robe as Papa sat in a nearby chair and read as well.

The noise at the lower door told us Stefano had returned. I set aside my book and rose to greet them. The children had returned tired and crabby so the Miro's nurse took them to bed. Claudia clung to her mother's skirt. Stefano chatted with Papa, but Polonia pouted and excused herself. *Why is Polonia sour and unhappy again? If the family wants me to know, they will tell me.*

When Stefano joined us in the salon, Papa offered wine. Glasses in hand we three sat, and Stefano reported they were leaving in the morning. "I want to be home before Epiphany. If we miss the new year's fireworks both here and at home, I care not. The children's gifts are at home, and I want to be there too."

Stefano informed Papa of Polonia's family's news. I learned her brother had been a successful transporter of goods from Venice to the northern regions and cities. Now he was in dire straits with no business. *At least we have the farm to save us. Is our city sinking? Not literally, but as a wealthy business center?* I just learned how bad it is for one family. *What of the entire city?* While I worried about the future, Papa had said buone notte and left for bed. I look up to see Stefano standing before me. *Do not upset him. Ask nothing.* "Stefano, you are a kind brother to escort me to my room."

"Before we go up, will you sing for me?"

"Of course." I stood, gestured for him to sit, grasped my hands before my waist the traditional way and sang the traditional song to greet the new year, "Capo degli Anno, Amico Mio." I finished and smiled at Stefano. "I wish you and your family a happy new year."

"You are a friend, dear sister. Grazie for being kind to my children and patient with Polonia. She does not want to return to the farm but we must."

"Your work there may save both our families. I am especially grateful for your warmth and affection, brother. If I may do something for you, you have but to ask." I took his arm as we walked to the stairs.

"Write to Polonia?"

"Without bragging or talking about the city." At his nod I added, "When is her saint's day? I will send a gift."

"She has none. Her name comes from Poland, the country of her grandmother's birth."

"I will think of something nice to do for her." *Write and send a spice or two. She complained about the cost.*

At the top of the stairs we spoke buone notte and separated to our rooms.

38

December 31

New Year's Eve Day is the Feast of Saint Sylvester's Day. We attended another High Mass and enjoyed an especially fine cena. At full dark we bundled into our outer wear and stood on the dock.

The fireworks in the Piazza Santo Marco exploding over the lagoon colored the night sky. Bits of diamonds and colored jewels fell into the lagoon and the canal. *I had had a better view from the terrace roof of Ospedale. Ohh. This is the first time I have thought something was better at Ospedale than here. Not that I would ever return.*

I hugged myself in happiness. Antonio pulled me to his side and wrapped his arms around me. "I will take the wind for you. Stay on the leeward side of me." *A good man who is even a better husband than I had hoped for. I have what I desired. A husband and a family. Soon a… do not even think it or ill fortune may befall me.*

1724

Winter

"We must be willing to get rid
of the life we've planned,
so as to have the life
that is waiting for us."
—Joseph Campbell

39

January 1

We attended High Mass to celebrate Capo degli Anno and returned home to another feast. We spent the afternoon in the salon; we three taught Lucietta the suits and the cards before teaching her how to play Sette e' Mezza. She finally won and squealed, "I won! I won! I want to play again. Again!"

We made her stop for cena. Afterward I played and sang for my family. Lucietta joined me for two songs, much to the delight of Antonio and Papa. Afterward Antonio and I escorted Lucietta upstairs and put her to bed.

Antonio held my hand as he walked me to my door. He kissed my palm and winked. "See you soon." At his door he blew me a kiss, opened his door, and disappeared.

I care not about hearing others' parties or the celebrations outside when I have him. I opened my door to see Garon was ready for me.

40

January 6

As Epiphany is only second to Easter in importance, the final High Mass of the Christmas season was long. The sermon was about renewing our vows to God and His Church and instructions on how to live a better life. *Different year, different priest, same message, same long service. I'm hungry; I hope he soon will be done.*

After colazione we moved to the salon for gift giving. Papa presented gifts to each member of the staff and to their children. Papa handed each to Lucietta, who carried it to the person and curtsied before handing it over. *How gracious she is, how sincere is her "grazie mille" and her saying her or his name. She has improved so.* After the last gift Papa handed a pouch of gold zecchini to the head of each household. He thank them for all they had done for the family since the last Epiphany. After they left we four stayed in the salon.

"Well done, Lucietta."

"Thank you, Papa. I wanted Nonno, you and Mama to be proud of me."

"We are," replied Antonio. "To our gifts. Per favore, Lucietta, find a gift for Nonno and present it."

I surprised Antonio with a hunting gun. "As you have your own and no longer need to borrow Papa's, you can hunt together." I answered his question with "Papa helped me."

Onto my lap Papa set a large item wrapped in dress fabric. From its shape I guessed what it might be. I stroked the fine pale green cotton and commented, "Such a beautiful fabric, perfect for a summer vestito." I unwrapped the lute and gasped. Its intricate inlay gleamed in the candlelight. I caressed the wood and strummed the seven strings. Only then did I notice the angle of the pegbox and the design on the peg tops. "Papa, this is very old."

"Almost one hundred years. From Cremona. Its stand is already in the music room."

I stood and carefully set down the lute. I hugged Papa hard. "You are too good to me, Papa. You spoil me shamefully. How did you know I play the lute as well?"

"Something you said the first time we met you."

I kissed his cheek. "I will tune it and play for you before we retire."

"My turn, if you will sit," requested my husband.

I moved the lute to a chair and wrapped the fabric around it against the chair back so it could not fall. I sat beside Antonio, who stood and walked behind a sofa. He returned with my summer cape wrapped around something large and flat.

"Close your eyes."

I waited, then felt something set on my lap and reached for it. Antonio stopped my hand.

"Open."

I gasped at the stunning colors. "What is it?"

"Peacock feathers. Very rare." As he held it up, fabric straps dropped, but I only saw the fan-shaped colorful array. At each end of stem was a feather with a green circle with a bright blue dot in the center. I reached and found them silky and delicate.

"This vibrant blue matches your festal gown. When you wear it at your back, you will resemble a peacock with its feathers extended." He reached beside me and brought up a matching Carnivale mask, swirled in blue, black and green with gold lines separating the colors. Small peacock feathers would rise above my left ear. "The sapphire earrings and ring will finish your Carnivale costume."

I opened my mouth to speak and closed it. I shook my head and tried again. "I..I..what to say?" I touched the feathers again. "I have never seen the like. So beautiful." I looked up at Antonio beaming at me. "You are right to be proud of yourself, Antonio. In my royal blue gown and with these additions I will be so unusual. When may I wear this?"

"When I take you to Carnivale. You must stay by my side. Carnivale can be raucous. Others will try to spirit you away from me, but you must not go."

"I will not let go of your hand."

"Good. But first we must attend the Carnivale dinner of the di Bennetos on the ninth day of February. There you will only wear your dress. The next night I will take you costumed to Carnivale."

I nodded. *Carnivale, a city-wide party we at Ospedale were told we may never attend. Full of drinking, dancing, and sinful doings. I can't wait.*

I leaned forward and whispered, "Antonio, she has waited long enough and has been so patient. Time for Lucietta." I looked at my daughter and said, "Lucietta, whose gift would you like to have first?"

She looked at her father, then at her grandfather. We saw which one she wanted. *Will she do what is proper?*

Lucietta gave me a knowing look and replied, "Nonno's of course. Nonno, may I have your gift first?"

Papa gave her a necklace of small pearls and small, matching stud earrings. Antonio presented her with a fur muff and gloves trimmed in the fur that matched the muff. Lucietta wore the jewelry and modeled the gloves and muff.

I gifted her a complete artist's set: an easel, an array of brushes, a dozen bottles of paints and a folder of artist's paper. "Your doodles are more art than scratchings and you need the supplies of a genuine artist." She hugged me and thanked me twice.

We separated to take our gifts to our rooms and to rest before the main meal at the fifteenth hour. Tired, I removed my slippers and pulled the coverlet over myself even though I was still dressed.

"Grazie Signora, for the fabric. Signor Delatesta was generous as well. I have enough to make two dresses."

"Charlotte, you deserve both. You are a good French maid and have served me well. Of course Papa noticed and rewarded you as well. I will rest my eyes until you call me for the feast." I did not hear Garon close the door; I was already asleep.

As was the Delatesta custom, everyone in the household ate the Epiphany feast crowded around the extended dining table. We filled the room and took turns serving each other. We passed bowls and platters and left them in the middle of the table. The wines flowed. When the children became bored, we excused them. Dinner over, we stood, took the leavings to the kitchen and followed Rosa's orders as to what to do with them. Desserts in hand, we trooped back upstairs to the dining room, called the children and enjoyed the last course.

Full and tired, Papa announced, "No more work tonight. Tomorrow after Mass we will help you clean and set the table for colazione. Everyone to bed."

As Garon brushed my hair, I sighed my happiness. *My first Epiphany of gift giving. What a day. Wonderful. Happy from beginning to end. Now I want to sleep.* Garon froze. I turned and saw Antonio in the doorway.

"Buona notte, Garon," he said.

She nodded at Antonio, curtsied to me and closed the door behind herself.

Antonio drew me into his arms, kissed my ear, my cheek, my lips. I opened my mouth to tell him I was too tired, but he placed his pointing finger on my lips.

"I am ready for my second gift, Cara."

I frowned. "What gift? I have no other gift."

He pulled away from me and placed his hands on my belly. "You cannot hide even the most subtle of changes from me. I know your body. Cara, tell me what I already know."

I pulled my lips into my mouth to keep from smiling and shook my head.

"Come now, Cara. Say what I want to hear." He drew me close.

I shook my head. Changing my mind, I unlocked my lips and whispered, "Augusto" into his mouth.

Antonio clutched me and kissed me with such passion I abandoned all thought.

41

January 10

After pranzo, Antonio said, "Cara, because you are a new wife, Papa and I decided this year we will not host a party during Carnevale di Venezia. Rather, we shall attend others. You will learn how the second hundred celebrate before Lent. Next year you will be a more knowledgeable and confident hostess. We will ask for an early party; they are less stressful, less grand and less costly than those closer to Ash Wednesday."

"A wise decision. The schedule?"

"Before the first Monday in May, we apply at the office that regulates Carnevale, both citywide and private. The first Monday of September. They announce the approved events and parties; they publish the schedule. If they have approved our event, we begin preparations immediately. Even before we decide who will attend, we must secure the services for food, decorations, flowers and more. Each of us must have new costumes for the parties and new clothing for each dinner. The planning is long and complicated, and the event is expensive. The party is both a celebration and a relief for the hosting family. The First Ten pay for the citywide events, and a private event is each family's responsibility. Each year some of the first Ninety-nine host parties for their rank; they rotate. Most of we second hundred host every three to five years. No one will think less of us if we wait a year."

"I understand. If you will excuse me, I want to look in on Lucietta's lessons." After I turned the corner, behind me I heard, "That went well," from my husband and Papa's retort, "Do not think you fooled her." I took the stairs.

Fooled, indeed! If the women will not visit me, neither will they nor their husbands attend a dinner or a party. When a family's Carnevale party is scheduled, whom they invite, and how lavish the event are proofs of their wealth and stature. I wager the highest inform the office the date they want; the rest must offer payment or invitations to be included in the list. Another proof I do not fit. At the top step leaned against Antonio's door to take deep breaths until I calmed. I thought of Lucietta as I tried to slow my breathing and my heart.

She needs to understand bragging before Claudia was not only bad manners, it was impolite and unkind to try to make someone feel inferior. She will her repeat politeness and manners for the rest of the month. Twenty-one days ought to fix in her mind how much we value manners, kindness and politeness. If she misses a day, she starts over at one. If she succeeds, she goes to the third lesson. No matter how long this takes, I will not yield on this to Antonio or Papa. She will become a better person.

Nurse stood in the corner and listened as I chastised Lucietta for her behavior toward Claudia. She was not happy about our talk or her new schedule, but she did not cry, just grimaced and gave me sour looks throughout my review of her behavior and our expectations. I required she repeat everything I said as I had said it. After an hour, I left for my room and sat at my desk.

Strange. Working in my accounts book, listing payments for Papa to make, and suggesting menus soothe me. I am skilled here. No one to correct, teach or lie to me. Afterward I lay under my bed coverings with my hands on my belly. *Oh my beloved bambina, he wants an heir. If God gives us a girl, at least one of us will be glad you are born.* Happy with my decision, I closed my eyes until Garon woke me for cena.

The next morning I sat with Papa and Antonio. In the old household accounts book I had examined every expense line by line. Before my arrival costs had been steady and then rose after my arrival. Costs declined after our marriage and rose for Christmastide and its gift giving. *How extravagant they are! We must economize now. No more waiting.*

"Papa, I have spoken with Sabina, and she confirms our house needs no repairs until we assess winter damage to the exterior. We should set aside a few coins each week so repair costs will not strap us when they occur." After Papa agreed, I turned to the more difficult matter. "The best place to be more thrifty is in our weekly food budget. Unfortunately vegetables are now more costly, and the prices of fish will rise with the coming Lent. I have asked Rosa and Perina to have less uneaten food left over. A waste. They say the pig gets those, and it will be fat enough for butchering after Lent. I will keep a sharp eye on purchases. I suggested coffee, and te' are expensive as is the sugar in the sweet rolls. "I asked Rosa to dispense with them, and she said to ask you. We could have a bowl of polenta grown in our own corn fields."

"No," said Papa. Antonio followed with, "Absolutely not! Papa, per favore, explain."

"Daughter, polenta is for the poor. It is cheap and fills their bellies for them to start the day. If we eat it, we are announcing we are destitute. Rumors will fly and no one will do business with us for fear we cannot pay our share or cover our expenses. Per favore, find another way to economize."

"I will drink water instead of te'. That is not much of an economy but it is something. Papa, will you accept having meat only on Sunday?"

"No. Twice. Sunday and once during the week. During Lent, you and I will re-examine the records and decide when to eat meat after Lent."

"Very well, Papa." I looked to Antonio for support, but I saw his closed face. *Even without his support, I must be brave.*

"Papa, may I now examine the business accounts book?" From the corner of my eye, I caught Antonio shrugging a shoulder, cocking his head and making a sour face.

Papa ordered, "Hand it over, son." Antonio lifted one hip, pulled out the thick ledger he had been sitting on and gave it to his father. I did not believe Papa when he said, "The numbers look worse than they really are."

This book starts 1720, two years after Venezia lost their seventh war with the Ottomans and lost their last island posts in the Mediterranean. Confined to the Adriatic and daring to go no further than Bari, we have no income from the near east and far east lands. I shook my head. *Bad, already bad.* I turned a page and saw the year's end savings had declined because expenses were a fourth more than income from the farms. More pages told me in 1721 and 1722 they had held their losses steady because of more farm income. With each page of 1723, my eyes widened. *Payment to Signora Pallavisi was reasonable, but clothing me and themselves to present ourselves to the doxe had cost a fortune. My cream outfit alone would have fed all of Ospadaele for a year! My clothing from Barbo was three times what I expected.* I covered my mouth with my hand to hide my shock. *Then I had added 100 zecchini to that. Had I known, I would have given her only a tenth.*

I looked up at Papa, shook my head at him and dropped my eyes to the page before me. Removing my hand from my mouth, I turned the last pages to examine the Christmastide gifts and other expenses. On each page our expenses were heavy. The last page started this year; I need not do math in my head. *The balance forwarded was half what it had been in 1720. We are heading toward disaster!* I closed the book, set it on my lap, laced my fingers together and set my hands on the book. *Start softly, but be firm. Raise not my voice unless they dismiss my fears.*

"Papa, Antonio, in just four years, you have spent half your wealth. At this rate you will soon have to sell ships, this house and everything in it. We dare never to sell the farms because we will be forced to move there. We will need their products to survive."

"Awww Grazia; you exaggerate. We are still wealthy."

I glared at my husband. "Half!"

Papa intervened. "Daughter, no Venetian lists all his wealth in his accounts books. Believe me when I say we have much more than I recorded in that book."

"Papa, I suspect that is your reserves. Perhaps the accumulated wealth of generations. Per favore, Papa, we cannot touch it. We dare not. Trade has gone north and overland. We may never recover. Not our trade routes. Not our wealth." I frowned at Papa. "No more new gowns for me."

"Daughter, you have no wardrobe. You need clothing for spring and summer."

He is right. "Only one for each season." Before he could say more, I added, "As I am not in society, that will be sufficient. Now to the matter of economy." I did not wait for either of them to interrupt me. "Whatever I do regarding household expenses will mean almost nothing in contrast to your business and our general living expenses. I expect to see this book on the tenth of each month. Both of you must find ways to economize at once." I stood and handed the book to Papa; I looked at Antonio. "I suggest you start now." Hearing only silence, I left the office and closed the door.

In the music room I sat on the bench with my back to the harpsichord and stared at the wall. *So much gone! Yet they say they are wealthy. Not for long if they keep spending like that. I will start with colazione to show them how to economize. Soup and bread for supper, first once a week, then twice and thrice or more. Until they object.*

Saturday a messenger delivered a large envelope into Papa's hands. Thinking it was business, I dismissed the moment and turned to the music room for my daily hour of solitude and music. I lit the candle beside the harpsichord. *Will anyone remember Sunday is my birthing date? No gifts. Just my favorite foods at pranzo and cena.* I sat. *Nineteen. A year ago I had no prospects and no hope for any. Now I have a husband, a daughter, a papa, and a bambina arriving.* I placed my hands together. *Good morning, God. Thank you for this year, the one I dreamed of and prayed for. I am honored You have answered my prayers and have given me a good husband and family. At Mass each morning I will continue to honor You, sing in praise of You, and be good to all in Your name. Amen.* I raised my arms, set my fingers on the keys, and played as I sang a hymn of praise to my Lord.

Sunday began with Mass and colazione. *Nothing was said. Perhaps they know it not.* I adjourned to the salon and picked up my book, a history of Venice. I opened to the chapter on the twelfth century, sighed and began. Two pages later movement caught my eye. Papa approached with Antonio and Lucietta on either side of him. With both hands, he was carrying in a beautiful green cloth. I set aside my book and smiled.

"Felice compleanno," they chimed in unison. Papa said, "Lucietta and I give you this woolen shawl." He set it on my lap.

"Grazie tante, Papa. Grazie tante, Lucietta." I stroked the soft fabric and felt something inside it.

"I wrapped my gift in your shawl."

"Grazie tante, Antonio."

Peeling back the cloth, I found a large, brown envelope. I lifted the flap, peered inside and pulled white papers halfway out. I read the title and the dedication, and gasped. "Oh, Antonio!"

"An original piece, and you have the only copy. I ordered it the first week of Advent."

Already paid for, I pray. I hugged the music to my heart. "Papa, have you seen this?"

"Antonio showed it to me yesterday."

"What is it, Mama?"

I gestured her to my side, and she sat. Lucietta squinted at the words.

"I see 'S' and 'G,' but I do not know the words."

"A Sonata for Grazia," and under it "Dedicated to my favorite not my student and her harpsichord." I pointed, "See his signature?"

"A … Ant … Antonio? Papa?"

"Antonio Lucio Vivaldi" and under it, "16th day of January in the Year of Our Lord 1724.

"This is the happiest day in my life. I have you, Papa, and you, my wonderful husband and now these thoughtful gifts. I am loved and I am grateful for each of you." I set my gifts on the sofa beside me and stood to kiss Papa's cheek and hug him. On tiptoe I threw my arms around Antonio's neck and kissed him hard. He responded in kind before setting me back on my feet. My cheeks warmed as I pulled back. I pulled Lucietta upright, kissed her on each cheek and hugged her hard. I whispered into her ear, "I love my daughter." Turning to Papa and Antonio as Lucietta wrapped her arms about my waist, I announced, "This is my best birthing date ever!"

"It's not over, Mama! Wait until you see pranzo and cena. We chose all your favorite foods. Rosa made a torte di cioccolato large enough for dessert at both meals.

Antonio asked, "While we wait for pranzo, will you play your sonata for us?"

"Of course." After I swirled the shawl around my shoulders, I picked up the music sheets and led my family to the music room. Because I had halted several times the first time I played the piece, the second time I played it was much better. At my family's applause, I nodded my thanks. When I stood, I reached for Antonio so I could hide my tears of gratitude and happiness. *I am the most fortunate of women. They love me, and he understands how much music means to me.*

The second day of February, we joined Candlemas to celebrate the Purification of the Virgin Mary. The Doxe and his entourage marched from Piazza San Marco to Santa Maria Formosa to attend High Mass. In our bursting church we had to jostle others to find a place near the back, and we stood shoulder to shoulder with strangers during the service.

42

February 9

I must calm myself, or I will be sick and unable to attend. As Garon supervised the bath being cleaned, I brushed my hair. The di Bennetos always invite the first ten of the one hundreds, so they must include us. At their party three years ago, they partnered Antonio with their niece, but it came to nothing. They have both since wed, she to a one hundred eight, and he to me. She will have to bob to me, but I need to worry only about the three ahead of us. I smiled to myself. Our host and his wife, who are one hundred, and two other couples. Antonio promised to stay beside me and point out the others. Breathe. Slow my heart. Remember all Papa and Antonio have taught me. Take deep breaths.

Alone with Garon I waited at my table and handed her the brush. Marita and Osana arrived. The threesome began a complicated pattern of braids, pinned curls, and trails of pearls through my hair that would create my elaborate style. As they worked I sipped well-watered white wine and nibbled on bread and sweetmeats for strength. Three hours later they finished by adding individual diamond hairpins and a cluster of diamonds clipped above my left ear. They cooed and complimented me on how magnificent I looked.

They are admiring how successfully they transformed this orphan into one worthy to be called a one hundred third. I turned this way and that. With the hand mirror I examined at the back and declared it even more stunning than the front. I complimented them on their work and said, "Grazie mille," to each individually as I looked into their eyes. Marita and Osana curtsied and left as Garon put away the leavings of their work.

"A late cena with many courses. Delicacies. Rare flavors. Wines to savor. Several desserts from which to choose! I am looking forward to a most wonderful meal."

"Signora, a proper lady does not eat. She tastes or nibbles. Her expressions show exquisite joy at each bite. She sips. She must be able to converse between tiny bites and almost invisible chewing. No genuine lady eats a full meal. She never fills her mouth."

"I will be famished."

Garon laughed and clapped her hands twice. My door opened; Zanetta set a table before me and Lavina placed a tray of food on it before they left us.

"Your hands are icy so I ordered hot broth. Half a chicken breast and a plain risotto will fill your stomach. No onions, nothing that will scent your breath. Afterward, you will clean your teeth and rinse your mouth with rosewater. Your breath must smell so sweet they think you are an angel."

As she talked I drank the broth and uttered an occasional "m-m-m" as I chewed.

"Signora, your first social event among your rank determines the success of your life for the rest of your days. You must be careful.

You must surprise them with how much you are like them and how well you fit in."

"Well I know it. But my stomach churns like a restless sea. I hope eating will settle it."

"I will leave you. When you finish open the door a crack, and we will dress you.

In the candlelight I stood before my mirror and stared. *My new peacock gown starts almost off the shoulders yet cannot fall because of the boning. My breasts are high, full, and showing as much as a woman of my rank should. Puffed sleeves at my shoulders then fitted sleeves to my wrists. Matching gloves with my rings over them and the sapphire necklace nestled inside the scooped front. For now I still have a tiny waist. I am wearing enough silk to set a ship sailing! I wish I had won him to my wish to wear the feathers. Tomorrow night. The whalebone stays of my corset are almost too tight. I must take short breaths and bend at my hips. Very stylish but uncomfortable. I hope all this is worth the evening.*

I will do what I must to make a good impression. Orphan no more. I am a woman of worth, married to a good man from a family well placed in a Venice so beautiful it is called Serenissima. Papa found me worthy. If I believe it and behave as if I, too, believe it, others will accept me. Should they reject me, I will still behave as a one-hundred-third should. Be proud and happy. I smiled at my image; I am ready to face them all.

Straight backed and with my head erect, I descended the stairs as if I were a Ten. As I turned into the hall Antonio dropped his jaw and stared at me with his mouth agape. I feared the smile Papa was giving me might crack his face. I returned a demure gaze. We stood in the silence for several moments. Papa nudged Antonio, who closed his mouth. He stepped forward, squeezed my hands and held them.

"Dio Mio, you are magnificent! You are your name; Grace from head to your toes. No mask should cover your beauty. The headdress would have spoiled your perfection. Wear it tomorrow night with your peacock spray."

I felt my cheeks color at his lavish praise.

Papa asked, "Feeling better, my daughter?"

Unable to look away from Antonio's adoration, I dropped my chin an inch then returned it to its proper height.

"Are you ill?"

"A nervous stomach. Nothing more."

"No need for nerves. Men will covet you and their wives will wish they could be you." He added, "Who are you?"

I spoke as I thought a royal might. "I...am a Delatesta."

"How proud I am you are." Antonio leaned over and kissed the tip of my nose. He straightened and ordered, "Garon, dress her."

43

Signor and Signora Valerio and Guilia di Benneto

Rio Nove

In the night gondolas slipped past each other without disturbing the water. Masked and swathed in hooded capes, their passengers only looked only ahead. Just before the Canale Grande a massive building appeared. At the dock a pair of boats waited for us to dock before them. *Do we arrive by rank? Of course.*

Between each torch that lit the di Benneto dock stood an attendant dressed in black and wearing a crimson sash. The men's black masks were rimmed with red, a fearsome sight. We alighted in silence. Antonio and I followed Papa. We passed wide double doors and walked into a large chamber unlike our entrance. *It has no water side warehouse and is all house.* A pair of liveried men held open the double doors. We walked across the space and reached gleaming teak stairs so wide four persons could enter abreast. The doors at the top of the stairs led into the antechamber.

Silent servants dressed in the family's colors helped us remove our outerwear and took them away. Antonio offered and I placed my hand on his forearm. Again we followed Papa as he climbed the set of stairs to the next floor and stepped into a long hall half as wide as our house.

Already, they are living as if they are among the Ninety-nine. Perhaps in the next listings they will be. Following Papa, we approached our host and hostess.

A maiordomo stated our titles and names. Signor di Benneto said, "Mille gracie for joining us this evening."

His wife spoke a formal, "Buone sera."

Papa said their titles and surname followed by, "You honor us with your kind invitation."

After Papa and Antonio greeted our hosts and shook Signor's hand, Antonio turned to me. I placed my right hand on his raised left, approached, and Papa introduced me. Signor spoke, and I responded; I repeated myself to his signora. Their eyes were as neutral as their voices. That hurdle completed, I kept Antonio's arm as we entered the salon.

The two couples in the room stopped talking and stared. Papa led us to the couples, and I curtsied and spoke the proper words. Antonio took us to another part of the room.

I saw the next couple do as we had done and then approach us. My first nod to one less ranked was to Signor Tuviani, one hundred four; and I received my first curtsey from his signora. When I met the Garzolos, one hundred five, I smiled at them before I nodded to Signora and commented how the color of her dress complimented her eyes. She thanked me and they moved on. Other couples followed, and each time I was a little warmer in expression and voice than they were. *Perhaps they do not like these forced formalities any more than I do.* I was relieved they were civil and returned a similar or neutral remark. *Signora Garzolo was the most pleasant. Remember her.* The full room was becoming warm when we lined behind our hosts for the procession into the dining hall.

A dozen pillars lined each long wall with a candelabra on each stand. Candelabra between floral arrangements lit the table. *This room is almost as long as our home! How glad I am we are not vying for a lower number; I hope we are not. We could not afford to live like this.*

A gold-edged card leaned against a small Murano vase holding a single rose to mark our places. Cream for men, but each woman's was a different color. I walked the length of the table to find my name below a pink rose. *Deliberate? To remind me I ought not to have her place? Ignore it. Maintain my half smile.*

I stood near the host's end of the table. To his right stood a priest, then Signor di Benneto's brother. To my immediate left, I saw Signor Alioni's name, one hundred two. I was next. To the host's left stood Signora Friuli, one hundred one, then Papa. *To see him so close gives me strength.* Near the other end of the table, Antonio stood on the opposite side of the table. Also seated by rank, he sat third right and between Signora Alioni and Signora Tuviani at the hostess's end of the table. Seated man, woman, man, the one hundred tens were seated at the center of the table. After the benediction we sat. Bodiless arms served Signor di Benneto and Father Capello first. Every liveried man served two persons. I knew to ignore Signor Alioni's and mine. His hand poured the first wine.

After three hours of course after heavenly course, our dolce arrived. I found my only one or two bites and one sip for each course had satisfied my hunger without my feeling heavy. As we dined I enjoyed conversing with Signore Alioni and Signor Garzolo. After asking a general question I listened to each gentleman, nodding, smiling and learning from them. I also had heard snippets from Signor Tuviani, who sat opposite me, and I conversed with the women on either side of him. No one said anything of importance. *I am becoming more comfortable being among strangers.* To show my confidence, I had looked Papa's way only once, but he was listening to Signora Friuli and did not notice me.

Signora Guilia di Benneto stood, and we women did as well. We followed her to their music room, which was filled with glistening-white chairs grouped in threes and fours. When I deliberately sat with three women of lower rank, they appeared uncomfortable in my presence. I felt safe because I knew they were required to be polite. Curving my lips in a polite half smile, I asked their names. I listened to their conversations and only entered them when I had something to add.

From behind me someone bent to my left ear. "Are you enjoying Lucia's dowry goods? How fortunate for you Lucietta is too young to marry and take them with her. You had none, so you have no value." Before I could think what she meant, from the right I heard a second voice. "Foreigner, we do not recognize your supposed nobility. You are not one of us and never will be."

I maintained my half smile. *Ignore them. Be deaf.*

"Signora Delatesta, please sing for us."

I looked to see who had spoken; her eyes held her challenge.

"Signora Fruili, I regret I cannot honor your wish. My vow to God prevents me from singing anywhere but in my home."

"You are famous for singing to gondoliers, workmen, and other unwashed."

What is she talking about?

She smirked, "Do you not realize that even through closed windows common laborers hear both your singing and your lessons to Lucia's daughter? Because they know you practice daily, they fill your rio. Have you never looked out your music room window and seen the crowd of boats bobbing below? You sing for them. Are we not more important than they—and more deserving of your talents?"

I looked about and saw other women smirking. *They may side with her, but I stand with God.* "Signora, I am singing in my own home. What happens outside it is beyond my control."

Signora Alioni continued the attack, "What is also beyond your control is your husband's visiting his mistress every Monday and Thursday. You seem to be oblivious to that as well."

My half-smile froze; I felt my heart fall into my shoes and my stomach wrench. *How do I defend myself? I need an ally.* I turned to our hostess. "Signora di Benneto, wise wives when to know something and when to choose to ignore. Are we not wise wives?"

Startled, she retorted, "Of course we are!" She glared at Signora Alioni and announced, "Wise wives also know what topics to avoid and when to remain silent."

Moderata Fruili dropped her stare and turned away, as did Camilla Alioni.

"Signora di Benneto, I see you have a very fine harpsichord. Perhaps the signore would like some music?" Signora Eugenia Garzolo added, "Signora Delatesta is skilled."

"I would like that. Per favore, Signora Delatesta, play softly so we may still converse."

Without looking at my attackers, I crossed the room and sat. *An escape. Grazie mille, Garzolo.* After lifting the lid, I played a glissando to get a feel for the instrument. *In tune, but stiff. Not been played in a long while. Think only of the music.* I began a sweet, romantic tune. Some spoke in hushed tones. A few may have looked my way, but I just smiled at the empty music stand before me and kept playing. *Heart, stop pounding. Think only of the music. Breathe. My stomach is upset again. Deal with it later.* I played two more songs and finished the last with a flourish. I turned to see Fruili and Alioni looking away as they whispered to each other. *Damn both of you for your treachery! I care not for the penance I must serve for that wish. Oh no, I have a need.*

When I stood others ignored me; only Signora Garzolo looked my way and gave me a quick smile. I walked to the servant at the door, made my request and followed her. After I had closed the door I heard the voices behind it rise. We walked to a corner of the floor, and the girl opened a door. Inside was a lit three-candle chandelier on a shelf and a bowl below a stool with a hole in its center. *An entire room just for this? What wealth to waste space.* I lifted my skirts and sat. I grabbed my middle and groaned.

Something is not right. I feel a need, but cannot orinare. My innards ache. I must return home. I closed the door and found a male servant beside my helper.

"Your signor requests your presence in the salon to sing for Signor di Benneto and his guests."

"Please send my regrets to Signor di Benneto that I am too ill to honor his request. Thank him for a wonderful evening, but I must return home as I feel unwell. Ask my signor to accompany me as I need his help. I will meet him where we left our capes." I grasped the girl's arm. "I feel weak. Please accompany me down the stairs." She crooked her arm so I could take it.

An attendant was behind me tying my mask when Antonio charged down the steps. "We cannot leave. You must return and sing for our host. I demand it." My knees buckled, and he grabbed me. "You must sing!"

Pale and shaking, I whispered, "I cannot. Per favore, get me home before I am sick on their floor and embarrass us." As he dressed, the girl held my elbows to keep me upright.

I clung to the railing as we descended the stairs. Refusing to look at me, Antonio grasped my arm and propelled me out the opened door. A blast of cold shocked me as Antonio pulled me. I stiffened my will and followed. Antonio was rough as he set me into a gondola. I leaned back and closed my eyes. The boat's gentle swaying made me nauseous, so I opened my eyes and lifted my head to avoid tossing my dinner over the side. The night air cooled my mouth and chin. At our pier Antonio left the gondola and extended his hand, but he dropped it as soon as I stood on the dock. Feeling better I followed him to the door. Inside I passed him and took the stairs. *I must relieve myself. Be at the pot to toss that meal.*

"I am ashamed of you! You embarrassed me, our whole family, to refuse our host with your false illness."

At the lower landing, I turned. "It was a test, and you failed!" I hurled at him. "You know my vow, yet you failed to support me at the same time two women insulted me before everyone. They planned it, and you walked into their trap. I did not. Where are you going?"

"Out."

"To your mistress? Even though it is not Monday or Thursday?"

When he turned back, I saw his stunned expression. Something deep within me loosed, and I felt a rush of wetness down my legs, soaking my stockings and slippers. I tried to cry out, but I felt myself falling into a dark pit as I faintly heard my name.

* * * * *

I roused to find myself in bed too weak to move under heavy bedding. A large hand stroked my head and cheek. Another hand grasped my hand under the coverings. A voice, both pleading and soft, said, "Cara, wake. Per favore, open your eyes. I am sorry. So sorry. Mi dispiace. Misero. I will not leave you. Cara, please wake." I kept my eyes closed and stirred not. Not wanting to be in my body, I let darkness take me.

44

Palaso Degli Delatesta

February 11

When next I woke, I saw light through my lashes.

"Cara! You are awake. I am so happy."

Still squinting, I saw his disheveled hair, unshaven face. I slammed shut my lids.

"Gracia, it is me. Please open your eyes."

"Too bright."

He ordered the curtains drawn. "Only candles now, my dearest. I am so sorry I was cross with you. I failed to recognize a trap; I should have supported you and your vow. You were ill and I was not kind. Per favore, forgive me, Cara."

With my eyes still closed, I confessed, "Forgive me. I orinare on my dress and ruined it. Slippers too."

He choke out, "Nothing to forgive. An accident. I will have them remade."

Within me, I felt an emptiness. *Had I tossed my meal?* Squeezing my thighs together, I felt something packed between my legs. *Fabric?* I smelled blood. *To stop blood?!* I cried out, "Bambina mea, bambina mea!" and rolled away from him. When I could not pull up my legs, I curled toward them.

I heard, "At Ospedale, when she said 'yes' and kissed you, did you feel her give her heart? You did not give yours; you still have not. You demanded she break her vow to God." I heard Papa's voice harden. "She learned your lie, and the shock caused her to lose the child. You have broken her heart." I heard Papa bark, "No! I will not hear it. The least you can do for her now is to stay with her while she decides to live or die of grief." I heard Papa's sob, hard steps and the door closing.

"Everyone, out!" I heard Antonio command.

I pushed Antonio away when he climbed onto the bed to curl himself at my back. Grabbing a sheet corner I covered my wet face. He left the bed. I felt cool air as he crawled under the covers before me. He grabbed me to hold me against his chest. My tears soaked the sheet, his shirt. When I failed to leave his tight embrace, I struck his neck with the side of my fist. "Leave!"

"No."

"Want alone." He pulled me closer. "I hate you!"

"No more than I hate myself."

In hopes he would leave, I stilled my body and reduced my crying to sniffles. He stayed. I blew my nose into the sheet. He kissed my head. Too weak to fight him, I straightened my body and stiffened my back.

"Cara, you must drink. Broth will strengthen you."

"Only if you leave." I heard him sigh, felt him leave the bed. I kept my eyes closed as he uttered instructions.

After the door closed Garon said, "Signora, you must be more upright. I have pillows.

Through my lashes I watched Garon add sticks to the brazier, fill a small copper pot with broth from a pitcher and put the pot next to the tiny fire. I drank even though the broth was tepid.

"Signora, the physician said you must sit upright to expel the last of the blood. If you do not, it will give you a fever that could take your life."

Do I want to live? I want Papa and Lucietta. Not him. Decide later.

With her help, I sat on the bed edge and dangled my feet beneath the blankets Garon had wrapped around me. The cloths between my legs made me uncomfortable. From the opposite side of the bed, Garon sat with her back against mine, so I stayed upright with no effort. After a time, I asked, "How long?"

"Two days."

"What happened to her?"

"All blood. Nothing to see. Burned your garments. Signor demanded your merito do it. He refused to leave you; Signor Delatesta did it himself."

That explains his furry face, wrinkled shirt and smell. His supposed dedication is not love; it is guilt. Not for having a mistress. For yelling at me? Not supporting me? It matters not. I will not ease his conscience; let him suffer as I do. I shed more silent tears for my lost bambina. From outside, Carnevale noises tried invaded a grief that overwhelmed me.

Garon interrupted my jumbled thoughts. "This evening, the physician will see you again. If your bandaging is fresh blood, he will give you medicine to expel what you must." Chin to my chest,

I covered my face with my hands. Garon instructed, "The broth is warm. Please stay seated. After you drink, I will help you to lie down."

"Signora Delatesta, please wake." I did as Garon had asked and found the curtains showed a crack of the last of pale winter daylight. She lit candles and placed them on my dressing table and on my desk. *Ignore cheerful sounds outside my window. Not my life any more.*

My door opened. Without speaking or even looking at me, a black-clothed man with a short gray beard watched Garon remove the cloths between my legs and cover me. She dropped the cloths to the floor; he left. I heard male voices beyond the closed door. When Antonio entered, I closed my eyes and clutched the bedding to my chin.

"Cara, you are safe from danger. You will eat beef and beef broth at every meal to regain your strength. Lent is close, and you must be strong enough for its rigorous fasting." I said nothing. "I will visit you every morning and every evening and stay until you speak to me, no matter how long it takes. If you refuse, expect me to sit with you all day and all night." I heard him step off the rug to the wooden floor and depart.

"His saw his face, Signora," reported Garon. "He means it."

We shall see. I rolled away and pulled the bedding over my head.

The next morning I finished a half bowl of meat bits and mushroom in a thick broth. He entered with a chair in hand. Instead of watching him set the chair bedside and take it, I watched Garon remove the tray and leave. To avoid his steady gaze I looked out the window at the gray clouds and shards of sunlight trying to pierce through. I waited what seemed hours. Finally, I looked back. "You mean it."

"I do."

We stared at each other. *Nothing in his face. No sorrow. Not even kindness. He is determined to stay; I will wait.* After a long time, I spoke. "What happened?"

"Blood dripped off the stair. You fell toward me. I caught you. Someone sent for our physician; I carried you to bed."

I imagined confusion and rushing about. *Where is Papa?* Seeing my hands were clenched tight, I loosened my grip. Without looking up, I asked, "Papa?"

"Arrived later. He wants to see you, but only when you ask for him. He feels terrible he was not with us."

"Per favore, tell Papa I want to see him whenever he wishes to come, as often as he wishes." *No response?* "I am tired and would like to rest now."

Antonio rose. "May I kiss your forehead?"

Staring at my hands, I shook my head. He latched my door so quietly, I had to look up to be sure he had left. Before I could sink beneath my coverings, the door opened, and in strode Papa. I grimaced to stop my tears and failed. Papa rushed to me, sat on my bed and drew me into his arms. I clutched him, buried my face in his chest and sobbed my grief. *Papa, dear Papa.* He kissed my ear and whispered, "My sweet girl, my dear daughter. Cry all you want. I am here."

45

February 13

The next day was as dark as my mood. Garon arrived. Hungry, I finished the beef bits in broth with boiled vegetables. As she left I sank under my coverings. I heard his footsteps, a chair dragged bedside.

"Buone giorno, Grazia."

If I speak not to him, he will stay. If I do, will he then go to her? How do I keep him here without words? I snaked my hand from under the sheet and blankets. Before I could feel air, he sandwiched my hand in both of his. I waited for him to speak, but he did not.

"How long since…?"

"This is the fourth day."

To keep him near, I curled my fingers around his hand.

"Why did you not tell me you were ill?"

"I thought it was nerves about the dinner. I did not want to disappoint you, so I said nothing." He drew my hand upward, opened his, and kissed my palm. *Talk of something else.* "It must be hard for you to have your birthing date during Lent. Do you celebrate it?"

"The Sunday before. My favorite foods, sweets, gifts. As a child,

I could not play with my toys until after Easter; I hated waiting."

At that thought I envisioned a boy version of him pouting. He did not speak. "I need to get out of bed, walk. I want to be at church on Ash Wednesday. When is it?"

"Seventeen days? You are too weak to walk to church and back. I have already arranged for a priest to bring the ashes to you."

"I want to be strong enough by then." *Show them. Words will not defeat me. Neither will this weakness.*

"For now you may get out of bed, but only on my arm or Papa's or Garon's. First this room. Next the hall. The first time you take the stairs, I will walk you. No more falling, Grazia. You frightened me half to death. I was terrified I was going to lose you."

He spoke with such fervor I almost believed him. Then I remembered. *He still needs a legal heir.* I sighed. "I am going to rest now. After pranzo I will only sit at the edge of the bed with Garon standing before me. After cena when you visit me, I will try standing." When he kissed my palm again, I curled my fingers as if to hold the kiss as I slid my hand under the covers. I waited until after he had closed the door. I opened my hand and wipe it on the bed sheet before I rolled to my side. *With me abed, he could visit her every day.* That thought kept me sad and awake until I surrendered to tiredness and slept.

That afternoon I sat on the edge of my bed, and Garon stood before me. Without looking up, I asked, "When did he last see her?"

"He has not left the house since you fell."

"Her name?"

"Maricella."

"Have they children?"

"Sons. Four and almost two."

"Is she with child?"

"No."

"How do you know?"

"Gossip. Also, talk is Signora Fruili's comments so shocked you, she brought on your loss. Another version is that Signora di Benneto is at fault. Both women are being blamed."

Say nothing. Let them talk until I decide what to do. I lifted my legs and let Garon cover me. I yawned as I pulled the covers under my chin.

Alone, my mind wandered. *If the elder is four, they have been together five years. After Lucia died. Two sons. What a hold she has on him! That he did not admit it is proof he will keep them. Proof he can father sons. I am less than a wife. Only a housekeeper and daughter raiser. A womb. He can give me sons, but can I hold them, birth them? Or even daughters? I do not know and dare not ask.* I closed my eyes. *Not tired—sad.*

Before I dozed off, I started at a thought. *Those two little ones, his sons, born innocent but will never be labeled so. No education, no chance to rise. All they can expect is derision and hard lives. If she dies will he send them to the boys' orphanage or bring them home? At least he loves them and takes care of them. That speaks a little to his character. I hadn't thought of that.* I rolled to my back. *Society is so unfair. They condemn the innocent for their births and demand rank in everything without regard to a person's goodness. How can I ask him to cut his ties to his sons for my sake? How do I live with him knowing about his other family? Will he give me children now?* I stared at the blue of the ceiling, trying to sort my feelings and desires.

After cena, I stood only long enough for Garon to help me into my vesta. I tied it around my camacia and sat. She stood before me; when Antonio arrived she left. I placed my hands on Antonio's and let him pull me up. "I feel silly."

"No matter." As he walked backward, I followed. At the door he turned and we stepped toward the window.

At my next turn I looked. "You closed the door between our rooms."

As we walked Antonio said, "The physician's orders. I may not lay with you until you have completed two cycles. In Confession padre extended the time to after Easter Sunday or two cycles, whichever is longer." Antonio paused before he admitted, "I cannot bear to see your lights or hear your sounds. Even your perfume wafts into my room. I closed the door to remind me of Padre's penance."

"As you closed it, you shall open it." *Give him something or he will go to her tonight.* "I promise to tell you the day my second cycle is over." At his nod, I asked, "Do you wish me to open the door to announce my news?"

"Certamente." We took two more turns before he said, "Enough for now. Per favore, sit."

I looked up to see his hopeful gaze. "You may kiss my forehead." His lips warmed my skin, and he held them on me longer than I expected. After his "Buone notte," he called for Garon, who entered. *Listening at the door? Remember to be careful with her.* Antonio kissed the backs of my hands before he released them and left the room.

A moment later we heard a knock, and Garon answered it. Antonio strode in carrying a red rose, which he handed to me. "Tomorrow is Saint Valentine's day, but I could not wait. I want you to wake seeing it and know I am thinking of you."

I held it to my nose and inhaled its sweet fragrance. "Grazie, Antonio. It is lovely and you are thoughtful." I paused and added, "I have nothing for you."

"Smile at me and I will count it more than enough."

I lifted my face and gave him an honest one. He kept his lips on mine and was gentle. Then he left.

I sniffed the rose again and asked, "Does the color mean something?"

Garon's response was a quiet, "In France it means admiration, affection, love."

After Garon put me to bed she left one candle lit. As I stared at the rose, I considered her answer. *Affection, admiration, yes. Love? I think not.* I dried my moist cheeks with the sheet.

In the dark, I looked about and noticed the candle partially lit the small painting of the Madonna and Child I had chosen from the attic. Instead of Mary with the baby Jesus in her arms, I imagined I was holding our lost daughter. Standing behind Mary, Joseph looked over her shoulder at the Christ child with pride and love in his eyes. I pictured Antonio in the same stance, protecting our daughter and me. I cried over what never will be.

46

❧

February 14

The next morning, Papa arrived. "Antonio is working on the account books; he is behind. I will take you down the hall." I took his arm.

As we walked, I asked, "It that noise Carnavale starting again?"

"Si. They rest Sunday, and party day and night until the midnight bell announces Ash Wednesday. Starting next week, fireworks will light the night skies. The last three days before the final Tuesday we sometimes have to shout inside the house from all the noise. We walked another length before he commented, "Lucietta is desperate to see you. Because we have kept her away, she is convinced you are dying."

"One more down and back, dearest Papa, and I will sit. Per favore, bring Lucietta to me; I will convince her I am recovering."

At my door, Papa leaned over and whispered in Lucietta's ear before she approached.

Lucietta curtsied. "Buone giorno, Mama."

"Per favore, Lucietta, hand me my shawl at the end of my bed. "

"Are you cold, Mama?"

"No." I took it from her. "Sit on my lap." At her "But Nonno said…" I opened my arms. She scurried into them and settled as I wrapped us together. I hugged her to me and asked, "What do you hear?"

"Your heart."

"How does it sound?"

"Thump, thump, thump. Steady."

"Just as it will until you are old, like Nonno." Lucietta snuggled even closer. "As this shawl warms you, your love warms my heart. I have been ill, but am better. Seeing you cheers me. Hugging you makes me happy."

She whispered, "I heard bad things. I heard Nurse say 'dying.' I peeked in your door. Nonno was wringing his hands. Papa was on his knees beside your bed, crying."

Shocked, I froze. *Crying? Think on that later.* "I was ill, but now I am better and even walking the hall to become stronger." I whispered into her ear, "You feared I was dying, but it is not so."

She threw her arms around my neck and drew me to her. "I do not want to lose another mama," she confessed into my ear.

I kissed her forehead, each cheek. "You will not, I promise." I leaned forward and back to rock her. She pulled her arms back under the shawl. Only she could hear, "I love you, Lucietta, my dear daughter. I am proud of my little girl." Holding her even closer, I kissed her. "Mama is better. Mama will be well. Soon we will sing together."

Antonio was standing beside Papa with an emotion I had never seen. *Might he love me? No. He loves Lucietta.* I stopped rocking.

Lucietta peaked over the shawl. "Buone giorno, Papa. Mama is better."

"And happy my family is together, Nonno, Papa, you, and me."

I smiled toward Papa. "I would like us to eat pranzo together in my room."

"A fine idea. Son, per favore, arrange it."

Lucietta stood beside my chair. Papa and Antonio perched on armless chairs as we ate around a small table. Despite a pleasant time of good food and polite small talk, I tired. Papa returned Lucietta to the nursery and I lay down. After supervising the removal of the meal, Antonio tucked me into bed with a kiss on my forehead. He promised to join me for cena.

At dinner, I told Antonio my plan to repair the damage done to Signora di Benneto's reputation. "Even if she refuses my invitation, she will know I support her. With your approval, I will send a letter."

"You have it."

After he departed, I considered. *I know him. He loves his sons; he will see they have as good lives as possible despite being born outside legal marriage, despite having no rank, no opportunities. What are his feelings toward her? Whatever they are, he cannot stop seeing her. He will see her every time he visits his boys. Can a man love two women at the same time? He may think so, but not equally. He may need me, but he has not said he loves me.*

I rolled over and stared at the shadows cast by the single candle on my dressing table. *Shadows. I am not living with one but two. He likes me, even admires me, but he is holding back his heart. Something has been missing between us. Even when we lie together. My heart felt it. He is not all mine. My heart knew but I refused to see it. I know I am living with his memories of Lucia. Now I know about the other, and she has his sons. She may even have his heart.* I crawled out of bed, blew out the candle, and returned to bed in darkness. My heart broke and left my body. I couldn't even cry.

47

February 17

After colazione Lucietta visited me before leaving for lessons. I sat at my desk as Garon straightened my room. I stiffened my spine. *Live each day doing what I must. Mother said soldiers march on even to their deaths. They face what they must and do what they must. I must soldier on. I chose this life. Now I must live it as it is. Banish my dream; it is no more. Today I must try to benefit Papa and Lucietta's futures.* I opened my desk drawer, withdrew a paper, and reached for pen and ink.

When I miswrote a word, I continued to write on the damaged paper. I turned over the sheet and wrote a copy for Papa to approve. While I waited, I sipped red wine to strengthen my blood.

To Signora Valerio di Benneto,

I am most grateful you invited the Signore Delatesta and me to your wonderful dinner and party. I regret having to leave hurriedly. When I reached home, I became ill. I am healed and ready to be social again. I dislike what I have heard of late. You had no part in what happened to me. I am distressed that anyone would speak ill of your kindness to my family. I hope you will come for afternoon tea at your convenience. Your joining me would honor me.

Hopeful of your reply, I am Yours in Christ,

Signora Antonio Delatesta

I clutched my hands in my lap; Papa paced as he read. "An excellent letter, but remove 'I dislike what I have heard of late.' The next sentence refers to the rumors without being direct. She will know why you invite her."

"Do you think she will come?"

"I do not know. Have Garon bring it to me. I will seal and send it."

On a new parchment, I copied the letter and handed it to Garon. "On your way to Papa please inform Nurse I want Lucietta."

Lucietta and I conversed in French, German, and Venetian as she recited her lessons. She dashed away and returned with her first sheet of inked letters. "Your first three capitals are excellent, but your D needs work."

She admitted, "True. Nurse says I must return to practice fingering the D before I may try again. When will we sing again?"

"I miss it as well. Papa said he would walk me down the stairs on Saturday. Perhaps Monday." Her sad expression touched my heart. "Garon, please set the small table; we two will have pranzo here." Lucietta crawled into my lap and gifted me with a kiss and a long hug. *I love her.* I told her so.

I napped while Lucietta returned to her lessons and sewing. Garon walked beside me as I strode around the room before being served cena. Lucietta returned and I read to her until our bedtime. I fell asleep to Carnevale celebrations. The next morning I heard faint noises and gazed at the door between us.

Behind me Garon reported, "He left after cena, was gone all night and has just returned home."

"Leave me." Alone, I covered my face with palms over my eyes and ordered myself not to cry. *What did I expect? He cannot not be with me for two months. He can have her whenever he wants. She gave him sons. I gave him failure. What is wrong with me?*

"Cara, are you all right?" asked Antonio as he approached my bed.

I lied. "I am praying for our lost bambina."

"Bambina?"

"You need a bambino. If it was a girl, at least one of us should want her.

He lowered my hands and held them. "I want all our bambini. Worry not, we will have them. Two. Four. Six?"

"Six. Seven children bring good fortune." I added, "I am ready to walk down the hall."

Afterward I stayed in my chair and Papa visited. After pranzo Lucietta arrived and we sewed together. *If I stay awake I will be tired enough to sleep.* Antonio joined me for cena; we walked. I yawned, and we returned to my room. I bid Antonio good night, hugged him around his waist and lifted my face. His kiss was tender, but lacked passion.

For hours, I turned from side to side. I heard Carnevale as my thoughts roiled, and sleep escaped me. *Nothing I consider can keep him with me. He is mine no more. Was he ever? What do I tell my heart? How do I live with what I know? Acting as though they do not exist is as* much a lie as acting as if his having a mistress and sons does not grieve me. He cried over me, but was it for me or his loss of an heir?

Round and round went my mind. *Do I say something? Do I not? How do I act? How do I treat him? Wringing my hands and crying will drive him away. How then do I give him the heirs he needs? Does he still want them? He can raise his boys and hand over the family to Stefano. No, he* won't *do that. He will keep both families even if I give him sons. I am left with half a life. Papa and Lucietta, but not him.*

As light peeked through the center of the draperies, I decided. *I love Papa and Lucietta and will take care of them, but I am no longer a wife. I am a puppet. Antonio pulls my strings, and I must do as he wishes. At home, I will do what he expects of me, keep the house and be Lucietta's mama. In public I will take his arm and smile at him, but my heart will not be in it. That he has lost.*

48

February 19

I closed my eyes against the coming dawn and listened to both birds chirping and the festive noises. Garon woke me after the others had left for Mass. I splashed cool water on my face and dressed in silence.

When Antonio arrived to escort me to colazione, I faked a smile, stood and took his arm. We descended with my hand on the railing and the other through his crooked arm. I let him keep my arm as we walked into the dining room. Turning the corner to Papa and Lucietta's applause, I gave them a genuine smile. *I doubt he noticed the difference.* I drank hot beef broth, scooped spoonfuls of a soup of mushrooms, onions, and beef bits, and enjoyed every bite. Surfeited, I sat back.

Tomaso announced our parish priest had arrived. As I had requested, Papa had summoned a padre to hear my confession. I took him upstairs to the first guest room and closed the door. He sat on a chair; I knelt on the floor. I had much to confess and advice to seek.

As I had expected, his admonishments were about my behavior not my husband's. Father informed me most of the Ninety-nine married for alliances and business reasons. Many had mistresses and second families. Others who could afford to do so followed the custom. He reminded me the other woman could never be in proper society and her children were the lowest class. He told me to remember my high rank, my good standing and that my children would be legal heirs and acceptable to all the world. His advice was to forget what I could not change and to be grateful for what I have.

He ordered me to be obedient to my husband's will as long as he did not harm me or my children. I nodded, accepted my penance and thanked him for his advice. His words had burned my ears, weighed heavy on my heart and left me in despair. *I hate his advice. Hate the custom. Hate how I am forced to live. The only choices I have are small ones.* He escorted me downstairs, and I left him with the men while I met Lucietta in the music room.

Distracting myself with music and Lucietta, I spent a pleasant morning warming our voices with scales and singing our favorite melodies. After pranzo I excused myself and napped until sunset. Again he escorted me down the stairs. After cena, we four spent the evening in the salon. He and Papa sipped wine as they chatted. Lucietta and I played Tressette, the simple version Violetta and Polonia had taught me. At the bells chiming the twenty-first hour Lucietta and I excused ourselves and went to bed.

Sunday morning Garon dressed me for Mass. He met me downstairs; we walked in bright sunlight that warmed us with a false promise of early spring. I yawned through colazione and took to my bed for the rest of the day.

"You exhausted yourself going to Mass."

"I do not sleep at night because I have been too long in bed. If

I exhaust myself, not only will I sleep better, but I will also force my body to become stronger." He escorted me to cena, and I read in the salon until bedtime.

Monday began the same as Sunday. Before I left colazione, Tomaso handed Papa a folded parchment. I watched him read it and refold it before handing it to me. Three watched with great interest.

My first message! I pray it is favorable news. Unbelieving of how pleasant was the formal wording, I reread it. Holding the paper in both hands, I looked up. "Signora di Benneto accepted my invitation to tea." I turned the sheet to the men. "May I have an emblem on paper like hers for myself?"

"Of course," Antonio replied. "We will print 'Signora Grazia Delatesta' beneath our family mark; I will order it and you will have twenty sheets tomorrow."

"Grazia, Antonio." *I will speak his name only when he does what I want or what pleases me. Eight days until Ash Wednesday, the best day to execute my plan. We will have been to Confession; the ashes will remind him of his sins.* I saw his smile. *He thinks he has won back my approval.* "Papa, Antonio, please excuse me. I will speak to Rosa about the tea."

Around the corner I leaned against the wall and heard, "She is fine. Everything is back to normal." *He is wrong. I waited, but Papa said nothing. Papa knows; Papa always knows.* I left for the kitchen.

After a hearty breakfast Wednesday, I returned to my room and skipped pranzo to prepare. I wore my dark blue wool. Behind me Garon fashioned my hair and buttoned the deep lace collar. I added pearl earrings, a bracelet and a pearl ring on my left hand. After having checked every detail with Rosa and Zanetta, I sat at the harpsichord to calm myself before walking into the salon and waiting.

"Signora, a gondola is arriving."

I stood at the top of the stairs and curtsied. "Buone giorno, Signora di Benneto. I am happy to see you."

"And I you," she replied as Zanetta took her mask and outerwear. I waited for her to enter the salon first and watched her examine the room before selecting her chair. Zanetta had followed and stood at the archway. "How would you renovate this room?" After I outlined my ideas, she commented, "Fashion has changed. Your plans are more modern and appropriate for your position."

"Your approval is important to me. I am wondering if I can complete my plans in time for Easter." *Asking that is only politeness. We cannot afford to renovate.*

"Many use the lack of social events during Lent to hire work done. Obtaining workmen and seamstresses can be difficult. I have a list of excellent people. I will write their names for you."

At my nod Zanetta disappeared and returned with a paper, pen, and ink pot, which she set on the table between us. Signora handed me the paper. "You may tell them I sent you. That should get you prompt service."

"Grazie mille, Signora."

The paper and implements disappeared and Zanetta delivered the tea. We visited as we sipped and nibbled. She asked about my singing and playing; I drew her out with polite questions about her family. She bragged about her children and grandchildren, and I looked as impressed as I was at their many accomplishments. *Lucietta has much to learn to match any of them.* After our second cups I asked if I might play and sing for her, and we left for the music room.

After I played a Vivaldi piece I asked, "Might you have a favorite song I may sing?" Afterward, I turned on my bench. "May I speak to you about a personal matter?" She nodded. "What happened to me the night of your party was no one's doing. Earlier I had experienced a queasy stomach, which I took for excitement. After it settled, I thought nothing of it. After dinner I thought my problem was my having eaten too much. Only in the small room did I realize I was ill and rushed home. I did not want to be sick before others."

"A wise decision."

"Signora di Benneto, I am distressed anyone would speak ill of you. How best do I quell rumor? Might you be willing to permit me to honor you with a tea and invite those you want to have attend?"

"That will help."

I knew she what she meant from the cruel gossip Garon had reported to me.

Signora said, "My favor will aid you socially. We both gain. I approve, but we must do it before Lent. Monday?"

"As you wish. And the attendees?"

"The Signoras Moderata Fruili, Camilla Alioni, Simona Tuviani Eugenia Garzolo."

"Signora, I cordially invite you to an afternoon tea to honor Signora Giulia di Benneto, Monday, the twenty-eighth day of February, in my home at the fifteenth hour. She asked me to invite you to attend. Yours in Christ. Signora Grazia Delatesta."

"A subtle command to appear. The details?" We discussed every element, even the music and how I will talk about my so-called illness.

She stood. "Signora Delatesta, we may have underestimated you. You are more like us than I thought. Escort me to the gondola. We will kiss each other's cheeks and hug. Wave farewell until the gondola disappears. Others will talk because I was here. Their curiosity and the gossip will assure the women's attendance."

I returned to find Papa waiting. "It went well?" I took his arm; in the salon I gave him details as we enjoyed dolce and fresh tea. "My Francesca would be as proud of you as I am. You have grasped the importance of an ally and possess the subtlety needed to gain her. Your playing and singing will please your guests and affirm you only sing at home. Daughter, you are doing well in advancing our family."

I kissed Papa's cheek and hugged him. After he departed I summoned Lucietta. With the leavings, we practiced her attending a tea. I complimented her on her good manners before I announced she had completed her twenty-one days of practice. She was polite and thanked me for my message. "The next task will add to your skills regards your lessons. After you do them without complaint, do your best every day, and meet Nurse's standards for excellence, you may choose the paint for your room. You may stand with me as I supervise the work."

"May I choose pink?"

"Certemente. You may even request they paint several shades in blocks on the walls, so you may select the one you like best."

She jumped up to hug me. "Mille gracie, Mama. I am sorry I thought ill of you. You want me to be a better girl than Claudia and I will be."

"Yes you will be. People will like you, and you will have friends."

"When will I have a friend, Mama?"

"Someday, in an invitation to our family will include you. If you meet another girl or boy near your age, that will be your chance to make a friend. For now, Nonno, Papa, and I are making you ready to do that."

"When I grow up, I want to be like you. Only I want to play the lute; the harpsichord is too hard."

I chuckled and hugged my girl. *Six in June. I can wait until a few more months before we try that again.*

49

February 28

Pranzo was five courses, including two meats. Too full, I did not even ask about dolce. Papa instructed Tomaso that cena should be the remains. "Have we enough food through Tuesday without cooking?" asked Papa. Tomaso reported we might, and Papa grumbled, "Lent. No meat, eggs, or dairy products for forty days. Only on Sundays until Easter. Serve it all or we must feed it to the pig." He shrugged and winked at Lucietta. "With luck our last meal before Ash Wednesday may be the leavings from the tea party. Just think, all dolce."

"Per favore, Nonno, all dolce!" chimed Lucietta.

As the Church permitted no work, card playing or other activities, I sent Lucietta to the nursery and napped. After cena I read in the salon. Too excited about the party, I crawled out of bed and wrapped myself in a blanket. I pushed aside a curtain and stared at a slip of moon.

Does it portend a new phase in my life? What it might it be depends on how goes Wednesday night. Bad I expect. He will not like what I say, but he will hear me. Think not so far ahead. This tea is even more important than the first. Complete that before I practice what to tell him. I crawled back into bed and curled myself into a ball to get warm.

The next morning the sun shined and waves rippled as boats slid through the canal before my home. The final partying of Carnavale sounded a desperate tone. *Ignore it.* After colazione Lucietta retired to the nursery for the day. I readied myself by wearing my deep green and pearls. *Papa hides in his office. He has already left the house.*

Moderata Fruili arrived first, with Camillo Alioni and Simona Tuviani following soon after. Eugenia Garzolo arrived last. All four guests waited in the salon as I greeted Signora di Benneto; they applauded when she entered the room. The tea and my playing and singing ended after two hours. *An hour longer than what is customary. A good sign?* Signora stood with me as we said farewell to my guests. As the guest of honor accepted being caped and masked, I mentally rehearsed my speech. Before she could say farewell, I said, "Signora di Benneto, I am grateful for what you have done for me. I owe you a favor. Even if you never see or speak to me again, know I am your supporter and defender."

Her mask hid not her twinkle and smile. "We will meet again."

I rested in the salon as the servants removed the tea things. I closed my eyes and recalled each expression, tone of voice, words and interaction. *The tea went as well as I had hoped.* After cena I sent Lucietta to the nursery. At my signal Tomaso refilled Papa's and my wine glasses.

"I heard pleasant sounds. No harshness."

"I took Signora Fruili aside and informed her I had arrived at the di Benneto dinner not feeling as well as should have. I assured her she had neither upset me nor had any part in my loss."

"You whispered it but within hearing of another?"

I nodded. "In the music room, I turned to Signora di Benneto. 'Shall I play your usual favorites or would you like to hear something new this time?'"

"The others thought your comment and her having come for tea last week significant. Well done, Daughter."

I excused myself to say buone notte to Lucietta and to retire early. Garon undid my hair and brushed it. "Signora, was your tea a success?"

"I am well pleased."

"Tomorrow will be a High Mass to celebrate Leap Year Day. Do you want me to set out something special? Request the pearls?"

"No. Mass is not for displaying fashion or wealth. I will wear no jewelry." Abed, I again recalled every moment of the tea. I reviewed each nuance or hidden meaning. *I pleased Signora, and all went well. This day holds triumph and loss. My tea went even better than I had hoped. He was not home for cena and will not return until early morning. I must wait until Wednesday. Until then I will be pleasant.*

He met us at Mass; I smiled at him as I took his arm to enter church, so he suspected nothing unusual. He spent the day with Papa in the office. I spent the morning in the music room. *Are workmen outside listening? No matter. I will not look, so I never know.* After pranzo I worked at my desk, and then reviewed Lucietta's lessons with her. I kept cena's conversation light and pleasant.

Wednesday we returned home with ashes on our foreheads to remind us from dust we came and to dust we will return. *If we are faithful to God and to Our Holy Mother the Church, we will reach heaven.* Colazione was bread and well-watered wine. No butter— not even vegetable broth. Pranzo was fish and vegetables. Cena, fish soup, and dry bread. *Thirty-nine more weekdays of fasting with only Sundays for relief. We do this to purify our souls. Be glad for it.* After sending Lucietta to the nursery, I gain his approval after saying, "We should be acting in unison even to say buone notte." After we left the nursery, I asked him to speak with me in my bedroom. When he balked, I said, "I have medical news to share."

I bid him sit in the upholstered chair and brought the wooden chair from my desk. I set it between him and the door. Our knees almost touched.

"Before the party my stomach ached; I thought it excitement. After dinner I thought I had eaten too much. My stomach hurt so I left the party. Your yelling at me was not the cause of our loss. It had already started."

"Are you telling me this to ease my conscience?"

"No. I am telling you the truth."

"Grazie mille, Cara. I have worried."

I bristled at his word for me, but only said, "Yesterday, I was uncomfortable; this afternoon I began my first cycle." He sat straighter as I added, "I suspect I will end my second cycle about Easter or shortly thereafter." I reached out and lay my shawl on the bed. "My other news is … I know why I lost our first bambina."

He frowned.

"First, another matter. I know about Maricella and your sons." He jumped up and I stood to block him. "I will not yell or cry or fight."

"I will not give them up!"

"Of course not! I will not let you. If you did I would think you had no honor. I would be ashamed of you." He sat with a thump. I sat. "I expect you to treat your sons well. Send them to school so they read, write and figure. I expect you to pay for a trade apprenticeship or for university so they can support themselves and live well. Your sons must have your support. They are the innocents in all this, and I will not have them harmed." Mouth agape, he leaned against the chair back. "Your sons need their mother. I expect you to support her even in these hard times. I would rather do without new dresses than deny them food, shelter and schooling."

"I do not believe you."

"Believe me." I stared into his eyes until he looked away.

I sat. "In exchange I want your promise you will never bring them to this house. I will never see or meet them."

"Done."

"Lucietta is proof you can father a girl. They are proof you can father boys."

"The problem is you."

I shook my head. "When you conceived your daughter, you had only been lying with Lucia. With your sons you lay only with Maricella. The problem is not me. You are."

Before he could object I rushed out, "You have been giving her your best seed, not me. I cannot carry a healthy child from your leftovers. I lost our bambina because you gave me less than your best. The problem is not mine; it is yours. Only you can decide what to do about it."

"I am a man! I can father as many children as I desire!"

"Do you still desire legal heirs?"

"Certamente!"

"I will give you heirs because I want children of my own, both sons and daughters. For that to happen you must decide how you will spend your seed. Every time you lie with Maricella, you give me less. Because of you, I lost our first bambina. Lie with her, and I will continue to lose bambini. You will have no heirs, not even another daughter."

"You are wrong." He looked away.

"You know I am right."

He accused, "You expect me to support them but never see them."

I swallowed hard. *I must give in to that.* "I did not say that. I am not asking that. I know you love your sons; they need you. I ask you if you want heirs." I heaved a loud sigh. "I am willing to risk my life to give you heirs, but I will not lose another bambina. My losing another bambina will be my proof you have chosen her, not legal heirs. I will keep your house, raise Lucietta and take care of Papa, but I will not just shut the door between us. I will lock it!"

Before he could speak I added, "You bargained well for yourself. You gained a mother for your daughter, a keeper for your household and a womb. I made a bad one. I gave you my heart and you gave me lies." I stood and looked down at him. "I have taken back my heart and am hiding it from you."

When he stood I stopped him with, "One last thing." I ignored his hard, angry look. "You do not mean it; I am not your 'dear one'. You call us both Cara. Even in bed you say 'Cara' so you do not have to remember which one of us you are with. Never will I answer to that word again. My name is Grazia. Say that or Signora Delatesta or nothing. From this moment, only when you say "Grazia or Signora Delatesta" will I answer you." I crossed my arms over my chest and stared back.

He sneered. "Shall I call you 'Zia'?"

"NO, you may not! My sisters called me 'Zia' because they loved me. Only those who love me may call me that. You do not love me. Of that I am certain."

He stepped around me and strode to the door before he turned. "I lay with Maricella because she gives me pleasure. You do not know how to be a wife."

I yelled at his departing back, "You do not know how to be a husband!"

I will not cry; I will not cry. The choice is his, not mine. He stomped down the stairs; I waited until his sounds faded. I removed my shoes and trod barefooted down the stairs. I peaked around the corner and saw Papa's office door ajar. With my back to the wall I approached. Through the crack between the door and the frame, I spotted a stripe of him. He was gulping wine, pouring more, and finishing that, too. I heard the goblet touch the desktop.

"Dio Mio, I have underestimated her!"

"You finally noticed," retorted Papa.

I crept backward, turned, and dashed up the stairs. After dismissing Garon I locked my door, disrobed and threw my things at the chair in which he had sat. Abed, I covered my head and cried into my pillow. When I had no more tears, I sniffled and rose from my bed to seek a cloth. My head felt stuffed and my heart empty.

With my back to my dressing table, I sat in the dark and pondered. *He likes his well-run household; he enjoys when I dress well and he can display me, but is that love? He wants heirs and enjoys trying for them. I thought that love, but what if it is not? For a time I pleased him, but now what? We made a bargain, but where is love in a bargain? He keeps her and the boys, and I keep his house and raise Lucietta.*

I stood and drew back the curtains to see a moonless night. *Someone always wants something from me. First, the sisters and their*

*need for donations. Now, his need for heirs, a well-behaved daughter,
and fitting into his world. What about what I need? I have my music; I
can live for that and Lucietta.* I dropped the drape and turned. *I am
in a loveless marriage I am forced to walk through the rest of my days.
Papa. Papa loves me. To Papa I will be warm and caring. But not to him.*
I crawled into my bed, lay on my side, and stared into the darkness.

50

March 2

He did not go to Mass with Papa and missed colazione. Gone all day, through the night, and still not here. With her. To punish me. Not speaking unless someone addressed me, I tried to cheer myself with music and failed. I plodded through the day and crawled into bed.

Friday morning before Mass someone knocked on my door. I sat up, leaned against my pillows and pulled my coverings to my chin. *Please God, let it be him. Let him agree with my wishes. Blessed Mary, give me the words. Dear Lord, let him choose* me. "Enter."

Papa entered, his eyes bloodshot and his expression haggard. I gasped. *What happened? Did he kill himself?* Holding the handle to steady himself, Papa leaned against the opened door. Antonio filled the door frame. *Thank you, God. Oh no, he looks as bad as Papa. I froze. Who died? Her? Did she kill his sons?* Papa closed the door and leaned against it while Antonio approached.

Still silent, he stood bedside and opened his hand to reveal a scrap of crumpled dirty parchment torn from a larger piece. I straightened it and read aloud, "Giacomo and Miro are safe. She burned the house. Only stone walls left. I need help. Please come."

At hearing those words Papa began crying and wiping his face with his sleeve. I sat upright. "Polonia? Claudia? Why does he not mention their safety? No date. When did this arrive?"

"Midnight. This is all we know."

"I am so sorry, so sorry. What can I do?"

"Papa wanted to go; I will."

He won that fight. "When?"

"Now."

"By ship?"

"Papa called for a crew and will fill one of our ships. I will ride overland. Papa insisted I tell you myself before I leave."

I threw Papa a nod of gratitude before I patted the bed and bade Antonio sit. "Of course you must go. Stefano needs you." I placed my hand on his forearm. "Gracie mille for telling me yourself. For saying farewell."

"May I kiss you before I leave?"

Despite this tragedy, he must earn my lips. I leaned forward and gave him my forehead. He pressed his dry lips against my skin; I waited for him to release me.

He whispered, "You send me away because you hate me. You want me gone from you."

"I do not hate you." Pulling back so he could see my face, I saw his sagging shoulders, his tear-stained face and his eyes full of fear. *Do not let him leave showing him a cold heart. At least be kind.* I placed my right hand against his cheek. "I do not hate you. I am not sending you away, but to Stefano. We are a family. When one of us is in need, we do what we must. Stefano needs help. For a time Papa and I must do without you." Seeing a glimmer of hope in his eyes. I continued.

"Every day you are away from me, I will pray for your safety, for your wellbeing and for your swift return."

He took my hand, held it in both his hands, and kissed my palm. I felt his gratitude, and my heart warmed. "Antonio, be careful; be safe. Come back to me."

Antonio clutched me in his arms. "I do not want to leave you. Not like this."

While I knew what he meant, I countered with, "I will be fine. I have Papa and Garon and the entire household to look after me." I pushed him only so far as I could see his face and gave him a small smile. "I will be here when you return. I am not going anywhere." His eyes told me what he wanted. *Send him away with it. Give him a reason to return.*

I placed my hands on his shoulders and tilted my head. I closed my eyes as our lips met and felt tenderness and need, fear, then desire. He drew me into his arms, and I let him lay my head against his shoulder as we kissed. I darted my tongue into his mouth and let his into mine. I gave in to the passion he offered; the heat that always fired when we kissed clouded my mind. When I could bear no more, I pulled away from him and saw his smile.

I whispered, "Antonio, you may be gone a long time, and they are so young." As he frowned, I kept speaking. "They will ask, 'Where is Papa?' Tell them you must go on a long journey; you do not know when you will see them again."

He rasped, "Even now, you speak of them!"

"Your sons will ask why you do not visit them. They deserve to hear it from you." I added, "Please give her enough to live for two months. If you need to be gone longer, send a message so Papa can see to their needs until you return." Seeing my advantage in his shock, I added, "They are your sons, Antonio. You love them. Always take care of them."

Antonio stiffened, stood, and announced in a flat voice, "I leave now. I will send messages when I can." He spun on his heel and exited my room.

As Papa closed the door, I heard him utter, "She is a remarkable wife. Endeavor to deserve her."

I withdrew under the coverings. When Garon arrived to dress me, I lifted the comforter from my head and uttered, "Two disasters in one week. Wake me when the third arrives." I waved her away and stayed abed.

Papa sent an invitation to dine. At cena Papa's answer to Lucietta's question was almost honest. "He left for Zio Stefano's home. Said it was time to inspect the fields and watch the planting."

After I escorted Lucietta to bed and bid her buone notte, I went to Papa's office as he had requested. We sat in silence a long time. I knew no words that might comfort him. As I waited, I prayed for Polonia and Claudia. When he announced our topic, I dropped my chin to my chest. "You did nothing wrong, daughter. The errors are all his. He did not explain his loneliness after Lucia's death. Antonio did not tell you about his sons and should have. He expected he could keep you happy and them secret. When did you learn of them?"

"A woman at the di Benneto party."

"She cost you your bambino. Her name."

I heard his hard voice. *I will not condemn her. Explain.* "Papa, my stomach ached before the party and after we ate. I thought it was excitement then too much food. I think I was already losing it before she spoke. Papa, per favore, harm no one for my sake. I beg you. Soon or late I would have learned it. At Christmastide I suspected something was amiss when he disappeared from Mass to cena even though the family was here." In silence we stared at each other for a long time. When he finally nodded, I added, "Papa, all I can do now is wait."

"I overheard you talk with Signora di Benneto. She is right; the salon needs to be redone."

"I was only being polite. Papa, we cannot afford the expense."

He ignored my remark. "Why not the primo floor? I did not favor Lucia's tastes; it needs refreshing." He added, "I like my office as it is. Not the music room for that is new."

"It will be costly. We cannot afford it."

"We can. Daughter, no Venetian records all his coins in his accounts book. We have more than we record. Much more."

Is that how he housed, fed, and clothed them? I saw no such entries in the accounts book. Do not ask. Papa has always told me the truth; trust that.

"Repaint the entry and the main hallway. Redecorate the salon and the dining room; they need it. Do whatever pleases you."

"Are you certain we can afford it?"

"I am. I want fresh, more modern-looking rooms. While Antonio is absent, redecorating will distract you." He added, "If anyone asks you about Antonio's absence, say he was called to the farms. You do not know when he will return. Go about your day." I stood and Papa stood. He hugged me. "Leave financial concerns to me, daughter."

Four days later, my first cycle ended. I closed myself in my room and cried. *My first mestruazione finished. Another chance gone, another loss.* I threw the last of my rags into the washing pail and closed my rags belt into a drawer. I moped through the rest of the day. Before

Mass the next morning Papa escorted me to church to be cleansed by a priest's blessing.

On the way home I looked up and saw the sun was higher in the sky and brighter for the time of day. After colazaione I walked the rooms and went to my desk to write my list of changes. At bedtime I did not correct Lucietta when she thought my sadness was because I missed him. I kissed her and left the nursery. In my room Garon fussed over me and hinted her questions, but I did not respond.

Sunday, the twelfth day of March, the second Sunday of Lent, was the reprieve I needed. We ate meat at both meals, enjoyed fresh asparagus from the south and dipped our bread in herbed olive oil. At the end of pranzo, Papa surprised us with a bowl of strawberries in cream.

"Papa will be sad to miss this dolce!"

"I expect Zia Polonia is also serving an excellent meal."

"Nonno, do you think Papa will write to us?"

"He will if he has time. Papa will be busy helping with the planting."

I agreed and scooped a berry from the cream. Afterward I took Lucietta with me to admire the pig and to inspect the gardens.

Monday morning Papa walked me into his office. "Remember the list Signora di Benneto gave you? I engaged workmen and seam-stresses who will arrive Wednesday. The secondo and terzo floors need nothing. You may decorate however you like. New looks may help my son think in new ways. Show me your ideas for each room."

He wants this for me. Papa, if we cannot afford this, I will bankrupt us. "Papa, one room will do."

"The salon, dining room, the hall and the entrance. No less. We have the coins, and the worker's families need to eat. If you dislike the music room, redo it as well."

By the end of the day the staff had stored what they could in the attics and had pushed the largest pieces to the center of each room. We covered the items with the sailcloth that had covered items in the attic. At Papa's instruction they also hung a curtain at the top of the stairs to keep dust from the secondo floor. That evening I asked Papa to sketch his view as he sat outside at our country home in the mountains.

"If it pleases you, Papa, I will commission a mural in the dining room on the fireplace wall. If not, I can commission a painting to hang above the fireplace or above the arch opposite where you dine. No matter the season you will see summer. If I had coins, I would make it a gift."

"That you thought it might please me is gift enough, dear Grazia. I prefer the painting. When I am too old to travel to the mountains, I can hang it in my room."

I raised my glass in the salute, "May that day never come," I said and sipped my wine.

"That day will come, my dear. The way of the world. My only regrets are losing Michielo and my Francesca."

I spoke the traditional response. "May we meet them in Heaven." We drank in silence.

Tuesday I supervised the staff removing draperies and rods and all wall decorations. They also washed walls. Wednesday morning, I was ready. As I had requested of Papa, seamstresses and upholsterers arrived after Mass. After examining their swatches and bolts, I informed which house would provide curtains for the salon and which for the hall. I shocked the seamstresses that I wanted them hung from the ceiling to the floor. I explained such height makes the rooms look grander.

They were even more surprised when I requested each window have a panel of the almost sheer white cloth with the traceries in pale beige one house had brought as a sample. *Looks like a large lacy pattern.* "The panels will let in light, but obscure what is inside. I like privacy." *No neighbors may gawk at us, but I will see them hidden behind the lacy pattern.*

I left the swatches of fabrics for the plasterers to match in the dining room, the salon, and the hall. The upholstery men agreed to compromise; one shop took the sofas, the other the chairs. When the workmen arrived, I showed their leader Pietro swatches of curtain fabrics the painters had to match.

The long hall has but one window at each end and needs to be light. I chose white linen drapes. *The dining room will be a warm blue so pale, it is barely there, like the sky during dawn.* Pietro informed me changing the deep gold walls in the salon to a warm cream would require two coats of white plaster, perhaps three, before painting two coats. We decided to put the paint in the plaster to cover the old color. Pietro set the men to work hauling ladders, patching holes, and covering the wood floors with sailcloth. The men left before cena.

We dined at the small table in the hall on chairs from the kitchen. "Papa, on Saturday when you pay Pietro for this week's work, I would like to give each man a bottle of wine."

"Is not their pay enough?"

"I want to set an example of rewarding good men who work hard. It does not have to be the best bottle or the worst, just a good one. A personal 'grazie' from the woman of the house." I smiled. "The next time we want work done we will not need the word of a higher ranked. They will come because we give honest pay and are generous with our thanks."

Papa looked at Lucietta. "Follow your mama's thinking. What is it?"

"Be good to workers because you will get more and better work from them."

"And because…?"

"It is the right thing to do?"

"Brava!"

"Mama, are you also giving them wine because you followed everyone around all day, supervising and ordering? I stood on the stairs and heard you. You inspected every hole to be sure the wall was smooth. You even had a patch of color laid on the walls to be sure you approved before they could paint."

"Their work must please us for a decade or more. We do not want to walk into a room several times a day and hate the color each time. Remember that."

"Si, Mama. I remember everything you tell me."

I sat back and asked, "Where are you in your behaviors?"

Lucietta straightened and smiled. "I have completed being polite, using proper manners, and doing my best in my lessons. I am three days from completing stitchery." She made a face and sighed. "Some stitches challenge me, which may make me take longer than expected."

"The workmen leave at noon on Saturdays. After pranzo, I will sit with you, and we will sew together."

"Gracie, Mama. May I know what I earn next?"

"You will choose your bedding, the fabrics of your summer and winter coverlets, hang pictures, and choose items for your dressing table from your mother's belongings. I will add what I want you to have, but that will be a surprise."

"What happens after I do all four and am obedient, too?"

"You leave the nursery and move into the big girls' room."

"Will Nurse move with me?"

"She will until we need her in the nursery. Then Papa will find you a maid of your own." *Let her move in before she learns she must share it with her younger sisters. My Lord, per favore, may she have at least one.* "Lucietta, I think Nonno wants to go to his office. I will join you soon in the nursery."

In Papa's office I broached a delicate subject. "Papa, I see almost nothing of your beloved Francesca in the furnishings and decorations. Have you anything you would like me to return into our home?"

Papa's slow grin showed me my question pleased him. "In the trunk at the foot of my bed I have several pillows she sewed. Also the draperies that had hung in the dining room. They are still good and will complement the color you chose for the room. I have other things as well."

"Might we look at them together and choose what to return to their rightful places? I stopped because Papa's eyes were becoming moist. We stood. Papa proudly showed what he had saved from Lucia's decorating. *I will return Francesca's blue brocade curtains to the dining room and her pillows to the salon.* I measured their length, hugged Papa hard and closed the door behind myself. *I love you, Papa. Anything for you.*

In the hall I turned to the nursery to bid my daughter buone notte. I returned to my room to write a note to the seamstresses that I need another lacy panel for the former dining room curtains and remembered to include its shorter length. *I will have Tomasso send the note in the morning in the morning.* Garon readied me for bed and I bid her buone notte.

Spring

"The most beautiful springs
are those that come
after the most horrible winters!"

—Mehmet Mural Ildan

51

March 18

By noon, the workers had finished the second coats in the dining room and the salon and the first in the hall. Papa paid the men, and I distributed the wine after giving two bottles to Pietro. Our staff cleaned the room, uncovered the dining table, and brought up kitchen chairs. As we enjoyed supper, I smelled the fresh paint and admired the color as the candles flickered. Lucietta bid us buone notte, and Nurse escorted her upstairs.

"Grazia, the painter will arrive Monday to see the room and my sketch."

"I hope he will have the work painted, framed and hung before Easter."

"Better it be done well than quickly."

I nodded and emptied my goblet.

Rather than ask what I already know, I said what is true. "Lucietta is Pontenuevo's granddaughter." He nodded. "How could he hate Antonio?"

"After Lucia birthed Lucietta, she bled to death. Horrible.

Antonio was devastated. Pontenuevo had loved her so much he had spoiled her. She had met Antonio during Carnevale, and they fell in love. Ponenuevo tried to convince her to marry among their rank, but she vowed she would marry no other. He gave in to her but he never liked us. He blames Antonio for Lucia's death and vowed to destroy Antonio and me."

"I had thought we might invite him to spend time with Lucietta to learn to love her as we do. Now I fear him."

"Well you should. At all costs, we keep him away from our little girl. Even when she is an adult. He will never again enter this house. When she leaves the house, we double the guards."

"Does the household know about this?"

"Oh, yes. Everyone knows about Pontenuevo. I permit no stranger entry. We accept no gifts unless the giver is trusted by me and hands them to me. We change vendors often; all know what will happen to them if anyone in our household sickens or dies because of their products. Pietro swore to me his men had been with him for a long time and that he trusts them. You were too busy to notice. While the workers are here, one guard stands at the top of the stairs and another before the nursery door. If any had attempted to reach the second floor, he would have died."

I tried to hide my surprise by pouring myself a half-glass of wine and drinking it. I put down my goblet. "Pontenuevo is dead to me. Not even the doxe could convince me otherwise." We stood and hugged. Papa followed and watched me as I climbed the stairs to see Lucietta.

On the way to Mass, Sunday's sun hid behind grey clouds, and gusts blew our capes around our legs. I cared not because the asparagus I had ordered from the South had arrived yesterday afternoon.

I had planned several courses for both pranzo and cena to celebrate the first day of spring.

After pranzo, I napped, but I awoke with a start and thought of him. *What are you doing? Thinking?* I stretched and re-curled myself beneath my warm coverings. *Lent is almost half over. Should I write a note? No. He left me not I him. At least not physically. I have no power to make him return. From the farm he could pass through the Veneto, captain one of his ships and sail south. Would he stop at Bari, or would he brave the Mediterranean and challenge the Ottomans? I fretted. Doing that could get him killed. Asking Papa would only worry him. Do nothing. Say nothing.*

I rolled over and peeked at the closed door between our rooms. *Grazie, Papa, for my need to be doing something productive. You understand why I want the garish colors and bright fabrics gone.* I sat up. *Thoughtless Lucia, you ordered silk draperies without lining them. Sun damaged, they shredded as they came down. Such an expense to lose.*

As I left my bed, I affirmed my choosing to save what I could for a few pillows. *Diminish her presence but not erase it. I smiled. Let Lucietta be our reminder; she is the best of both of them. Lively and loving, yet strong willed, clever and determined.* I summoned Garon and sent for my daughter. We knelt and prayed the rosary for her Papa's wellbeing and safe return home. Lucietta chatted about the contents of her new room as we walked hand in hand to cena.

That night, after I had dressed for sleep, I entered his room and stared. *Why I am thinking of his bed? My thoughts ramble between hating my situation so much I want him to stay away and wanting him to return to be only with me. Nights I toss and turn. One time I am glad his smell is gone from my pillows and another time I miss it. My emotions confuse me. What do I want? Really want?* Stepping backward,

I left and closed the door. I stared at my empty bed. *A mess I cannot fix.* At my dressing table I started brushing my hair to calm me. My thoughts continued to shift between the worst and best outcomes for me. I sat at my table for hours.

By midweek, Pietro showed me he had not completely covered the gold in the salon walls.

"Might another coat be enough?"

"I am hoping so, but I fear not. Darker, older colors often bleed through. You chose a suitable color because cream has just a hint of yellow, which may still influence your color. I think you need four coats."

"I know it is best to add a coat each day, so the new coat sticks to the former one. Let us decide after each coat what needs to be done."

By Saturday noon the salon wore its final coat of paint and the pale cream matched the swatch. Papa paid the men in coins and I in wine. In the middle of the room, I turned a slow circle. *Two weeks to Palm Sunday. We still have much to do.*

Tuesday while working at my desk, I froze when my door creaked open. Garon tiptoed to the center of my room. At my "Garon, what are you about?" she shrieked and threw up her hands.

"Face me." I gazed into her eyes. "You need no longer fear. The workmen are gone. The messes are gone. You had been acting frightened, worried and upset. Why? The worst work is over." I remembered to ask, "Why are you tiptoeing into my room? Has a third disaster struck?"

Garon covered her face and burst into tears. I let her cry for several minutes. "Garon! Look at me! What has happened?"

Still weeping into her hands she mumbled, "I am the third disaster. I do not know how to stop."

Setting my quill next to the accounts book, I lay my hands on my lap. "What have you done?"

Garon swayed forward and back. *Do not faint, per favore.* She dragged her sleeve across her eyes and clutch her hands to her breasts.

"I met a woman. She was friendly and asked about my life and my work. I told her only good things each time she asked about you. How beautiful you are! How kind. She complimented me on my fine position. After a time, she told me what others said about you. I defended you. Truly, I did, Signora."

"What happened next?" Still looking away from me Garon shrugged.

I guessed, "Gossip" and she nodded. What about?"

"His mistress, their sons. I knew before you did, but I said nothing."

"That was wise of you. I would not have wanted to learn about them from you."

Were you spying? What does this woman want? "Did she ask you to tell her about our household?" At her nod, I added, "Does she want you to spy on us?" Another nod. "Why did you not send her away?"

"I had told her how I came here. She said you would dismiss me if you knew. She threatened to tell you unless I spied for her. She ordered me to convince you to run away. I told her you promised your signor you would be here when he returned. She does not care." Garon wailed, "If I do not convince you to run away, she said she will have me killed!"

I stood and called out the door. "Someone come to me at once!"

Sabina's daughter Zanetta appeared.

"Fetch Signor Delatesta. Tell him it is an emergency." I turned and saw a yellow puddle at Garon's feet. I closed the door. "Do not leave this room. Clean up your mess and yourself before Signor arrives." Arms crossed over my chest, I watched her scurry about and then disappear behind my dressing screen.

The door flew open. "Daughter are you all right?"

"I am fine Papa. I have information about which you must decide." I gestured. "Please take this chair. I will fetch our speaker." Head in her hands, Garon was sitting on the vaso di orinale stool. I took her elbow, lifted and said, "Tell the truth. He will be fair." I walked her to Papa. "Tell Signor Delatesta everything from the moment you met this woman to the last thing you told me."

Eyes closed, Garon swayed as she talked. She shared every time they had met, every detail of conversation, every threat. As Garon spoke, Papa glanced my way. I shrugged to show him my ignorance. He raised his brows to me before he turned back and continued listening.

When Garon stopped, she opened fear-filled eyes and dried them and her cheeks. In an even voice, Papa asked, "Garon, when do you meet?"

"At Mass. I attend the dawn service to be here when Signora wakes. She stands in front of me and whispers, 'Report.'"

"Where are our women?"

"They stand in front of me. She slips between us."

"What hold has she on you?"

"In Provence I ran away from Madame. She pinched and hurt me and was awful to me. I could never please her, no matter how hard I tried. After I ran away, I lied to the agent that I was free to be hired. My father had sold me to Madame; I was her slave. She threatened to tell you. Said you would return me."

"I would never return a slave, no matter how you gained your freedom."

I saw Garon's tears spill again.

"When I hired you, you promised to be loyal to this house. You have broken your promise."

"S'il vous plaît, Signor, do not return me to Madame. She will be so angry she will burn me again." Garon pulled her garment off her left shoulder and showed us two scars.

Papa asked me, "Will you keep her?"

"Garon, swear a holy oath to God you will never tattle to this woman again nor to anyone. Swear you will be loyal to this household, never sneak about listening and never share what you hear."

"I swear to God I will be loyal, Signora, Signor. I swear, no sneaking about, no sharing. Not even with other staff. As God is my witness!"

"Papa, with your permission, I will keep her." I turned to Garon. "Attend Mass with the staff and stand among the women. If this gossip seeker speaks to you, say, 'I stand with my house. They know everything. If you hurt me, the Delatestas will punish you. Never speak to me again.' Repeat what I just said." After she did, I commanded, "Say it again. This time in a strong, proud voice." She did so. "Signor Delatesta, we await your decision."

Papa approached Garon, who dropped her head and trembled. Standing close to her, he threatened, "Make this mistake again, and we will do worse than throw you out." He spun on his heel and left.

Again, Garon burst into tears. *She is only a year older than I and she is as innocent of the world as I. Be kind.* I drew her into my arms and let her cry against my shoulder.

Cried out at last, Garon pulled away. She looked at my chest. "Merci. Merci bien. Mercie, avec tout mon coeur. Madame, I will be faithful all my life."

With all her heart. She means it. "I know you will. Now tell me. How did you know I had promised my husband I would be here when he returns?"

Garon heaved a sigh. "When you two are in this room, I sneak into his room and hear you through the opened door. I swear I will do it no more."

"No, you will not." I turned away and then back. "Garon, if you ever marry, you will understand why it is so important for a husband and wife to be alone."

"Oui, Madame."

"Garon, you are now skilled enough in Venetian. Dispense with 'Madame.' Use Venetian and say 'Si Signora.'"

"Si, Signora Delatesta."

After cena I dismissed Lucietta and asked Papa, "This woman who wants gossip. Does she work for Lucia's father?"

"No, she is a rumor monger. Sells what she learns. To him and others. That she has lost her source will upset her and displease him."

"Why would the gossip monger advise her to convince me to run away?"

"If that was Pontenuevo's doing, your leaving would prevent Antonio from marrying again and never having an heir."

I shook my head and decided. "If he is that unhappy and vengeful, never again will he see Lucietta. To make us suffer, I, too, fear what he might do to her." I paused. "Does that woman work with men who do the same?"

"Yes, but our men refused them years ago, and her agents no longer bother them. I spoke to our women; they will protect Garon."

They are good people. They will spy on her and tell us if she fails.

52

Palm Sunday

April 9

After Mass we placed palms in every room to remind us of Jesus's journey into Jerusalem. We feasted as usual, napped as usual and enjoyed the gentle warmth of the late afternoon sun during our garden walks. Lucietta bubbled about vegetables peaking from the dirt, the nascent blooms beside the walkways, bird sounds and the breeze. She reported her plan to have completed her five tasks before the end of April.

At cena Lucietta frowned and asked, "Nonno, might Papa be home for Easter? Do you not think Papa should be home for Easter?"

"Papa knows the date. I have not heard from him so I cannot answer you." He glanced my way and finished with "Papa has many duties and he must attend to them. We will wait and hope to see him soon."

Nodding agreement, I looked away and picked up my wineglass to hide my mouth. As I sipped, I watched the coming sunset light the drapery edges and pool on the edge of the newly cleaned rug under the table. "The furniture will return Tuesday morning. We will be ready for Easter." Tired, I excused myself, and took to my bed.

Monday I tallied my accounts before writing the menu for Easter. After pranzo I met the staff in the kitchen and handed my sheet to Rosa. I reminded everyone of the upholsterers' arrival. "I expect you to start on your floor and clean all the way to the entrance. After the men have placed everything as I desire and Signor pays them, I expect you to re-clean the primo floor and finish at our entry door. Everything must gleam."

"Si, Signora. I promise it will," affirmed Sabina.

At bedtime I stared at the door between our rooms. *Why not? I opened the door, lifted* Antonio's *covering and dabbled a drop of my perfume under his pillow before I remade his bed.* Closing the door behind me, I returned the bottle to my dressing table. *When his pillow becomes too warm, he flips it. He will smell my perfume and remember I am on the other side of the door. Perhaps he will miss me.*

Early in the morning our sofas and chairs arrived. After the men had left, the staff brought out the stored items. I supervised the hanging of pictures, the laying of rugs and the placing of statues, vases and other items where I pointed. More tired than I expected, I plopped into my chair wishing cena was chicken or beef. *Five more days of fish; then none except on the required Fridays. For weeks. Until Papa asks for it.*

Halfway through dinner, I felt myself lose control. I jumped up to avoid staining the newly upholstered chair, excused myself and rushed to my room. By the time Garon arrived, I had pro-tected myself, doffed my clothes and lay in bed in my camicia da notte. Garon put away my shoes and vestito before she took away my underskirt to be washed. My second moon cycle had begun; I counted it would be over after Easter Sunday. *If he returns home, do I want him in my bed? How long could I delay him?* I banished my thoughts, crawled deeper under the coverings and closed my eyes.

Mass on Maundy Thursday had been long. During Mass the priests had blessed both holy oils for the baptism of new Christians on Easter night and all the Church's oils for the coming year. After colazione Papa dismissed Lucietta to her lessons before he escorted me to the salon, bade me wait and left the house. I picked up my pamphlet and looked at the drawings of fashions in Paris before picking up my latest book.

An hour later Tomaso arrived. "Signor wishes to see you in his office."

"Has Signor Antonio returned?" He did not answer and left. I closed the office door behind me. Papa was sitting at his desk with something under his right forearm. His flat expression gave me no hints. I sat on the edge of the chair opposite him.

"Antonio asked that I hand you documents. This is the first." Papa lifted his hand, and I spotted a small square. He extended his hand.

I unfolded it and read, Grazia, I wrote you a letter of my love for you. Per favore, I beg you to read it. Antonio. My eyes filled, but I looked up and nodded.

Papa opened his center desk drawn and took out another square. "He instructed you read this first."

Eyes closed, I held the letter to my heart. *Small but vital. May I feel his heart in his words.* I cracked Il Conto's wax seal and unfolded the sheet.

The neat handwriting was not Antonio's. I dropped my eyes to the bottom before I read:

Dearest Sister,

Much to say and little space, so I will be direct. Antonio first went to Stefano. Since Antonio left you, he came here often, left, and returned.

He and my husband have been in secret conferences. I also know Antonio has been to Venezia several times without seeing Papa or you. Antonio is in great distress. Drinking too much and walking the floor all night. Whatever he has decided has been done, though I know not what. Lucia's death devastated Antonio; now he guards his heart.

Too much, I think. I know you care for him. I believe my brother cares for you. Antonio asked me how to show a woman he loves her.

My answer: Words can be lies. Do not say. Your actions reveal your heart. Act. My advice to you. Be careful what you say and do. Whether you two come together and are happy depends on your decisions, words, and actions. Unfair, I know, but Antonio is more fragile than you realize.

I am your sister who loves you.

Violetta

Under her signature, I read tiny letters.

Antonio forced me to let him read this before I sealed it.
He vowed he would send this with the rest.

I reread the note and lay it on my lap. I dried my eyes with my sleeve. "Violetta wrote 'the rest.' What rest?"

Papa removed several sheets from his top drawer, closed it and handed them to me. I took the papers with two fingers and held them at arm's length as if the black marks were acid to burn me. *Antonio's writing but addressed to Papa. Do I want to know?* I looked up.

"I hope you will be pleased, daughter. He worked hard to set things aright for all of you." When I moved not, Papa added, "He instructed me to stay with you while you read."

My future is in these words. Dear God, Jesus, and the Virgin Mary, give me strength. I took the sheets in both hands.

Papa,

After you and Grazia read this, burn these pages to protect us. This is the only written proof of what I have done.

Maricella and her sons now live in Padova in a four-bedroom house. Her supposed late husband's supposed family bought it for her. She will rent two rooms to house and feed four students attending the university. Walls surround the back, and the yard has room for a large garden. If she is careful, she will have enough income to live well.

She also has all the documents she needs. A new baptism certificate. Her marriage and her late husband's death certificates. I had him die when the Ottomans sank the Mediterranean Zephyr. The boys each have baptism certificates with her and his names listed as their parents. They count her a widow, a respectable position. She lives in a respectable part of town and has a respectable income common in a town with a university. She already has two students in residence.

In addition she has a letter from the company who owned the Zephyr informing her of the money owed her at his death. Her late husband's family lawyer is holding it for her, will manage it on her behalf and will report to the family quarterly. This sum should enable her to educate her sons or to send them into an apprenticeship. I have done this for them and for us.

I vow never to visit Padova, to seek neither her nor her sons. I vow to pass around Padova on our way to our farms or on visits to Il Conto and Violetta.

Grazia, I was wrong. You do know how to be a wife, a good one. You demanded I be honest with you and to behave with honor. You insisted I take responsibility for the innocents I brought into the world. You expected the best of me even when I behaved badly toward you. You left me free to decide what to do.

I choose you. I want you back. Not a parallel existence of distant, polite conversations from a man trying to live two lives. I want one life with you. I desire our lives joined in every way. I am your faithful husband now and forever.

You fill my mind, My heart hungers for your love. Per favore, Grazia, be my wife again.

Your Antonio

Papa, after Grazia reads this, please ask her — Does she want me? If not, I will captain a ship and live on board. If she wants me, you know how to reach me.

My eyes spilled as I re-read the missive. I clutched the pages to my breast as I rocked back and forth. "He set sent them away."

"He did more than that. Antonio provided the documents she needs. No matter what anyone suspects, she has proofs she is an honorable widow, and her children are legitimate. She will tell them their father died at sea; they are too young to know differently. Her husband's family purchased her house; it is they who gave control of the money to invest to a lawyer. It is they who will supervise her life. The family who helped construct and will verify her story is in our debt. They claim her and the boys and will do so to anyone who asks. Antonio well paid someone to produce her documents."

"He kept them in the Veneto region. He could still see them."

Papa shook his head. "If he does, all will come apart and people will throw his sons out of society. Remember, she only speaks Venetian. In another region, she would not understand or speak as they do. That region's citizens would find her out, and his efforts would be destroyed."

I recalled Papa's other words. "He had the papers made." At Papa's nod I added, "I told him to provide for them, give them a good life. He did as I had asked." I reread his letter. I lifted the pages and looked in my lap at Violetta's words. Your actions will reveal your heart. Be careful what you say and do.

"Is there anything else I need to know?"

"Only what your heart tells you."

I looked at the book-filled shelves but saw them not. *I want a family. This family. I want a husband—him. Children—his. I want him to look at me the way he did that day we waited for the doxe to interview us. From what Violetta wrote, I know for him to love me, he first needs to see mine. Dare I love him again?* I asked my heart and held my breath.

In my mind heard, *Choose to try.* I looked at Antonio's signature. "Do you have a scissors?" Papa opened a drawer and handed it to me. He watched me cut out Antonio's signature and tuck the slip over my heart. In a firm tone I said, "I want my husband back. Per favore, please ask Antonio to come home. Where is he?"

"In town. Awaiting word."

Papa did not move. Again the tears came; they coursed down my cheeks. I recovered and wiped my face again. After standing and handing Papa both letters I asked, "May I watch them burn?"

Papa laid the parchments on the grate, touched a candle to a corner, and gently blew until flames rose. Poker in hand he stood beside me and stirred as black bits fell through the grate onto the cold ashes below.

53

Papa walked me to the salon and bade me to sit. He said, "I will be in my room; the servants have their instructions. You two will have this floor to yourselves until you ring the servant bell. I will bring Lucietta down with me."

Papa walked to the front window, pushed back the lacy panel, and waved back and forth. As he turned to depart, I stood, hugged him hard and kissed his cheek. "Papa, did you and your Francesca ever become so divided you had to restart your marriage?"

"More than once." He chuckled. "My Francesca was a strong-willed woman. Yet she said I was the stubborn one. You two are as strong willed as we had been. If you truly love, you can come together again."

"Gracie mille, Papa. I love you." Papa kissed my forehead, patted my cheek and left.

Standing at the window where Papa had signaled, I recognized the form of the man looking up as a gondolier rowed to our dock. I jumped back from the window panel. *Did he see me? Stand? Sit? Which chair? Which sofa? Should I speak? To say what? Volante said actions.* When the front door closed, I almost did not hear the latch click. I stopped in the middle of the room and faced the hall. Antonio stepped into the archway and froze. *Thinner, with the drooped eyelids of an exhausted man. Hands clenching then unclenching. Do something or he could flee.*

I smiled, lifted my arms and took one step forward. "Welcome home, Antonio." He came to me. I stood on my tiptoes and flung my arms around his neck. He threw his arms about me and pulled me so close my breathing became pants for air. Into his ear I whispered, "I missed you." I kissed his cheek and left my lips against his skin. He made a strangled sound against my shoulder and hugged me even more tightly. "Antonio, I cannot breathe! You must give me a little space."

Antonio loosed his grip, but he kept his face from me. He kissed my shoulder and then a path up my neck. Antonio rasped, "Mi dispiace. Tante, tante dispiace."

Forgive his fault. Forgive all his faults and start again. "I am glad you returned to me."

Antonio pulled back to see if my face matched my words. Smiling I kissed him on the mouth and felt his confusion, then gratitude, then the full measure of his passion. *Dio mio, never kissed like this! Have I all of him now?* I gave him all of myself. My lips burned. My heart thundered. When my womanhood throbbed, I remembered.

When I pulled back and struggled to escape, he abruptly released me. "Oh Antonio, I forgot. I am in mestruazoni. I am unclean." I hoped he would hear my regret. "You must not touch me."

He shrugged. "Priests. What do they know of marriage? What a man and woman mean to each other." He smirked. "Just as easy to confess more kisses than only one." He lifted my hands and kissed the back of each. He turned them over and planted a moist kiss and a lick in my right my palm. He kissed the inside of my wrist; I locked my knees to remain standing. By the time he finished with my left, I wanted to pull him to my bed. Nay. Lay with him right there on the salon floor. Only that I was a mess stopped me. I pulled back. "You are a devil!"

"Temptress! Only a taste. I hate waiting."

"As do I!" I mirrored his expression. We laughed together for the first time in so long I could not recall when last we had. I stepped back and walked a half circle around him. He matched me in our silent dance. Having exchanged places, I curtsied and said, "Buone giorno, Antonio."

He bowed. "Buone giorno, Grazia." He gestured; I sat. Antonio looked at the floor. I heard him inhale a deep breath before he turned.

Is the fear in his eyes reflected in mine? We are a sorry pair. Who will speak first? Before I could decide, Antonio approached and knelt. Hands together in prayer, he looked up at me. I held my breath.

"As God is my witness, with all the archangels, angels and saints in heaven beside Him watching me, I, Antonio Delatesta, vow to be faithful to you, my honorable and faithful wife, Grazia Delatesta, until my death."

I breathed.

"Grazia, no matter where I go, what I do, or whom I see, I will keep my vow. You need never worry or fear otherwise. May God strike me dead or punish me in the most horrible ways if I prove faithless to you and my vow to Him."

I looked into his eyes. *He means it. He means it!* I un-clutched my hands. "I believe you. Before God and all the others, I vow to care for you, and to remain faithful until my death. Let this be our second marriage ceremony. Our private one." I waited. When his face relaxed and moved to smile, I said, "We are husband and wife again." I added, "If you can wait a few more days. Monday, Tuesday at the latest."

"I count the days."

"I must attend to myself upstairs. Shall I send down Lucietta? She is most eager to see you." At his nod I reached for the bell on the table and left.

I met Papa and Lucietta on the stairs and winked at our daughter. At her "Papa?" I nodded. She flew away, and I heard, "Papa! Papa!" as Lucietta jumped the last two steps. Tears filling my eyes; I patted Papa's arm as we passed. I did not let myself cry until I had closed my door. I took care of myself, washed and dried myself. I wet a cloth and dabbed my eyes. I lifted the stopper of my perfume bottle and touched under each ear and at each wrist.

At the salon entrance I saw Lucietta clinging to her father as she sat on his lap. Behind me Tomaso announced pranzo. I took Papa's arm so Lucietta could have her father's attention.

As we dined Antonio reported the Po had flooded as usual, and of having had to delay planting some fields. He stated Stefano thought the corn would do well after the ground had dried. To me he explained that, at first, corn from the new world was so valuable only the very rich could afford it. "That the ranked paid so much for the luxury crop was to our advantage." Antonio finished with, "Our ancestor was wise to spend so much for the seed. He cultivated it two years before selling the first bit. These days corn is served in almost every worker's home almost every colazione. We bought more farmland; now our corn earns us more zecchini than the rest of our grains combined."

While Antonio escorted Lucietta to the nursery for the night, I walked into the salon and stood before the Canaletto. *Did he see that my relief at his coming home is real? Even though I had kept Lucietta between us? Because I must keep him at a distance until the priest blesses me? I kept my face pleasant and conversation light. Does he think I have forgiven him? Have I?* I heard his steps stop behind me.

"Our daughter is in bed, and Papa is in his office."

I said nothing.

"Papa was wise to buy that before Canaletto left for Roma. After he delivered works to the Prince of Liechtenstein last year he became famous. I hesitate to guess what Stefano Conti of Lucca is paying Canaletto for his next works."

His talk is his effort to re-engage with me. I relented. "The view from the lagoon of Piazza San Marco and the doxe's palace. When I look at it, I remember the whole day."

"A good day."

"Indeed." *Let him lead. See where his mind is.*

"As I entered, I recognized your hand. Door re-stained and nailheads polished. Scrubbed steps and balusters repainted white. They painted the posts and the hand rail gray, not white."

"Less likely to show nicks and dirty hands; makes the balusters seem brighter." *Very well. Talk about my changes.* I turned to him. "What do you think of this room?"

"The paintings and hangings seem more important against the neutral wall. What happened to the striped drapes?"

"Unlined, the edges had turned brittle from sunlight and

shredded when we removed them to plaster. I could not save them, so I had a few pillows made of what remained." *Say nothing of how much I wanted her decorating gone.* "Lined drapes will last much longer." At his nod, I added, "From outside, the white panel between the drapes gives us more privacy."

"Mama's cushions are back, as is her favorite woolen shawl lain across her favorite chair. I also see the cushion you sewed while we awaited news from the Council. Two from the drapes Lucia chose. An excellent combination."

Antonio picked up the candelabra and requested we tour the rest of the floor. As we strolled I told him my reasons for every choice, every change of placement of furniture and decoration. He said nothing until we ended in the dining room, gazing at the painting above the entry arch.

"The view is even more beautiful. I will show it to you when we travel there in four months."

"I look forward to it." He moved; I followed. When Antonio stopped at the base of the steps, I turned to face him. *What is he about?*

"Grazia, I never courted you before we wed. We have these days together yet apart. Will you let me court you now?" I nodded. "Goldini has written a new comedy. After your confinement would you like to attend?"

"As you wish." When I saw him start to frown, I added, "Grazie tante for thinking of it."

He stared at me.

What will be your next attempt to regain my favor?

"Lovely lady, I am grateful you are kind. I will drift to sleep, recalling how beautiful you are and of your many accomplishments.

Eager to spend the day with you, I will rise with joy in my heart and wings on my feet. Know I will wake before you and will be waiting for you here. Buone notte, beautiful Grazia." He bowed and looked at me with hopeful eyes.

"If your words are courting, I want more." I curtsied and smiled back. "Buone notte, Antonio." I took the steps alone. In my room I asked, "Garon, what is courting?"

"A lovely time between meeting and marriage. He sends you flowers and writes you letters of his love and admiration. Sometimes poetry too. He tells you how beautiful you are, how accomplished and how much he desires you to be his. He promises you a good life, his undying devotion, and whatever you desire. Sometimes some of it is true."

"He lies?"

"Not really," she sighed. "He imagines himself the perfect husband for you, but real life intrudes and none of us is perfect." As she prepared me for bed, she added, "We French women do it best. He implores; we ignore. He pleads; we shrug. He begs; we consider. If he continues and we find him acceptable, we let him win us. But slowly. I do not know how you Venetians court, but French women no matter their rank are slow and careful. Once we wed, we are stuck with him for life. As you already are."

As I already am. I want to be much more than stuck. Pray it will be so. I crawled into bed. After Garon had left, I considered. *He praised me for what I do for him. Tried to give him an heir. Keep his house. Raise his daughter. Perhaps he wants to live a more pleasant life with me. He is trying now because he did not love me then. Perhaps he is trying to convince himself he might love me now. Garon is right. I know what I want. Let him earn me, but at my pace. When I must relent my body, I will be pleasant, even sweet, but not give my heart. Not speak the words until he does, and I believe he means them.* I rolled to my side and slept.

54

Easter

April 16

Friday and Saturday started with a Mass for everyone but me. All day we fasted. After the evening service we dined on fish, vegetables and bread. Because these days were the most important of the year, at home we prayed silently, reflected on the sermons and stayed apart from each other.

Easter, a joyous celebration of our faith, began with a procession to High Mass. We wore new clothes that symbolize a new year of following the Christ. After a sumptuous colazione, Antonio and I walked in the garden side by side but not touching. I stopped and lifted my face into the sun's warmth and heard Antonio's smile in his words.

"You are a flower raising your face to the sun for warmth. You are my sun, and I seek the warmth of your smile on me."

Too much and awkward, but he is trying. I looked his way.

"I know. A poor effort. I am no poet, no Dante Alighieri. I lack the skill for pretty phrases."

"Not words, but deeds."

"What deed would please you?"

"Honesty."

I watched him look away and keep his face from me. "Ask."

"Not on a holy day. I hear nothing of the outside world, but I suspect problems. Tomorrow I want to sit with you and Papa and learn the true state of our affairs. Business problems, losses, debts, all of it. What about the farm and Stefano? I cannot help if I do not know what we face."

"Not on a holy day."

"I have seen Papa's expression when he returns home. Worry, concern, even fear. I overheard your voices through the office door. More sounds of anxiety and worry. The good sisters taught me economy, conserving and reusing. I know more about those things than do you; I can be more help than you think. Will you arrange it with Papa?" He nodded. "Let us walk through the vegetable garden so I can show you what I ordered planted."

Monday, I slept while everyone else attended Mass. Garon arrived to dress me. Colazione was a poached egg on a fire-toasted slice of bread. Papa and Antonio drink caffe and I water.

"I want to stay with Papa," said Lucietta after she had finished eating. "Mama, you had him all day yesterday. Today is my turn."

I cocked my head at her. "What is this week's word?"

Lucietta glowered at me, turned away and responded in a flat voice. "Obedience." She added, "When do I get what I want?"

"When you have earned it. Have you earned it?"

She huffed a "No."

"What do you need to do to earn a coin today?"

"Be obedient," Lucietta replied in a childish sing-song.

"When does it start?"

"When I open my eyes."

"Earn a coin today or not. Your choice." Lucietta looked to her father for support. I did not need to glance his way; I saw his answer in her face.

Lucietta placed her napkin beside her plate, stood and pushed her chair toward the table. "Nonno, Papa, Mama, per favore, excuse me. I must go to my lessons." She departed with the measured steps of a young lady.

"Grazia, is that her last lesson?" At my nod Antonio added, "Her hardest."

"She is determined to have completed all five tasks by the end of the month. You just helped her. That she knows I have your support will make this easier on all of us."

"Is her reward ready?"

"Si. Afterward I want her to be so secure in her new behaviors that she thinks of them as normal, not ones that need prodding and rewards. After I think her ready, there is a further reward if she wants to win it. To earn an even more important gift than her own room, she must do all five tasks every day for thirty days in a row. If she misses a day, she starts again at Day One."

"What could that be?"

"Will you keep my secret? Not even a hint?" At his vow to remain silent, I whispered "Hems to her ankles."

Seeing his eyes pop pleases me. "Even if she takes a year to earn it, she will be early by over two years."

Papa asked Tomaso to take a fresh caffe and water to his office.

After Papa rose, Antonio and I followed. Antonio closed the world against our private matters. "It is with Stefano and his family we must begin."

Antonio reported Stefano had caught Claudia choking Miro. He beat her. He was going to send her to a convent school with no contact from her family. Stefano told Antonio he had planned to have Claudia remain there for as many years as it took for her to reform. She could not return until her brothers were old enough to defend themselves against her. Polonia threatened to go into the convent with Claudia. Stefano took the boys to the next farm for their safety and a fire started.

The farm manager ran to the house to see Polonia in the doorway on fire and screaming. They grabbed Claudia to keep her from running to her mother. Before they could beat out the flames, Polonia burned to death. Their priest declared the fire and Polonia's death accidental and buried her in holy ground.

I saw Antonio's pain and was too afraid to see Papa's face. I waited. Antonio looked away. "He found the melted money chest in the ashes, but the coins and Polonia's clothes were in a satchel outside the house. A second satchel held Claudia's clothes and some valuables."

Antonio continued, "Stefano thinks Polonia set the house aflame. It burned too hot to be an accident. He thinks she poured oil in the rooms. When Polonia dropped a candle on the oil, some may have landed on her clothes and flamed. Claudia is in shock; she does not speak, will not answer and stares at nothing. Their priest took Claudia to a nearby convent in hope the sisters can help her. Stefano is a broken man. Blames himself."

Polonia *will be a long time in Purgatory; she needs my prayers.* "I will pray for the repose of her soul every day of my life." I mouthed "I am so sorry, Papa" and watched him close his eyes.

Antonio repeated my words. We sat in silence until Papa was ready to speak. They admitted our business situation is in disarray. The Ottomans are sinking any ship that attempts the Mediterranean. With no imports or exports north of Bari, our former trade in luxury goods and rare spices is arriving on the continent by overland routes. Venezia and the Veneto region are closed to foreign trade.

"Papa, Antonio, I spoke with Rosa. The price of sugar doubled after the war and has doubled again since. I know sweetening wines, cafe, te' and foods is part of demonstrating wealth, but we can no longer afford it. I have instructed Rosa sugar and dolce to be reserved for Easter, Christmas, Epiphany." Before they objected, I added, "We can conserve coins by omitting colaziones of breads, sweet rolls and sugar in our drink." *Try one more time.* "If you hunger, we could eat polenta."

"Never! said Papa and Antonio in unison. "Remember why." announced Papa. "We are far from that. I would rather have just cafe or te' after Mass, eat one main meal at pranzo, and have soup and bread every cena. I will not touch polenta." Antonio nodded his agreement.

Papa just gave me permission. Start that menu in the morning. First remove the sweet rolls, then reduce the breads to one kind, then none. Soups of vegetables in season. If either complains, I will remind them what Papa said.

Papa changed the subject. "Because everyone is vying for any shipping on the Adriatic, our ships sit at port. They are unsalable in the overflowing international market, and we have no way of delivering them to another country without risking them being sunk. What is left of the military is in disarray. Ship building has stopped. With no work many sailors' families are starving. The lagoon and marshes are being overfished and overhunted. Our economy is sinking fast."

We adults ate pranzo in silence and let Lucietta talk of her lessons. Our responses were perfunctory. After we sent her back to her lessons, we left the table for the office.

"We have more advantages than others." As I had expected, my remark surprised them. "May I begin?" At Papa's nod I said, "We are fortunate we are not of the first Ninety-nine, who must continue to pay to maintain the city. Too proud to reveal their losses, they would hide eating polenta for every meal rather than admit they can no long afford their lifestyle."

"I agree," said Antonio.

"Your ancestors were right; never sell land. From the farm we can shift selling crops from our secondary to our primary source of income. Not as lucrative as importing luxury goods but it will sustain us." I looked at Papa. "We need to support Stefano and spend more time with him. He will listen to both of you."

"He asked me to return after Easter. I told him I would," reported Antonio.

"Papa, when you suggested I remodel this floor, I wish you had informed me of our situation. I would not have done so."

"The house needed refurbishing. Spending for it was worth seeing you happy."

"Grazie tante, Papa, but now we can delay no longer; we must economize." I looked at Antonio. "Others' dislike of me is now to our advantage. Papa no longer needs to feed his business associates, and no one wants to visit us or invite us. Our business and social obligations are almost nothing. Tell me how I may help, and I will do it."

"Grazia, I am glad I married you."

"If things continue as they are or get worse, how much do we have? My wardrobe, the doxe's dinner party, the remodeling and now the expenses of restoring the farm. I estimate we have spent half our wealth."

"Not quite half," admitted Papa.

Half! How can he remain so calm? What if we never regain any of it? Half gone could mean losing this house! Speak not. Do not share how frightened I am. Breathe. "How long can we stay in Venezia before we need to close the house and return to the farm?"

"Never!"

"Antonio, I understand your desire to sail and to be profitable again, but it is too dangerous. We must face what is true. Our markets have moved far north of the Veneto. They will not return as long as the Ottomans rule the sea. Perhaps not even then. Wish all you like, but we must live in reality."

Antonio reached for my hands, but I pulled back. He remembered and leaned back as well. "Grazia, Lucia would have understood none of this. She would have continued to spend and drive us into poverty with her demands. If I have not said it before, I say it now. I thank God you are my wife. You see what we need to do. Not what we want."

He sees me! Perhaps he will no longer compare me to his memory of her. Not what he wanted to make of me but who I really am. Perhaps saying it may make it true. "Antonio, I am blessed you are my husband." *There. I said his name again. Had he guessed when I did and I did not? End that now.* "I know you will take good care of our family when we have it."

"We will do it together." When I saw Antonio's promise in his eyes, I showed him mine.

"Finally!"

"Finally what?" asked Antonio without looking away from me.

"You are a pair. Acting as one. You are the head; she is the heart. You two were raised so differently, know such different worlds. I feared you might never come together. Thank God I am alive to see this."

I blushed and did not care Papa saw it. Antonio placed his hand on the arm of my chair as close to my hand as he dared. Continuing to seek the warmth in his eyes, I gazed at his face and did not pull back. I forced myself back into our situation.

"Papa, how long? Months? Perhaps years?"

"Four, maybe five years. If we are careful, if the crops do well, seven, maybe eight." He added, "Maybe longer."

"Long enough for the Spanish to drive the Ottomans back or to sink all their ships," said Antonio.

"Whether or not they do, we will survive," I promised them and myself.

55

April 18

My second cycle ended before bedtime. *Wednesday holds a terrible memory. Dare we start on a Wednesday? Will a new start tomorrow diminish the old memory? I pray so. Tomorrow morning I will wash and ask for the priest's ritual cleansing before Mass. He hinted he will stay until we are together again. Trying to hold him off would be futile.* I went to bed earlier than usual.

Tuesday the priest blessed me before Mass, and Antonio took my arm as we entered the church. The day passed too swiftly for me; my fears overtook my reason. *Would it go well? What can I do to ensure it does? What if it does not?* After I prepared, I opened the door between our bedrooms.

Robed in brown, Antonio walked halfway into my room. He smiled at seeing me wrapped in the same cover over the same camicia di notte as on our marriage night. I sat on the same seat and stared at him in the shadows from candlelight as I had then. "Why is your scent on my pillow?"

"I scented it to punish you for leaving me." I shrugged. Antonio, spoke not as he kept a neutral face. "I know what I want now." I smiled at seeing his brow rise. "I want a second start."

"How?" came his throaty response.

I stood and opened my robe so candle light flickered against my strip of a gown. "In my arms." Antonio stepped toward me. "In my bed." Antonio lowered his head and kissed me.

"What of your heart?" he whispered against my mouth.

I dropped the robe to splay my fingers against his chest and lean into him. "Oh Antonio, anger is not abandonment. I want to be with you. Will you come to me? Not for a child. For us."

Our lips met in a languorous kiss. Antonio thrust his tongue into my mouth and pulled me closer. I pushed my hips forward. Among the tangled bedding he was loving me again when the last candle sputtered and left us to continue our pleasures in darkness.

The next two evenings we departed for our rooms as soon as it was respectable and slept little. He was tender, caring and loving in everything we did. He curled me into his arms and slept against me. Woke me in the middle of the night to repeat our pleasures. Friday near dawn, I awakened but kept my eyes closed and stirred not. *Better than the first times. Much better. I know what to expect and more what to do. Send him away happy. My turn to wake him.* While still within his arms, I turned, kissed him and thrust my tongue into his mouth.

After Mass and a quick meal we three stood on our dock and waved. Antonio's gondola swung left then right up Rio del Mendicanti. The gondola shrank and disappeared as it turned northwest toward our shipyard on the mainland.

"Will Papa be safe?"

"Certemente Little One. He will sail to the Po River and into the delta. If need be, smaller boats will take all with him up the river to our farmlands." We turned homeward.

"Nonno, will I ever see the farm and the animals...and things?"

"Perhaps. We shall see."

Following Papa, Lucietta and I walked hand in hand, and she looked up at me. "When Papa says 'perhaps' or 'We shall see,' he means 'no.' I am thinking Nonno is the same."

While I admired her shrewd assessment, I did not reply. *I, too, want to board a ship and spend time on the farm. It all depends on what he finds.* We sent Lucietta to the nursery and sat in the salon. Papa sipped caffe; I drank water. While enjoying our being silent together, I wanted answers. I waited until Papa looked relaxed.

"Papa, what can you tell me of Lucia?"

Papa smiled as if he knew I would ask one day. He picked up his cup and saucer and sipped before answering. "Above all else, Lucia was charming. Vivacious and lively."

"Beautiful, too?"

He nodded. "Borne to wealth and privilege, accustomed to having her way. She saw Antonio after he had returned home from a sailing trip and pursued him. Her father had arranged a marriage to a thirty-second, but Lucia declared him too old and would not have him. She was relentless. Pontenuevo finally gave in and let her marry Antonio. For a time they were very happy. Especially when she became with child. Fourteen months after they had wed, she died giving birth. Antonio named their daughter after her."

"Pontenuevo still blames Antonio for her death."

"He swore revenge on all of us. Tried to destroy our businesses and almost succeeded. For two years before your arrival, he had bribed or threatened every father Antonio had approached. Pontenuevo had sworn if he could not have his daughter, Antonio would have no heir."

I have no family to bribe. O-oh. That is what she meant that night asking me if I was enjoying Lucia's dowry. Lucietta's dowry will include her mother's.

"How much have you saved for Lucietta's dowry?"

"She will have her mother's jewels." Papa shrugged.

"You have little scudo or zecchino set aside." I counted his silence as admission. "The ranked know the Pontenuevo jewels. Her future husband's family will expect them. The household goods and coinage we offer will determine how well we can place Lucietta among the ranked. It will also determine her worth to her new family and how well they will treat her."

"What do you suggest?"

"We start now. Save soldi, turn them into gazzetti, then scudi, and zecchini. Hide them in the attic and forget we have them until she comes of age. In nine or ten years, we will be ready and she will have a large dowery because we will have been saving all along."

Papa finished his caffe and set his cup and saucer on the table between us. "Any other questions?"

"May I ask about the ships?" At his nod, I continued, "They are valuable and I am concerned for their safety. Just sitting docked and unused and with no crew aboard. Might thieves strip them bare?" He grinned. *How have I amused you?*

"About that you need not worry. A trusted former crewman guards each ship. Part of his pay is living on board with his family. That saves them rent. We pay them to guard the ship, keep it clean and scrape the barnacles from the hull. Each family has several children who run about, squawk at seeing strangers and are better guards than dogs."

I chuckled at the image his words had created; his broad smile told me he was again at ease. I relaxed against the chair back. "What of the foreigners? They stay for weeks during what they call their 'grand tour.' Might they enjoy sailing down the Adriatic to a coastal city like Ravenna to spend the day touring and dining? We could be their transport. Wait for enough patrons for a profit, leave early and be home in time for cena and their evening entertainments. The income might be seasonal and dependent on this new foreigner travel, but it could be an income. Being the first to think of it, organized it and do it might be a significant advantage."

"I will think about it." Papa shrugged and looked away.

Because April 25 is St. Mark's Day, all the faithful are obligated to attend High Mass. We attended early and enjoyed special meals. Instead of our joining city-wide celebrations, Lucietta and I played and sang for Papa. Draped in our capes we stood on the dock and looked south to spot some of the fireworks over the lagoon.

56

May 3

All morning, Papa had been in the city, Lucietta at her lessons, and I in the music room. We met at pranzo. Holding a square parchment with its broken seal visible, Papa strode into the dining room and sat.

"Before we begin, I have an announcement." He held the parchment before him and read, "Signor Giovanni Delatesta. You and your family are cordially invited to join us on our barge to observe the Marriage to the Sea. Please arrive at our pier at the eighth hour. We will serve a cold colazione before we board. After the ceremony we invite you to the party to follow." Papa paused for effect. "Signor Pasquali and Signora Eugenia Garzolo."

"What did you do to garner that invitation?"

Papa winked at me. "Garzolo and I have done business together many times. When last I spoke to him, he mentioned his wife's approval of your behavior at the di Benneto dinner. They may be two ranks below us but I think you may have made a friend, Grazia."

"How did I do that?"

"Unlike the others, you create your own fashions. You choose to be kind. You respect the Garzolo position without demeaning or challenging them. Because of that you differ from many of the ranked."

Lucietta leaned over and whispered, "Mama, Papa is not here. May I attend?"

Instead of confirming her hope I replied, "Ask Nonno."

"Nonno, am I invited as well?"

"You are. As this is the first time you will be in society, how you behave will determine your future among the ranked. That Signor Garzolo invited you is both an honor and a test. Likely his grandchildren will be present. This will be a time for you to impress your elders and to make friends with their children."

As we dined Papa gave us a history of the ceremony and the symbolism behind Festa La Sensa. After describing every feature of the Doxe's gold barge, he explained the ceremony. Papa ended with, "Lucietta, Mama will train you how to behave, how to speak and what to do. At the ceremony you will hold mama's or my hand and not lean over the railing. At the party you will be with other children. We expect exemplary behavior."

"Si, Nonno. May I have a new vestito for the ceremony?"

"Her mother's daughter," Papa mumbled.

At a nod from Papa, I told her, "You may."

"Mama, per favore, may I have it remade from one of my mama's pink dresses?"

"Not this time. Your first outing in society should be in a new dress." Papa answered my question with "When you go to Signora Barbo's shop, choose either blue or green for Lucietta."

Before we left the table Papa said, "I almost forgot. At the end of the ceremony, some adult will announce, 'Now is time for all children to jump into the lagoon.' Do not do it! You are supposed the laugh and reply, 'Not this year!' Remember, the only things that go into the water are the ring and the flowers we throw after it."

"Si, Nonno."

Tuesday,I brought Lucietta with me to the fitting for my fall vestito. *Glad Papa agreed to only one new gown each season. I care not for display and better to save coins.* We exited the gondola and looked at the Rialto Bridge. Fascinated, Lucietta slowed us as she looked at shop fronts and people while we took the lane to the shop.

"Remember, no touching anything unless I hand it to you. Do not speak unless she addresses you directly. Stay beside me. When she measures you, do not fidget."

"Yes, Mama."

I took her hand, and we entered. In the gondola on our way home, Lucietta spoke, but I leaned to her and whispered, "No conversation in public." She nodded and we finished our journey in silence.

Two days later Papa sent for me. "Should anyone ask about Antonio's absence, reply he went to see about a matter at the farm. Only admit he has not yet returned."

"They will ask, 'What is so important he would miss this event?'" I answered for him. "I will reply, 'He did not say.' Papa, lies show on my face. With your permission, we tell Lucietta only what we already have. We will behave as if nothing untoward has occurred." I stood. "Tell me what else to do, and I will do it. I leave you to your plans." Schooling my face into a serene expression, I waited for Papa to dismiss me. When I left, he was staring into the office's unlit fireplace.

I set aside the first piece and took out the new music Padre Vivaldi had sent me. Working it out took all my concentration.

After I had finished a decent rendition, my heart settled but my mind turned to May eighteenth. *Practice a calm, accepting demeanor. Express no concern about Antonio's absence. Deflect questions with a shrug of innocence.* Without seeing it I stared at the sheet of music as I tried practicing smiling with a vacuous expression. Lucietta's entrance broke my concentration. Together we warmed our voices before I taught her the new song Padre had gifted me.

57

May 18

Three previous days of rain had ended at sundown and the sun rose in a cloudless sky. As Papa had predicted, the day would be sunny and warm. The bottom of the sun was not yet visible when the gondolier pushed from our dock. When we arrived at the Garzolo dock, the others were already aboard. Signor escorted us onto the barge.

"A gondola is holding our place in the lagoon, but it is filling fast and we leave now. We will eat as we travel."

As we sat, the rowers on the level below our seats took us toward the Canale Grande. Papa, Lucietta, and I sat opposite Signora Garzolo, her son, his wife, and their youngest, a girl. At the front of the barge on our side sat their daughter, with Signor and me to his left, then Lucietta and Papa. Each of us received a small tray of bread, cheese and a cup of hot, sweetened tea. We perched the trays on our laps as we ate. A servant removed our trays to place the contents in a basket. Down another rio and a third we went. At the intersection of the Canale Grande, we stopped because it was full of boats, barges and gondolas.

The lead bargeman ordered the rowers to push into the fray. In unison the river of boats traveled down the canal. After passing Piazza de San Marco the vessels separated as they entered the wide lagoon. Our barge surged forward and far into the lagoon before turning to face the city. It stopped beside a gondola and the bargeman leaned to pay the gondolier. Now high in the sky, the sun warmed us as we stared at other boats and waited. A light wind relieved us of the rising heat. Signor introduced us to the rest of his family and made small talk with Papa. The servant offered glasses of fruit-flavored water. The throngs created waves of talk that rose and fell as we waited for hours.

As the tide started to sea beneath us, the lagoon remained calm from the swarm of vessels holding it down. Festooned with red and gold ribbons and flags, the doxe's barge first appeared tiny. As it grew Papa reminded Lucietta and me of the order of procession: the doxe's barge with the bishop and the first ten; barges that held the next thirty and their families; the boats and barges of the remaining first Ninety-nine. They formed an inner ring around the doxe and blocked our view. At the bargeman's order our boat moved into a better position to the objections and cursing of those crowded around us. I saw every rooftop filled with tiny people. I looked away from the red dots atop the Ospedale roof.

The barge bright with golden plates everywhere gleamed in the sunlight. The bishop raised a gold, jeweled cross. We knew he was marrying Venice to the sea from which it gains its wealth and prosperity, but we were too far away to hear him. The doxe raised his hand. I held my breath as I heard the same from the thousands around us. A gold ring glinted in the doxe's fingers as he turned in a slow circle to display it. The doxe drew back his arm and threw the ring into the sea to a great shout from everyone in the boats and on the rooftops. He waved as we cheered and cheered. His barge turned back the way it had come and the procession followed it.

After a long wait vessels near us began moving, but the lagoon cleared slowly. As we neared the spot where the ring had met the sea, we saw hundreds of flowers floating on the waves the boats created. Seeking the same blessing of prosperity for our family, Papa removed our garden flower pinned to his coat and tossed it onto the pile. Signor Garzolo did the same for his family.

By the time we reached the Garzolo dock, I was hot, hungry and thirsty. Lucietta tugged at my sleeve and expressed a desperate need. At the necessary I used our rank to move us ahead in line. Then we rejoined Papa at the foot of the stairs. He lead Lucietta to the children's table and sat her beside Bianca, a Garzolo granddaughter. Because I saw a servant standing behind each pair of children, I felt Lucietta was somewhat protected from the others.

We moved into the dining room and took our places. This time I sat to Signore Garzolo's left, the third seat of honor after Papa. A servant filled my water glass twice. The other two families were their son's and their daughter's. *The third family appears to be a business associate or a partner and his family. I hope they introduce me so I may make a new connection.*

What I had thought would be a light pranzo was a full meal of a cold leek soup, roasted lamb chops, vegetables, and breads. We left the table to enjoy the garden. Signora Garzolo linked our arms together as we walked. She introduced me to the rest of her family and to her husband's business partner and his family. *Three new connections, a sign of her acceptance, and her expectation they will follow. Mille grazie, Signora.*

I left and returned with goblets of Prosecco, which we sipped in unison. I moved away for others to speak with Signora. At a long table I stood with a small plate in hand as I chose two small dolces.

"Signor Delatesta, why is your signor not with you?" asked the Garzolo daughter.

I smiled. "My signor left to see about a matter at our farms." I turned her away from other questions with "Do you live in Venice as well?" We chatted about nothing important. I looked for Lucietta and found her laughing and talking with two other girls who looked to be her age. They walked off holding hands.

As a light wind picked up and cooled me, Papa arrived to take us home. He had sent a servant for Lucietta, who arrived two minutes later. We spoke our farewells to Signora Garzolo, who asked me to call her Eugenia and took my hand in hers as she spoke a warm farewell. Signor Pasquali did the same first to Papa then to me. Lucietta curtseyed, thanked her hostess and host for their kind hospitality and spoke formal farewells. *Well done, daughter.* I smiled down at her and she smiled back as we followed Papa to the dock.

Seated in the salon Lucietta yawned, but I did not dismiss her. I said to my daughter, "Last Saturday you honored me because it was St. Grazia of Zaragoza saint's day. Today, what are we doing for Nonno?"

Before Lucietta could respond, Papa interjected, "Nothing more need be done. I was the guest of honor at an important event and served a feast. Several men congratulated me for this being my saint's day."

I gave Lucietta a tiny nod. She took the hint, went to Nonno, and hugged him. "Happy saint's day, Nonno. What may I do to honor you?"

"A kiss and two hugs."

After she delivered them she asked, "Nonno, may I be excused? I am very tired and want my bed." Papa dismissed her. I told Papa why I wanted to follow her.

After I dismissed Nurse, I turned Lucietta around to undo the bow at her waist. "Please tell me about your time with the other children." Lucietta reported who sat at the table with her, what they were served, who said what and every other detail. She said Bianca's sister had sat at a second table with the older girls, and the boys sat at a third. Near the end of the party Adrianna had said to her, "You are nicer than they say, more polite and kind. I think they are wrong about you."

"What did you say?"

"I nodded my head. That was right, was it not, Mama, because my rank is higher than hers?" At my assent she continued, "I thanked her for her kind words and said I hoped we would meet again." She replied, "'I hope we do.' and walked away to talk to a boy."

After I pulled down her camicia di notte, I hugged her hard. "You did very well, my daughter. You made a good beginning. I am proud of you." After we knelt and Lucietta said her prayers, I lifted her to her bed and covered her. She raised her arms to me so I sat and hugged her.

"Mille grazie, Mama, for making me a good girl. I like being liked. I want you to be proud of me always."

"You are a good girl and people will like you because of it. Sleep well, my dear and kind daughter. Your guardian angel, Nonno, Papa, and I will always watch over you."

I returned to the salon wearing tears. Papa set down his glass of Soave and jumped up to ask what was the matter. I hugged him and told him, "Oh Papa! She hugged me hard and thanked me for making her a good girl. She can be so sweet. Now I understand why it was so easy for Antonio to spoil her." I wiped my eyes.

"True. In her way Lucietta told you she is your daughter. As if you had birthed her. In a way you have. Birthed a better girl, one who will become all you hope for her. Not because you are firm, even strict with her, but because she now realizes what you do is for her benefit. Come, I will pour a glass for you, and we will toast our little girl."

58

June 1

Surely, I am healthy enough to bear a child now. Five weeks gone. Will he return home? If he chooses he could live aboard the small ship and trade on the Adriatic. I might never see him again. Pray, pray hard. I want to be a wife, not a housekeeper. I keep the pattern of my days, but I miss him. As angry as I am at being lied to, I still miss him. I considered why as Garon dressed me for Mass.

Lucietta and I had finished our morning singing practice and ate pranzo with Papa. I sent Lucietta upstairs for her afternoon lessons and returned to the harpsichord. I was playing a piece when someone coughed. I finished the measure, lifted my fingers, and turned to see Papa. He gestured and I followed.

I closed the door behind me. Papa said he had seen that Lucietta would not leave the nursery and that no one else would come to this floor. I looked about, satisfied my bedroom was neat. I opened the window a bit and felt the afternoon breeze. *Stay standing to move. Closer or away, depending on his words and actions. His promise to be faithful opened the door between our rooms. He wrote 'forever.' Do I believe he has stayed faithful? How many days, months, years before I believe that? Stand halfway between the bed and my dressing table. No expectation of intimacy.* With my fingers entwined before my waist, I faced my door. The handle moved and I held my breath.

Antonio entered while looking at the floor. Without looking at me he turned to face the closing door as he locked it. I heard him inhale a deep breath before he turned. *Is the fear in his eyes reflected in mine? We are a sorry pair. Should I speak first?* Before I could decide, Antonio approached and drew me into his arms.

"You continue to do the right things for all of us. I am proud of you. That you are an honorable man is one thing I love about you." *Not "I love you," but as close as I dare go for now.* His kiss told me what he desired. "After all this time, only one kiss? Where are the others?" I teased.

"Where would you like them?"

"Surprise me."

He pulled back and kissed one closed eye, then the other. I sighed. My forehead, the tip of my nose, my chin. He touched his lips to mine. As I responded his ardor increased. *Not yet.* I pulled back, and he released me.

"I would like to talk." I pointed to my desk chair. "Will you sit?" After he pulled it out and sat, I approached. "May I?" At his nod, I sat on his lap and put my arm about his shoulders. "Why did you return to me?"

"I thought of living on the small ship, but Stefano was adamant that I should not. At the end of each day we talked over wine. He admitted he had been wrong to keep Polonia from Venice. He said he should have promised her three trips a year. After the crops were in, while Papa and I were at the mountain villa, and one holiday. Then surprise her with a fourth trip. He charged I was worse than a fool to have treated you as I had."

Antonio loosened his hold as I shifted. I placed my arm about his waist, lowered my head to his shoulder and snuggled against him. "And…"

"He reminded me I only have one heart to give. I knew he was right on both counts. I went to Il Conto, who said almost the same things. He advised me well and knew the men and resources I needed."

"You mean plenty of coins and forgers and lawyers who would not ask questions."

"Mm-heh."

"We must repay Il Conto."

"Papa already said he would." He broke our silence with, "She… I was lonely. When my sons arrived, I was happy again." I thought about what he meant. Then I asked, "How is Maricella?"

"Resigned. She cried and begged to stay in Venice. I explained the advantages to her and my sons over and over; finally she agreed. She wanted the boys to have respectability. She never had that; now she will. She was born into no rank, but she is not a bad woman."

"I never thought she was." I left it at that.

"Are you going to ask about them?"

"You love your sons very much and miss them terribly. I know you do. I wish I could help you with that. Your actions display your good character, Antonio. Your love for them. Here they would have been close, but their lives would have been a misery. No rank, no education, no chance to improve their lives. With what you have given them, now they can have good lives.

"I will never see them again."

The regret, sorrow, and misery in his tone tore at my heart. *He needs hope.* I lifted my head and kissed his cheek. "You will see your sons again. If things go bad for them or if they need you, she will tell them. When they are old enough, she will tell them the truth." When Antonio shook his head, I added, "Si, you will see them again. You may have to wait until they grown men, but they will return to you."

"Should they appear at our door, what will you do?"

"I will do what you do. If you welcome them with open arms and a glad heart, so will I."

"Vow you mean it."

I held his eyes. "They are your sons. I vow I mean it." *Speak truths.* "I pray we have a family of our own, God willing. By the time they become adults, I may feel more secure."

He stared back at me. "You are secure, and we will have a family of our own."

Until I give him two sons, she still has the upper hand. To dispel that thought, I kissed his cheek and moved toward his mouth.

He stopped me with, "I admire you. I respect you. I appreciate my life with you." He looked into my eyes. "I also admit I held my heart from you. Out of fear. When I realized you were with child, I was both thrilled and terrified. What if you died in childbirth? Then you almost did die. I could not bear losing you, so I used Stefano's disaster to flee."

My heart knew; he had been withholding his. He lost her to childbirth. Why not me as well? Violante is right. I nodded as if I understood. *Reassure him, even if God makes it a lie.* I turned his head to face me. "I am as strong willed as you. I am also stronger and even more determined than you know. Believe me. I will survive every childbirth, and I will live to be very old. Even older than Papa is now."

"Promise me."

"I promise."

"Have I ever said, 'I love you'?"

I shook my head.

He caressed my cheek. "I love you, Grazia, and everything about you. From your head to your toes. I love the way your hair curls when I twist it round my finger. I love your expressive eyes that tell me what you are thinking. I love the way you crinkle your nose when you are unsure of the food placed before you. I love how your long fingers dance over the keys and pluck strings. I love how you care about our finances and obligations. I love how you adore Papa and gaze after him when he leaves the room. I love how you fluff your skirt after you remove your cape. At every turn, you amaze me. I also love how you hold Lucietta's hand when you walk together. Even when you are strict with her, you do it with love in your voice. Your voice! The angels must weep with jealousy when they hear you. When you sing, I stop what I am doing to listen. I have even crept to the music doorway to be close to you."

"I did not know that."

"That evening you stood before the Canaletto. I stood behind you and thought of our day at the Council. I remembered your strength, your courage, and your fearlessness. I realized I started loving you when you refused to sing on command. I was afraid to say it. Now I fear I have waited too long. I love you, Grazia. Per favore, tell me I am not too late."

"It is never too late to say those words. You could say them every day for the rest of our lives, and I would never tire of them." I caressed his cheek. "You know my answer. I love you, Antonio. I love your sense of honor, your strength, your dedication to our family. I love so much about you I don't know where to begin. I love your kisses. Such power in them! I melt and hunger for more. I love being in your arms; I feel protected. In my worst moments, your saving me from Ospaedale, and after I lost our bambina. I chose to live because of what I felt when you held me. Your smile is my sunshine. The twinkle in your eyes delights me. My voice? Yours is deep and calming. I also hear determination, kindness, patience, and love. Yes, even love. I thought I heard it that night, but I was unsure. You are right; I need to hear the words. Per favore, say them again."

"I love you."

I answered him the same. "Like our first ceremony, we should consummate our vows. Not in here. In your bed. A new start, a new place." I kissed his cheek. "Our marriage has had several starts. Perhaps that is what marriage is. We go through a difficult time, some trouble, or something bad. We renew our promises of love and constancy and come together again. As long as we hold on to each other as we face the world, we will be fine."

"Yes, we will. I would like to carry you into my room."

I nodded against his shoulder and kissed his neck. "Close the door behind us. No one exists but us."

Slow and sweet was his every touch as he undressed me and I him. He drew back the coverings in invitation, and I crawled between the sheets. We shared our love for hours. Spent, we fell asleep in each other's arms.

I woke in the night and found Antonio wrapped around me, peacefully sleeping. *Every kiss, every touch, this night. True, for the first time. He does love me.* My eyes filled. A ragged sob escaped. Another followed. I could not stop crying. I felt Antonio wake.

"Grazia, what happened? What is the matter?"

I turned and sobbed against his chest. I sobbed for all the fears I had carried, all the worries I had hidden behind false smiles. I cried for every time we had come together with a lie between us. When I had stiffened my spine and closed my heart after the dinner party. For every time I had lied to myself about accepting his past. But mostly for relief. Relief that it is all over. Finally over.

"Dio mio, what did I do to you? I have so much to make up for. Grazia, please stop crying. I promise everything will be better. Every day, everything will be good between us. You will know how much I love you. Oh, my darling! Please stop crying. You tear at my heart. Now I realize how yours felt. All those months. The time I wasted. No. I am wrong. You cry as much as you need to. I will hold you and cry with you. I harmed you so much. All the damage. I will repair it. I swear I will."

I had cried all my tears, and my sobbing had become dry, heaving breaths. Somehow his telling me not to stop crying was what I needed to hear. At my silence Antonio gently wiped my face and neck with the sheet. Against his wet chest, I heard his heart. As his slowed so did mine. In the quiet I asked for what I wanted. "Say it again."

"I love you, Gracia. I love you so much. I have harmed you, and I have much to make up for. From this moment everything between us will be good. I promise. No matter what happens next we will stand together against it." He kissed my hair, my forehead, my nose. "You are the wife I have always needed, always wanted. Until I die I will say it every day. I love you, Gracia."

I nodded against his chest. Then I lifted my head, raised my chin and kissed him. For a moment he froze then he returned my kiss. I rolled to my back; he kept his arm under my neck. "I am tired."

"Then sleep."

I rolled to my side and pulled his wrist until his arm was over my waist and he lay behind me. When he cuddled me I kissed his wrist and tucked his hand under my chin. As I fell asleep I felt his breath against my hair.

I do not know how long I had slept. I only knew I woke hungry. Antonio had rolled away and was sleeping beside me on his back. *A new day. How will it start? With my face washed and me clean.* I slipped off the bed and felt my way to the door. I saw a light as I stepped into my room.

The window had been closed. A half-burned candle on my dressing table sat on a large tray of bread, cheeses, and cold meats. Beside it stood two goblets and a bottle of red wine with the cork almost out. *Good woman. Brought what we needed without disturbing us.* I washed, donned a clean camicia and reached for my robe. The glimmer of dawn lit the drapery edges and made a thin stripe into the room. After I cinched my robe, I turned and saw Antonio leaning against the door frame.

"A waste of time to put that on. I am only going to remove it."

"Not before I eat. I am hungry." I picked up the wine and the glasses. Antonio entered and picked up the tray. As I followed him into his room I looked down only as far as Antonio's waist. "Per favore, wear your robe with the ships while we eat."

"Why bother?" he shot back.

"I also want something to remove."

"Promise?"

"Promise."

59

June 2

Antonio sat beside me as we enjoyed colazione. Papa and Lucietta returned from Mass. Surprised, Lucietta froze in the archway.

"Papa!" she yelped. Lucietta looked at me for permission, and I nodded. "You are home!" She ran into his waiting arms and they hugged. She spoke a muffled, "I am so happy! May I sit beside you?"

I sat back and enjoyed listening as Lucietta peppered her father with questions. Antonio insisted she take two bites for every answer. Papa and I grinned at each other as we enjoyed caffe and water. The meal over Lucietta announced, "I have earned my own room. Mama wanted me to move in when both of you are present. May I show it to you, Papa?"

After they departed I asked Papa, "What have you decided about a pleasure cruise on the Adriatic?"

"I spoke to hotel owners, gondoliers and shopkeepers. They agree. The touristi tell us what they think we want to hear but they do only what pleases them. They enjoy concerts and the theater and touring churches and palaces. The touristi like traveling in the gondolas on the rios and think our city is both classical and quaint. They also sleep late, laze away the days, and at night party and keep company with women."

"Donna della notte."

Papa tilted his head and shrugged at me. "They may say they will order a trip but they will not. We will bear the cost of making preparations and have no clients. "

"Grazie Papa, for looking into my idea. I regret it would have been more cost than profit."

Papa's voice lifted. "I do have two contracts for deliveries down the coast. Another contract will give us an almost full ship on return. Our men are preparing the small boat. I renamed it Adriatic Zigzag to imply we will go anywhere. Daughter, I must remain here to reconnect with my contacts and host pranzos again. Antonio must captain the Zigzag. He will leave the fifth and will be gone almost two weeks."

Good timing. By the time he returns, my next cycle will be over, and we can make a bambina.

"You have worked hard and made wise moves, Papa. I have prayed for renewed friendships and income, and we have started to remake them. If you are able, I would appreciate knowing about feeding guests in advance. Even two hours is enough."

"Monday, I will extend invitations for the eighth, and I will know how many to expect by Wednesday."

"I will inform Rosa. This pranzo must be the best ever, so they will want to return."

Holding her father's hand, Lucietta re-entered the room. "Papa said I may ask. Mama, may I move into my room before my birthday? Today? Now?"

"You may. Papa and I will assist you." I rose and followed them into the nursery. Nurse had already cleared the chests. We picked up stacks of clothing from the beds, followed Lucietta across the hall, and laid the items on her new bedding.

"Papa, Mama, with your permission, I would like to put these things away myself. After the chests are moved, Nurse and I can finish the task."

Suddenly, so grown up. Asking permission but expecting agreement. I saw Antonio nod and added mine.

Antonio asked, "Is everything as you desire it?" At her assent he added, "Buone."

I said, "Lucietta, we have a gift for you. They are in the top right drawer of your dressing table."

Antonio moved beside me and put his arm around my waist. Lucietta opened the drawer and her eyes widened. She picked up the top garment, held it before her and hugged it as she swayed side to side. "Mine?"

"Yours. A child wears cotton chemises. A girl becoming a young lady wears silk against her skin."

"Oh! Mama, Papa, grazie. Grazie tante, grazie, grazie mille!"
She hugged me first!

As Lucietta hugged her father, he said, "We are proud of the young lady you have become. You have earned our gift; wear it with pride."

"But do not brag about it. Corretto, Mama?"

"Si. If anyone sees an edge and comments?"

"I say nothing; I just smile."

Antonio patted her head and said, "That is what a girl becoming a young donna does." He smiled at me.

That night,I had dressed for bed and was brushing my hair. I stopped when I spotted Antonio leaning against the door frame. "Do not stop; I enjoy watching you. Grazia, per favore, wear your robe."

"I shall because I like the way you remove it."

"Stop smirking."

"You first." I felt my cheeks warm and looked away. *Do it. You know you want to.* "Do you remember when I told you only those who love me may call me 'Zia'?" He nodded. "You may call me 'Zia' if you like." As he approached, I stood so we could embrace. "Only I may ever call you Zia," he bargained, "and only when we are alone."

I felt his kiss from my lips to my toes, which curled into the rug. I pulled back so I could say, "When you kiss me like this, I cannot think. I cannot even breathe!" Then I pulled him to me and kissed him back. After a long time we parted. I said close to his mouth. "When we are like this, what shall I call you?"

In a husky voice, he answered, "Zia. You are my heart, and I am your 'Tonio,' but only when we are alone. Even fully clothed and standing upright. Until my dying breath."

1725

Summer

"We must let go of the the life
we have planned
so as to accept the one
that is waiting for us."
—Joseph Campbell

60

Northeast of Venice

in foothills above Udine

August 22

"Papa and his namesake are napping. Walk with me? I have something to show you."

"Lucietta?"

"Sketching the valley with her maid beside her. She knows where we are going."

Hand in hand we strolled over grass to the path and up the hill. When it narrowed he led. "Tonio," I chided, "this is more a climb than a walk. Where are we going?"

"To a view." Ten minutes later we halted because the path had washed out. "The last storm. I will have it rebuilt." He led me through trees until the path was again safe. I held onto a tree while he jumped onto the path. Tonio raised his hands to me and I let go. He caught and kissed me before he set me on my feet. Taking my hand he led me past a wooden bench, and we trod uphill until the path stopped at a grassy promontory.

"Echo Valley." He turned me toward it and instructed, "Yell something."

I looked sideways. *Even if I think he knows, it is time to say it.* I faced the valley and yelled. "I am happy!" came back to me three times, each time fading, until the last 'happy' was almost a whisper. "Your turn."

I grinned at his deep throated, "I love you!" as it echoed back to me. He turned me into his arms and kissed me so passionately, I gasped for breath. "Now this place knows it, too." He held my hand as he led us the way we had come.

Passing the wooden bench on the upside of the path, I saw "For My Francesca." burned on the top back board. I stopped us. We sat and faced mountains. *A distant haze softens their curves and cliffs. A cloudless sky above us and over them. That white ribbon might be a waterfall, and the cuts between the mountains might be passes. Are there more mountains beyond?*

"Why does Papa always say 'my Francesca?' Does he think he owned her?"

Antonio exclaimed, "No one owned my mother! No one would dare try!" He paused. "In my mother's family, one of her brothers married a Francesca. My uncle's wife was 'Petro's Francesca.' Father's cousins' wife was called 'Magno's Francesca.'" Each said 'my Francesca" when speaking of their own wives. A habit Papa still uses. Do you not hear his love when he says her name?"

"Si, but I still wondered."

Antonio twined my fingers in his and laid our hands on his thigh. "Someday, you will become 'my Grazia.'"

"Why?"

"Custom. Gio's first son will be named after me; his first daughter will be named after you. Only I may call you 'Zia,' so we cannot shorten our granddaughter's name. Already, you are 'Mama'; then you will also be 'Nonna' and 'my Grazia.'" He paused. "After Papa is gone we will call Gio by his full name."

"We name every other generation the same?" Tonio smiled at me and nodded. "I have no…what do we name our second son?"

"With your permission, I would like to name him Michielo, after my brother and my grandfather. Keep the name in our family."

"Michielo is a good name." I slouched as I remembered I know not my mother's Christian name. *I have nothing for a second daughter.*

"If you like, you could name our second daughter after one of your sisters."

Again, he reads my mind. "We have time to think about it."

"If you stopped nursing Gio, we could try for another now."

Is that why you brought me to this pleasant place? To ask me to give up Gio? "In a week he will be only four months. Tonio, he must be nursed until he eats soft foods."

"A milk mother could nurse him."

I held his eyes. "I will not give him to another. I cannot explain the bond nursing makes between us. I only know I must continue. Also, to give my body time before I have another bambino. Seven, eight more months, at most. I will stop then and be most eager for another bambino."

"Papa said you would argue that." He squeezed my hand and grinned. "Papa also told me Mama reasoned the same. Of course she won. Now I know why we four are about two years apart."

Mille grazie, Papa. Once again, you know my heart. I looked a long way off. "So beautiful. The mountains seem far away. Are we not on a mountain?"

"We are on a foothill. The valley below us is the divide to the next foothills and the mountains." He pointed high above me. "The snow-topped behind those hills are mountains." I looked forward to spot the bottom of our foothill and leaned back from the distance.

"What lies beyond?"

He pointed left. "That way is Switzerland; they call this range Alps." He pointed ahead. "This way, we call them the Dolomites. Beyond is monarchia austiaca."

"And Vienna?"

"Si."

I looked that direction. "She travelled far to give me a good life. I am grateful she brought me all the way to Venezia."

"So am I, my beloved. So am I."

I turned to kiss Tonio, and he met me halfway.

Author's Notes

Antonio Lucio Vivaldi
March 4, 1678 - July 28, 1741

While Antonio Vivaldi is a minor character in this story, he is of major importance to me. From the Contents page, you may have guessed I organized this novel like one of Vivaldi's major works, *The Four Seasons*. It is the first piece of his music I heard and is a favorite. Because of Vivaldi, I fell in love with the Baroque period of music. Then I found George Handel, Henry Percel, Johann Sebastian Bach, and others.

I just realized I gave Antonio Delatesta's first wife the female version of Vivaldi's middle name. I must have seen it long ago; somewhere in my memory I had latched on to it until now. Vivaldi's life story and music has affected me deeply; I hold Vivaldi, his many works, and Venice in my heart.

Other Real Persons and Places

The Anna Maria in Chapter 2 was a real person. In 1723, Anna Maria della Pieta', aged 27, was a renowned violinist who chose to remain at Ospedale her entire life.

Five -year-old Chiara della Pieta', a child prodigy, sang as well as played the violin and the organ while in Ospedale. In some accounts, her name is also written as "Chiaretta," an endearment meaning "Little Chiara."

Alviso III Sebastiano Mocenigo was elected the doge (modern word) of Venice in 1722 and served until his death in 1732. He was called Monsignor el Doxe (My Lord the Doge), and his titles included Serenissima Principe (Most Serene Prince) and Sua Serenita' (His Serenity).

If you research the Vivaldi house in Venice, you will see it is on a corner on a street, not on a canal, as I have written. I am not wrong, and the historical maps of Venice agree. When Napoleon conquered Venice in 1797, he made two significant changes. He gave a huge portion of the northeast part of the Veneto to his allies, the Austrians, in exchange for Lombardy. In Venice, he ordered some rios filled and turned into streets or walkways. At that time, there were few bridges across the rios, which hampered the movements of his troops. Now Venice boasts over 400 bridges. Fortunately, Napoleon left the path of the Grand Canal untouched.

The original building that housed Ospedale is gone. The site is now the location of the Hotel Metropole, Riva degli Schiovoni 4149.

Vivaldi's Church

The modern Church of the Pieta (Chiesa della Pieta') sits adjacent to the Hotel Metropole yet also on the site of the earlier, small, wooden church, which had been attached to the Pio Ospedale della Pieta. Begun four years after Antonio Vivaldi died in Vienna, Austria, the new church was built from 1745 to 1760. Likely, this newer structure is called "Vivaldi's Church" because of the his association with the orphanage and because his works are now often performed there.

Italian Foods

Terrone

In Cremona, Italy, in 1441, Francesca Sforza married Bianca Maria Visconti. The celebration buffet featured a delicious sweet made of nuts in a honey and whipped egg white confection in the shape of the famous tower of Cremona, called the "Torrione. The sweet became as famous as the tower and is known as Torrone.

I included a piece of Terrone on the dessert plate at the Delatesta dinner for the Signor el Doxe, in Chapter 34 because, by that time, Terrone was served on special occasions in northern Italy.

Today, you, too, can eat this dessert, now shaped into small rectangles, covered with a thin wafer, sealed in foil, and sold in small boxes. True terrone is still made in Italy and is distributed in the United States by several reputable companies. I purchase mine in Italian grocery stores, but they are also available online. I was raised on La Florentine Terrone; the Ferrara brand is also very good. Buon Appetito!

Wine

I have never had bad Italian wine. At home, I prefer Prosecco to champagne for special occasions. I choose wines based on what my brother, a wine expert and connoisseur, recommends. I favor reds more than whites, but I let the meal dictate what I serve.

In Italy, I order the house red or white in most restaurants, and have always liked the waiters' choices. During my last trip, I found a new favorite white. Soave wines are produced in the province of Verona, which is within the Veneto.

The Italian Language

In 1861, Giuseppe Garibaldi completed the unification of the city states on the Italian peninsula, as well as joining Sicily and other islands to the new country, Italy. Statesmen debated which regional language would become the official language of Italy. After much internecine conflict, the country rallied around the dialect of their beloved, most famous poet, Dante Alighieri, who read, wrote, and spoke Florentine, a Tuscan dialect. The language authorities included words from all regional dialects into the Italian language we know. Most of the old regional dialects are still spoken by a minority in each old city state area, including in Venice and the Veneto region.

I hope my including a bit of Italian enriched your enjoyment of the story and gave you a flavor of what you might experience when you visit Italy.

A Surprise

During my research, I learned select Venetians could join the ranks of the nobility through membership. In 1580, the cost was 50,000 ducats, which would be 8.3 million U.S. dollars today. In the 1630s, the cost was 60,000 ducats. In the early eighteenth century, one gained the status of "nobility through payment," by paying 100,000 ducats. That's 16.6 million dollars today!

Disclaimer

As I researched the Venetian laws which I used, I found the years and the substance of the laws. I obtained neither the laws' numbers nor access to the actual documents. Honestly, I doubt I could have read eighteen century script. I am sure I could not have translated the Venetian dialect even with an Italian/English dictionary in hand. I decided to create the numbers of the laws and amendments. Those are fiction.

Coming Soon

Madeleine

A Daughter of King Louis XIV

"Sister Marie-Claire, that man slouched against the wall. This is the third time he's been here, yet he does not stand in a girl's line. Does he not want a wife?"

"His wife arrived with the first group two years ago. She died in childbirth. He cannot have a second wife until every girl has chosen from among the single men. Only then, may he approach and ask for an interview if a girl remains."

I gazed down the tables at the four girls who, like me, were still unmarried. Again, each girl but I had a suitor in her chair. They had additional men standing in line waiting to be interviewed. I stared at the empty chair before me. *The girls who arrived on the first ship in May had the best choices. Arriving ill in June has cost me. August now and only five of us left. If no one chooses my chair, I must leave Quebec City for Montreal. Perhaps, there I can find a man who does not know I arrived sick almost unto death.*

Behind me, Sister ordered, "Stop!" as she pointed to a suitor who was leaning over the table too close to a girl as she leaned back. Immediately, he straightened, scowled, and turned away. The man behind him quickly took his place.

When none standing in line would meet my gaze, I again looked toward the man with arms crossed over his chest. *Taller than I with a thick neck, thick arms, trim waist. His well-muscled body shows me he works hard. His brown eyes appear guarded but not unfriendly. Is my staring at him causing his half smile?* As he returned my gaze, I felt unsettled and looked away.

After looking at the empty chair opposite me, I pursed my lips, thought, and decided. I straightened my back, lifted my legs, and swung them over the bench. I did not answer Sister Marie-Claire's "Where are you going?" as I marched to the man by the door. He stood erect and unfolded his arms. Sister followed me.

"Do you have a ship?"

"No. I have a flat-bottomed boat I row to transport goods to the city and home."

"Bon!" I declared. "I am Madeleine Cordon from the Normande' region. I sailed from Dieppe. You are?"

"Charles Bosseur from the Bretagne region near Bruz."

Surname means hard worker. I hope it fits him. "Why does no one sit before me?"

"They carried you off the ship on a cot. You looked to be dying. Word is you are weak and will not survive this harsh land."

"Mal de mer and terrible food. After a week on land and good food, I was myself again. I am not weak, and I will survive. With the right husband, I will thrive. I plan to live a long time."

"I hear your determination."

"You were married before?"

"She came from Paris. Complained of living in the wilderness, hated farming life."

I will say a prayer for the repose of your wife's soul."

His flat "Merci" may mean he cared not for her. What if he has no heart? "Your babe lived?"

He nodded. "A son. Eleven months. He will live with his milk mother until a woman chooses me."

"How did you come to New France?"

"In servitude for my passage. I paid the debt and earned coin. I requested land on the south side of Île d'Orléans, an island in the river, and the government granted me 475 arpent carr'e. I built and grow enough to feed a family. When I have more land cleared, I will also have crops to sell."

"You need a wife; I want a husband with a home. S'l vous plait, tell me more.

He lifted his chest. "I do not do things usual. I dug the well; then I built the barn around it. The water never freezes, and you brave no storm to get it. The house is attached to the barn."

"Clever. You think ahead."

His eyes light when he smiles. I like that.

Acknowledgements

Margaret, you are the only editor I trust with my "babies," my works in progress. You are, encouraging, an expert at analyzing my works, and the ruthlessly honest editor I need. I follow your advice and become a better writer. I don't know what I would do without you, and I hope I never have to find out. (Secret: So far, I have three more novels in my head. Please stay with me.)

I am so grateful to you, Ann B. for coming to my rescue. You are a skilled proofreader, and this story is better for your sharp eyes and mind. Thank you for your friendship and your hard work.

Teri E., thank you for traipsing around Venice with me as I completed my research. I greatly appreciated your company, your observations, and how well you planned our trip to Padua.

Thank you, Nadia Kimm, for visiting me while I researched in Venice and for your gift. I cherish Nigel Kennedy's violin performance of *The Four Seasons* and will think of you every time I play it.

Spencer Smith, you are an organist, pianist, and musician extraordinaire. Thank you for lending me books about Antonio Vivaldi, for being my music resource, and for your friendship. I miss your playing the harpsichord.

Once again, Joyce S., you have been an invaluable resource. This time of Venetian history, customs, and the Italian language. When I told you I had been up all night writing because my research had sparked an idea, you were so encouraging.

Thank you, Linda, for the map of Grazia's home. Your beautiful work exceeded my expectations, and I hope we will work together again.

I am also grateful to Joanne M. Ferraro. *Venice: History of the Floating City,* her non-fiction work, is so engaging, I enjoyed every chapter. Because Ferraro's work is also so thoroughly researched and documented, I trusted her information.

Francesco da Mosto wrote an extensive history of Venice, his birthplace and his heritage, in his book, *Francesco's Venice.* The many beautiful photos and the history he shared inspired me. I also enjoy his YouTube episodes.

About Victoria

Victoria's journey to writing about Grazia and Antonio began at a symphony concert. The program notes explained Antonio Vivaldi had been commissioned to write two concertos a month for six years for the girls at a famous Venetian orphanage.

While listening to the Vivaldi piece, she asked herself: Who would be playing Vivaldi's music? What if she were a singer and had perfect pitch and a pure voice? Would she become famous? How might she succeed in leaving the orphanage? Would anyone want to marry her? What was Venice like when Vivaldi was composing those concertos?

By the end of the concert, Victoria knew what Grazia looked like, how she left the orphanage, and who her romantic interest would be.

She writes historical romance because she realized that is where her heart lies. "In every age, love is the force driving people. Even in the story of Lady Margaret in the Henry's Spare Queen Trilogy, it was love and her determination to survive that defeated her enemies."

If you enjoyed this book, please be sure to leave a review, so other readers are more likely to discover it as well.

You feedback and support mean the world to me.

Thank you.

Victoria

Also By Victoria

Henry's Spare Queen Trilogy

Lady Margaret's Disgrace, the Prequel
Lady Margaret's Escape Book One
Lady Margaret's Challenge Book Two
Lady Margaret's Future Book Three

Find Victoria online and on social media:
Author Website: *victoriasportelli.com*
Facebook: victoriasportelli

Dear Reader

If you enjoy this book,
please, leave an honest review
on your favorite review site.
I deeply appreciate your feedback and support

Thank you so much!

www.VictoriaSportelli.com